HOW TO LIVE AN UNDEAD LIE

HAILEY EDWARDS

Edited by Sasha Knight
Proofread by Lillie's Literary Services
Cover by Gene Mollica
Tree of Life medallion drawn by Leah Farrow

HOW TO LIVE AN UNDEAD LIE

The Beginner's Guide to Necromancy, Book 5

When a fledgling vampire arrives at Woolworth House searching for his maker, Grier is forced to relive her time in Atramentous. Most of those years are as dark and empty in her memory as she was in her cell. She can't remember her progeny, or the night she resuscitated him, but she can protect him from the Society. As long as she's willing to barter with her grandfather to do it.

But Lacroix has plans of his own. He envisions the city—*her* city— under his rule, and Grier under his thumb. Now all he needs is the right leverage to force her cooperation, and he has just the person in mind. Grier is ready to trade her freedom until a grim truth is revealed that splits her heart in two. Yet another person she loves has betrayed her, and Grier is left agonizing over how much of their relationship was real and how much is a lie.

ONE

"Shiver me timbers." I swung my foam sword in an arc to clash against the bent one Oscar had brandished with a bit too much enthusiasm against a tree earlier. "Batten down the hatches."

"You're the best pirate I know," he said, black eyes shining up at me in adoration.

Pretty sure I was the only pirate he knew, and I wasn't much of one. All I had done was memorize the lingo from a Talk Like a Pirate Day blog post. I was hazy about all the definitions, but Oscar cared more about exuberance than authenticity. "You're not half bad yourself, matey."

Soft laughter huffed behind us, and I cut my eyes toward the lean figure crossing the lawn at Woolworth House.

Linus wore his hair down, the dark-auburn length brushing his shoulders. His gray slacks kept their crease despite the humidity, and his white button-down shirt was starched within an inch of its life without a sweat stain in sight. His black leather shoes probably shouldn't get dew on them, let alone the muck we were wading through. But his eyes were more navy than black, his lips bent in a shy smile, and suddenly I was ready to foot the bill to have his oxfords repaired or replaced if only he kept looking at me like that.

"Arrrgh, me hearties." I rested the soft blade of my weapon at his throat. "I spy a landlubber."

"I believe it's *arrr*," he said, leaning into the foam sword until his cool lips hovered a fraction of an inch above mine. He let me close the distance, and he exhaled when I did, like he still doubted his welcome. As much as I wanted to linger, I broke off the kiss before we scarred Oscar for life. Or death. Undeath? "Unless you're a particularly frustrated pirate."

Chuckling, I smiled against his mouth. "You can't help it, can you?"

Pink flooded his cheeks, and he eased away from me. "Habit."

"I know." I lowered my weapon and slid my arms around his trim waist. "I don't mind."

"You enjoy being corrected all the time?" He sounded doubtful as he held me, his hands featherlight where they met at my spine. "It doesn't bother you? I can—"

"It's not *all the time*." I wasn't a total dunce. "Only some of the time." I propped my chin on his sternum and gazed up at him. "And it's adorable."

Yeah, yeah. Mushy to the extreme. I know. Cut me a break. We're in our honeymoon period.

The first week of a new relationship is the most intense, or so I'd always heard. I had never had a new relationship, so maybe this felt bigger to me thanks to the lack of experience.

Boaz had always been a dull ache behind my breastbone, a second beat I had felt since we were kids. Linus was more of an addictive taste I was starting to crave, and I didn't mean his blood. I meant *him*. The soft looks, the gentle touches, the tender words. All of it. All of him.

"*Grier*." Oscar sank as much annoyance into the word as humanly—ghostly?—possible. "Pirates don't kiss. It's gross. Make him walk the plank."

"Sorry, Linus, but you heard him." I breathed in the herbal and copper scent of his skin, my mouth watering. Fine, so part of the craving did involve his blood. "Rules are rules, shark bait. You boarded without the cap'n's permission." I raised the sword and pressed the tip of my blade against his heart. "To the poop deck, ye go."

"Poop deck." Oscar cackled. "You said poop."

Boys, pulse or no pulse, enjoyed toilet humor.

Linus smothered a grin, and it was all I could do not to kiss him until it surfaced again.

Hormones.

What can you do?

Apparently, having a *real* boyfriend agreed with me.

"It's Davy Jones's locker for you." I nudged Linus until the foam bent, and he backed toward the house. "Woolly, the cellar doors if you please."

The twin halves leading into the false basement used for storing preserves and mundane nonperishables swung open, the hinges groaning with the old house's laughter.

"Step lively now." I tried keeping a straight face, but it was a losing battle. "This plank was made for walking."

"Drown already," Oscar sighed over my shoulder. "We have treasure to find."

Thanks to a tropical depression moving through the area, we had postponed our treasure hunt for a week after the ball. It was past time to let Oscar have his promised fun.

Eyes glinting with amusement, Linus sank into the murky depths of the cellar, and the warped doors closed over his head.

"Hoist the mainsail," I called, and we resumed our trek to where the map I had drawn for Oscar indicated treasure awaited us. "Batten down the hatches."

A peculiar sensation wedged itself between my shoulder blades as we set out, but there were eyes in the woods.

Lethe.

Hood.

The vampire bodyguards Lacroix had assigned to me.

And High Society necromancers who hadn't lifted a finger to aid in the Grande Dame's release efforts who were willing to make my acquaintance after my demonstration at the ball.

Most requests were confined to emails, texts, calls, or physical mail. But a few wanted to skip the nonexistent line, and those I left to the gwyllgi to hunt or snack on as they saw fit.

Shrugging off the sense of unease, I got back in the pirating mood.

"Arrr." Oscar held the parchment spread out in front of him. "I can smell the booty from here."

I waited all of three seconds before he floated higher than the lowest tree limbs in a laughing fit.

"Booty." He squeezed his eyes shut, but inky tears dripped down his cheeks. "That's funny."

"On your feet, buccaneer." I tugged on the back of his sailor outfit. "There's no time for lollygagging."

After drifting onto his feet, Oscar fanned out the map and resumed his quest.

A throaty baying noise raised the hairs down my nape, and Oscar spun toward me, his eyes black pools.

"Shark," he screamed gleefully, pointing between two trees. *"Run."*

"We're on a—" I started, but it was too late. "Guess this captain ain't going down with his ship."

Lethe padded out on all fours, her lips peeled away from pointy teeth, drool stringing her jaw. Even with the foam shark fin belted around her middle, she looked fierce.

Behind her, Hood strolled on two legs while humming the theme from *Jaws* to set the mood.

"Swim for your life," I yelled to Oscar's retreating back. "I'll handle these coxswain."

"Pretty sure a coxswain is a helmsman," Hood said dryly.

I cut him a flat glare that only made him smile wider.

Gwyllgi had a *lot* of teeth.

Undeterred by my wrath, he continued. "I'm guessing you've never been to Tybee Island Pirate Fest?"

"I don't have a serving wench costume Lethe can borrow, if that's what you're asking."

Odette hated the crowds, so she often came to stay with us during the weekend pirate festivities. Since the rules of Southern hospitality forbade me from abandoning a guest, I had missed every single one to play hostess alongside Maud.

"Now, a little more *dun-dun-dun-dun* and a little less lip, Shark Number Two."

"What kind of shark is he?" Oscar called back to us, clearly offended. "They don't even have lips."

Sticking the fingers of one hand together, Hood propped his wrist on top of his head in a makeshift fin. "The kind that eats ghost boys for breakfast."

The gwyllgi shot after the squealing apparition, and I followed at a much more sedate pace, half hoping the landlubber would shake off his drowning and catch up to us.

"Hey, none of that." Hood circled back for me. "You're in our waters now."

That raised an interesting question. "What happened to the ship?"

"We released the kraken." Mischief glinted in his eyes. "You must have missed that part while you were making out with your captive."

Heat rushed into my cheeks. "I was not—"

"Less stalling." He snapped his teeth at me. "More running."

Without Lethe's golden-haired brother Midas to crack the whip, I had taken up running with Linus at dusk before training with Lethe. He was fast, and his endurance was off the charts. If I asked, he would tell me it was a side effect of bonding with a wraith, but his lean muscles told a different story. He gave Cletus too much credit for abilities he had earned himself, but that was how Linus thought. Always so quick to brush aside his worth.

Growling, Hood charged me, and I didn't have to fake my scream as I sprinted after Oscar.

Fifteen minutes later, a stitch pulled in my side, and my lungs strained for oxygen, but I kept pumping my noodly legs. Even so, I knew Hood was letting me win. He could have overtaken me ten times by now. Still, I made him work to maintain his smug grin.

A feral snarl rose behind me, the deep rumble a threat no human throat should make, and I startled. "Hood?"

Muscles rigid, eyes locked on a pool of shadows, he had adopted a pointing stance usually seen while in his other form.

"Stop right there," a hard voice snapped from the darkness. "Grier, get behind me."

Sweat dripping into my eyes, I blinked in the direction of the command like a shipwreck survivor who had spent too long in the ocean. I really hoped he was a mirage, but I doubted it.

At last, the creeping sensation lodged between my shoulder blades all night had been given a name.

"You've got...to be...kidding me," I panted as Boaz emerged. "What are you...doing here?"

Milk-chocolate irises striated with lighter bands, liked swirled caramel, raked over me, searching for injury. White scars stood in stark contrast against his tanned skin, which was darker than the last time I had seen him. He must be spending more time outdoors during the day. His platinum hair, shaved on the sides and worn longer on the top, showed the bleaching effects of the sun as well.

Odd. Very odd. But not odd enough for me to ask. Curiosity would only encourage him.

"Visiting Amelie," he said, the gun in his hand wilting. "I heard screaming and came to investigate."

With my history, I couldn't blame him for being alarmed. That didn't mean I wanted his concern.

"As you can see, I'm fine." I limped in front of Hood, placing myself between the barrel of Boaz's gun and my friend. "Just a training exercise that got too intense."

A flutter of robes caught my eye as Cletus took point at my shoulder, and I winced at the knowledge he was broadcasting this scuffle live to Linus.

"I heard you all the way from the garage." Boaz squinted at my hand. "Is that...a foam sword?"

"Like I said—" I tucked the blade behind my back "—training exercise."

After clearing his throat, Boaz stepped closer. "Grier—"

"You did a good deed, and I thank you for it, but we're done."

"As long as I'm here..." He rubbed a palm over his head, ruffling his hair. "I've been wanting to talk to you. About the ball. About Adelaide."

Pride kicked up my chin. "There's nothing to talk about."

Boaz had made his bed when he broke up with me to propose to her, and now she had to lie in it with him. Adelaide was a better fiancée than he deserved, but maybe her goodness would rub off on him in time.

"I'm still your friend," he said, the words a silken promise. "I worry about you."

"The sad thing is, you believe that."

Fury, scalding in its intensity, far more heat than my single comment warranted, ignited in his eyes, but he was no longer focused on me.

I didn't have to look behind me to know Linus had arrived.

"You dropped this." He extended the rolled treasure map toward me, the paper damp and mud-flecked, while tucking his other hand into his pocket. "I thought returning it might earn me a place in your crew."

Poor Oscar. And poor Lethe too. She hadn't meant to scare the ghost boy so badly he dropped his map.

She was getting more paranoid about her impending motherhood by the day, and this incident wouldn't boost her confidence in that department.

Accepting Linus's offering, I tapped it against my thigh. "There are always decks in need of swabbing."

Linus didn't kiss me in front of his longtime rival for my affections. He didn't reach for my hand or touch me in a physical, claiming way. He didn't cast me any meaningful looks, either. He gave no outward signs our relationship had progressed beyond friendship, though Boaz had overheard us at the ball and had to know better.

The fact Linus was fine not crowing his victory didn't surprise me. He was a quiet man, and his victories were often kept just as silent. Even the word—*victory*—was mine, not his. He wouldn't see it that way.

"What are you talking about?" Boaz slid his gaze past us to Hood, who kept his fin proudly in the upright position. "This is—"

"None of your business." I cut the gwyllgi a pleading look. "Escort Boaz to the carriage house, please."

"Sure thing." Unashamed, Hood kept his hand propped on his head. "Swim this way."

Boaz frowned at him, and then at me, but he left without further comment.

Sadly, he didn't *swim this way*. Too bad. It would have been *hilarious*.

"I saw you drown." I faced Linus. "Does this mean you're an aquatic zombie? An undead merman? A zerman perhaps?"

Amused, he ducked his head. "I am whichever fits best into your narrative."

Tempted to chastise him about his malleability, I swallowed the words when his cool lips found mine.

"Mmm." I smacked a few times. "No fishy aftertaste."

"I did brush." He kissed me again, slower this time, and my knees melted. "I even used mouthwash."

"That must be it." Nails biting into the hilt of my sword, I glanced up at him from beneath my lashes. "You didn't stick out your tongue or chant *nanny nanny boo-boo* at Boaz. I can't decide if I'm impressed by your restraint or offended you let his latest infraction slide."

"I don't need to prove you're mine." Linus skated chill fingers along my jaw, and prickling flesh rose in response. "You're not a thing I possess. I hold no ownership over you."

But he belonged to me. I had a piece of paper that said so. I meant to destroy it, but I kept dreaming up excuses not to strike a match and watch one more possible future burn when I had already lost so many.

"And here I was thinking of getting matching tattoos." I wrote my name across his heart with a fingertip.

A spark of interest lit his eyes, black creeping in along the edges, but he quenched the flare of possessive heat all too soon. "Maybe one day."

Maybe.

One day.

Linus speak for *If you don't get tired of me before then.*

"Step lively." I set off at a jog, hauling him after me. "There's still one shark in the game."

A few minutes passed during which I was reminded I was the least fit person in our group. A fact emphasized when I stumbled over Lethe's outstretched foot and almost ate dirt. She sat beneath a tree, legs crossed, eating a hamburger. The elastic belt sagged around her waist, and she had twisted the fin to one side to avoid crushing the foam against the trunk.

"Did you hide a snack in the woods," I wondered, "or did you have one in your pocket when you shifted?"

"Wouldn't you like to know?" She crammed in the last bite then wrinkled up not one but three wrappers while I looked on with wide eyes. "I'm pregnant, okay? I get hungry."

"That's not as comforting as you might think," Linus mused. "Coming from a shark."

Lethe stuck her tongue out at him, and proud tears welled in my eyes. I was such a bad influence.

"Where's the kid?" I scanned the area, but there was no blue glow in sight. "Did you spook him?"

"He's a ghost." She grunted as she stood. "What do you think?"

"He memorized the map." I tamped down the instinctive worry stemming from Oscar and Boaz sharing the same woods at the same time. The Elite had no use for a ghost boy now that the dybbuk had been contained. But still, the concern lingered. "Let's see if he's discovered whether X marks the spot."

The three of us walked together, on two legs, to the location where I had asked Lethe to dig a hole deep and wide enough to accommodate a battered trunk I salvaged from the attic. Filled with glass gems and doubloons cast in brass and zinc, it was a discount pirate's dream come true.

Oscar wasn't gloating over his find or scratching in the dirt. He didn't jump out from behind a tree to scare ten years off my life, either.

Dread pooled in my stomach as I knelt on the undisturbed earth. He hadn't been here. He couldn't have dug up the chest alone—he didn't have that kind of strength—but he wouldn't have been able to resist getting a head start.

"Spread out." I dusted off my knees as I rose with a grimace. "We've got to find him."

"He's a ghost." Lethe straightened her fin to get it out of her way. "He can't get hurt, right?"

The question brought memories of Ambrose rushing back to me. The dybbuk Amelie had bonded with fed on spiritual energy. He consumed ghosts, among other things, and he had tried devouring Oscar. That's why the Elite had used the ghost boy as bait for a trap that nearly killed me.

"Even the dead can be diminished," Linus said gently, for my benefit.

"I'll shift." A grimness settled in the lines around Lethe's mouth. "My nose is better that way."

Grateful they supported me and what must seem like helicopter parenting, considering the child was already dead, I waited for her to transform and then pick up his trail.

She backtracked across the property, stalling out between the last place I saw them and where we found Lethe enjoying her snack. The rigidness of her spine warned me I wasn't going to like what I saw, and my chest crumpled inward when a discarded foam sword, bent in the middle, came into view.

"Oscar," I called as I rushed over to reclaim it. "*Oscar.*"

There was no answer as the red magic of Lethe's transformation splashed up her legs, signaling the end of the trail.

"I was tracking your scent on the sword." Her nostrils flared, but her lips pinched. "Without it, I've got nothing. Ghosts have no smell. They're visible to us, and we can feel them, but that's about it. Does he vanish on you often?"

"Sometimes," I admitted, tucking the foam weapon under my arm. "He was so excited about the treasure hunt. He begged me for weeks. It's not like him to flake mid-game."

"He might have expended too much energy." Linus touched my elbow, offering comfort. "You two got into a sword fight earlier, and he carried it and the map during the hunt. He's stronger now than he was, but his natural state is incorporeality."

Intense focus was required on his part—tough for a six-year-old—for him to hold on to objects, no matter how lightweight. Anger helped him manifest too. Yet another reason why I didn't want to arm him with anything sharper than molded polyurethane foam. Not after what he had done to Marit.

"Maybe you're right." The map crinkled in my fist when I tightened my fingers. "You don't think Boaz...?"

"I doubt he would risk falling further from your good graces while his sister lives on your property."

"Guess there's nothing left to do but go home and wait." I set out in that direction but pulled up short when Hood, sans fin, came into view. "Have you seen Oscar?"

"No." He searched my face. "What's happened?"

"We found his map and his sword." Guilt bowed Lethe's shoulders, and misery thickened her voice. "I gave him a head start so I could take a snack break, like it would have killed me to wait an hour before stuffing my face again."

"This isn't your fault." I unstrapped her fin. "Besides, we don't know for sure that anything is wrong."

"I'm going to have a flesh-and-blood kid soon," she fretted. "What if I park his or her stroller at a food truck, get preoccupied inhaling calories, and walk off without him or her? Or worse—what if he or she is kidnapped? The grandchild of the Atlanta alpha is a major bargaining chip."

"Hear how panicked you are right now?" I rested my hands on her shoulders. "That's how I know you're going to be an amazing mom. You would never forget your kid, not even on Two for One Taco Tuesday."

Eyes glassy with unshed tears, she pushed out a slow exhale. "Thanks."

"No problem." Unable to resist, I gave her a playful shake. "Now if it was a churro stand..."

"That's your kryptonite." Her watery laugh made me smile. "Not mine."

"As much as I enjoy hearing you two rank which foods are most likely to result in the child abandonment or kidnapping of our first-born, we need to focus." Hood rubbed his jaw. "Oscar is tight with Woolly. She might have an idea of where he's gone. We should check with her next."

Hope surged through me in an electric tingle. "I could kiss you right now."

"Please don't." He shot Linus a pitying look. "I remember what happened to the last guy."

A teensy smile curved Linus's mouth, but he dropped his chin to conceal his amusement.

I saw it, though. I had gotten good at noticing what he hid from the world. Or maybe he wasn't hiding so much as no one had bothered looking. He was seen now. And when his gaze met mine and the corners of his eyes crinkled, I was flustered at the uptick in my pulse from a simple glance.

Linus meshed his fingers with mine. "How close do we need to get for Woolly to answer?"

The chills racing up my arm had nothing to do with the temperature of his skin, and my chest tightened.

"I can sense her whenever I'm on the property, but our connection is strongest when I'm in sight of her." We set out again, and in a little bit her pitched roof came into view. "Close enough."

I shot the question to Woolly along our bond, and alarm flared, sinking my hope she had a bead on Oscar.

"No luck." I sweated against his palm. "She hasn't seen him since we left."

"Go to work," Lethe suggested. "Get your mind off things."

"We'll worry if he hasn't checked in by dawn," Hood agreed. "Lethe will keep an eye out for him and call if he beats you home."

"All right." I exhaled. "I don't have any better ideas, so we'll go with yours."

"Where are you guys patrolling?" Lethe cut into my swirling thoughts. "Downtown?"

"River Street," I said, deciding I would check the *Cora Ann* in case the magic binding Oscar to the brass button I wore around my neck had faltered long enough for him to be sucked back to the scene of his death.

"Bring home some of those churros you mentioned." She patted her flat stomach. "Baby likes cinnamon."

"Mmm-hmm." I didn't bother hiding my eye-roll. "Does baby like caramel and chocolate sauce too?"

"Yes, he or she does." Lethe ignored my sarcasm. "Thanks for asking."

Back at Woolly, Linus and I left the gwyllgi to discuss security protocols while we stepped inside to dress for the night.

Since I no longer held a job as a Haint, River or otherwise, I had started joining him during his nightly patrols. While it didn't pay much—or anything at all, really—I enjoyed getting to know my city through his eyes. The contacts I made now, with him at my side to vouch for me, would prove invaluable after he returned to Atlanta.

Ouch.

The pinch in my heart when I thought of him going home no longer took me by surprise, but it still hurt.

I didn't want him to leave, but he had a job, a duty. And it wasn't to Savannah, or to me.

"You're quiet," he murmured at the base of the stairs. "Oscar, or something else?"

The man was perceptive. I had to give him that. But telling him I was dreading Atlanta yet again was out of the question. My insecurities would drive a wedge between us if the topic kept popping up in every conversation. Instead of venting, I reminded myself I had known what I was getting into, and with whom, and shook my head.

"Let me grab my bag." It wasn't an answer, but he didn't press. Like I said—perceptive. "Be right back."

I had a thing about ignoring my feelings, bottling them up until pressure built under my skin, ready to explode. I was getting better about letting off steam before I reached that point. Lethe's friendship was slowly filling the hole where Amelie used to fit. There would always be a gap, a space no one else could fill, but such was life.

Old friends left, new ones took their places. Even if the old ones still lived in your carriage house.

Up in my room, I went to check on Eileen where she gazed out into the yard from the oak podium I had rescued from the attic. I kept track of my goddess-touched sigils within her pages, but she seemed otherwise content to bask in the moonlight like a cat in the sun.

I was scratching her eyelids with my fingernail when the force of Woolly's mental *ping* made me gasp.

Images of Oscar flipped through my head, each one brighter than the last.

"We'll find him," I promised, regaining my balance. "The kid is family."

Her relief gusted from the floor registers to flutter the curtains above my window.

"He played hard today." I located a black nylon backpack crammed with necromantic paraphernalia. It was nowhere near as elegant as Maud's leather doctor bag, but that statement piece hadn't exactly been vintage chic when she started carrying it, either. "He might have gone...wherever it is he goes when he's not here."

Oscar never volunteered the information, and I had never asked. I wasn't certain he was aware when he began fading, and if he wasn't, I didn't want to be the one who told him.

A knock on the front door brought my head up, and I strained to hear who Linus greeted, but Woolly's consciousness flared, and a jaunty melody crashed through my mind with her incandescent joy.

"Oscar?" I asked, not quite believing our luck. "He knocked?"

How unlike my little sneak, who preferred popping in and scaring the pee out of people. Mostly me.

Thanks to my connection with Woolly, I was aware of Linus approaching before I heard footsteps on the stairs, and I met him in the hall.

"We have a situation." His lips thinned, and his hand tightened on the banister. "You have a guest."

"I thought..." I peered around him, but he stood alone. "Oscar isn't here?"

Linus hesitated. "He's downstairs."

Certain the last thing I wanted to do was find out what put that look on his face, I followed for Oscar's sake.

The front door stood open, and a young man around my age waited on the porch. He jingled a ring of keys hooked around one finger while clutching the glowing blue hand of my adoptive son with the other hand. The man's hair was black as midnight, and the soft waves fell across his shoulders, clashing with the hard set of his jaw and the piercing green eyes that measured me from top to bottom. He was handsome enough, but wiry. Lean like he was hungry. And he was...angry.

No, that wasn't quite it. He was nail-spitting furious. With me. Over what I had done to him.

How I knew all that at a glance made me question my sanity, but his truth beat against my senses.

Behind him, in the shadows, lurked the gwyllgi. Lethe had already shifted, but Hood remained upright.

As I stepped closer, a prickle of awareness swept up my spine, alerting me to the fact our visitor was a vampire, but...there was more. Not the lure of Last Seed, but a resonance that vibrated in my back teeth, an urge to reach out and touch him. Soothe him. Make amends.

"Oscar." I waved him over, not trusting myself any closer to the vampire. "Come here."

The ghost boy continued staring a hole in my thigh through unseeing eyes.

"I call to spirits," the vampire explained. "I don't mean to summon them." He opened his fingers, but Oscar kept gripping his hand. With a sigh, he pressed a guiding palm between Oscar's thin shoulder blades and nudged his toes right up to the threshold. "I figured you'd want this back."

Ghosts tended to be drawn to necromancers, not vampires, but stranger things had happened.

Just look at me.

Reaching through the wards, I pulled Oscar to me and then demanded, "Who are you?"

"Corbin Theroux."

"That doesn't give me much to go on." I examined his face, trying to place him, but memory failed me. "You look familiar. Have we met?"

"Only once." His hard smile showcased elongated fangs. "I'm your progeny."

"Oh."

Fiddlesticks.

TWO

P rogeny.

    My progeny.

    Corbin Theroux.

Black edged my vision, and Linus cupped my elbow to steady me. "Why are you here?"

Never is a long time for a necromancer, but I hadn't expected the Grande Dame to allow this meeting.

Labeling Corbin as an accident was harsh, but that's how I viewed his creation. I had no memory of coaxing my first vampire into existence after his mortal death at the hands of a fellow inmate. Most of my time in Atramentous was spent in a drugged haze, and I hadn't blinked clear of it when I made him.

"I escaped from my cell." He flashed the keys in his palm. "I stole a car and drove to Savannah." Bitterness tightened his mouth. "I can't go home. Not like this. My parents would kill me."

"You can't tell them you're a vampire," I said through numb lips.

"They would see me coming from a mile away. My folks know all about you, and your world." A world of pain darkened his eyes. "I'm not being dramatic. I'm being literal. They would see their son had fangs, and they would plunge a stake through my heart for the sake of my immortal soul." He spread his hands. "That's why I'm here. I have nowhere else to go."

A human with working knowledge of our world was rarer than hen's teeth, at least one not confined in a cell for life, but he wasn't human. Not anymore. Thanks to me. "How...?"

"I come from a family of hunters."

"Hunters," Linus repeated softly.

"Break it down for me." I massaged my temples. "I feel like my head's about to explode."

"That's why he was in Atramentous." Linus raked his gaze down Corbin. "Few humans are sent there. He must have committed a major crime against the Society. Killing vampires is the worst offense, due to the loss of revenue. It's punished more severely even than the murder of a necromancer."

The Grande Dame had once mentioned I might be surprised by the diversity of my cellmates. I don't recall her ticking vampire hunters off her list, but there was a lot the night she reinstated my title that I had been too stunned to retain.

"I got sloppy. I was recorded beheading a vamp who had been preying on homeless kids. The clip went viral, and the Elite showed up at my day job two days later." Corbin examined me with naked curiosity, his gaze roving my face. "If you hadn't done what you did, I wouldn't have seen the sky again. Granted, in my fantasies, it was blue, but I'll take black." A sigh moved through him. "That makes me the worst kind of hypocrite. Death over undeath is the family motto, but I didn't hesitate."

The twisting in my gut eased. "You...chose this?"

"Yes." He looked at me oddly. "You let me decide my fate."

Eyes pinched closed, I exhaled through the knot of guilt unfurling in my chest. "I didn't know."

A portion of that white-hot anger in him fizzled when he understood I had no idea what I had done.

"I don't remember doing it." Yet here stood the proof I held power over life and death in my hands. "Not that patchy memory absolves me from responsibility, but I didn't know you existed until the Grande Dame informed me I had progeny."

"The drugs." Corbin raised his lip then tapped one of his fangs. "For a long time after, I thought these were a hallucination."

Clear in his tone was the wish they had been. I had turned him into what he must hate the most.

Funny how relieved I had been a moment ago to learn he had chosen this life.

That small reassurance hadn't lasted for long.

Linus derailed my guilt trip before I traveled far. "Mother will be searching for him."

"The Grande Dame will be desperate to get him back," I agreed. "He's proof of what I am."

"Clarice Lawson is your mother?" Corbin took an involuntary step back. "The Grande Dame?"

"Try not to judge him too harshly." I smiled over at Linus. "You don't get to choose your parents."

"No," Corbin agreed slowly. "You don't." His shoulders loosened. "She told me about you."

Too bad she hadn't returned the favor on my end. "I'm sure it was all very complimentary."

"She explained what you are and how I came to be." Laughter twisted in his throat. "She wanted me to understand, to be grateful."

Having been on the receiving end of *you can thank me now* talks from her, I could sympathize.

"She told me you live in Savannah." He raked his gaze over Woolly, the garden, and the carriage house. "I knew your last name, so finding you was easy."

Woolly swung the front door in a questioning arc that helped me remember my manners.

Oscar shuffled over to me and latched his arms around my legs, his eyes heavy with sleep he had never required until now. I palmed the small knife I kept finding reasons not to return to Linus and pricked my index finger. I touched Oscar between the eyes, drawing on a crimson sigil supplied by genetic memory.

"Grier," he rushed out on a shocked breath.

"I'm here, kid." I kissed the top of his head. "Feel better?"

"Mmm-hmm." He reached for me, and I boosted him onto my hip. "I'm sleepy."

Pulling back, I fretted at the dull glow in his cheeks. "Do you want me to tuck you in bed?"

"Nah-uh." He curled his fists in my hair. "I wanna stay with you."

"You got it." Holding Oscar close, I waved Corbin in. "This is not a conversation for the front porch."

Behind him, Hood caught my eye and gave a tight nod while Lethe trotted off into the yard.

As soon as Corbin stepped across the threshold, Woolly snagged him in her wards like a gnat on flypaper. His eyes flared with betrayal, pinning me on the spot like we were trapped together. Loathing morphed his features next, and that he hurled at Linus.

"This won't take but a minute," I reassured him. "I have to know I can trust you before I let you in."

A quiver rose through my feet from the hardwood, a tremor of anxiety from Woolly that she would pick wrong. Again.

"You got this." I placed my hand on the nearest wall. "Volkov tricked his way in. That wasn't your fault. Trust your instincts."

The tremble beneath me eased, and she refocused her energy on scanning Corbin from top to bottom.

After much hemming and hawing, she concluded he wasn't a threat. And with his energy signature humming at a similar frequency to mine, we couldn't deny he was my creation.

Corbin stumbled upon release, but he recovered before tipping into me. "Your home is *alive*?"

"You're a vampire, he's a ghost, I'm a necromancer, and a haunted house is what you find odd?"

"We all have our hard lines." He scanned the room. "Guess mine gets drawn at animate buildings."

Welcoming our second-ever vampire guest into the living room, I indicated the sofas. "Have a seat."

Warily, he sank onto the cushions, muscles tense and ready to uncoil if the couch so much as twitched beneath him.

I could have explained the phenomenon was limited in scope to Woolworth House herself, not her contents, but I figured keeping him on his toes was a good idea.

Eyelids lowering, Oscar levitated out of my arms as if he were a feather blown on an air current.

Woolly rustled the curtains in the nearest window, and I nudged him in that direction. She wrapped him up tight in the scratchy fabric, allowing him to drift nearby while I returned my attention to our guest.

Linus indicated I should take the chair, and he perched on the armrest. Bracing my elbow on his thigh, I propped my chin in my palm and awarded Corbin my full attention. "Start from the top."

"Like I said, I got caught taking out a vampire." His voice came out strained. "The Elite arrested me, tried and convicted me, and then they tossed me in Atramentous."

Black edged my vision, and the room shrank until I was back there, sitting in my familiar cell.

The cold seeps into my bones. The putrid stink of my own filth clogs my nose until I part my ragged lips and suck in rank air swirling near the floor where I press my cheek.

With a violent tug, I wrested myself out of the memories before they sucked me down into oblivion.

Cool fingers brushed my cheek, smearing tracks while hot tears dripped off my chin.

The stairway into my mind, the one curving away from my problems, loomed. The path was a quick escape from what I longed to forget even when I barely remembered the details. But instead of retreating, I set my jaw and linked hands with Linus. Tears wet his skin, and I used his touch to anchor me in the present.

The time for burying my head in the sand had passed. Chin up, I had to see where this journey took me.

"You claim you escaped." Linus addressed Corbin while tracing an absent line from my elbow to wrist. I wasn't certain he was aware he was doing it, but it soothed me. "Where were you held?"

"A facility in Reno." Corbin clenched his hand around the keys, and blood leaked between his fingers from the strength of his grip on the jagged metal teeth. "The Grande Dame offered me a deal. If I allowed them to study me, my condition, they would call my time served in one hundred years."

"You took the deal." Otherwise, he wouldn't be sitting here. He would be chained in a cell.

"What choice did I have? One hundred years in the span of forever is..." A shiver rippled through him, like the thought of eternity chilled him to the bone. "I obeyed their every order and smiled while I did it. Faking compliance earned me extra privileges. Laundry detail got me access to the docks and the trucks." He noticed his hand and wiped the blood on his pants. "One night, I wheeled in my last cart of dirties then crawled under the semi and worked out hand and footholds. The trailer skirt hid me, and I held on until the driver stopped for the night."

"They didn't search beneath the trucks?" Linus cocked his head. "What about the dogs?"

"Cadaver dogs." Corbin snorted. "I don't smell like a vamp to them. I noticed it my first time in the yard, and I tested the theory for weeks before I tossed away my only avenue of escape."

"A soul has to leave the body before it can return," I said, thinking it through. "You died, and I brought you back. You ought to smell the same as any vampire, or close enough for the dogs to point when they scent you." I shared a look with Linus. "Woolly recognized similar notes in his energy to mine. Do you think that might have altered his scent as well?"

Linus pursed his lips in consideration. "We'll have to ask the gwyllgi for their opinion."

"I don't know what to tell you." Corbin shrugged. "I discovered a loophole, and I exploited it."

"A loophole that size is unlikely." Linus radiated calm. "Society prisons are very good at what they do."

"Call your mom and verify my story," Corbin taunted. "She's probably spitting nails right about now."

Used to taking hits below the belt where his mother was concerned, Linus raised an eyebrow as if to ask, *Is that the best you can do?*

"When I call, should I mention you're here?" Linus kept his tone cool, but black gathered in the corners of his eyes. "That you're my source of information?"

The vampire swallowed hard. "No."

"How else would I explain my sudden interest in a minor facility in a town clear across the country?"

Corbin had no answer for that.

Linus knew his mother better than anyone. He was Corbin's best hope of avoiding detection, assuming we decided to help him evade capture. I wasn't sure I wanted Clarice Lawson as an enemy, even if I was responsible for Corbin's current predicament.

"I'm sorry for being an ass." Corbin raked his fingers through his hair, tugging on the ends with frustration. "I haven't eaten since I broke out six days ago."

A hungry vampire was a dangerous vampire. Corbin was a ticking time bomb until he fed.

"I don't know how to..." A grimace twisted his features. "They didn't teach me to..."

"Feed," I finished for him.

"Yeah." Relief he didn't have to say it bowed his shoulders. "That."

Vampire hunter or not, sympathy welled in me. "They served you donor blood?"

"Yeah." He wet his lips. "Heated. In a mug."

Not teaching a vampire how to source his own meals wouldn't

handicap him in the long run. When they got hungry enough, they turned savage. Their biology demanded blood, and their brains flipped a switch to make sure they got it. Rip out enough throats and rogues learned finesse. That or they got put down.

"Look, I get that I put you in a tight spot." Corbin stood with a resigned sigh. "You're under no obligation to help me, but I don't want to hurt any innocents. Can you at least point me in the right direction?"

I hooked a thumb over my shoulder, indicating the stairs. "Fifth room on the left."

"You're going to let me stay?" He glanced between us. "Here? With you?"

"With *us*." I patted Linus's thigh. "He lives here too."

Corbin wisely kept his mouth shut about our living arrangements.

"Dawn is four hours away, and you chose a heck of a city for your escape." Vampires aware of his family ties would kill him on sight, and most necromancers would pay someone to do it for them. Being Deathless didn't mean he couldn't be killed. It just meant he wouldn't die on his own. "Giving you a place to crash for the day is the least we can do." Stashing him also meant we knew where to find him until we decided what to do about him. "Linus and I have errands to run, but we'll leave Lethe and Hood with you in case there's any trouble."

"To keep an eye on me." His eyes glinted in a flash of temper. "That's what you mean."

"That too." I gestured around the room. "This house isn't just my home. She's family. Hurt her, and I will deliver you to the Grande Dame with a big red bow stuck to your forehead. That goes for Oscar and the gwyllgi too."

Squeaky barks carried from the bay window where Keet bounced along the bottom of his cage, snapping his beak at the bars.

This was all Lethe's fault. I told her not to sneak him pieces of hamburger patties. Now she was his hero.

"The same goes for the parakeet." I indicated the small banana-yellow bird scratching his earhole with his foot. "Usually, he has grand delusions he's a bat. Right now, he believes he's a dog. Just go with it."

"Oookay." Corbin looked ready to bolt out the door and take his chance with the dawn. "I guess."

"I'll bring up a towel and fresh sheets in a minute." I hadn't changed the ones in that room since Amelie moved into the carriage house. After getting to my feet, I crossed to the window and unwrapped the bundle of ghost boy cradled in Woolly's embrace. "Oscar, can you show Corbin to Amelie's old room?"

His mumbled reply sounded mostly like a *yes*, so I nudged him toward the stairs.

Corbin stared at me a moment too long then ran his tongue over his teeth in preparation for what he was about to ask.

Linus picked up on the tension between us, and he slid his hands into his pockets. It did nothing to hide the way his fingers curled into fists, but no black clouded his eyes, and I doubted Corbin noticed the slip.

"I need..." Corbin's gaze caressed the length of my throat. "I can't put it off any longer."

"I'll bring you dinner," Linus said in a voice that threatened my ears with freezer burn.

A soft growl tickled the back of my throat, and he whipped his head toward me.

"Not you."

"I offered to bring him dinner." His tone thawed, his eyes dancing. "Not *be* his dinner."

The temperature in the room cranked up a few degrees as I blushed. "Nanny nanny boo-boo?"

The joke was weak, but it was all I had to offer after snarling over him like he was a bloody steak caught between the jaws of two ravenous dogs.

After Oscar tugged on his sleeve, Corbin took the hint and headed upstairs, leaving Linus and me alone.

Linus waited a minute before allowing his lips to curve. "I don't mind you being possessive."

"You're not a hunk of meat." I exhaled through my teeth. "You act civilized, so can I."

"Don't feel the need to conform on my behalf." He eased his fingers under my hair, cupping my nape, his fingers spreading chills. "No one has ever wanted me for myself. I don't mind. You wanting me."

"Good." I let him guide me against his chest, where I buried my face in his shirt and linked my arms at his spine. "I don't plan on stopping anytime soon." I felt the hitch in his breath, the uptick of his heart. "One day, you'll believe that."

He hummed an answer that didn't satisfy me, but it's not like I could beat him over the head with a stick. I mean, I could. He would let me. But it wouldn't drive home his worth. It would only prove I was a crazy girlfriend.

Hmm.

"Am I your girlfriend?" I mumbled against his shirt. "We didn't exactly define this." I swallowed. *"Us."*

"I don't require a label," he said, tension drawing his back tight against my fingertips.

"What if I want one?" I peeked up at him. "Do you have any objections?"

"No," he breathed, the word softer than the relieved exhale that parted his lips.

"Wait here." I ducked into the kitchen and dug out a permanent marker and a pack of yellowed labels Maud used to stick on preserves and various other concoctions. Linus kept a wary eye on me while I filled in the blank space where he couldn't see. "Done." I peeled it off, walked over, and stuck it to his shirt with a pat. "There."

"Grier's boyfriend," he read, his fingers tracing the curling edge. "I suppose that means the reverse is true for you."

"I'm not sure." I gestured to all the empty real estate on my shirt. "I don't have one."

Unable to stop the smile crinkling the corners of his eyes, he walked into the kitchen and jotted down a line. He peeled off his label, returned to me, and smoothed it on my shirt, right over my heart. I worked up the nerve to glance down, uncertain what title he had settled on so quickly, and my voice broke when I read simply, "Mine."

I had never belonged to someone before and had them belong to me too.

This felt big, larger than stickers and more permanent than the markers we used to stake our claims.

"You guys heading out?" Lethe strolled into the room and plopped on the couch. "Or making out?"

Huffing in annoyance, I picked up a pillow and threw it at her head. "Ever hear of knocking?"

"Ever hear of not inviting strangers into your house?" She caught the pillow and tucked it under her head. "Oh! Or better yet—ever hear of not inviting strangers to sleepovers? Seriously. You have trust issues. As in, you're not suspicious enough."

"Woolly cleared Corbin," I reminded her.

"He won't cause any problems," Linus agreed. "We have too much leverage over him."

Hearing his certainty bolstered mine. "If he shows his butt, we'll toss him out on it."

Linus excused himself to the kitchen.

The fridge opened, glass tinkled, and the microwave hummed.

Lethe examined her fingernails. "What do I get for babysitting your spawn?"

"Whatever you want from Black Dog Brewery."

Her eyes lit up, and she rubbed her hands together.

"Keep it under a hundred this time," I warned. "I can't afford to keep bribing you otherwise."

"I did," she protested. "My bill was like ninety-nine dollars and ninety-six cents. A new record."

"The charge was for two hundred and sixty-five dollars."

She twirled a strand of vibrant blue hair around a finger. "I can't help that you didn't put a cap on Hood or Baby Kinase."

"One hundred dollars," I said slowly. "Total."

"Fine," she huffed. "I'll go light."

"Thank you." I lifted a finger. "On the topic of my spawn, how does he smell to you?"

"Like he spent one too many days in a car without taking a pee break."

"I meant species-wise."

"Oh." She thought about it a minute. "Mostly, he smells human, but not *human*. Know what I mean?"

"Uh, no."

"Vampires carry this undertone of humanity in their base scent. It sours over time, but it's still present, even on fledglings. Decay starts as soon as they turn. Corbin smells like you, but not like a necromancer, and like a vampire, but not a dead human."

"As confused as that explanation makes me, I'm guessing inhaling it would also give a cadaver dog pause."

"Probably." She snickered. "They're not exactly gwyllgi to know the difference, are they?"

Linus returned with a steaming mug he raised to Lethe. "Can you run this up to Corbin?"

Nose wrinkling, she reached for it. "Sure thing."

Arm extended as far as it would go, she couldn't run up the stairs fast enough.

Eager to get out of my head for a few blocks, I turned to Linus. "Do we patrol, or do we run away?"

Locks snicked on the front door, and I realized my mistake, but by then Woolly had latched the windows too.

"I'm kidding," I told her. "It was a joke."

The old house was not amused, and she refused to budge.

We were locked in for the night thanks to me and my big mouth.

"There's more than enough to keep us occupied in the basement," Linus pointed out.

Basement access had been a tender spot between us, but relationships were built on trust, and he had earned mine ten times over.

"That works." I massaged the base of my neck. "I wanted to stretch my legs, but it's probably smarter to stay home considering we have an unexpected guest."

The chandelier in the foyer dimmed with Woolly's suspicion that I had accepted being grounded so well.

Little did she know alone time with Linus was far from a punishment.

The lock on the basement door got thirsty from time to time, and tonight it must have been parched. That, or it tasted the remnants of old blood on my hand from where I pricked my finger to give Oscar a boost and got a hankering for more. I had to reopen the cut, stick the persnickety brass key in the lock, and bleed liberally on both before I could twist the knob.

"That never gets easier," I grumbled.

"Paying a tithe never does," Linus said, then took my hand, turning it over in his. He knew better than to offer to take away the pain, and it was too minor for a healing sigil. Before I could tell him so, he guided my finger into his mouth and swirled his tongue across the hurt. "Better?"

I managed a whimper.

"Grier?" He caught me around the waist as my knees liquified. "What's wrong?"

"Her ovaries exploded," Lethe called from the living room, having returned from her errand in record time to torment me. "I heard the blast from here."

"How do you know what happened?" I yelled back at her. "You don't have super vision."

"I smell blood, and I heard you gasp, all breathy-like. It wasn't hard to figure out what you're up to back there."

Linus's cheeks managed to redden within a shade of his hair. "Oh."

"No, no, no." Lethe cackled. "It was more like *Oooh, Linus.*"

I died on the spot. I was dead. Done. That's how it felt anyway.

"I'm just going to..." I indicated the open door leading downstairs. "Uh, basement."

The claustrophobic press of a starless night sky swirled around me as I descended into what had been Maud's private sanctuary. The walls closed in on me, the maw as cruel as my cell in Atramentous, the abyss ready to swallow me whole.

Usually, I darted straight through the enchantment that discouraged nosy visitors to the bottom. Tonight, I lingered in the magical gloom while my blood cooled from Lethe's taunting.

The problem with hiding in absolute darkness is no one can see where you're standing.

Linus bumped into me, and I stumbled down a few steps. He caught me in a steely grip and lifted me back onto the stair below his. "I thought I gave you enough time."

"You did," I panted, clinging to him now that I had lost my sense of place. "I was dragging my feet."

More certain in the dark than me, he took my hand and escorted me into the library.

The spell dissipated on the lowest stair, and Woolly flicked on the lights, her consciousness hovering.

"We're not going to jailbreak," I assured her. "There's no way out of the basement."

Unconvinced, she settled in to watch us start cataloging the treasure trove that was Maud's life's work.

"This is where we left off." Linus dropped a box onto the research table where we had taken our lessons with Maud. "Do you want to skim or sort?"

"You read faster." I pulled out the chair for him. "I'll sort. I want to burn off some of this energy."

Floor-to-ceiling bookcases lined the walls. Scrolls and books and pamphlets overflowed the shelves. We had never paid much attention to the upper rows. I say *we*, but Linus would have asked about them. She must have kept their contents to herself since he appeared as overwhelmed by the process as me.

Necromancers lived a long time, and we accumulated a lot of junk during those years. People like Maud, the academics, the innovators, collected more than most. Their private thoughts carried weight, and she had safeguarded every single handwritten note by sealing it in the library, the lab, or her private office.

"These are letters from her former lovers." Linus tossed a packet of envelopes bound with twine on the table. "I would rather not read those if it's all the same to you."

Wrinkling my nose at the content, I lifted them with a fingernail hooked through the knotted bow.

I didn't want to read about more of her exploits in graphic detail. Once was plenty. More than enough. We had stumbled across enough love notes between her and her beaus to realize she enjoyed describing her sexual encounters down to her partners' recovery time.

A few of the racier excerpts included sketches and read like instruction manuals for new hires.

It was more than any child ever needed to know about a parent.

"I'll file these under *Naughty*," I said, wishing for hand sanitizer, "and we'll keep going."

"We're within two years of when your mother arrived in Savannah," he offered. "We're getting closer."

The goal was to reach the point when Mom and I showed up on Maud's doorstep. The hope was we could determine if Mom had written to Maud about her condition—or mine—prior to her arrival. Then we could read forward, absorbing Maud's observations over the years in the hopes we could learn what she had discovered and build our knowledge base on hers.

"Are we not going to talk about Corbin?" Linus asked into the quiet. "You must be reeling."

With my back to him, I took longer than required to tuck the letters into the correct box.

"I never thought we would meet. That was silly, wasn't it? He's immortal. I'm the next best thing. It makes sense that he would seek me out eventually. He would have been curious about me, about his unicorn status, even if his resuscitation happened under normal circumstances."

"You prioritized. There's no shame in that. It's not like you've been sitting on your hands all this time."

"No," I agreed, facing him. "I've been trying to survive."

"Do you feel drawn to him?" A hint of the clinical seeped into his voice, the professor at work.

"He makes my back teeth ache." I turned to him and leaned my hip against the box. "Is that normal?"

"Each practitioner has a different response to their progeny. This might be normal for you. It's hard to say without a second progeny for comparison." He drummed his fingers on the table. "How do you feel around Keet?"

"My heart gets squishy, and I want to coo at him, even when he's being a weirdo. Can you believe he barked at Corbin?"

"That's not what I meant, and yes. I can."

"Keet and I have been together since I was a kid." I rolled a shoulder. "I might have grown used to him over the years." Linus inclined his head, awarding me the point. "What are we going to do about Corbin?"

"We?"

"Pretend this is dodge ball. I picked you first. You're on my team. Sorry not sorry, Grande Dame."

"I'm always on your team." He leaned forward in his seat. "I always have been."

A burst of warmth ignited in my chest and spread through my limbs. "You're spoiling me."

"No." Wisps of black swirled through his eyes, there and gone. "This is how relationships work."

The mention of his greater experience doused the heat suffusing my limbs with icy reality.

It was stupid, I was stupid, for wanting him to be a paragon of virtue to spite Boaz. Linus had had a life before I crash-landed back in his. He had no reason to hope he would ever see me again. He had been free to pursue whatever, and whomever, he pleased, and it was obvious he had taken lovers.

He had told me as much himself.

"I bow to your wisdom," I said lightly. "I don't have much to compare us to."

Hands braced on the tabletop, he rose. "I didn't mean—"

"That wasn't an invitation to share." I swatted the air like it might knock down what he wanted to say. "I really don't want to go down that road with you. Memory Lane is my least favorite street for cruising."

"All right." His lips thinned. "Back to the matter at hand. Corbin. What do we do about him?"

"How much trouble will we get in when your mother finds out we aided and abetted him?"

Linus sat. "A significant amount."

"You have a firmer grasp on the political ramifications of whatever choice I make. What do you think?"

"You sound like you've made up your mind to help him disappear."

"Unless there's reason to believe he's a threat to innocents, I won't return him to a cage. I just...can't."

"I know."

"You have more to lose if this goes south. You don't have to back up my decision with your mother."

"Yes," he said, his fingers pressing along the peeling edge of his name tag. "I do."

Unable to resist the temptation, I crossed to him and plopped down on his lap. "I like you."

"I like you too." He leaned forward, his mouth an exhalation from mine. "Very much."

"Kiss me already." I threaded my fingers through his silky hair and guided his face down to mine, our lips brushing as I spoke. "I'm tired of doing all the work for you."

"This is a dream." His cool breath whispered across my cheeks. "That I can touch you, that you want me to touch you..." He laughed softly. "None of this feels real. One wrong move and I'll find myself in bed, alone."

The roots of my heart twisted until I worried they might snap. "You haven't slept since the ball. Not once that I've seen. Please tell me this isn't what's keeping you up days."

"I'm afraid of waking."

"Oh, Linus." He was breaking my heart. "I'm sorry for this in advance."

While his brow gathered in neat little rows, I pinched the soft part of his upper arm with a vengeance.

The shock blasted him out of his seat, dumping me on the table as he stood. "Why did you—?"

"Congratulations!" I clapped for him. "You're wide awake."

And he had probably bruised my much-abused tailbone. I really had to add some padding back there.

Note to self: Eat more churros. Add extra caramel. With a side of chocolate sauce.

So far, I had gained fifteen pounds thanks to the high concentration of Vitamin L in my diet, but I wasn't as curvy as I used to be even with the blood smoothies Linus blended for me at breakfast. I missed having boobs. A butt would be nice too. Most of my hard-earned weight was settling in my hips and thighs. I never had an hourglass figure, but I was starting to look like the bottom half of one. Until I turned sideways. Oh well. Curves were curves.

Maybe I expected Linus to laugh. Maybe I expected him to rub his arm and scowl. Maybe I expected more sweet words exchanged in whispers. However I expected he would take the wake-up call, it hadn't been like this.

The darkness in him beat like a second pulse in his temple, his tattered wraith's cloak a smudge across his shoulders. Black churned in his eyes, devouring the blue, and he flattened his palm against my sternum. He pressed, not hard but firm, forcing me to lie back on the table. Bracing his palms on the wood to either side of my shoulders, he lowered his head until I could have stuck out my tongue and licked his chin. I was tempted to do just that.

Linus gazed down at me, ravenous, a buffet of his favorites he wanted to savor one item at a time.

I joked to cover my nerves. "Cletus isn't going to get an eyeful of what's happening down here, is he?"

Mentioning the wraith broke the spell, and Linus blinked his eyes clear. "No."

Gathering my wrists in his hands, he hauled me into an upright position and claimed my mouth in a blistering kiss full of sharp edges and flavored with hope. I didn't understand where either came from, but they both cut just as deep. His blood hit my tongue from where my teeth clashed with his lips, and my head spun, my stomach tightening for an entirely different reason.

The force of his embrace had me reclining again, this time with a smile on my face.

Tap-Tap-Tap

"Ignore it," I breathed into his mouth, hooking my legs around his hips. "Whoever it is will go away."

"Sun's up," Lethe yelled against the door. "Corbin's out cold. I'm heading to bed."

Footsteps thumped away from the basement door, and I relaxed into his embrace with a low moan.

"Ha!" Lethe shouted loud enough to raise the dead. "I thought I heard heavy panting down there."

"I give up." I dropped my legs, scooched off the table, and sidestepped him. "I'm going to die a virgin."

"Whoa." Lethe sucked in a sharp breath. "I'm really going now. As you were, lovebirds."

More footsteps tromped away from us, but I called out, "No one believes you."

She answered a heartbeat later, "I was totally leaving that time."

After jogging up the stairs, I shoved open the door, which bounced off her forehead.

"Fuck." She rubbed the red spot between her eyes. "That fucking hurts."

"Such language," I said sweetly, not feeling the least bit sorry for whacking her. "Think of the baby."

"You weren't thinking of the baby when you gave his or her mother brain damage."

"You're fine." I pried her hands away from her face to examine her. "You'll have a goose egg, but that's it."

"I wouldn't have bothered you if I'd realized that's what Linus meant about you two staying occupied." She sighed with her whole body. "Okay, I still would have done it, but I would have quit after the first time."

"No, you wouldn't have." I took the modified pen out of my pocket, grateful each time I used it that I didn't have to resort to brush and ink to draw on sigils these days. "Hold still."

"You just want to erase the evidence before Hood sees what you've done to his darling mate."

"You're not wrong." I tapped her on the end of her nose. "Now stop wiggling."

"I have to pee. The baby is jumping up and down on my bladder."

"You're not that far along yet." I narrowed my eyes as she darted a quick glance out the window and then to the door, as if measuring the distance. Motion caught the corner of my eye. Hood, strolling into view as he made his rounds. "You're trying to beat me to Hood and get me in trouble."

"You're not wrong," she parroted, baring her teeth in a grin. "So long, sucker."

Faster than anyone on two legs had any right to be, she bolted out the front door.

Before Woolly could latch it behind her, I leapt over the threshold and skidded across the planks.

Lethe was fast, her feet hitting the grass as she sprinted toward her mate, who stopped to watch our mad dash with an indulgent shake of his head.

"You're teaching our child to be a tattletale," Hood warned, amusement brightening his eyes.

Five yards ahead of me, Lethe slid to a stop, almost knocking him to the ground. "I have a boo-boo."

"Poor baby." His arms came around her, steadying her. "Did you drop another cookie?"

"That was one time," she protested, "and it was still warm."

Mallow hired a new baker last week, and he worked magic on the selection of cookies, brownies, and cake pops they sold. Usually, I was all about the hot chocolate, but Lethe was broadening my horizons.

The incident in question occurred when she promised me the last cookie then waited until I left to pour us glasses of milk before she stole it. Suspecting treachery, I ducked back in the room and caught her with her hand in the glassine bag. I tackled her from behind, and she dropped the prize, which rolled under the coffee table. After a growl to warn me away from her food, she wedged herself under there. When she popped the treat into her mouth, she cracked her head on the underside of the table.

Leaning down, he kissed his mate's forehead tenderly. "Better?"

"That's it?" A growl revved up her throat. "I'm injured."

"The rest is waiting for us at the gate." He indicated the driveway with his chin. "I ordered breakfast."

"I love you more than bacon," she said, peppering his face with kisses. "More than ham. More than hot wings. More than steak."

"Let's not go overboard." He took her hand then pointed a finger at me. "Get in the house."

"You're not the boss of me."

Woolly opened the door, beckoning me back in, but a throat cleared behind us.

Amelie stood in the doorway of the carriage house dressed in nice pants and a cute top with her hair pulled back into a neat tail. "Do you have a minute?"

Already tired from the early hour and goofing off, I slumped. Her appearance exhausted me. "Sure."

For the first time since moving her into the carriage house, I entered its living room. I paused on the threshold and shot a glance at the kitchen, but it was just a room filled with appliances. Without Linus, the warmth was gone. The heart of this home now beat in his childhood room in Woolworth House.

"You look nice," I told her when she didn't manage to come up with a reason for wanting to see me.

"Online classes." She smoothed her hands down her pants, and I noticed her feet were bare, her toenails painted a flaking orange color. "Usually I can fudge it with brushed hair and a clean shirt, but tonight I had a presentation."

"Your brother stopped by," I said, and I could have strangled myself for providing the segue.

"That's what I wanted to talk to you about." She reached out, her fingers curling, like she worried I might sprint for the door and she planned on stopping me before I escaped. "Not him, I promise."

Unable to bring myself to sit, to get that comfortable around her, I stood with the backs of my knees pressed against the couch cushions. "I'm listening."

"Odette is gone."

Happy this was one mystery I could solve on the spot, I let the coil of tension in my chest unwind.

"She's visiting a client," I informed her. "Trips are so unusual for her, she warned me ahead of time."

"Her house is empty. There's nothing left." She tore her finger-nail to the quick. "She's gone, Grier."

The room spun, and I was grateful the couch caught me when my knees buckled. "How do you know?"

"I've been talking to her every Monday for weeks. This last time, she promised to visit, to teach me control..." She made a vague gesture that I assumed referenced Ambrose, her dybbuk shadow. "I worried when she never got back to me, so I asked Boaz to drive out to Tybee and check on her. That's why he stopped by tonight."

"He didn't say a word about this to me."

"He brought the matter to his commander's attention and requested permission to launch an investigation into her disappear-ance." She linked her hands at her navel, and her knuckles turned white. "He wasn't going to bring this to you until he had answers, but Odette is your family. You deserved to know, so I overruled him." She smiled to herself. "He just doesn't know it yet."

"I appreciate the heads-up." I propped my legs under me. "I'll go take a look around at dusk."

"Let me know what you find?" The hope in her expression gutted me. "I'm worried about her too."

"I'll give you an update when I have one." I started for the door, intending to walk right through without saying goodbye, but guilt cramped my belly. "I hope this won't cause problems between you and Boaz."

"I've been doing a lot of thinking." A self-deprecating laugh escaped her. "There's not much else to do in here."

The taste of old pennies flooded my mouth as I bit my tongue to keep from pointing out she wouldn't be exiled to social Siberia if I could trust her.

"I have a chance to reinvent myself." She dragged her gaze to mine. "I made a list of traits I think a good person should have." Her smile went limp and sagged on her mouth. "Honesty was at the top." She unlinked her hands, and they trembled. "This is my first step on the path to a new me."

A new me.

Soon she would cease to exist as Amelie Pritchard—no, that version of her had already been erased. She was Amelie *Madison* now. The reminder left me with a ringing in my ears. She stood in front of me, an arm's length away, but I couldn't have crossed the yawning abyss stretching between us if I had wings.

"It's dangerous wanting to be someone other than yourself," was all the advice that popped into mind.

Amelie wanting the elusive *more* was what had gotten her into this mess.

"I'm a caterpillar these days. First Ambrose turned me into his host, and now Adelaide is turning me into her dead sister." Her toes bunched on the hardwood. "When I burst from my cocoon this time, I'm hoping for butterfly instead of moth wings."

"I want that for you too." And I meant it, every word. "I want you to be happy."

But until she loved herself, the person she was born to be, I worried misery was all she would find.

"Thanks," she said softly. "You'll let me know about Odette?"

"Yeah," I promised. "I will."

The walk across the lawn to Woolworth House was too short to grind down the edge of my panic. I strode in, jogged the stairs, and took advantage of Linus's open-door policy. I found him propped up in bed, wearing black-framed glasses, dressed in a white tee with striped pajama bottoms. The book in his hands drooped at whatever he read in my expression.

"Odette is missing."

He set aside his research and opened his arms to me. He didn't have to ask me twice. I climbed up the mattress and rested my head on his shoulder.

"How do you know?" he murmured against my hair. "Who told you?"

"Amelie." I breathed in his scent and relaxed. "She got worried when Odette wouldn't return her calls and asked her brother to check out the house on Tybee. That's why he came out earlier. That, and to spend some time with her."

"How does he know she's gone?" His fingers traced soothing lines down my arms. "You mentioned she was traveling. Does he know her well enough to tell what's missing?"

"No, they aren't close." I shivered in his arms, the chill of his skin clearing my head. "That doesn't matter in this case. The house was empty. Cleaned out, according to Amelie."

"I'll check it out." He kissed the top of my head. "You go rest."

Jitters prompted me to offer him company. "It's not far. I could go with you before I crash."

"Your truce with Hood is delicate." He set me aside with gentle hands. "It's in your best interest to remain here."

True, Hood was still sore about me trapping him in a circle while I faced off against vampires solo, and I had given my word not to interfere with him protecting me again, within reason, but he had extended my leash a bit. He didn't shadow me everywhere I went, so long as Linus or Cletus did the job for him.

Unhappy to be rousted from my spot, I frowned. "Are you telling me to stay put?"

"No." He stood and selected an outfit from his closet. "I'm making an observation."

"Hmph."

"Come with me," he offered. "I won't stop you."

"This is a trap," I grumbled. "You're using logic against me."

"I will support whatever decision you make," he said on his way into the bathroom to change.

The old house groaned through her floorboards until I worried they might snap.

"I'm not going with him," I assured her. "I respect Hood too much to sneak out without him."

Plus, the guy had really sharp teeth, and he knew how to use them.

When Linus reemerged, dressed and ready, I let him reach the door before clearing my throat and pulling out my pen. "Where do you want your sigil?"

When he glanced back, his eyes were warm. "I thought you might have forgotten."

"You're going to examine the scene of a possible crime. Alone."

"I've done it many times over the years."

"Yes, well, you didn't have me then. You're going to have to suck it up and learn to live with it."

"Somehow," he said, his fingers working over the buttons on his shirt, "I think I'll survive."

"You better," I growled, then set to work on the sigil that would keep him safe when I couldn't.

THREE

The dream swirled into my head before I understood that I
had fallen asleep waiting on Linus.

*He has a new girlfriend. His third one this week. Just as
mundane as all the rest.*

*Why not me? Why won't he ask me? I would say yes. He knows I
would say yes. Maybe that's the problem. Maybe I should play hard to
get. Maybe then he would see we were meant to...*

*The carpet squishes under my feet, and cold slime seeps between
my toes. I shiver, confused, my anger at Boaz forgotten. The smell hits
me then, copper and rose water and thyme.*

Maud.

*I collapse to my knees beside her and scoop the icy blood back into
the gaping hole in her chest.*

"Maud?"

*The sobs start, and I can't stop them. I'm working as fast as I can,
but her heart—*her *heart—it's missing.*

"Wake up. Please wake up. Please, Maud. Wake up. Please."

Shivers dapple my arms, and my teeth chatter, but it doesn't matter. None of it matters if she won't open her eyes. I'll be alone again. All alone. Maud is all I have, and she's...

She's gone.

She's dead.

Dead.

Using her blood for my ink, I start drawing a sigil, one I've never seen in any textbooks.

"No, Grier," a voice pleads behind me. "Stop before it's too late."

"I'm not losing her too. I won't." I keep going, slipping and sliding, covering her head to toe in the foreign sigils. "Come on, Maud. Try. For me."

"You have to let her go." Footsteps pound closer. "You don't want her back. Not like this."

"You're wrong." I scream so loud my voice shreds to ribbons. "I want her back any way I can get her."

"You don't mean that. Please, Grier. Think."

Snot clogs my throat as I close the sigil with a defiant swoop of my finger.

Magic explodes into the room, knocks me backward, and my head cracks against a wall.

"Grier."

Darkness swirls around me, and I embrace it, grateful when it blinds me to the corpse at my feet.

Cold seeped into my bones, frigid as the grave, and I turned away from the source, still half-asleep.

"I'm here," Linus murmured from some great distance. "Sleep."

I sank deeper into the blackness, and this time I dreamed of nothing at all.

I WOKE with shooting pain in my tailbone. I was ready for a spine-ectomy. Mine was faulty. It hurt all the time. I'm sure sleeping upright on floors and getting knocked on my butt daily had nothing to do with it.

"You're awake."

Eyes still heavy with sleep, I mumbled, "I am?"

"Your stomach is growling."

"I swallowed a tiger."

Linus laughed, really laughed, and the sound was so bright I had to open my eyes to see for myself.

"Breakfast is ready whenever you are," he said, and he handed me a chill tumbler that smelled like herbs and copper, like him, like fresh-cut mint rubbed between a thumb and finger and the tang of old pennies. I sipped, and my appetite dialed down from a roar to a purr. "Do you want to eat first or shower?"

"I'll shower." Setting the smoothie aside, I groped behind me, intending to push myself upright using the vee made by the corner where I slept, but there was only one wall supporting my back. "What in the...?"

"You slept in the hall outside my room," Linus explained, rescuing my aperitif before I knocked it over with my flailing. "I found you when I got home."

"I must have fallen asleep in your bed." Slumping down, I rubbed my eyes. "Sorry about that."

"I don't mind." He shifted to his left, but I saw the chair he had positioned into the doorway of his room. A new sketchbook rested on two hefty tomes under it, and a jar full of colored pencils topped it off like a cherry on a sundae. "I wasn't sure if you walked here from your room." His gaze tagged the landing. "I worried you might fall down the stairs if you got turned around, so I kept watch."

Embarrassment propelled me to my feet. "Please tell me you didn't draw me."

Linus blocked the doorway to guard his prize. "How could I resist?"

"Show me." I held out my hand. "I want to see."

"Are you sure?"

Not really. "Yes."

"Promise me you won't destroy it." He scanned my face. "I'm partial to the subject matter."

"Fine," I grumbled, crossing my toes. "I won't destroy it."

Poor, trusting Linus retrieved his sketchbook, lifted the cover, and spun it on his palm. I was about to make a liar out of myself when I saw what he had drawn. Me. Asleep. Curled up in his blanket outside his door like a baby bird kicked out of her nest. I looked... peaceful. Content. Safe. Clearly, he had taken liberal artistic license.

"Well?" He nudged my foot with the tip of his shoe, proving he knew me too well. "What do you think?"

"I'm not sure who the model is, but it's a lovely piece." I traced the dark strands of hair fanned across the hardwood. "You're a talented artist."

"Your dreams aren't all nightmare," he told me. "The worst comes before dusk."

"That sounds about right." I passed the drawing back to him. "The nightmare feels longer, though."

"Nightmares always do."

An unsettling quiet filled the space between us, and the light dimmed in his expression.

Out of time for make believe, I gathered my nerve. "What did you find?"

"Boaz was right. The house is empty. There's no furniture, no art on the walls, no pots in the kitchen, no clothes in the closet." He flattened his lips into a hard line. "There's no trace of Odette, and no sign she plans on returning."

"I don't understand." A childlike whine threaded my voice. "I spoke to her last week. She told me she was going to visit a client. She wouldn't have just left. Not without telling me. Something must have happened to her."

"There were no signs of a struggle."

"I want to see for myself." I touched his arm. "It's not that I don't trust you..."

"I understand." His hand settled over mine. "I've already informed Hood we'll be driving out to Tybee."

"I'll go change." I slipped past him. "We can deal with Corbin when we get back."

Tiny brackets framed his mouth, but he let me go and went to ready his things.

Woolly, the little eavesdropper, informed me Corbin was sleeping in with a flash of insight through our bond. He was probably exhausted from his escape and the drive here. Good. He could catch eighty winks as far as I was concerned. Odette was family, and family trumped progeny in this case.

After I pulled on jeans, sneakers, and a clean tee, I braided my hair and slung my backpack across my shoulders.

Linus met me on the stairs, and we walked down together.

Hood and Lethe waited for us in the living room. She was snacking her way through a bowl of popcorn, but she stopped cramming her face long enough to smile at me. Hood stole a piece, and she growled at him. He tweaked her nose, finding her adorable, and Lethe snapped at his fingers. Before they progressed to full-on love bites, I clapped my hands to get their attention.

"Lethe, can you stay here and watch Corbin? He's still asleep, but he'll wake up hungry."

"There's more blood in the fridge," Linus added before a smile crinkled the corners of his eyes. "From all the donors Grier rejected. Corbin might as well drink up. She won't touch it."

"You're lucky I don't have one of those juice box straws with a tapered end." I mimed piercing his carotid artery. "Otherwise, I would so stab you right now."

The man was far too pleased with himself for being tasty. But I wasn't much better, snarling over my preferred vintage when vampires got too close to him, so I had no room to talk.

"Sure thing." She stomped Hood's instep on her way past him to the couch. "I'm always left behind. Why would tonight be any different?"

Glancing between them, I had to wonder if I hadn't walked in on a fight larger than food. Granted, not much ranked higher than grub with Lethe, but she wasn't usually this violent over non-meat snacks.

Hood tossed the van keys in the air. "Do you want to drive them?"

"No." She shoveled a handful in her mouth, giving her chipmunk cheeks. "That's your job."

"I'm staying with the vampire." Hood folded his arms across his broad chest. "You go with Grier."

"I won't, and you can't make me." She reached for the remote, smearing butter all over the buttons. I bet Linus—my little neat freak —was dying inside, but he kept his agony to himself. He could always wipe it clean later, when there wasn't a cranky gwyllgi guarding it. "I'm going to sit here, stuff my face, and veg out while this parasite bloats me."

Parasite? That was a new one.

"You okay?" I inched closer. "You're more bite than bark tonight."

"I'm fine," she snarled at me. "Back. Off."

I took her suggestion literally. Gwyllgi reflexes put necromancers to shame. "This is me, backing off."

When Linus took my elbow, I didn't fight him as he led me outside and away from Lethe. Hood followed, but he kept glancing behind him to where Lethe was eviscerating her snack with brutal chomps.

"I'm not going to suggest it's hormones," I told him, "but I would like to know what's up with her."

"She got challenged for her position as second in the Atlanta pack." He scoffed. "Via text message."

"The cowards waited until she was pregnant and out of town to hit her with this? Even then, they didn't have the courage to do it to her face?" I curled my fingers into fists at my sides. "Can she fight in her condition?"

Blanching, Hood checked to see if she'd heard, then exhaled with relief when she continued ignoring us.

"*Never* imply she's not fit to defend her rank. She'll kill you for the insult to her pride." Pinching my arm in a viselike grip, he hauled me stumbling to the gate. "Though she would feel bad about it later."

"Oh, well, that makes it hunky-dory," I whisper-screamed. "I'm warning you now that if she eats me, I'll give her indigestion for the rest of her life. Your children and great-grandchildren will rue the day she gobbled me like a Thanksgiving turkey."

"Slow down, drumstick." Hood chuckled. "Thanksgiving is a human holiday."

"No, it's a major food holiday," Linus reminded him. "Grier celebrates all those."

"There's no law against a necromancer celebrating Turkey Day," I pointed out, and they both laughed.

Being raised with a foot in each world, the way I and most Low Society necromancers were, was an invitation to adopt the human holidays that suited us. For me, that involved most all of them. Any excuse to eat was a good reason to celebrate in my book.

"She has her priorities straight," Hood said, amused. "You're definitely pack with that bottomless pit you call a stomach. You're practically gwyllgi."

"I choose to view that as a compliment." I passed through the gate. "Let's go to Tybee."

On the way, I used an app to order Lethe five burgers, five fries, and five chocolate shakes with whipped cream and cherries.

With any luck, the extra calories ought to make her easier to live with until her inner beast settled again.

FROM THE MINT-GREEN siding to the peppermint-pink shutters, from the white trim accenting the eaves to the clear plastic sealing the windows to keep it cool, Odette's bungalow on Tybee Island had always reminded me of hard candy still in the wrapper.

Hood parked in the sandy driveway, and I approached the front door. I knocked, waited. No one answered. I knocked again, waited longer. Still no response. I gave it a go for a third time, but the results were the same.

Odette wasn't here. No surprise there. I was only prolonging the inevitable.

"The door was unlocked when I was here earlier," Linus offered. "I didn't lock it after I left."

Gathering up my nerve, I tested the knob. As Linus said, it spun without resistance. I pushed in, and the sight punched me in the gut.

The bone-white couch, the driftwood coffee table, the local art hung here and there. All gone.

When I breathed in the air, it tasted stale. Old. Faded. The perfume of her incense was a whispered suggestion.

A loud sneeze blasted from Hood as he entered the living room. He glanced up at me through red-rimmed eyes and sneezed again. Water poured down his cheeks, and snot dripped from his nose.

He looked like someone had hosed him with pepper spray.

"What's wrong?" I gripped his arm when he swayed. "Hood?"

"Get him outside." Linus took his other side. "He needs fresh air."

Thankfully, Hood walked out under his own power. He allowed me to navigate since his puffy eyes were swelling closed. With his sinuses blocked, he was nose-blind too. Depending on me was a huge show of faith for a predator, and I firmed my grip on him, determined to be worthy of his trust.

"The house..." he panted, "...has been...dusted with powdered...bronze."

"They expected a gwyllgi." I helped Linus ease Hood down onto the sand. "Don't move."

Hood wrapped his palm around my ankle. "Where are you going?"

"To the van." I rested a hand on his shoulder. "I'm going to get some water out of the fridge so we can flush out your eyes."

"Stay with him." Linus cut me a look over Hood's head. "I'll fetch the water."

I mouthed *Thank you* then knelt beside Hood. With his senses impaired, he was bristling for a fight. As someone he had sworn to protect, that he claimed as pack, he was fighting instincts that must be howling at him to act to keep me safe even though he was the one who had been attacked.

"Do you want me to call Lethe?" I let him keep his grip on my leg. "Do you need a healer?"

"Yes." He coughed, his breath whistling through his abused lungs. "Both." His eyes, red-rimmed and puffy, focused on me. "Tell her what happened, but don't let her get near me until I'm clean."

Linus returned with a few bottles in hand and passed them to me. "What can I do?"

"Call Lethe." I cracked open the first lid. "He's going to need medical attention prior to her arrival."

"Hopefully," Linus said, dialing as he walked away, "she'll take this news better with a full stomach."

"I'm going to pour this water over your face," I told Hood. "Hands down. Don't touch your eyes."

A growl pumped through his chest, his hand tightening on my ankle, but he held still.

"One bottle down, three more to go." I watched Linus out of the corner of my eye. "Almost done."

"We need to sterilize him before he gets around Lethe," Linus said, rejoining us, "or in the van."

"I didn't even think about contamination." I looked at him. "We've been exposed too."

The van cost too much to risk its functionality. That left us with two options. Neither were great.

"Open your eyes." I finished with Hood and collected the bottles. "Better?"

"Before it felt like someone had blowtorched my eyeballs."

"And now?" I prompted him.

"More like someone sandpapered them."

"Sounds like progress to me." I passed the empties to Linus, who walked the trash over to the bulky can waiting at the curb for pickup. "Just sit tight, and we'll figure this out."

Linus crossed back while pressing buttons on his phone, and I got a bad feeling about his plan of action. Not that I had a better one.

"I called Mother's driver. The Lyceum is sending someone for Hood. They'll take him to the Elite barracks on Habersham Street, stick him under a shower, then arrange for a ride to Woolworth House in a different vehicle." Linus pocketed his phone. "The driver will take Hood to the healer then pick up Lethe and drop her off there."

"That takes care of them." I got to my feet and helped Hood to his. "What about us?"

"I made arrangements" was all he said, but he didn't seem happy about them. That all but guaranteed I wouldn't be either.

"You searched the house earlier." I aimed the comment at Linus. "Why didn't the bronze dust affect Hood when he met us at Woolly?"

"I sent Cletus in to scout," Linus admitted. "After I tested the door and found it unlocked, I thought it best to leave the house undisturbed. There weren't enough shadows for a lengthy reconnaissance, since wraiths can't manifest in daylight, but I did the best I could under the circumstances."

The force of his meaning struck me, that he was preserving evidence, and I almost wished I had left well enough alone.

This really was a crime scene now, but not for the reason I first imagined. Dusting the house with powdered bronze had been a deliberate act of malice.

"Lethe might have miscarried if she'd breathed in enough of that poison," Hood said, his voice scratchy.

Thank the goddess for small mercies. Lethe was safe inside Woolly and not mired in the sand with her mate.

"Odette didn't leave of her own free will." The confirmation rocked me. "She was taken."

"You said she was visiting a client." Linus lifted his head. "Do you have any idea who?"

"Confidentiality agreements tied her hands." I had no clue who used her, and her clients banked on that anonymity. "All she told me was she made allowances for him that she wouldn't for anyone else. It made me think they must have become friends over the years. She did say he was one of her first and still one of her best clients."

"One of her first," he said, sounding thoughtful. "That might help us narrow the scope of possibilities."

A sleek car painted the exact shade of wet blood pulled into the driveway, and a man in a suit stepped out wearing the blank expression of someone who did as his employer required without asking questions. He got within several feet of us before Hood caught his scent and started growling.

"It's your ride," I murmured, soothing his overprotective instincts. "No worries."

His grumble implied he wasn't thrilled to be crammed into a car with a stranger but would cooperate.

"We got this," I called to the driver. "Can you open the door?"

"Yes, Dame Woolworth."

With help from Linus, I wedged my shoulder under Hood's armpit, and we lifted him together.

"Do you want me to ride with you?" A cold sweat broke along my skin. "You don't have to go alone."

"I can't afford to show more weakness," he panted. "Not after the challenge to Lethe. The pack will have eyes everywhere, and I can't let them see me like this."

"We'll send Cletus with you." I made it an order. "He's inconspicuous."

A weak growl rattled up the back of his throat, but he didn't press the issue as we stuffed him in.

"Cletus." I waited for him to join us. "Can you escort Hood on his errands?"

The wraith fluttered overhead, his attention fixed on the bungalow.

"What is it?" I touched the wispy edge of his tattered cloak. "What do you see?"

Unable to voice an answer, he drifted lower, until he stared at me from his empty hood and extended a bony arm toward me. I reached out, and he dropped a white ark shell on my palm.

"Ah, thanks." I turned it over in my hand. "Linus, any idea what this means?"

The bleached shell could fit on my fingertip, and it was perfect except for a tiny dot near the hinge made when a moon snail drilled a hole through the shell with the sharp teeth on its tonguelike radula.

A frown knitted his brow. "He's not projecting to me."

That probably wasn't a great sign, but there was nothing to be done about it right this second.

Having given me his gift, the wraith took position over the car, ready to do his duty.

The driver gave us a polite nod then pulled away.

Once they were out of sight, I got antsy about this latest kink in Cletus's wiring.

"Can you pick up on Cletus now?" I searched Linus's face. "Can you see Hood?"

Black swallowed his eyes as he stared down the single lane. "Yes."

Before I could summon relief, a familiar van streaked with dirt and finger-written obscenities rolled up to the curb. The window lowered to reveal our old pal Tony, dressed in a stained tee and pajama bottoms, who toasted us with the last swallow of his energy drink.

"It's been a while." He tossed the can onto the growing pile in the front passenger floorboard. "You two go on vacation or something?"

"Bermuda." I smiled brightly. "The triangle is awesome this time of year."

Tony stroked the few scraggly hairs protruding from his chin. "Where are you headed?"

"Johnson Square." Linus held the door for me then joined me on the bench seat. "Near the Nathanael Greene Monument."

I shot him a look, but he wore the mask of Scion Lawson, and there was no prying up the edges for a peek underneath while in mixed company.

We rode in silence, minus the boisterous slurps from the front scent as another energy drink met its untimely death.

Ah, the fragrant scents of pepperoni, unwashed feet, and armpit funk.

I must be feeling nostalgic.

My eyes were certainly watering.

Linus slipped Tony his requisite fifty-dollar bill when the van slowed, and he had a grip on the handle before it came to a full stop. He got out, helped me onto the sidewalk, and we left our former driver before he finished swallowing.

After a few laps around the monument, I got curious about our destination. "Feel like going for a walk?"

"I wanted to make sure he was forced back into traffic. I don't want him to see where we go next."

I wanted to see where we went next. "Do you think the Marchands are still bankrolling him?"

"No." He sounded certain of the fact. "Heloise is the one who struck the bargain. Eloise cut ties with him after he demanded payment for services rendered. She knew we were aware of his betrayal and that he was compromised. He is no longer of any use to her. She squared her sister's account with him after using the app to book a ride across town, but she told him not to bother contacting her again."

A coil of Spanish moss hit my shoe, and I scanned the old oaks overhead until I spotted the chittering squirrel responsible. "How do you know all this?"

"I planted a bug the last time we rode in his van." Linus made no apologies for that fact. "My team has been monitoring him for weeks. The transmissions cut out a few days ago. We had the confirmation we needed, but I prefer to keep tabs on my enemies."

Setting aside the fact he was playing spymaster, I wondered, "What happened to the original bug?"

"Filth." He took a handkerchief from his pocket and unfolded the halves to expose a tiny device staining the fabric brownish-red. "He must have tossed a can or container in the back that jarred it loose. Some combination of pizza sauce and energy drink fried its circuits." He rewrapped it and tucked it into his pocket. "I was more careful with placement this time, and the casing is waterproof."

"Boys and their toys." I bumped shoulders with him. "You're kinda cute when you go all James Bond."

"I didn't tell you." The curtain of his dark-auburn hair swung forward, hiding his expression. "I'm sorry."

"I'm not going to shake a finger at you and call you a liar if you forget to clue me in every now and then. You're used to working alone, making your own decisions, and acting on them." Easing my fingers through the silky length, I tucked a few strands behind his ear. "Don't hold back with me about us, and I'm good."

The way he palmed his nape and rubbed like he had narrowly avoided stretching his neck over the executioner's block broke my heart. "It's hard for me, letting you in."

"I know." I took his hand. "It's not exactly easy for me, either." I laced our fingers. "We'll figure it out."

"I have something to show you." He searched the street one last time. "Promise you'll let me explain before the screaming and hitting starts." He ducked his head. "It's not a gift, really."

"Oh, goddess." Dollar signs flashed in my mind's eye. Linus might be getting better about showing his affection rather than buying it, but if he was warning me, he must have spent big. "This is going nowhere good."

"Will you come with me?" His hesitation was priceless. "It's not far."

"I might as well." I bit back a laugh. "I'm curious what's put that look on your face."

The last time he looked this particular combination of anxious and excited, he gave me Eileen.

We crossed left onto East Congress Street then took a right on Abercorn Street. On the corner of Abercorn and East Park Avenue sat a two-story house turned business with faded blue clapboard siding that had seen better days. A realtor's sign stapled to the power pole out front read SOLD in red letters.

The bottom fell out of my stomach. "Tell me you didn't buy that house."

"I did."

"You said it's not a gift."

"It's not."

I narrowed my eyes at him.

"Technically," he amended, "it's not for you."

"Then *technically*, who is it for?"

"Me."

"You bought a house in Savannah?" I frowned at the eyesore. "*That* house?"

The address promised he had paid at least a half million dollars for the location, but the house itself was in sad condition. Only a significant cash infusion could save it, and love. *Lots* of love.

The keys jingled when he removed them from his pocket and unlocked the front door.

"The downstairs was originally an art gallery, but it's been remodeled and reimagined several times over the years." He glanced back at me. "Upstairs is a fully renovated two-bedroom, one-bath living area."

"Are you...?" I stepped back, almost into the street. "Are you moving out?"

Our living arrangement had nothing to do with our relationship. Us sharing a roof, or at least a property, was a condition his mother insisted on. There was no reason to feel rejected, but I did. Just a smidgen.

"What?" Fumbling the knob, he dropped the keys. "No. Of course not. Nothing like that." He crossed to me and set his hands on my shoulders. "I'm doing this all wrong."

I sucked in a breath, expecting the worst. "Spell it out for me."

"You've been lost lately."

Cutting ties with the Haints had left me adrift, true, but I had found new purpose in rededicating myself to my studies, to my past, and to my city.

No.

This city.

Savannah wasn't mine. My home, yes. But *mine*? One potentate in this relationship was plenty.

"Okay," I said, "so far I'm following you."

"You loved being a Haint, and I thought..." His arms fell to his sides. "What would you think of starting your own ghost tour company?"

"Competing with Cricket?" The blood drained from my face. "To quit on her then open my own business feels like a betrayal."

Linus nodded like I had stuck to his mental script. "What if you didn't have to compete with Cricket?"

"How do you figure that's possible? She's cornered the market in walking tours downtown, and the *Cora Ann* is a huge success. What's left that's not in direct competition with her?"

"What if you specialized in...the truth?" He shoved his hands into his pants pockets. "You tell historically accurate stories from the human perspective. Why not tell a niche clientele what actually happened at a select few locations throughout the city?"

As much as the scope of the project overwhelmed me, I couldn't deny the flutters in my belly.

"The Society would have a cow." The reality of presenting the idea for his mother's approval left me cold. "They would never let me share necromantic history with the masses."

"Not the masses," he corrected. "Vampires, necromancers, witches, gwyllgi, wargs, and whoever else is willing to pay twenty-five dollars for a two-hour walking tour led by none other than Dame Woolworth herself."

I didn't notice I was wiggling in a happy dance until he started laughing under his breath.

"Incoming," I shouted and flung myself at him. "I cannot believe you did this for me."

Linus caught me, a hint of his tattered cloak exploding from his back as his eyes shot wide. *"Oomph."*

Arms cinched around his neck, I screamed, "Early-warning system *activate.*"

"It's too late to activate." He laughed. "You already launched."

Raining kisses over his face, I hung on tight, climbing him like kudzu until he wore me like an apron.

"What am I going to call it? *Oooh.* What about a theme?" I chewed my bottom lip. "Not Southern belle, but a costume. Something to set us apart. Too copycat? Allowable? What do you think?"

Face buried in my neck, he murmured, "I love...your enthusiasm."

Lips pressed against his throat, I murmured back, "I love...your thoughtfulness."

"Let's go shower."

"Are you serious?" I fluttered my lashes. "Do you think buying me a building is all it takes to get me naked?"

Linus flushed so hot, so fast, he turned purple beneath his freckles. "That's not why I—"

"You think I don't know that?" I cupped his face between my palms. "I'm teasing."

"There's something I need to confess." He covered my hands with his. "I..."

The warmth fled his expression, black swallowing his eyes as he zoned out on me.

"Cletus checking in?" I released him and shimmied down his body to my feet, not expecting an answer.

"Hood has showered and changed. All traces of bronze powder have been erased. He's with the second driver, in a clean vehicle, and they've picked up Lethe."

A buzz in my back pocket caught my attention, and I whipped out my phone. "Crap."

Linus came back to awareness. "What's wrong?"

"Lethe shot me a text to remind me since she's gone, Woolly and Oscar are babysitting Corbin alone."

That meant no more teasing Linus and no more grand tour. We had to get home.

"We can use the upstairs shower and change clothes to decontaminate ourselves. You can go first." He led the way into the building, through the cavernous downstairs with poured concrete floors that echoed with our footsteps, and up the black metal stairs near the back. A few steps past the landing, he indicated a small bathroom with clean towels stacked on the lip of the sink. A few still had price stickers. "There's a shop a few buildings down. I'll procure us clothing and then work on transportation."

"Should you do that before you shower? Won't you just transfer the powder?"

Replaying it in my head, it sounded like I was offering to let him join me, and he must have thought so too if the tips of his ears reddening were any indication.

"I'll give them our sizes and have someone else bag my selections. That ought to minimize any cross contamination."

I trailed my fingers over the terrycloth. "Did you stock the place yourself?"

His gaze touched on the shampoo and soap in the shower, both his favorite brands. "I did."

"Hmm."

He followed me one step into the room. "What does that mean?"

"You expected to shower here?" I noticed the other things then. Toothbrush, toothpaste, deodorant.

"Work," he said, and his eyes went distant. "Some nights I wash it off before I go home."

"Even in Savannah?" Lately, we tromped home together, dirty or otherwise.

"Especially in Savannah," he said, voice soft as he left.

The reminder that secrets lingered between us shouldn't have stung as much as it did, but there you go.

I got naked, eager to drown the carousel of thoughts circling through my head under the shower.

Having full control of the water was odd. The lack of running commentary was peculiar too. I didn't like it much. I was too used to having Woolly in my head, her presence a vibrant spark that brightened my days. This building felt like a brick-encased corpse by comparison.

After I scrubbed until my skin turned pink, I emerged from the shower smelling like Linus. No complaints there. I dried off then wrapped the largest towel around my torso to keep me modest while I scrubbed the contents of my pockets clean of bronze powder then went exploring.

The upstairs apartment was all pine heart floors and elegant period details, lovingly restored. Whoever had lived here sank a substantial amount of time and money into renovating the living area. Too bad the economy couldn't support many boutiques or galleries long term, even if their unique offerings charmed the tourists. I hated imagining the previous owner sacrificing this labor of love to salvage their finances.

The first bedroom, the larger of the two, caught my eye. Well, the king-size bedframe made from twisted wrought iron did. Foam wrapped the elegant posts, and a plush mattress still in its plastic sleeve leaned against the wall. Sheets in their zippered bags and pillows stuffed in boxes filled the far corner.

The prickling awareness I was being watched brought a smile to my lips, but when I turned, I was alone.

"Bathing here I get," I called, figuring Linus must be in the hall. "But do you really need a bed?"

No response.

"Linus?"

No answer.

Proving I could learn, I didn't investigate. I darted for the bathroom and the knife I had left to dry on the sink after its cleaning.

Quiet pervaded the space, and I almost convinced myself the noise had been the unfamiliar building settling around me, but a sixth sense warned me I wasn't alone. I didn't waste time wondering. I sliced open my index finger and drew protective runes down my arm then set myself in a protective circle.

A soft chuckle echoed up to me from the stairwell, and then the heavy presence retreated.

I counted the seconds by the pounding of my heart until I heard the front door click shut.

Clutching my towel, I lowered the seat on the toilet and sat down to wait on Linus.

FOUR

Linus arrived ten minutes later dangling a large paper shopping bag from his fingertips. He held it as far away from his body as the length of his arm allowed to avoid contaminating its contents. It hit the floor when he spotted me sitting in my magic bubble on the toilet.

"Have any luck?" I indicated the toppled contents spilling across the floor. "I'm getting chilly."

"What happened?" He righted the bag, but his eyes never left mine. "You're in a circle."

Using the edge of my towel, I rubbed off the sigils. "I sensed a presence and called out, but they didn't respond except to laugh at me before they left."

Thankfully, he paid me the courtesy of not asking if I was certain my mind hadn't played a trick on me.

The vampire archers hadn't attacked since the incident on River Street, the truce with my grandfather appeared to be holding, and the Marchands hadn't left their sprawling family estate in Raleigh since the night of my ball. A necromancer pressing their case was a possibility, but why would he—and the laugh had sounded masculine—flee after cornering me in a vulnerable position?

The lull in activity was one of the reasons Linus embraced me joining him on his patrols. All the trouble we found was someone else's drama. A refreshing break from the insanity that was my own life.

"I want to hold you." He lingered in the doorway. "But you've showered, and we don't have much time."

"You can make it up to me on the ride home."

I eased around him, gathered the clothes, and carried the bundle into the master bedroom. I left the bag with its contaminated handles on the floor. We would have to come back later and clean up after ourselves.

A flicker of black near the tall window startled me.

"Oh, Cletus." I exhaled with relief and waved him in. "It's just you."

This building wasn't warded against wraiths, not yet, so he drifted through the glass and joined me.

Hopefully, this meant Hood and Lethe were safe and not that Cletus had abandoned the gwyllgi for me.

"Turn around, please." I sorted my clothes from Linus's. "This won't take but a minute."

The wraith faced the window, the wisps of his cloak more substantial than the first time we met.

I pulled on clean underwear, each piece taken from a padded hanger, and slid a floral sundress over my head. A pair of classy flip-flops, a thing I hadn't known existed, had been wrapped in the material. The dress would have been too small if not for its trapeze cut, and the toe thong pinched the top of my foot, but all in all, he did good.

"All right." I started finger-combing my hair. "Let's clear out and give Linus the room."

I bumped into him in the hall, and I wish I had bumped him a little harder, maybe copped a feel in the bargain.

A large towel wrapped his hips, and the intricate tattoos branding him were on full display. I pretended not to gawk. It didn't go very well. Despite the number of times I had seen his bare chest, I couldn't get used to the sight.

So much skin. So much corded muscle. So much ink.

"You can't look at me like that when I'm only wearing a towel," he said, water dripping from his damp hair. "Let me get dressed first."

"The fact you aren't dressed is what's causing the problem." I fanned myself. "I'm getting hot flashes."

The wall kissed my spine before I saw him move, and then his lips were on mine. I took it as an invitation to explore his back with my fingertips, and I moaned into his mouth when he broke away to plant stinging bites down my throat.

Heat pooled low in my gut, but I startled when icy fingers brushed my shoulder. Weird. Linus was gripping my hips, pinning me to the wall, and he hadn't sprouted a third arm that I had noticed.

The wraith faded through Linus until I was almost kissing the black hole of his fathomless cowl.

Recoiling from the grim visage, I gagged. *"Cletus."*

A flick of Linus's wrist ordered the wraith away. "I'll try not to take triggering your gag reflex personally."

"I like Cletus, but I'm not ready for that level of kink." I laughed. "I still have my training wheels on."

Linus made a pleased sound low in his throat as he rested his forehead against mine and shut his eyes.

"You sound happy," I pointed out. "I didn't just greenlight a threesome with Cletus, did I?"

"Ah, no." A powerful shudder rippled through him. "Necrophilia isn't a fetish of mine."

Snorting at the comment that left me wondering where vampires fell on that scale, I smiled. "Glad to hear it."

"And..." he kissed the tip of my nose, "...I am happy."

Heart full to bursting, I jerked my chin toward the wraith. "What blew smoke up his cloak?"

"He's concerned about us staying here." Linus withdrew, but the pleasant chill of his touch lingered. "He shouldn't be capable of worry." He cocked an eyebrow at me. "He shouldn't have emotions at all."

"Oops?"

"Oops indeed."

"Does the fact he's back mean Lethe and Hood are with the healer?"

"Hood has finished treatment, and they were on their way to Woolly when Cletus left them."

The wraith would have escorted them all the way home if he hadn't picked up on Linus's concern and come to investigate, but this latest evidence of Cletus's independent thought process made me wonder.

Had the wraith come to me because Linus was rattled or because the wraith itself worried?

And how much trouble would I get in if the answer turned out to be the latter rather than the former?

"Get dressed." I shoved Linus through the bedroom door then regretted putting my hands on him again. More to the point, I regretted not putting my hands on more of him. "I have to get home before Oscar and Woolly blow up the house. Plus, we need to check on Corbin."

Fine, so she *was* the house. I doubted she would set herself on fire or allow Oscar to manifest near a box of matches, but I still didn't trust those two. They were troublemakers, the both of them.

Linus dressed in the time it took me to work up the nerve to investigate the stairwell for signs of my visitor. No convenient footprints led the way, no lingering cologne perfumed the air, and there was no message written in the settled dust.

"See anything?" He examined the walls and steps as well. "I didn't notice any oddities on my way in."

"Nothing." I rubbed the base of my neck. "I'm starting to wonder if it was a figment of my imagination."

Yeah, yeah. Him doubting me was one thing. Me doubting me was—any day ending in Y, honestly.

"Don't discount your instincts. You wouldn't have raised that circle if you hadn't been certain someone was there." He took my elbow and guided me downstairs. "I believe you." He held me close, and I suppressed a grin at the subtle protective gesture. "We'll set wards before we begin rehabbing the building."

Outside, I used his keys to lock up the place while he scanned the street for lurkers. "Who's giving us a lift home?"

"You'll see." Having deemed the area safe, he escorted me to the curb to wait. "It's a lovely night."

"I hadn't noticed." I tipped back my head. "Clear skies. Bright stars. Quarter moon. Not bad."

That's when I heard our ride approaching with the *clip-clop, clip-clop* of hooves on asphalt.

Laughter bubbled up in me. "You booked us a horse and carriage?"

They were popular with tourists, and I loved watching them parade around downtown, but I hadn't ridden in one since the year I begged Maud to rent one for my birthday. I was nine or ten, I think. I had fallen asleep on the bench seat, curled around Amelie, and Boaz had to carry me in before dawn.

Pleased with himself, Linus waved to the coachman. "I thought the fresh air might do us good."

And the longer trip promised extended cuddle time. "This is perfect."

"Evening, folks," the older gentleman said with a syrupy drawl. "These are my friends, Prince and Bowie, and we're pleased to be your escort home."

Linus opened the half door on the carriage and helped me up onto the bench facing forward. He joined me a moment later, and I tucked myself under his arm before he finished lifting it.

"I won't break," I promised. "You can hold on as tight as you want."

Permission granted, he pulled me across his chest and rested his chin on the crown of my head. His arms came around me, and he held me like he might never get another chance.

Maybe my run-in with the chuckler in the hall had made him nervous, but a tiny part of me worried there was another reason.

These were the moments when I braced for the worst, when I expected the other shoe to drop. I waited and waited, and the longer I kept vigil, the more convinced I became that the impact would level what I was building with Linus.

He told me once that he was a secret bound in a thin skin of humanity.

I knew that. I accepted that. I respected that.

But I had been hurt so many times I couldn't shake the dread this would be the deepest cut yet.

Linus might worry that I would get tired of him, that I would leave him, but I was the one who hadn't burned our marriage contract.

After the driver set out, I took the liberty of testing a sigil I had been toying with for the past few days. I used the modified pen to draw it on each of us then settled in to discuss options for dealing with Corbin.

"How certain are you that this sigil works?" Linus twisted his hand back and forth, admiring my work.

"I tested it out on Hood. I figure if a gwyllgi can't hear me blasting music through my Bluetooth speaker, then a human won't hear me having a conversation." I worried my bottom lip between my teeth and then admitted, "I'll be honest. It's had a fifty percent success rate. I also tried it on Lethe, but she found me."

"Why do I feel there's more to the story?"

Pulling back to see his face, I tried to act offended. "Why are you so suspicious?"

"With you two, there's always more. Hood had no idea what he was unleashing when he introduced her to you."

"I might have been eating a cheeseburger at the time," I confessed. "She sniffed me out."

"That I can believe."

"She's eating for two," I reminded him in the same tone she used. "She needs those extra calories."

"Mmm-hmm." He tightened his arms around me. "I'm glad they're your responsibility and not mine."

"On the topic of responsibilities..." I buried my face against his chest. "Corbin needs to learn how to vampire. He's a danger to humans until he's taught how to feed. He needs outside connections for blood when donors aren't an option. Given his history, he'll never forgive himself if he hurts someone."

"We could send him to Reardon." Linus cupped the back of my head. "He would be safe at Strophalos."

"Reardon is a dysfunctional vampire, and a shut-in."

Reardon McAllister was a made vampire with no clan affiliation since his necromancer wife turned him against his will after he sustained life-threatening injuries in a carriage accident early in their marriage. He was a human victimized by vampires, and that placed him under the Grande Dame's purview. Since Corbin was running from the Grande Dame, no matter how secure Strophalos was, he wasn't safe there.

"I will admit Reardon might not be the best choice to teach a fledgling vampire to hunt when he can't leave campus. The faculty frowns on eating students."

"I have a crazy thought." I looked up at him. "What if we dump him in Grandpa's lap?"

"Your grandfather would take him in." His lips thinned. "He would love to have a Deathless in his ranks. I worry what it would mean for your relationship with Mother. She won't take kindly to losing her prize."

"I've been thinking about that." I sat up straighter. "You had trouble believing he busted out of prison. I can't speak to the facility where they sent him—it sounds like minimum security at best—but I can tell you the sentinels take their jobs seriously. I can't see him escaping without help. I'm not saying he's lying. He might believe he got lucky, but I don't."

Any narrower and his mouth would disappear. "You think she let him go."

"Why would she feed him all that information about me—down to my city—if she didn't intend for him to run straight to me? She knew his history, knew his family would shun him, knew the vampires would kill him outright, knew the necromancers wouldn't dare hide him for fear of retribution. He has no one, nothing. He's alone in the world, and she knows me well enough to guess I would take him in."

"You saved his life."

"Did I?" *Life* was a loaded word for the existence he faced now. "Or did I condemn him?"

Most humans would be grateful for this turn of events, but most hadn't grown up hunting the very thing he now was either.

"Ultimately, that's up to him to decide. Eternity is what he makes of it."

"You're very Team Grier." I leaned in closer. "Has anyone ever told you that?"

"No." He pitched his voice low. "Though I'm sure others have suspected."

The reality of what we were contemplating sank in as the humor of the moment faded.

"Your mother knew I wouldn't shelter him long term." I might help him disappear, but I wouldn't make a production out of it. "Given Lacroix's doting-grandparent act at the ball, she must be gambling he would be eager to make amends for his transgressions. He wants to give that appearance anyway. She expects me to yank on those family ties to protect my progeny out of a sense of obligation." I whistled softly. "She wants a plant among Lacroix's vampires."

Lost in thought, he let the scenery draw his eye. "The trap does appear to be set."

"Corbin fosters with Lacroix, learns the ins and outs of vampire-hood, and maps how the organization works." I put it all in words to test how crazy it sounded. "Assuming the intel is good, your mother offers him amnesty for his past crimes."

The sales pitch was easy to imagine with all the Society's resources at her fingertips.

Join the Undead Coalition.

Have your pick of clans—or maybe even start your own.

Just keep playing mole, stay buried, and share all the dirt on Lacroix's plans.

"The timing is suspect," Linus admitted. "Mother met Lacroix at the ball, and a week later your progeny arrives on your doorstep with him the logical haven."

"Hmm. Then it's decided."

A wary expression crossed his features. "Dare I ask?"

Snuggling in for the remainder of the ride, I confessed, "I'm going to make Corbin an offer he can't refuse."

CORBIN WAS SITTING on the couch, watching television, and eating a bowl of cereal left over from Amelie's marshmallowism days. I watched through the window, expecting a flash of red or pink to coat the small frosted pieces, but when he turned up his bowl to slurp, milk dribbled down his chin.

Plain. White. Milk.

"Are you seeing this?" I murmured to Linus. "He's eating. Actual food."

Volkov once ate a grilled cheese sandwich in my kitchen, but he was a Last Seed. They were born from a newly turned male vampire knocking up a willing surrogate before his sperm died too.

Deathless, even though they were made, must share more traits with LS than your standard vampire.

"Interesting." Linus came up behind me. "The blood wasn't

enough."

"This might explain why your mother left hunting out of his curriculum. He can't require much blood to survive if he can still process food for nutrients."

We watched a moment longer before Corbin felt eyes on him. He wiped his mouth dry with the back of his hand then scowled at our huddle and started for the kitchen with his bowl.

The eaves creaked overhead, Woolly snickering at us getting caught, and she opened the front door.

Once inside, I glared up at the foyer chandelier. "You couldn't have flicked a curtain to hide us?"

The crystals tinkled with her laughter, and the sound made my heart light.

"How's Oscar?" I glanced around, but he hadn't come to greet us. "Still sleeping?"

The floorboards made a groaning noise that conveyed her worry over the ghost boy.

"I'll check on him before I go to bed." I lingered in the foyer. "What about Corbin?"

The lights brightened, giving the impression the old house liked him. How much of that was my energy coursing through him versus his own merit, I wasn't sure.

"We're not keeping him," I warned her. "We're not running a B&B here."

Odette once accused Woolly of being a halfway house for broken dreamers. She wasn't wrong. We had taken in our fair share of strays. I preferred to believe most would be rehabilitated during their stay, and I could release them back into the wild.

Thinking of Odette made my chest pinch until I rubbed the spot, not that it soothed the ache.

Corbin was loading the dishwasher when I came upon him. Tidy. I liked him better already.

"You eat," I stated the obvious. "Actual food." Well, cereal. "You couldn't have mentioned that sooner?"

"I'm a freak of nature." He leaned against the counter. "I didn't want to spook you."

"Hey, freak of nature is my line." I dropped onto a barstool. "And you're not going to scare me. You can't be worse than I am. I made you, remember?"

"Hard to forget."

Ouch. "Last Seeds can eat food. Most don't. It's so plebian." I snorted. "All this means is you're more like them than made vampires."

"Last Seeds? What are those?" He looked at me funny. "Aren't all vampires made?"

"They didn't tell you anything." I groaned, letting my head fall back on my shoulders. "No wonder you're so confused." Linus stood in the doorway, giving me the floor, but I waved him in. "You're better at lectures than I am. You've had a *lot* more practice. Would you care to fill in the blanks for him?"

Linus smiled a tiny smile that told me he was aware I was teasing him. "I'm happy to be of service."

While he began outlining Vampire 101, I slipped onto the back porch and squinted into the darkness. Hood and Lethe hadn't been with me long, but I had grown to rely on them so much. I would have felt braver with one or both by my side, but I had to do this right. That meant I had to do it alone.

I walked until my spine tingled, took a breath, and stopped where the garden ended in a copse of trees.

"I need to speak to my grandfather," I said in a cool voice. "Tell him the matter is urgent."

"Yes, mistress," two voices replied in tandem.

Keeping my shoulders squared, I walked back to Woolly as Amelie opened the carriage house door.

"Any news?" she ventured, her gaze sliding past my shoulder to the trees. "Did you find Odette?"

"Boaz was right. The house has been cleaned out." And doctored to screw with the gwyllgi, meaning we couldn't track her using our best resources, but I couldn't tell Amelie that. "There were complications, so we just got back. I was going to text you before bed." At least that had been the plan up until I had forgotten with everything else going on. "I'll update you in a few days, unless we find her before then."

"Okay." She attempted a smile. "I'll do the same. When I hear back from Boaz."

"I'd appreciate it." I hesitated before producing the shell from my pocket. "Does this ring any bells for you?"

"You're joking, right?" She sobered upon realizing that no, I was not. "There are a million of these on Tybee, holes and all. It's where a moon snail—"

"—drills a hole with its radula so it can slurp out the clam." Odette had taught us that when we used to spend the summers gathering shells and stringing necklaces on her porch. "Just thought I would check."

"Send me some pictures in better light," she said after a minute. "I'll look them over and see if it shakes anything loose."

"Sure." I waved then rocked back on my heels toward Woolly. "Night."

Guilt prickled my nape as she watched me go, but I had nothing left to give her.

Linus strolled out the back door, hands in his pockets, as I hit the steps.

"You didn't run screaming into the woods after me," I observed. "Impressive."

"I did consider it." He swept his gaze over me. "Any minute now, I was going to start flailing."

"Just make sure you wait until I have my phone ready and my camera on." I climbed the stairs to meet him. "Can you imagine the boost in your rep when the denizens of Atlanta see their potentate shrieking and doing the *ants in my pants* dance?"

A tic in his cheek betrayed the smile he was hiding. "Evildoers will tremble with fear."

"Hey, it's my duty to send you home in better shape than when you arrived."

The joke fell flat, and I gritted my teeth to avoid apologizing or compounding the faux pas.

"I have to go back," he said softly and gathered me in his arms.

"I know, I know." I rested my cheek over his heart. "I don't want to think about it. Or talk about it. Which is why I'm amazed it keeps popping out of my mouth."

"Corbin is ready to discuss his options."

Grateful he didn't press the issue, I packed away all those messy emotions and nodded. "Good deal."

I pulled away, and he let me go. I tried not to read anything into the moment, but panic beat against my breastbone every time I thought of him packing his bags.

Lethe had advised me to give him a reason not to go.

She never explained what would happen if I wasn't enough to make him stay.

FIVE

C orbin looked resigned to his fate when I reentered the kitchen and claimed the stool next to his.

"You have a couple of options," I started. "You can stay here and haunt my attic, so no one will ever find you. You can run and take your chances on your own. Or you can go live with my grandfather, and he can teach you how to vampire."

"How would that work?" He canted his head to one side. "There are no vampires like me."

"We don't know that for certain. I can almost guarantee Gramps has run across your kind during his life." I twisted aside and leaned back against the counter. "The problem with that option is I don't know him very well. He's had me kidnapped, promised me to one of his Last Seed followers, and encouraged his clan to collect me and return me like a coat from the lost and found."

Corbin waited, expecting a punchline, but I was already here. The joke was on him if he didn't take me seriously. "You're not selling me on that option."

"We recently declared a truce. I don't know if it will hold. I don't know what it means exactly. But I can tell you there's no love lost between the Grande Dame and my grandfather. He would protect you just to spite her."

And because he wanted something from me. What, I wasn't certain. But it was enough he was willing to bind me to his clan through vampire law by marrying me off to Volkov. It was enough that he smiled as I stepped all over his toes at the ball. Enough he had taken direct orders from me through a clenched jaw.

He would foster Corbin, and I would owe him a boon. What he wanted in exchange...would be nothing good.

At least he was aware Linus and I were a thing. Hopefully that ruled out any plans on his part for arranging a match.

A tiny voice in my head assured me this was yet another reason not to burn the marriage contract between Linus and me.

Bawk. Bawk.

I was such a chicken.

Cricket should have kitted me out as Yellow Belle instead of Blue Belle.

There were no nets to catch you when you fell in love. I learned that the hard way. The only thing waiting for you at the bottom after you took that leap of faith was the other person.

Choose well, and you lived happily-ever-after, or at least happily-for-now. Choose poorly, and you went *splat*.

Corbin considered me. "You don't sound like you want to be on the hook for this."

"Oh, I don't." I wriggled on my seat thinking about it. "The last place I want to be is between the Grande Dame and what she wants." The second-to-last place was handing the Grande Dame exactly what she wanted, which I might very well be doing. "You're a murderer."

He opened his mouth to contradict me, I cut him off before the excuses started.

Undead people were still people.

"What you do might be viewed as noble among the mortal set, but a vampire was a human who paid a necromancer a small fortune to enjoy near-immortality, and you robbed them of that. I'm not saying all vampires are saints. Far from it. We're all flawed: humans, necromancers, gwyllgi, etc. Vampires are no exception. But you're in our world now. There won't be any pats on the back or fang necklace stringing parties—whatever hunters do to celebrate their killing sprees—but there will be a whole heck of a lot of pissed-off vampires once they figure out who you are and what you've done. That means you need the protection of a vampire who can shield you from a stake to the heart until you can prove yourself to whatever clan takes you in."

"You think your grandfather can do that?"

"I know he can, if he decides you're worth the effort."

"Worth the effort," he repeated, unable to hide his disgust. "I won't beg a vampire for shelter."

"Then I'm glad we had this talk." I saluted him. "You've just saved me the hassle of meeting with him to discuss your case. Thanks."

Corbin shoved away from the counter and stormed out into the backyard.

"Kids these days." I clucked my tongue at Linus, taking a moment to send the promised shell pics to Amelie. "What can you do?"

"I'm not sure." Linus stared at the floor. "I've never maintained prolonged contact with my progeny."

"I need to check in with Lethe, and then I'm going to bed." I dusted my hands together. "Today was trash. Bag it, and set it at the curb."

A flinch twitched his shoulders, so slight anyone else would have missed it, but I saw.

"I'll keep an eye on Corbin," he offered. "You go on up, shower, and dress for bed."

The taste of foot clued me in to the colossal mistake I had made by painting today in such broad strokes with the same brush.

"There was one bright spot." I slid off my stool. "This guy I know took me downtown and showed me this building he's pretending he didn't buy for me, but we both know he totally did. He even pitched me a business plan and let me use his shower." I approached slowly. "FYI, the water pressure is ah-*mazing*."

"You could have been attacked in that building, and that guy you know would have been too late."

"I can take care of myself." Not one hundred percent, but I was thinking in the sixty or seventy range.

"I hate that you have to, that it's a skill you have no choice but to acquire."

"I hate that you put your life at risk every night to keep others safe, but those are the breaks."

"Yes." His gaze shot up to me then, his surprise almost comical. "They are."

I invited myself into his arms. "When are you going to stop being surprised that I want to protect you?"

That I wanted him, that he was wanted. Period.

"When the sun fails to rise, when the stars wink out, when the moon falls into the ocean."

"Are you quoting at me?" I squinted up at him. "I can't tell."

"A failed attempt at being romantic, I'm afraid." Pink suffused his cheeks. "I'm not very good at it."

"I like that you're practicing on me." I felt heat on my nape. "I'm glad some of this is new to you too."

His lips parted, like he might say more, but he cleared his throat. Twice. "I better check on Corbin."

"I'll do my best not to wind up outside your room again."

"I don't mind."

But I did. Drool was not sexy. Bedhead, not great either. Screaming and writhing on the floor?

Ugh.

Leaving Linus to reel in my progeny before the sun rose and turned Corbin to a crispy critter, I headed upstairs to check on Oscar. Quietly, I opened the door then ducked my head in his room.

He was gone.

I chose to read that as a good sign. When he came back from wherever he went, he was always recharged. I hoped that held true this time too.

Woolly nudged the door closed, squeezing me out into the hall where she prodded me toward my room.

"Will you let me know when he gets back?"

The old house groaned assent then turned on the shower in the bathroom.

I didn't need a shower, but I embraced the chance to wash today off me before I climbed into bed.

HE HAS A NEW GIRLFRIEND. His third one this week. Just as mundane as all the rest.

Why not me? Why won't he ask me? I would say yes. He knows I would say yes. Maybe that's the problem. Maybe I should play hard to get. Maybe then he would see we were meant to...

The carpet squishes under my feet, and cold slime seeps between my toes. I shiver, confused, my anger at Boaz forgotten. The smell hits me then, copper and rose water and thyme.

Maud.

I collapse to my knees beside her and scoop the icy blood back into the gaping hole in her chest.

"Maud?"

The sobs start, and I can't stop them. I'm working as fast as I can, but her heart—her heart—it's missing.

"Wake up. Please wake up. Please, Maud. Wake up. Please."

Shivers dapple my arms, and my teeth chatter, but it doesn't matter. None of it matters if she won't open her eyes. I'll be alone again. All alone. Maud is all I have, and she's...

She's gone.

She's dead.

Dead.

Using her blood for my ink, I start drawing a sigil, one I've never seen in any textbooks.

"No, Grier," a voice pleads behind me. "Stop before it's too late."

"I'm not losing her too. I won't." I keep going, slipping and sliding, covering her head to toe in the foreign sigils. "Come on, Maud. Try. For me."

"You have to let her go." Footsteps pound closer. "You don't want her back. Not like this."

"You're wrong." I scream so loud my voice shreds to ribbons. "I want her back any way I can get her."

"You don't mean that. Please, Grier. Think."

Snot clogs my throat as I close the sigil with a defiant swoop of my finger.

Magic explodes into the room, knocks me backward, and my head cracks against a wall.

"Grier."

Darkness swirls around me, and I embrace it, grateful when it blinds me to the corpse at my feet.

Except it doesn't last. I'm not passing out, I feel like I'm waking from a nightmare of my own making.

The blackness thins, swirls, coalesces, and I sob like my heart is breaking.

What have I done? What have I done? What have I done?

Her heart is gone. There can be no culmination now. How would we ever find it in time?

Goddess, what have I done?

A figure kneels on the floor, shrouded in black, hands clawing their face, their chest, their arms.

The room spins, a vortex of midnight, as all that grim power funnels itself into a new host.

I rocketed toward consciousness, soaked through with sweat and trembling. I came awake stretched halfway across my threshold, my fingernails broken and fresh claw marks on the hardwood. I swallowed and I swallowed and I swallowed, but the lump in my throat persisted. I tasted old blood and salty tears.

Chill hands hooked under my arms and lifted me to my feet, but my legs might as well have been jelly.

"I remember..." I wet my cracked lips with my dry tongue. "I tried to bring her back. Maud. I tried to resuscitate her."

Linus shut his eyes, but it did nothing to conceal his pain, and it didn't dull the edge of mine when I realized what this meant, what ought to be impossible but made so much sense.

"You're not surprised," I rasped, locking my knees to keep me upright. "You knew."

The rich navy of his gaze was a punch to my gut, a wordless confirmation.

The smidgen of resolve I had gathered around myself crumbled. "How did...?"

Black mist spun across the surface of his skin, hiding his expression, the vortex cloaking him in midnight.

A vortex of midnight.

"It was you. In my dream." Legs buckling, hope failing, I sank onto the floor. "You were there."

All that dark power had cocooned him, embraced him...devoured him.

"I—" I bit my lip, tried again. "I remember now."

The voice pleading with me to heed his warnings, the figure clawing at his face after I failed to listen...was Linus.

Linus had been there, in Woolly, with me, when my world ended for the second time.

Just like that, the other shoe dropped, and it squished my hopes and dreams flat as pancakes.

A gasp broke free of my chest, and then another and another.

Lungs burning, I gulped oxygen until I choked from swallowing. Not enough. Never enough. I scratched at my throat, raking furrows in my skin. I couldn't breathe. The walls pressed closer, suffocating me. Air whistled through my teeth. No use. It was no use. None of it.

Linus caught my hands and pinned them down at my sides before I clawed myself bloody.

The peaceful afterlife I had imagined for Maud had been just that—a dream.

The nightmare—that was reality. Hers and mine. And neither of us could wake from it.

How much of what I dreamed was real? Accurate? How much was tainted by drugs and time and Atramentous? There was only one way to find out, and that was by asking the man across from me to tell me the truth, even if it hurt, even if it left us both raw and empty.

"Let me go," I rasped, and he folded his hands in his lap.

Wiping my face dry on the hem of my shirt, I focused on my breathing until my pulse stopped roaring in my ears and my breaths came easier. I don't know how long I sat there while my hiccupping sobs tapered into a breathless quiet that ended with puffy eyes and a graveled voice.

"I found Maud sprawled on the carpet like she had fallen. Blood everywhere. Her chest..." I rubbed my throat, but it didn't help. Maybe nothing would ever again. "Someone killed her and cut out her heart."

"They wanted to punish her," he said softly. "They took the heart to prevent us from performing the culmination."

"They must have hated her," I whispered, "to do that."

The culmination was a ceremony where, hours after death, the heart was removed and burned to ash to release the spirit. The remains got swept into a box for the mantle. Necromancers didn't bother with the rest. The graves. The flowers. Our bodies got incinerated then left for the wind to collect. It was the heart that mattered, and someone had taken hers.

I dropped my face into my hands and wept. I'm not sure where I found the tears. I should have run out by now. No one person should be able to hurt so much at once without dying.

The Grande Dame had entrusted Maud's heart to me, the remains encased in a gold box, meaning they had recovered it at some point, but it must not have offered them any leads as to her killer's identity.

Woolly gathered her consciousness around me, soothing as best she could, but I was hollow.

"Tell me the truth." I couldn't look him in the eye. "All of it."

"I came to spend the weekend with Maud." Entire minutes lapsed before he continued. "I was on break at Strophalos, and she had a new project she wanted a second opinion on. I met Mother for lunch. She wanted to see me, pretend hurt that I hadn't stayed with her, but she wanted to know what her sister was working on more. When I got back to Woolly..." A horrible finality laced his voice. "I was too late."

"Maud was dead when you arrived," I said, not exactly a question.

"Yes." Exhaustion made it sound like he had dragged the word up from his toes to his mouth. "You must have beaten me there by minutes." He drew his knees to his chest and wrapped his arms around them like a child in need of comfort he knew better than to expect would come from anyone other than himself. "You were covered in blood, scooping handfuls off the floor to fill the hole in her chest."

I crushed my eyes shut, but that didn't stop me from hearing the rest.

"You were in shock. I was screaming at you to stop, to listen, but you didn't hear me. You had covered her body in sigils I had never come across in all my studies." He rested his forehead on his arms. "I couldn't read them, but I could guess what they did."

"I was trying to bring her back." The horror of it struck me anew. "I was trying to resuscitate her."

But necromantic magic doesn't work on necromancers. We have one life, and that's all. No extensions.

"Maud had no heart. She couldn't return to her body. She wouldn't have survived." He kept going, voice going lower. "You called her soul, and it had nowhere to go." He was barely whispering now. "I did what I had to do. I did the only thing for her—for you—that I could. I claimed her soul, bonded her to me as a wraith. That way at least she would be released into the afterlife when I died. Otherwise..."

Maud, one of the greatest necromancers of our time, would have been reduced to a flickering lamppost.

"But your sigil changed her." Linus kept going, his voice muffled by his knees. "She was...something I have never seen before or since. I didn't understand until I bound us. I had never bonded to a wraith, only read about it, but she...altered me."

At last the true reason for all the side effects of bonding with a wraith were revealed.

Cletus was no ordinary wraith, and Linus no ordinary necromancer after their union.

Without the culmination, Maud would have been doomed to afterlife as a shade. The necromantic equivalent of ghosts, shades were imbued with the magic of their former lives. That power, and their ability to absorb energy from others, made them dangerous. Their hunger, over time, bloated them on power until they grew strong enough to possess the living.

That's what happened to Ambrose.

That's what created a...dybbuk.

Oh, goddess.

Someone must have hated Maud very much indeed to condemn her to an eternity as a parasite.

"I stopped sleeping, and then I stopped eating. My core temperature dropped, and I started manifesting the tattered cloak. The scythe came later, after I became hungry for...other things." He glanced up then, and I met his gaze on reflex. His smile was brittle and terrible, and I wish I had never seen it. "I documented it all."

"Of course you did," I said softly, mind reeling with the implications.

"I'm not a dybbuk." He tossed it out there before I could shape my thoughts, my words, into the damning question. "She and I struck no bargain, and our joining was only voluntary on my end. Even wraiths get a choice. They can bond or decline. She had none. I took it from her."

The old house pressed in on me, and I sensed Linus through her. The scope of his pain was staggering. No wonder he sat before telling his side of the story. He might have collapsed otherwise.

"All this time, Amelie and Boaz have blamed me for the decisions they made in their lives, of their own free will." I wiped my face dry with the backs of my hands. "I did this to you. I made you what you are."

"An Eidolon." He stared at the wall in front of him, at nothing. "A phantom."

Eidolon. First a dybbuk and then vampires had hurled the word at Linus. But it wasn't a title, it was a classification. "What does it mean?"

"The essence of other wraiths sustains me. I don't devour them the way a dybbuk does, I gather them to me. They're each a patch in the cloak I wear. Our joining is...symbiotic. They could separate if they wish, but I give them substance. Most choose to stay, at least for a little while, until they grow strong enough to leave again. Maud is the only wraith within my control strong enough to manifest."

All those wraiths tied to him. Maud bound to him. Because of me. Because I was weak. Because I was selfish. Because I had been a child who had lost too much and refused to be alone again.

"How can you stand to look at me?" I hid my face behind my cupped hands. "How can you stand to be in the same house as me, the same city?" *The same city...* But he didn't live in Savannah. I dropped my palms to the floor to steady myself after this latest wretched revelation. "You moved to Atlanta because of this, because of me. You're a potentate because I—"

"What I am," he said, cutting me off, "I've done to myself. I'm unnatural, an aberration that shouldn't exist."

"No."

"I'm a predator, Grier. Don't pretend otherwise. You've seen me.

I hunt because the urge drives me, not because I'm a good or decent person. I didn't accept the mantle of potentate for Atlanta's sake. I took it for myself." He unfolded a bit, but not for the sake of comfort. He still looked miserable. "Potentates do bond with wraiths. Powerful necromancers do take on more than one. The position gave me a reason to hunt, an excuse for violence. It protects me, camouflages me, and I do my best to atone for my deceit by giving my all to my city."

Giving his all. He had certainly done that. He had given everything he had and then some. For me.

"I have to see...Cletus." I stood before I lost my nerve. "I'm going to the porch."

Linus kept his head bent, his gaze distant, his hands laced on his lap where they twitched like he wanted to reach for me but didn't dare try.

Downstairs, I procrastinated under the foyer chandelier, telling myself I was waiting for Linus to join me. But he didn't come. Through Woolly, I saw he remained where he'd set down his burden, the twisted chains of his past anchoring him to the spot.

Finally, I worked up the courage to ask the old house, "Do you remember how Maud died?"

The lights dimmed, the walls leaning in, and the wet gurgle of the water heater sounded like a sob.

Hands balled into fists, fingernails pricking palms, I readied myself for the truth. "Can you show me?"

Eyes shut, I waited for the deluge, for the movie to play along the backs of my eyelids that would put the past to rest.

Only the blackness of expectation greeted me.

"I don't understand." I probed her consciousness. "Why can't you share what happened that night?"

Woolly broadcasted a series of images: Maud climbing the stairs from the basement, the front door opening, and then...nothing.

"You don't know, do you?" I placed my open palm against the door. "You didn't see."

The list of people Maud would have welcomed into her home wasn't all that long. The list of people able to bypass Woolly in her heyday was shorter still. Other than myself, Linus was the only one I could name off the top of my head. Odette would know the details, if there were any, but she wasn't here to ask.

"What's the first thing you remember after that?"

An overhead shot of me kneeling in blood, screaming for Maud, flashed in my head. The perspective was skewed, but the scene came straight out of my dreams.

Through her, I watched Linus choose to finish what I started. I watched him buck and writhe as her soul knitted together with his, heard him scream until he lost his voice. And when it was done, when he had condemned himself, he looked at me with eyes gone full black. I recoiled from him, from what I had done, and the mask of Scion Lawson snapped into place, obscuring the fathomless pools of his gaze.

Even then, he had shielded the worst of himself from me, and I had been too blind to notice.

"It will be all right." His hands were bloody when he reached for me, but mine were too, and he was all I had in that moment. I hugged him close, sobbing against his shoulder, his arms stiff as wood around me. "We'll find out who did this, and I promise they will pay."

The rest of Woolly's recollection showed him calling for help that would come too late, and the way the Elite stormed the house. Their gazes fastened on me, on the blood covering me from head to toe, and the verdict was passed on the spot.

Guilty.

Traitor.

Murderer.

One sentinel hooked his arms around my middle, hauling me away from Linus like I might pose a threat to him, while another one clamped down on Linus's shoulders to keep him kneeling. Linus held on to me, our hands grasping, but the blood made our fingers too slick to clasp, and the Elite pulled us apart.

Three more Elite piled on Linus when he started swinging at them. They knocked him down and shoved his face in the blood to keep him from coming after me. I was howling for him, for Maud, for anyone to help me.

Woolly had been oddly inert. I remembered that now. How the Elite burst into my home and dragged me kicking and screeching out the door without any pushback from the old house who would have given her life, such as it was, to protect me.

The last flash showed the black look Linus turned on the Elite while he struggled to hold on and not explode into the grim creature now prowling beneath his skin, eager for the fight, ready to kill for me.

As a boy I sometimes ate across the table from, he had been willing to end lives to save mine.

This was in the aftermath of Maud's death. How much worse must his reaction have been when I was sentenced to Atramentous? How much deadlier had his rage grown before he harnessed his new appetites? How much agony had he endured knowing I had bound him to a creature, a shadow of a woman he loved like a mother, who bore no resemblance to her at all, who would never be more than an extension of his will?

Until I started changing the wraith, twisting its purpose, opening its eyes.

The dark pulse of hope that she might continue to heal I crushed underfoot with each measured step onto the porch. It would hurt too much to believe she might be restored when there was so much we didn't know about my condition and how my blood affected others.

Cletus waited for me with a rose torn from its bush dangling from one hand.

Linus must have sent him.

Her.

Maud.

"Thanks." I accepted the flower, Maud's favorite variety, and inhaled the fragrant bloom. "I don't know what to say." I reached for the wraith, and he—*she*—took my hand in her bony fingers. "This is all my fault. I did this to you. I don't know how much you remember, how much you understand, but I'm sorry. I'm so sorry, for all of this. I should have let you go. I shouldn't have tried to hold on. It was wrong of me, and..." A fresh sob from a seemingly endless supply choked me. "What can I do? How can I make this better? For you? For Linus?" The papery skin covering those long fingers stroked my cheek in a caress I should have recognized a thousand times over but hadn't given a second thought. "Are you...?"

Okay.

What a stupid thing to ask. What a stupid thing to wonder. What a stupid, selfish wish.

Stupid, stupid, stupid.

A low moan rattled the wraith's throat, the closest she could come to speaking, but I swear I heard my name in the sound.

"I'm going to spend the day on Abercorn."

I spun away from the wraith to find Linus standing a few steps behind me. "You're leaving?"

Surprise widened his eyes before he shuttered them, hiding his emotions behind a mask.

Hurt, anger, and grief welled in me, and I was about to light into him, but he raised a hand to silence me.

"You need time to think." He adjusted the strap on the bag slung over his shoulder. "You have decisions to make."

"I want Ma—*Cletus*—to stay with me." I kept hold of the wraith. "I don't want to let her—*him*—go just yet."

"I understand." He eased past me, careful not to brush my shoulder. "Lethe is waiting for you in the kitchen with Corbin. Hood is on patrol."

"Linus?"

He took the steps but hesitated in the grass. "Yes?"

"Why didn't you tell me?"

"The Cletus you first met is the only Cletus I had ever known until you. Wraiths are spirit and bone. They follow orders, they don't make their own decisions. They don't think, they don't feel. They exist. That's all." He almost glanced back, the muscles in his neck twitching, but he wouldn't look at me. "I would have told you if there was anything left of her, but there wasn't, there still might not be, and giving you hope would have been cruel." His head came up when lights splashed over the driveway. "I broke your friendship rules." *No more lying, no more omissions, no more skulking, no more attempting to get in the basement.* Those had been my rules. "I omitted the truth about Cletus. It was a choice within my control, and I made it. Punish me however you see fit. I accept your ruling without question."

Punish.

Of course, he would expect me to hurt him. Tit for tat. That's what he had been taught. That's all he knew. And I had warned him if he broke my trust again, I was done.

The urge to follow through with my threat, to cut him off cold turkey, was there. I didn't want it to be. I wanted to be better than this. But I was heartsore. And I was so very tired of being hurt by those I cared for most.

That didn't stop me from following him to the gate, taking his hand, and drawing the protective sigil on his wrist.

I didn't say anything, and neither did he. He was out of words, and I had yet to find mine.

A crimson sedan pulled to a stop at the curb, and the driver got out, nodding to me and then Linus.

I turned away, unable to watch him get in the car, unable to bear him leaving, unable to ask him to stay.

Tires crunched as the sedan pulled back into the street. A wrenching pain in my chest made me wonder if this was how Maud felt having her soul ripped from her body.

Lethe met me halfway to the porch, tackled me with a bone-crunching hug, and we sank onto the grass in a tangle of limbs. Collapsing against her, my head on her shoulder, my tears soaking her shirt, I let the grief sweep me away, right up the stairway into my head, where there was no pain.

A long time later, when I was down to hiccups, Lethe gathered me in her arms and lifted me against her chest. She carried me to my room, laid me on the bed, and then climbed in behind me. She held me until I stopped trembling, her grip unbreakable, like she might hold me together through sheer will alone, but there was nothing to be done for my heart. It was breaking, shattering into a million glittery pieces, each edge sharpened with a memory that cut. I should have bled to death from all the tiny slices, but death was easy, and nothing in my life had ever been that.

SIX

When I jerked awake from the first full day of natural sleep I'd had since my release from Atramentous, Linus wasn't back. I didn't have to check with Woolly to be certain.

I had never felt alone in Woolworth House. Not really. Not like this. But his absence was a hollow ring in my ears.

The door to his bedroom stood open—he'd left it that way—but the welcome was absent without him.

A brush of Woolly's presence across my senses forced me to uncurl from the tight ball of limbs knotting the center of his mattress. His, not mine. I must have found my way in here sometime during the day.

"I feel better." I stretched my fingers through the slats in his headboard to brush them along the wall. "How are you coping?"

The floorboards groaned—no. That was a moan.

Cletus drifted into the room from the hall and came to hover at the foot of the bed.

Sadness radiated from Woolly, overlapping my own melancholy, but she had let the wraith in.

"Can you tell?" I put the question to the old house. "Do you sense...?"

Maud.

Woolly reeled in her emotions, blocking me from her thoughts, and that was answer enough.

She would have seen beyond the cloak, through its bones, to the soul animating the creature when it first crossed her wards. Had there been anything of Maud left in Cletus, Woolly would have rejoiced to find her mistress, however diminished, had returned.

But there had been no celebration.

Woolly had allowed the wraith in for my benefit, because that's how she viewed Cletus—as a generic manifestation of necromantic will—not as Maud. Not as a creature with its own identity. And with her silence, she wanted to spare me that final nail in the coffin of my hope that Maud was still in there, somewhere.

"No one can know," I warned them both. "No one can ever discover what I've done."

A bolt of fear thrown by Woolly struck me in the heart.

"I'm not worried for myself." I rubbed my chest. "I'm worried about what this might mean for Linus."

Eidolon was not a designation I had heard until it started getting tossed around about him. He might not be a dybbuk, but dybbuk were hunted, their hosts executed or sentenced to the grave of Atramentous. He walked a fine line even his mother might not be able to smudge if the Society learned the truth about her son, and about Maud.

"I hate to do this. It feels like I'm erasing the only scrap left of your identity, but I can't call you Maud." I wet my parched lips. "I'll have to keep calling you Cletus. It's the only way to protect us all."

The wraith nodded, a low moan escaping its maw, and Woolly's consciousness bolted from the room.

Tremors shook the house, her heaved sobs shifting the structure on its foundation, but I let her grieve.

"She'll adjust," I promised Cletus, uncertain if he had the

capacity to understand what I had told them, or Woolly's reaction to the news. "She just needs a little time."

Maud would never have violated Woolly the way Cletus had the night we met—when he stole Keet, who she never would have touched, and left the Grande Dame's invitation in his place. Maud wouldn't have had to stoop so low. Woolly would have flung open her doors to welcome her home. Instead, she still smarted from that stark breach of trust, even if she had forgiven Linus. Learning her former mistress, the person she trusted above all others, had done that to her...was hard.

The wraith gave no indication how it felt about Woolly adapting to its presence, but it did drift to me, its hand tucking into the depthless void of its robe. It withdrew the ark shell it had given me at Odette's and the knife I had forgotten at the property on Abercorn.

The property Linus bought for me, to give me back some of what I had lost.

"Thanks." I set both on the bed, dressed in jeans and a tee, pocketed the items, then ducked my head into Oscar's room. His bed remained empty. With a sigh, I set out for the kitchen. Lethe sat on Amelie's old stool, hunched over seven takeout boxes with a familiar logo on the lids. "Do I smell bacon?"

"You had a rough night. Ordering in was the least I could do." She nudged a box toward me. "I charged the food to your account, so don't thank me too much."

"Still, I appreciate it." I went to the fridge and found exactly what I expected—a smoothie rich in Vitamin L—waiting on me. There was no card this time, no note, but I didn't need one. Even when Linus expected the worst, he gave his best. "How much did you hear?"

"The wraith is your adoptive mom, Linus is something called an Eidolon, and he bound Maud Woolworth to him after you called her soul from her body in a failed resuscitation."

Mouth hanging open, I cranked my head toward her. "Anything else?"

"I also heard Linus tell Woolly to keep you safe and to call if you ever need him." She tossed a wedge of buttered toast aside with a frown then crammed a sausage link in her mouth. "*Ever* implies he won't be here to hear if you call. *Ever* implies he's not coming back. *Ever* implies last night was goodbye."

A tremble started in my fingers and spread into my palm. The spasm released the smoothie from my grip, and it spilled across the tiles. "He's staying on Abercorn to give me time to think."

"He's the Potentate of Atlanta, Grier. He put off his responsibilities while he was tutoring you, and that's fine, but you haven't polished his apple in weeks." She grinned with chipmunk cheeks. "And yes, I know exactly how that sounds."

"He wouldn't lie about that." He had never outright lied to me. Omission was his greatest sin.

"He told you he was spending the day there. He never said what he was going to do after he woke up."

Quick as I could, I mopped up the mess then washed my hands. "I need to get to Abercorn."

Corbin entered the kitchen on autopilot. He pulled down a bowl and filled it with cereal without looking at me or talking to me. I wasn't certain he was aware I was there. His eyes weren't all the way open yet.

"Keep an eye on him," I told her. "I'll be back as soon as I can."

"I'll text Hood," she mumbled through a full mouth. "He'll meet you at the gate."

"Cletus." I lost precious seconds waiting on the wraith to appear. "Come on. We're leaving."

The wraith followed, his bony fingers curling over my shoulder when we reached the front door.

A second later, Woolly alerted me to the presence of a guest. No, not a guest, a vampire.

Great.

Just what I didn't need right this second.

I had the door open before he could knock and backed him out onto the porch. "What?"

The vampire recoiled at my tone before packing away his affront. "The master will see you."

"Oh. Good." I reordered my thoughts. "When?"

"Now." He stared back at me, expectant. "You did say it was urgent."

"I—" I wanted to hop on Jolene and drive her like a bat out of hell to Abercorn. I wanted to find Linus in the apartment before he got any ideas about going back to Atlanta. But I had to offload Corbin. With his history, his connection to me, it was too dangerous to keep him in my home. Not to mention the fact he couldn't feed himself, which meant I might as well go stab a few humans to death if I didn't get him the help he required to mature into a self-sufficient vampire. "Give me a second. I'll be right back."

I retreated into the house and shut the door. Backtracking, I found Lethe texting her mate while scrambled egg clung to her bottom lip.

"New plan," I called. "I'm getting my gear, snagging Corbin, and we're going to see my grandfather."

"What about Linus?" She set down her fork, never a good sign. Actually, I'm not sure I had ever seen her do it up until now. "You need backup."

"I'll have Hood." I smiled at her. "And you, if you're interested."

"Hell yes." She pumped her fist. "Gimme a sec. I need to pack a few snacks."

"Shocker." I left her rummaging in the cupboards while I went to find Corbin, who was bleary-eyed but more alert than he had been. "A vampire is here to escort me to see my grandfather. This is your only shot with him. You either come with us, or you move on to Plan B, whatever that is."

"I'll go." Tension bunched his shoulders. "I want to hear what he has to say before I agree to anything."

"Get dressed, and meet me on the porch in ten." With that done, I found a quiet spot and called Cletus in close. "Tell Linus where we're going and why. I'm going to give Amelie a heads-up so we have a backup for our backup."

Using the back door let me escape into the rose garden without encountering the vampire stationed at the front door. That was a blessing. I didn't want witnesses for this conversation.

Amelie had the door open when I got there, proving she had been spying on the yard. Not that I could blame her with so little else to entertain her.

"What do they want with you?" She stared past me to the front porch where my escort waited. "Are you in any danger? I can—"

"*Don't* call your brother."

"I was going to offer to go with you."

Lifting her house arrest would be more trouble than it was worth. Plus, it would get me in even hotter water with the Grande Dame if she found out I had allowed Amelie to slip her leash.

"Lethe and Hood volunteered." I ignored the hurt in her eyes. "I just wanted to let you know I'm going to see my grandfather. I don't expect any trouble, but trouble has a way of thwarting my expectations."

Hearing the name left off that list, she checked to either side of me. "Where's Linus?"

"He's in town. His wraith is with me. He'll be getting live updates."

"I saw him leave with a bag last night." She reached for my arm. "Are you guys okay?"

"I don't know." I looked at her hand, wishing her touch still meant comfort to me. "Ask me tomorrow."

Her eyes brightened in an instant. "Does that mean you're coming to visit again?"

I walked right into that one. "Sure." I started backing away. "I have to go."

"I won't call Boaz," she said softly. "You have my word this doesn't go further than us."

Uncertain how much worth her words carried these days, I

nodded without conviction then turned back to the house, wondering how much her attempts at atonement stemmed from guilt and how much from boredom. Loneliness bred desperation, and foolhardiness had landed her in this mess in the first place.

If I wanted her to get better, I had to do better by her. That didn't mean putting myself in the line of fire, but it did mean bringing in someone who could help her adjust to cohabitation with Ambrose, since we had no clue how long their essences would mingle before his dissipated enough she could evict the jerk.

With Odette skittish about the gwyllgi and currently unavailable for consultation, I would have to cast a wider net. That meant asking Linus for tutor recommendations of a different kind.

If I caught him before he did something drastic like give up on us faster than I could digest all I had learned in the last twenty-four hours.

Lethe met me in the kitchen, pockets bulging with snacks. "You visited the ex?"

I gave her a look. "Yes."

"What?" She popped a mini donut in her mouth. "We both know I'm your new best friend."

"We do, huh?" It was fun to watch her sweat in the wake of that bold statement. Not much got to Lethe. She was fierce, tough, and... she had never had a best friend. Never had a friend worth promoting. "You offer to throw one baby shower..."

"How do we do this?"

"Do...what?"

"Make it official?" She tapped her chin. "Do you want me to spit in my palm then shake your hand? Cut your palm and mine then smear them together so we can be blood sisters? Do I create a right-eous mixtape then blast music beneath your window at noon?"

"Um, I think those are mostly things that happen in eighties movies or at summer camp."

"You're not going to make me get down on one knee and ask, are you? I have *some* pride."

After fishing a donut out of the bag, I dropped to one knee at her feet and took her hand.

"Lethe Kinase, we haven't known each other long, but I get this feeling whenever I'm around you. I think it's hunger, because you're always eating something that smells good, but maybe it's my gut telling me that you're the one. Will you accept this donut as a token of my affection and agree to be my BFF?"

"What the actual hell?" Hood roared into the kitchen. "What are you two doing? And why is there always food involved?"

Ignoring her mate, Lethe sniffled. "I do."

I slid the donut on her pinky finger with a grin while Hood looked ready to tear out his dreads.

"Now to consummate our union." Lethe waggled her eyebrows at me, dancing aside when he grabbed for her. "You can't stop me, Hood. This is fate. It's destiny." She bit into the donut. "It's *delicious.*"

Face straight, Hood glanced at me. "How long did you say Linus would be gone?"

"Linus can't help you now." Lethe crammed the other half of the donut in my mouth. "We're *official.*"

Hood just shook his head. "She wasn't like this in Atlanta."

"What do you mean?" She stopped goofing off to listen, and her pulse jumped in her throat.

Since I'm *not* a vampire, I pretended not to notice that or the smell of my ruined smoothie lingering in the air.

"She growled when others got near her food," he said. "She didn't share. She picked fights that ended in bloodshed. Now she picks fights with you that end in takeout. She spent too much time alone, even though our packmates were always around. Now she crashes on your couch, raids your fridge, and eavesdrops on all your private conversations." He crooked his finger at her, and she inched closer to him while staying out of reach. "She smiles and means it. She's... happy. She hasn't been that in a long time."

Keeping to the balls of her feet, she cocked her head. "Does this mean you're giving us your blessing?"

The smile he shot her way hit its target, and she swayed like a lovestruck teenager.

"I'm happy you're happy." Lightning fast, he caught her by her upper arms and yanked her to him. "That's all I want, all I've ever wanted. If that means letting you feed other women donuts off your fingers, or whatever the hell I just witnessed, I can deal. But don't invite her back to the den with you. That's where I draw the line."

Clamped against his chest, Lethe didn't have much wiggle room. She still could have broken free if she chose—I had seen her do it a hundred times in practice—but she melted against him. "Deal."

I left them to their mated bliss and went to check on Corbin. I found him waiting in the living room. "Are you ready?"

"Yeah." He ducked his head. "You?"

Taken aback that he would ask, I had to dig for the right answer. "Yes."

"Have you spoken to your grandfather since you declared a truce?"

"No," I admitted. "This will be the first time we've seen each other since."

Corbin lapsed into silence, and I let him think while I veered into the hall. I had wavered on bringing the goddess-touched artifact with me. It was dangerous—to me—and valuable. But it was also a powerful weapon I was willing to bet had some impact on vampires since it had affected me. When Heloise jabbed me in the spine, I lost touch with my magic, leaving me defenseless against her power. While I wasn't eager to experience that sensation again, I wasn't above inflicting it on others as a last resort.

Plus, it was a stake. Where magic fails, pointy ends prevail.

The gwyllgi entered the living room as I was leaving, and I pointed to clue them in to my intentions.

Thankfully, the basement door didn't fight me. I got in, beat the gloom, and hit the library.

I hesitated a moment when I passed the cabinet where I was storing the marriage contract, but there was no time for lingering. I strode past it and retrieved the artifact from a locked bin filled with palo santo sticks.

As far as I could tell, the artifact was an ancient ash stake, which spoke to its possibilities as a weapon against vampires. Shaft worn smooth from handling, tip unnaturally sharp, it fit my palm like it had been carved for me alone. Magic? Perhaps. I hadn't spent enough time on this end of the point to decide.

I tucked the stake in the waistband of my pants at my spine like I saw people do with guns in the movies. Aside from giving me an insta-wedgie, I worried it might also stab me if I sat down wrong on the way to see my grandfather. Clearly, the movies had no clue what they were talking about.

Next idea. I put my boob deficiency to good use and tucked it in the band of my bra, tip up, figuring the odds of me stabbing myself under the jaw were slimmer than jabbing myself in the gut.

That was better. Not great since fitted tees didn't forgive much, but doable thanks to the fact this was a recent purchase, a size bigger than I was now, the one I expected to be after I regained those last few pounds.

"Good enough."

I took the stairs, rejoined the gwyllgi, collected my progeny, and met our vampire escort.

"Sorry about the delay." I plastered on my best innocent smile, one that said, *No, there's not a stake down my bra, why do you ask?* then gestured toward the van. "I hope you don't mind if I use my driver."

As much as I disliked treating Hood like *the help*, he didn't appear to mind the ruse. Granted, he worked as a doorman for myriad reasons, so he must be used to fading into the background. Crazy when you considered who he was, who he was mated to, and the power their pack held in Atlanta. But I could attest to the fact the Society never looked beyond the end of their nose. They didn't value other races, species. Their interest began and ended at home. Vampires were an offshoot of ours, so it made sense they were insular as well.

"Not at all, mistress." The vampire did a better job of acting like he wasn't mocking my limitations than I did acting innocent. "I expected as much." He gestured for me to lead. "Please, the master waits."

"Hood?" I was grateful he took the hint without arguing and went to fetch the van. "Cletus?"

The wraith joined me, resting his bony hand on my shoulder in a show of solidarity I hadn't realized I needed until that moment.

As much as I wanted to believe the reason his touch steadied me was Maud was in there, somewhere, I knew in my gut it had more to do with who controlled the wraith than who the wraith was to me.

Linus.

The urge to ditch this meeting and run to him instead, so I could yell at him until I got out all the hurt, was there. But my alliance with the master was too tentative for me to risk his offense if I bailed on our first meeting, one I had initiated.

Hood rolled up, and we met him at the gate. Our guide claimed the front passenger seat to better give Hood directions. That left Corbin and Lethe with me in the rear. I sat in my preferred spot, and he sank beside me. She took the plush half seat next to the door that Linus favored. Cletus, as usual, preferred to meet us there.

From where I sat, it was hard following our exact turns, but tension coiled tighter and tighter in my belly until I pressed my palms against my stomach to rub the miserable ache.

Lethe was staring at me. "You good?"

Forcing my hands into my lap, I glanced over at Lethe. "I think I know where we're going."

Her green eyes rounded in comprehension, and her lips peeled away from her teeth. An urgent warning flashed in her eyes, but when she opened her mouth, no sound escaped, and she ground her molars.

I leaned forward, pitching my voice low. "Are *you* good?"

She nodded once, but her jaw remained clenched hard enough to break teeth.

I met Hood's gaze in the rearview mirror, and a faint red sheen rolled over his eyes.

Something was happening to the gwyllgi, who were my backup, and they might not get a chance to explain before we arrived for our audience with my grandfather.

Paranoia danced up my spine en pointe, and foreboding chills pirouetted in its wake.

Corbin leaned over, his lips brushing my ear. "What's going on?"

Despite his caution, there was nothing gwyllgi wouldn't overhear in a space this size. "I'm not sure."

"Gwyllgi work in security," Lethe gritted between clenched teeth. "We sign magically enforced NDAs."

Sweat popped on her brow, and she slumped back in her seat, panting like she'd run a marathon instead of making a vague statement about her work habits.

A chill settled into my bones as a new certainty blossomed in my mind.

The only way that applied to this situation was... They had worked for Lacroix.

SEVEN

The farther we drove, the harder I fought to hold on to my calm. The urge to dash up the stairs in my head and find solace in the quiet of my own mind left me staring out the window behind Lethe. This time there was no Linus to anchor me, to give me a reason to stay, but it was dangerous giving another person that kind of power over you, even when you trusted them, so I pulled myself back from the edge for a change.

After what felt like an eternity in the stifling confines of the van, the vampire pointed to a dirt road. "Turn left. You may park beneath the portico."

On the edge of my seat, I leaned forward and had to roll in my lips to stifle an outcry.

The drive was familiar.

The landscaping familiar.

The garden...horribly familiar.

And the house...the estate...

I had been held prisoner here. I had wasted away to nothing here. I had almost, *almost* given up here.

The physical scars on my wrist might have been smoothed away, but the emotional ones remained.

"Do not be dismayed, mistress," the vampire said smugly. "The master could hardly welcome you in our new clan home while your loyalties remain divided."

This was a power play. Plain and simple. Lacroix wanted me off kilter. He wanted me spooked. Paranoid.

Mission accomplished.

Unsurprising, given his age, he had seized the upper hand before I even got in the van. I hadn't expected to meet him on level footing—a man like him saw no one as his equal—but I hadn't anticipated him to hit below the belt this soon. Clearly, overestimating his sentimentality toward me had been a grave error.

But, since he struck the first blow by selecting this location, I couldn't find it in myself to feel all that bad about the stake nestled against my sternum.

Our escort got out, and a nod from me had Hood locking the doors to keep him that way.

After removing the modified pen from my pocket, I lifted my shirt and drew the protective rune I had redesigned for Linus on my lower stomach, careful to keep the stake hidden in the folds of material in case the vampire pressed his nose to the glass. When I finished, I arched an eyebrow.

Lethe raised her shirt, no hesitation. The tiny swell giving her a slight paunch made me pause, but a baby was an even better reason to protect her. I drew it on her stomach then turned to Hood. It wasn't graceful, but he climbed into the back with us, and I drew him one between his shoulder blades.

Corbin I saved for last. If he saw my friends sporting theirs without experiencing any adverse effects, he might volunteer for his own. That was the hope. I wasn't certain if he understood what sigils were or that the red ink was mostly blood. He didn't appear confused as he peeled his faded tee over washboard abs puckered with cruel scars earned in his trade. I wore my reminders on the inside, just beneath the skin, so I didn't linger over his marks or ask any questions.

With all of us protected, we let Hood get the door from the inside and finish his chauffer act by helping me step onto the driveway.

The vampire's nostrils flared, scenting blood, and he understood that I had worked some magic, but he couldn't be certain unless he asked me outright. I was willing to bet he wouldn't go that far—I was still Lacroix's granddaughter—and he didn't out of respect for his master.

I might have entered through the front door on the night Volkov and my stalkerpire smuggled me here, but I had no memory of it thanks to the strength of Volkov's lure. Escape brought me out here from the side of the house, near the rear, and rescue happened on the manicured lawn.

Boaz had led the charge to save me. He had been there, arms wide open, to help me limp to freedom.

Our relationship had been simpler then, and I wished I could turn back the clock, but I wouldn't have listened to myself even if I could go back in time and shake my shoulders until my brain rattled. I had wanted him too much for too long to be satisfied without experiencing him for myself.

Now that I had, I had regrets. But without getting my heart stomped on, I would have been skipping a necessary step to my recovery there in the middle. And without that wake-up call, I might have missed out on Linus.

As if the turn in my thoughts had summoned him, Cletus materialized at my shoulder.

I glanced back to check on Lethe and Hood, both of whom refused to look at me. Not a great sign.

The details of their NDA must have been a doozy if they were locked down this tight. Admitting they had signed the paperwork left Lethe breathless. More information might cut off her oxygen altogether. I had heard of gag orders, but this was ridiculous.

Corbin stuck close as I followed the vampire through the ornate front doors, down a long hall tiled in the wheat-colored stone I recalled glimpsing through a crack in the door to my room when Lena came and went. Lena, who had been my nursemaid as a child, if my stalkerpire was to be believed.

Lena, who let me waste away to nothing without lifting a finger to help. Lena, who would have dressed me for my wedding and been hurt when I refused to kiss my groom...until he cranked up his lure anyway.

There were no fond memories for me here. I had to pack away the grim reminders and hope I got the chance to unload on someone later.

"He thought you might be more comfortable in the study." The vampire, who had still not given his name, knocked on a door that looked the same as the dozen others lining the hall, then pushed it open. He bowed so low, he could have kissed his shins. "Your grand-daughter is here to see you, Master."

Before I was revealed, I arranged the mask of Dame Woolworth on my face, using every trick I had learned from Linus to make my persona seamless. Without knowing me, Lacroix had no hope of prying it up or peeking beneath.

"Grier, my darling girl. You look well."

Gaspard Lacroix was frozen in his late thirties. His hair was long and black, and he kept it bound at his nape with a simple ribbon. Power rolled off his skin, giving the air a tangible weight, and my already unsettled stomach lurched. Only the tattoo between my shoulder blades kept me standing while his magic hissed I should fall on my knees before him, kiss his feet, lick the tiles beneath his shoes.

The gwyllgi had a natural immunity to vampiric lures. Other-wise, they couldn't take odd jobs for vampires without being enslaved by them. Why pay when you can get it for free?

Corbin was the wild card, and I regretted playing him. I wasn't certain if he had any natural immunity to a vampire of Lacroix's caliber, or to lures at all, but I had to find out before I left him to my grandfather's tender mercies. Now all I had to do was wait for Lacroix to strong-arm him and see if Corbin buckled.

"I appreciate you taking this meeting with me." I arranged a polite smile. "I have a bit of a situation, and I was hoping you might counsel me."

"Tell me more." He gathered my hands in his, warm and dry, pressed a kiss to each of my cheeks, then pulled me toward an elegant wingback chair opposite the one he had been in when we arrived. "Sit, sit. Let us discuss this problem." He reclaimed his seat without acknowledging anyone else was in the room. As much as I wanted to be flattered to be the center of attention, I knew a snub when I saw one. "What can I do to help? Anything. Name it, and it will be yours."

"This is Corbin Theroux." I gestured him forward, and he came without a trace of the nerves he must be experiencing. "He escaped a secure facility where the Grande Dame placed him for observation." I let that sink in. That he mattered to the Grande Dame, that she had set him aside, that she wanted him observed. "He came straight to me and begged for asylum."

I was laying it on thick, but Corbin didn't contradict me, thankfully.

"Interesting." Lacroix shifted his focus to Corbin, and already I could breathe easier. "Why would she...?"

"He's Deathless." I suppressed a flinch when Lacroix shot his gaze back to mine. "He's my progeny."

"Welcome." He bounded to his feet, eyes sparkling, and shook hands with Corbin. "It's a pleasure to meet you. Forgive my earlier rudeness. I have not had much occasion to converse with my granddaughter, and she was all I saw."

Guess I wasn't the only one laying it on thick. Maybe it ran in the family. Perish the thought.

"I understand, sir."

Sir. I was shocked when Corbin didn't choke on the word, but the militant cadence to his voice betrayed that it was all an act. Good news for us, since Lacroix's touch didn't appear to influence Corbin's distaste for the man.

"Well-mannered, I approve." He indicated Corbin should take the other vacant chair. "Take a seat, son."

The endearment set alarm bells clanging in my head, but I couldn't pinpoint why.

"You understand the delicate nature of the issue," I said, readjusting my mask. "I'm betrothed to the Lawson scion, but the Lawson matriarch has a vested interest in my progeny. There are no other known Deathless vampires in existence. The temptation to observe one has proven greater than the sum of his past crimes in her estimation."

"Past crimes," he murmured, clearly interested. "Elaborate."

Corbin kept his head straight, eyes forward. "I come from hunter stock, sir."

Surprise he had shared the truth of his past radiated through me, but Lacroix would approve of that killer instinct. Provided he could hone it and redirect it.

"Fascinating." Lacroix all but rubbed his hands together. "I suppose that must have been the crime that led you to be held in the black pit they call Atramentous."

"I was careless," Corbin admitted, "and I got caught."

"None of that, now." Lacroix clucked his tongue. "You can learn, you *will* learn."

The volume of the warning bells doubled, tripled, and I finally processed why his attitude grated.

I was female, to be given into an advantageous marriage. Corbin was male, and he was, by vampire law, the closest thing I had to a biological son.

Lacroix was showing his age, falling back on old prejudices, and losing mega points with me.

He was reaching if he meant to proclaim Corbin the new Lacroix heritor using that thin connective tissue, but he had embraced Volkov for less. And Corbin had the benefit of being able to sire children, which Volkov, as a Last Seed, couldn't do. Corbin could establish a ruling bloodline. A *pure* bloodline.

The children of Deathless vampires were said to be true immortals, though their grandchildren were believed to be mortal, but mortals could be made immortal easy enough if you had, say, a goddess-touched granddaughter on speed dial.

I had expected Lacroix to barter with *me* for Corbin. *I* had expected to be the leverage. But I was a known entity, and Corbin was a shiny new toy, ripe for the claiming since I had as good as admitted he was a clanless fugitive.

"I will offer him asylum," Lacroix announced. "How can I not? He is your progeny, and that makes him clan."

Corbin, who had done a bang-up job of appearing calm and collected, shot me a sideways glance.

"You make a generous offer, Grandfather." Unable to comfort Corbin, I got ready to dump bucketloads more shade on the Grande Dame. "They caged him, refused to teach him how to feed. He lives on donor blood. He's ignorant to his vampire heritage."

Lacroix couldn't have looked more affronted than if he had been a fluffy cat who fell into a bathtub.

"Vampires are predators." Lacroix bared his teeth, but he kept his fangs tucked politely away. "They are made for the hunt, for the kill." He must have remembered not everyone present was on Team Murder Good. I was Team Murder Bad, but I doubted there was a local chapter. "Those were the old days," he said, injecting nostalgia into the sentiment. "We feed without killing in this era. That is the wisest and best course to maintain our species' anonymity."

There was no mention of killing being wrong, not that I had expected one. Still, I felt better about Corbin's potential immunity after he made fists so tight I was amazed he didn't swing them at Lacroix's head.

Corbin had dedicated his life to saving humans from The Vampire Threat. I didn't have to be an active member of that chapter to know they used all caps for that kind of thing. Bad enough he was a vampire, that he had chosen this life, betraying his old one, but for Lacroix to expect Corbin to kill humans to survive? That was a rookie mistake.

Lacroix had grown too used to preaching conversion to the members of the Undead Coalition. And I suspected he had let slip the bait he was using on accident: the unregulated hunting of humans. A return to the old ways. *His* ways. He wanted to pass out sunglasses in all his *Welcome to Clan Lacroix* kits so that his converts might view the future through the rose-colored lenses of his past.

But Corbin hadn't bought his way into a clan—he hadn't wanted immortality, he had chosen it as an alternative to death. That was it. Expecting him to clap his hands and squee over a chance to spill oceans of human blood proved how out of touch Lacroix was with this demographic. Corbin would grit his teeth and starve first.

"Humans do tend to glorify the supernatural" was the most neutral response I could cobble together.

"That doesn't mean the poor boy can't be taught to feed from willing partners." Lacroix didn't hear me over the plans he was making. "I would be happy to oversee his education personally."

He slapped Corbin on the back, his fingers digging into the meat of his shoulder, and old magic hit me.

Bend, bend, bend, it seemed to whisper across my senses, but I refused to break, and so did Corbin.

Much to my relief, he didn't exhibit any signs he was aware of Lacroix's grasp to strangle his will.

Touch boosted the power of a Last Seed's lure—Volkov had illustrated that firsthand—and Lacroix was giving it all he had, pumping his lure into the room until I coughed as it lodged in my throat. The tattoo on my spine burned, the ink pulsing with my heart, the design holding Lacroix's compulsion at bay.

Perhaps this meant Deathless were immune to Last Seeds. Perhaps they were immune to all lures. I was happy to let Linus puzzle that out. All that mattered to me was that Corbin's eyes remained clear, and my mind remained my own.

"You have much to learn, but it has been an age since I had someone to teach." Lacroix did a poor job of concealing his annoyance, but he appeared more intrigued than put out by this discovery. "My son, George, was adopted. Last Seeds can't produce children, so when the time came to name my heritor, he was chosen from among the descendants of my line as the most qualified."

The offer to Corbin was clear, but I was too busy savoring the morsel he let slip about my father. While I had been holding on to the hope Lacroix and I weren't blood related at all—as with Volkov, sometimes a LS adopted an heritor—it was good to have confirmation.

This meant Lacroix had been cultivating his bloodline, as some vampires chose to do. They reached back to find their closest living relative and then set about ensuring their line continued, usually supporting the humans financially in return for pick of the litter as heritors or clan members were needed.

Ah well. Linus had the Grande Dame, and I had Gaspard Lacroix. No one was perfect.

Before that thought marinated for too long, Lacroix snapped his fingers.

"Say your goodbyes," he told Corbin, "and then we will leave for our clan home."

Corbin strode to me, eyes bright, pleading, but I had to pretend not to see, not to react.

Lacroix had to believe Corbin was buying into his spiel, not ready to snap off the nearest chair leg and stake him with it, if this was going to work.

"Corbin and I haven't spent much time together," I said to Lacroix. "Would you allow us a stroll through the gardens before you leave? He is my first progeny, and I have questions."

"You will be able to maintain a relationship with him." Lacroix smiled, and there was real cheer behind it. "I would never dream of keeping the two of you parted." He grew wistful. "It is a shame you're already spoken for, Grier. Just think of the children you two could give me."

Progeny incest wasn't really a thing, but that didn't help me feel better about what he was suggesting, or the fact he wanted children from us. Not grandchildren. A slip of the tongue? Maybe. But I doubted it.

"Sadly, I'm engaged." *Thank you, marriage contract.* "Those are only slightly less difficult to break than wedding vows."

"Ah, well. You are still young, still fertile." He made a gesture in the air. "The Lawson scion might not prove to be as long-lived as his mother. You can never tell about these things. A time might come when you consider the match with Corbin."

The mask flaked off and left my face bare. I wasn't as adept at this as Linus, and hearing Lacroix threaten him ignited a caustic blend of raw terror and panic in my chest that nothing short of setting my eyes on him would douse.

"Linus is very important to me," I enunciated carefully. "Today, tomorrow, in a century, I would take the black if we married and he died."

Dames and matrons who chose the black after the death of a spouse fell into two categories. Either they could afford not to wed again, and they led their family alone. Or, less commonly, their heart-brokenness and refusal to entertain marital offers drove their families into the ground.

"You're young," he soothed. "Hearts change with time."

"Mine won't." I hadn't framed Linus and me in that light in my mind. I still wasn't sure how the future looked when I had been so single-minded in the past. But I knew I couldn't lose him. Not to Atlanta, and not to my grandfather. That had to be enough until we figured out the rest. "I hope I'm never given occasion to prove I mean what I say."

Temper sparked in his eyes, but he kept his tone civil, even if the tic in his cheek betrayed his fury.

"You are young," he repeated. "You do not know what you say."

"Sir," Corbin said, calling Lacroix's attention back to him, "if you don't mind, I would like to escort Grier to the gardens now."

Pleased one of us had manners at least, Lacroix chuckled. "Go on." He smiled. "Have your walk."

Corbin cocked his elbow and presented his arm to me, and I looped my hand through. The move was one I had come to expect from Linus, and I wondered if that's what had given Corbin the idea. I clung to him like a lifeline, and he escorted me past Hood and Lethe, who stood posted on either side of the door but peeled aside to follow us.

We didn't wait for our vampire escort to set out, and that explained how we ended up at the entrance to a room I had never seen from this angle but would have recognized anywhere. The paintings, I realized, hung on the opposite wall had given it away. I remembered them from all the desperate glances I shot in the hall each time Lena entered or exited my room.

Cletus, who had waited in the hall, drifted to the door and tapped his finger against it three times.

"You want us to go in there?" I bumped against the far wall before meaning to take a step.

The wraith tapped three more times, then he lowered his bony hand to grasp the knob.

The gwyllgi exchanged glances, but they kept their mouths shut.

I bit back a whimper when the door swung open on a room I remembered all too well.

The covers were thrown back, the French doors left open onto the patio. Leaves and other debris littered the floor, and the gauzy curtains danced in the breeze. Cletus drifted out into the small garden enclosed by stone walls. He paused at the patio furniture and pointed a damning finger at the concrete.

I drifted out, aware of what I would find but not understanding its significance.

A perfect seashell had been pressed into the concrete along the farthest edge. During my captivity, I had oriented myself by its curve. The patch of dirt beyond it was where I hid the porcelain shard I used to open my veins to ink on the sigils used during my escape.

I hadn't reached the shell before the wraith crossed to me and *tap, tap, tapped* my front pants pocket.

"What does it want?" Corbin crowded in, looking around in confusion. "What is this place?"

"Remember the difference of opinion between me and Grand-papa? It started here, when he let his protégé, a Last Seed named Danill Volkov, kidnap me with intent to marry me. This is where they held me after a panic attack incapacitated me in my original room, which I later discovered was my nursery. Turns out my personal jailer was my nanny back in the day. How's that for irony?"

Corbin stared at me, lips parted, but my family drama appeared to have stumped him.

When I considered how a hunter must have been raised, I wasn't sure how that made me feel.

Until I decided, I awarded the contents of my pocket my full attention.

The ark shell from Tybee filled my palm, its sharp edge pressing into my fingertips. I withdrew it, running my thumb over the ridges, and when I could no longer resist, I knelt and placed it on the concrete beside the one embedded there.

"I don't get it." Corbin scratched his cheek. "What does your shell have to do with that one?"

"I'm not sure." I pulled out my phone and snapped a picture of them side by side. "Maybe nothing."

"Your wraith seems to think otherwise."

"Wraiths don't think," I lied. "They're nothing but spirit and bone."

Disbelief was written across his face, but he elected not to argue with me.

Breathing out his frustration, he said, "I can't stay with him."

"Hush." Eyes darting around, I pricked my finger then drew the privacy sigil that had worked so well during the carriage ride with Linus on the back of my hand. Pressure filled my ears, and they popped as a bubble of silence enclosed us. Any vampires we encountered would smell the fresh blood and assume I had been up to something, but they wouldn't know what. That was as much a guarantee as we could ask for. "Okay, go ahead."

Taking what must be peculiar magic in stride, Corbin repeated, "I can't stay with him."

"He's willing to teach you, protect you. You'll have a clan at your back."

"You heard him," Corbin growled. "He wants me to kill humans."

"He wants you to live up to your potential," I countered, keeping my tone neutral.

"I won't do it." He set his jaw. "I'll figure out another way."

"You're willing to risk your life to save others? You would rather die than kill a single human?"

There wasn't an ounce of hesitation in him. "Yes."

"That's what I was hoping you'd say," I admitted, tossing aside my Dame Woolworth mask. "We need to figure out his endgame. He's splintering the Undead Coalition. Why? He's folding the most powerful members into his own clan rather than killing them. Why? Others are allowing their clans, some centuries old, to vanish beneath the Lacroix flag. Why?"

Corbin exhaled a slow breath like he was sorting through everything I had thrown at him.

"The vampires have been under Society rule through the Undead Coalition for as long as anyone living can remember. As far as necromancers go, anyway. Lacroix is old enough to recall what led to the Society founding the Undead Coalition. He's old enough to know what they gave up by existing under the ruling Grande Dame's thumb. He reemerged after I was released from Atramentous. I wondered why for a long time, but I understand now. For the first time in my life, I had no protector. My mother is dead. Maud is dead. The Grande Dame...has never cared for me. She didn't lift a finger to liberate me until you." I hadn't realized it was true until the words hit my tongue, but "You saved me as much as I saved you."

Maybe that was why, despite his past, I wanted to save him back. Second life, second chance.

"What if he wants me to...?" He rubbed his face. "I can't hurt others, not even to live."

"You don't have to kill anyone," I assured him. "Blame me. Tell him our bond compels you to admit the complete truth when I ask you a question. He can't be sure it's a lie. How many goddess-touched necromancers are walking around with their Deathless progeny for him to ask? Better yet, tell him I forbade you to kill. He holds power over his subjects. Why shouldn't I?"

A fraction of the tension eased in his shoulders. "I can do that."

"I can't promise his intentions are any more nefarious than rebuilding his own clan from the ground up, but I have to believe if what he offered them was anything they wanted, he wouldn't have to use compulsion to get them to defect. He cast his net for new clan members wide, and there might be innocent vampires tangled in the mesh too."

"Compulsion?"

"Do you remember when Lacroix put his hand on your shoulder?"

"Yeah." He rubbed the spot. "Pretty sure he left bruises."

"He was trying to nudge your mind." A shiver rippled down my spine. "He almost succeeded with me, but you appear to have a natural immunity."

"We always assumed vamps got in their victims' heads. It was the only thing that made sense. Hearing it confirmed, having a name to go with it—a lure?" He shook his head. "I saw a jogger almost break her ankle once to stop and follow a man dressed in baggy jeans and a hoodie off the track, away from the streetlights, into the shadows. I saw a guy on his way to his daughter's ballet recital stop on the last step, smile at someone I couldn't see, and walk off without entering the building. There have been kids too. Out playing basketball in the street after dark. They just got this look in their eyes and walked off without a word to their friends."

"You killed those vampires." I hadn't meant it as an accusation, but the tone rankled him.

"I did." He challenged me with a look. "I tracked my targets, made sure they were killers." He rolled his shoulders. "It doesn't make me any less of a murderer, but it helped me sleep at night. I have no innocent blood on my hands, and I plan on keeping it that way."

"Lacroix might hammer on you until you crack."

"I won't." Corbin infused steel into his voice. "Not on this."

"Can you do this? Stay here, with him? I can't promise he won't make you cross lines, but you could save a lot of lives, a lot of *human* lives, if you help us get ahead of this."

Corbin cast his gaze across the garden. "You just want to know what he's planning?"

"Yep."

"How do I get out?" He stopped his perusal on me. "When the time comes, what's my exit strategy?"

"I hope you won't need one."

"You think he'll bring me in that close?"

"He already considers you clan. Part of that is your connection to me, part of it is his need to secure what he's identified as a valuable resource and a potential heritor. He's going to want you to be happy to make me happy. He's going to want to prove he can protect anyone I place in his safekeeping. Such as future progeny. He's also going to want to stick it to the Grande Dame. He doesn't care for her or the Society. He's not thrilled by what they did to me, either. But seeing as how he didn't have me sprung either, he wasn't invested until he knew what I was and what I could do. Until I became valuable to him."

"That's brutal," Corbin murmured. "I thought I got a raw deal."

"We both had families who loved us. We might not have kept them long, but that's still more than a lot of people get."

Kids blessed with two families, like me, whose second mother loved them like blood, were rare. People who lost them both through violent and sudden means, well, we were probably as common as unicorns.

Corbin scratched the dark stubble on his jaw. "How am I supposed to get word to you?"

"Don't trust Grampy to keep the lines of communication open?"

"No."

"Your immunity complicates things. He would honor the offer to let us stay in touch if he thought he could control what you were saying and doing. Since he can't, he's going to ease you over to the dark side one cookie at a time."

"Lucky for us, I don't have a sweet tooth."

"Will your power affect a wraith?" I raked my fingers through Cletus's tattered cloak. "Drain him?"

"We can find out." His gaze hooked into Cletus, and with an effort of will, he *tugged* on the wraith.

Cletus drifted closer to him, head cocked, then froze, the mist of his cloak darkening.

"I can't call him," Corbin said, sweat popping on his brow. "He can hear me, but he's not receptive."

"Good."

Calling off his experiment, Corbin exhaled. "Why is that good?"

For one thing, it meant he couldn't drain Linus through their connection. For another, it kept Maud safe.

"I'm sending Cletus with you. He'll get a lock on your location and report back. That way Linus and I can keep an eye on you. I'll send the wraith to your room each night until you're confident you can go for longer stretches. The new clan home can't be far. Lacroix has roots in the area, and old vampires prefer staying close to home."

"Okay." He blew out a breath. "What about afterward?"

"I'm going to talk to the Grande Dame about an immunity deal. You bring us intel on Lacroix, she grants you a pardon for your past crimes. It's a fair trade, even though it won't protect you from retribution unless you join a clan willing to keep you safe in exchange for the novelty of having a Deathless in their ranks."

"You're half vampire." He gave me a measuring look. "Ever consider starting your own clan?"

"I'm already Dame Woolworth. I don't want to be Master Woolworth too."

"I get that."

"Linus has thriving progeny and a solid reputation. One of the clans in his debt might be more willing to host you for his sake. A favor owed by the Grande Dame's son carries weight."

"Linus isn't here," he pointed out. "Are you sure you can speak for him?"

"Yes." Even if the bottom fell out between us, he would honor this bargain. That's the kind of man he was: honorable. "I'll send details with Cletus when it's safe."

Linus would know how to make our note-passing scheme work. He had used the wraith for multiple covert ops in the past.

"Ah. There you are." Our escort had located us at last. "I searched the gardens."

Before turning to him, I scratched off the sigil with my fingernail. "I got sidetracked with a stroll down memory lane."

"The nursery is untouched if you'd like to see your dollies." The cruel edge in his voice made me wonder if he had been here during my stay, if he had been one of the vampires who escaped. "You remember your old room, don't you?"

"I've wasted too much of my grandfather's time." I poured as much regret as I could muster into my voice. "I'll have to request the grand tour of the estate on my next visit. I didn't spend much time outside my room the last time I was here."

"There were casualties the night you escaped," he said softly. "I lost friends I've known for centuries."

"Your friends should have never locked me in a cage. I don't deal well with confinement."

The vampire took a menacing step into my personal space, and Lethe *moved*. She palmed his throat and slammed him against the stone wall, a dozen feet away, pinning him with his feet dangling above the grass.

"Bad vampire," she tsked. "Grier is under our protection."

"You can't—" He coughed. "The master—"

"That deal is done," Hood said. "His secrets are safe, and so is his clan, but Grier is pack."

Confirmation they had ties to Lacroix smarted worse than expected, but I concealed my reaction to the sting.

The vampire's eyes widened in shock, his lips moving over the word pack like he wanted to spit out the taste.

Grandpa would love hearing that I didn't want to be a member of his vampire clan but had accepted a spot in a gwyllgi pack.

"Put one finger on her," Lethe snarled, their noses touching, "and I'll bite it off then shove it up your nose into your brain. If you have one, which I'm beginning to doubt. Grier is Lacroix's granddaughter. You're a lackey. You're a predator, start thinking like one. She's so far up the food chain you can't see her from where you're standing."

"Let him go." I reached into my pocket. "I got this."

The second she relaxed her grip, he broke away and charged me. I let him. Welcomed the confrontation, as a matter of fact. I couldn't afford a hit to the reputation I had started building the night of the ball. I had to prove I could hold my own, that I didn't need protectors, that I was more powerful than the familial baggage leaving ruts in the road of my life from dragging it behind me all these years.

Impact drove me to the grass. The vampire straddled my hips, clamped his hands around my throat, and squeezed.

I could have pulled the stake, but it was a last-resort kind of weapon. I would have to kill him if I drew it. I wanted my legend constructed on powerful bones, not bloody ones, so I took the modified pen in my hand and...stabbed him in the meat of his thigh.

Okay, so a little blood was required for a necromancer to get the job done.

The vampire howled and reared back as I dove into my genetic memory.

Sigils whirled through my mind, and I discarded each suggestion while searching for a statement piece.

The vampire was doing his best to strangle me while Hood restrained Lethe, whose snarl kept grabbing my attacker's attention. The distraction gave me all the time I needed to isolate the perfect sigil. Grampa would *love* this.

Too busy wrapping his hands around my throat to restrain my arms, the vampire made it easy for me to dip a finger in his blood. The poor guy must have thought I was about to dig my nails into his wrists to pry him off me, but I only painted a sigil above his former pulse point.

Before higher reasoning caught up to primal instincts, I closed the design with a satisfied grin.

Power shimmered over him in a rippling cascade that left pebbled skin in its wake. His pallor, a hallmark of vampirism, only highlighted the gray sweeping over him in a second current of magic.

Eyes gone dull, he released me to touch his face. "What...have you...done?"

With him suitably distracted, I planted my left foot and right shoulder on the ground. Snapping my hips to the right as I kicked off with my left foot, I flipped the vampire onto the grass beneath me.

"I'm proving a point that I don't need anyone to fight my battles for me." I patted his cheek. "I'm leaving you here as a monument to stupidity that Grandfather can gaze upon as a reminder. Maybe if you play your cards right, he'll move you into the front gardens. The view is better there, trust me."

"You...can't—"

Whatever he thought I couldn't do, I had already done. His lips froze in a horror movie scream. Eyes wide, hands clawing his face, his pose left something to be desired, but a few perennials planted in the earth around him might brighten his morbid expression.

Dusting myself clean as I climbed off him, I almost smacked face-first into Lethe. "What?"

"You turned him to stone." She toed him with her shoe. "Are you half gorgon too?"

"I would have to be a third gorgon," I said in my best Linus-lecture voice. "But no. I'm not."

"Let's get out of here." Hood grabbed us each by the upper arm. "Our hands are tied unless you're in immediate danger."

I dug in my heels, turning back for Corbin, but he shot me a lopsided smile and said, "I got this."

For his sake, I hoped he was right.

EIGHT

A call from Amelie left me staring at my phone, debating if I wanted to answer. Since I had engaged her, I had no one to blame for this but myself. Raw after the meeting with Lacroix, I felt like his magic had scoured away the topmost layer of skin and left me all sinew and bone.

The worst part was deciding if it was the confrontation or the absence of Linus that wearied me.

I missed him, and I hated that he had put me in the position of doubting him yet again.

Lethe nudged my foot with hers. "Want to talk about it?"

"Can you?" I frowned at her. "You guys have been giving me the silent treatment for miles."

"You ought to find it comforting," she said, but her scowl told me she hated the secrecy. "Consider this a live demonstration of how tight our lips can seal."

"The farther we get from the estate," Hood added, "the easier it is."

A jolt of understanding arced through my brain, but I locked down the revelation, scarcely daring to turn the possibilities over in my head. There was no point asking the Kinases. Lethe was right. They had given me a chilling demonstration of what happened when someone tread on their magically enforced NDAs.

They had lost their will. The binding hadn't forced them to act against their natures, but it was clear that having two clients, former and current, in the same room gave them static. But the location must be a consideration too. They had interacted with Lacroix at the ball, in the Grande Dame's home, without issue. That must mean...

The true reason they clammed up on the way there, before they were anywhere near Lacroix, wasn't so much *who* we met but *where* our meeting was held.

Hood and Lethe—and I was willing to bet Midas—had worked at the estate, for my grandfather.

Doing what I did best, pushing down those uncomfortable realizations, I called Amelie back to avoid Lethe. "What's up?"

"Boaz just left." She hesitated. "I didn't mention you to him at all, and he didn't ask."

Bullet dodged, I relaxed against the seat. "Okay."

"He told me they found a note taped to Odette's refrigerator."

Cletus might have missed the significance of a note in an otherwise-empty kitchen, but what did it say that whoever packed up Odette hadn't been willing to leave even a magnet behind?

"The handwriting is hers." Amelie let that bomb detonate before dropping another. "It was a note to her realtor about a leak in the master bathroom in need of repair before the property was shown."

The roaring in my ears reminded me of the first time Odette held a conch shell to my ear to hear the ocean.

"It's a fake." I yanked on the seat belt, unable to breathe. "A forgery." Lethe tried to help, but I got us both so worked up she sliced through the strap with a clawed fingertip. "Tell him to have it tested."

"They did," she said in a small voice. "That's why he waited to tell me. They just got conclusive results."

"No."

"Grier—"

A brutal mash of the *end* button silenced her voice in my ear. "You heard?"

"Hard not to in close quarters." Lethe shifted on her seat. "We can't help it. Sorry."

"I need to visit the Grande Dame." A bitter taste flooded my mouth. "Take me to the Lyceum."

VISITING THE LYCEUM, and its mistress, ranked up there with other such enjoyable pursuits as root canals, fillings, braces, having braces tightened, using rubber bands on said braces—basically anything orthodontist related—and having your foot flattened by a steamroller.

This visit might earn a spot in the history books for it being the first time I asked to go and the first time I went in alone.

"Wait for me in the van," I told the gwyllgi. "This won't take long."

Lethe ignored me, no real surprise there, and trailed me right up to the front door. "I'll wait here."

Glad for the backup, even if she was about to be too far away to be any help, I pushed into the lobby.

Until the vampire-assassin incident, I hadn't possessed a key to access the secret panel that allowed the elevator to go all the way down to the Lyceum. I should have. I was Dame Wool-worth now. Maud had most likely stashed her key in her office, but I didn't want it bad enough to search her personal effects for it.

And anyway, Linus corrected that oversight after the ball. Once we learned the Lyceum was no longer secure, he gave me his key and requested another from his mother. He had armed me with every weapon at his disposal, even when it meant him doing without, even when the lack put him in danger.

But he had never valued his own life. Learning what he had done to Maud, for me, made perfect sense if you knew him as well as I was coming to understand him.

Oh, Linus.

Using his key, I coaxed the elevator into the bowels of city hall. The doors opened, and I stepped out onto marble the color of wet blood. I wasn't squeamish, I couldn't afford to be in my line of work, but there was something about the coagulated swirl of richer crimsons that had me tasting bile.

Eyes downcast to avoid taking in the scenery, I made my way to the Grande Dame's private office.

"Grier."

"Oh." I rocked back on my heels, surprised to find her stepping out of an office a few doors down from hers. I wasn't aware she made the rounds instead of making the rounds come to her. "Hi."

"This is unexpected." The Grande Dame peered around me, noticed the lack of Linus, and frowned. "You're alone?"

"The Kinases are waiting for me upstairs."

Her arched brow prompted further explanation, but I stood there, as fragile as if my bones were spun sugar, afraid any wrong move from her might cause a deluge that washed away my resolve.

After a hushed word to her colleague, the Grande Dame escorted me into her office and shut the door behind us.

"I spoke to Linus not ten minutes ago." She rounded the desk and sat in her high-backed chair. "He sounded...odd."

"I remembered something about the night Maud died." That wasn't what I came here to say, but it was too late to call back the confession once given. "I remembered he was there."

"I see." Her glistening crimson nails drew her attention, and she studied them. "Are you implying he had a hand in my sister's death?"

"No." I linked my fingers in my lap. "I remember him comforting me after I..." *found her body*, "...and he tried to intervene with the Elite. That's it. That's all."

"The Elite were forced to sedate him after you were taken away." As her hand dropped, so did her pretense. "Linus almost killed three men before they restrained him long enough to paint a sigil on his throat to slow his pulse. He was kept in a private cell until you were sentenced. I released him myself, explained you were bound for Atramentous, that he couldn't save you. He walked out of the Lyceum that night, drove to Atlanta, and never looked back."

Without leveling the accusation, I understood she blamed me for the loss of her son. She was right. It was my fault. Just not for the reasons she imagined.

Atlanta had become his haven, his mantle as potentate armor to protect his secret, and the distance from Savannah guaranteed to keep his mother at arm's length.

"I've wondered if bringing him back, calling him home, to you, was the right thing to do." A brittle quality entered her voice. "I couldn't see another way to heal you, to prepare you, but it costs him. He's paid a little more each time I see him, Grier, and he's not wealthy. Not in that way. You could bankrupt him if you set your mind to it. Bleed him dry. Leave him holding a cardboard box filled with memories of you."

Heal me. *Prepare* me. She made it sound like...like...she cared about me. Enough to risk Linus's feelings.

"Linus has one of the biggest hearts of anyone I've ever known."

"I know that," she whispered, "but I'm surprised you do."

"I deserve that," I admitted. "I didn't see him before."

A glimmer veiled her gaze, but she would never let those tears fall. "You do now?"

"Enough I want to see the rest."

She closed her eyes, collected herself, and when she raised her head, her voice was strong. "What can I do for you? I assume you didn't pop in just to discuss my son."

Back on track, I pushed Linus out of my thoughts. "Odette Lecomte is missing."

"Missing."

"Yes."

Leaning back in her chair, she leveled her stare on me. "How do you know?"

Outing Amelie meant outing Boaz. Neither were great options. She was in enough trouble, and he was a lucrative informational source I wanted kept available in case this plea for assistance dead-ended.

As an Elite, he could petition his fellows for help without involving the Grande Dame. That must be nice. Given her line of questioning, it sounded like he might have chosen that route, not that I would blame him. Sadly, she was my only remaining avenue for aid, so I had to handle this with care.

"Odette called to tell me she was heading out of town to visit a client." The best lies were laced with truth, and I was going to have to do some tight stitching for this to hold water. "Amelie is taking online classes, but she could use some face time with a live person."

"You don't feel you're equal to the task."

"Amelie and I are not what I would call friendly at the moment, no."

Lips pursed, she appeared thoughtful. "You're allowing her brother access to her, correct?"

"I am."

That was hardly a newsflash considering his "higher-ups" had assigned him to shadow me.

While the Grande Dame was as high up as it got, the Elite operated outside the laws of the Society. She might have been responsible for his appointment, but I doubted it. She wanted us kept apart, not thrown together. A more plausible scenario, in my mind, was she caught wind of his new duties and turned him into a special project. Still, even with him tucked under her wing, she wouldn't be privy to all the details of his assignments.

As easy as she made it to vilify her, I fell into the trap of underestimating her all too often.

As I got to know her son better, I was learning about her too. Not through direct conversation, but small tells when Linus talked about her, interacted with her, gave away more than either of them realized.

"What makes you believe foul play is involved?"

A chill swept down my spine. "I didn't say I did."

"Why else would you be here?" Her smile was red as blood. "You must be desperate to come to me."

"I saw her house on Tybee. It's empty. And whoever made it that way left behind bronze powder."

"To incapacitate your guards."

"And prevent them from picking up the scent of the person responsible."

"Odette Lecomte is a seer of some renown," she allowed, though she downplayed Odette's fame to suit her pride. "There are several members of the High Society who depend on her services. I doubt anyone would complain if I launched an inquiry under the circumstances."

"I would appreciate any help you can offer."

Nodding that, of course, I should be thankful, she asked, "How are the gwyllgi?"

"Hood required medical intervention." Hanging around me was bad for his health. "He's fully recovered." I flexed my hands in my lap. "Thanks for asking."

"Lethe Kinase is the firstborn daughter of the Atlanta alpha. We can't afford an incident with her, her unborn child, or her mate."

The edge of her concern being political shouldn't have surprised me. "I'll do my best to keep them in one piece."

"They're your friends. I can tell by the bite in your voice. That means you'll do better than keep them in one piece. You're loyal to a fault." She made it sound like a bad thing. "They couldn't be in safer hands."

The backhanded compliment didn't bother me half as much as the knowledge of how well she read me.

"Oh, don't look so surprised." Laughter quirked her mouth. "I've known you since you were a child. I've witnessed your stubborn streak rear its ugly head more times than I can count. Maud may not have given birth to you, but you are her daughter in all other ways."

A lump tightened my throat, and I almost hated her for giving me the opening I couldn't resist walking through in light of recent events. "You told me you knew how she died."

"I do." She lost focus, and her voice went soft as a whisper. "She was stabbed in the heart with a slender blade, likely an athame, perhaps one of her own. The killer carved open her chest and removed the organ." A fragility overlaid her usually sharp features. "That's how my sister died." She tried for a laugh, attempted to rebuild her façade, but its cracks gaped too wide. "The lie was close to the truth, you see. An attack on her heart did kill her."

Heat rolled in wet tracks down my cheeks, and she watched the tears fall, her own eyes dry.

Mouth a brittle line, she thinned her lips. "Have you opened the box?"

"No." The thought had never crossed my mind.

Nodding as though she expected my answer, she said, "I recommend you leave it sealed."

"Why would I—?"

"I'm tired," she said, rising. "You should go."

"All right." I let her usher me out into the hall then leaned against the door after she shut it.

A grim certainty hollowed out my stomach, and I rubbed the knot until I made it worse.

The gold box she had given me, the one holding Maud's heart... It was empty. It had to be.

Until this moment, I hadn't realized I was holding on to the hope that the Grande Dame had exerted her influence to locate the missing organ. I had wanted to believe I still had a piece of Maud with me, almost as much as I wanted to pretend the box and its gruesome contents didn't exist.

The Grande Dame had given me the box, I assumed, to punish me. But had she meant for it to give me closure instead?

While I doubted she had spent the days of my incarceration pacing the floors of her home and weeping at the injustice of it all—that wasn't how one became the Grande Dame—it did appear more and more that she had seized the first real opportunity to have me released without it blowing back on her.

She dethroned Balewa and reopened my case. She exposed her own—albeit fictional—ailment to the entire Society to have her *evidence* of a heart attack accepted as fact. And foisted Linus on me as a tutor and guardian since his status as potentate guaranteed his ability to protect me.

The uncomfortable possibility that Linus's difficulty in putting his feelings into words had been learned at her knee occurred to me in a flash of insight that made disliking her harder than it had been before I walked through her door.

I didn't trust her. I would never do that. I had known her too long and understood, the same as Linus, that she hungered for power more than she craved affection.

But maybe, just maybe, she wasn't the monster I wanted to imagine her.

Mulling that over, I hit the elevator, crossed the lobby, and nodded at Lethe.

She fell in step with me. "You good?"

"Not yet, but I'm getting there."

We got in the van, and Hood glanced back at me. "Abercorn?"

"Yeah." A tired laugh sawed out of me. "Abercorn."

LINUS STOOD with his back facing the street when we arrived at the building. A large suitcase sat near his feet like an obedient pet while he worked the locks. Sensing he had company, he turned from the door.

I held Hood's gaze in the rearview mirror. "Make a couple of loops?"

"Sure." He cut his eyes to his mate. "Hop up here and keep me company, gorgeous."

Lethe draped herself over his seat. "How about you find somewhere to park then join me back here?"

"I would say *don't do anything I wouldn't do*," I said, "but *don't do anything that requires stain remover* works too."

"Don't be silly." Lethe glanced over her shoulder at me. "That's why Hood suggested leather."

Wiping my hands down my pants, I scooted out the door while touching as little upholstery as possible.

Linus didn't call out a greeting, and he didn't close the distance. He stood there, watching my approach.

Mouth dry, I nodded to the luggage. "Going somewhere?"

His gaze swept over me, assessing, and he frowned. "Upstairs."

"Not Atlanta."

"Unless an entire city exists on the second floor of this building, no. Not Atlanta."

"I worried you might leave, after we fought."

"Friends fight," he said softly. "Friends also make up, and life goes on."

That was what I told him the first time I forgave him. He remembered it word for word.

"Sometimes they don't," I repeated his lines, proving I remembered too. "And it doesn't."

Head down, he said, "I won't leave."

His mother would be less than thrilled if he left before she granted her permission.

Chin lifting, he amended, "Not until you tell me to go."

"I don't know what to do." All I knew for sure was I wanted to break his suitcase over my knee if it kept him from leaving. "This is the start of a cycle. You omitting things, me finding them out, me getting hurt, you apologizing." I exhaled through my mouth. "I don't want that kind of relationship. Not again."

His nod of agreement came slow. "You deserve better."

"That's the problem." I met his gaze, a rich navy, and held it. "I'm becoming convinced there isn't anyone better."

He visibly startled, black wisps clouding his irises, and he parted his lips on a question he didn't ask.

"How do we do this?" A raw quality scraped through my voice. "How do we make this work?"

"You're a strong woman, Grier. This only has to work if it's what you want. You don't need me."

"If you believe that," I said, "maybe we should call it quits and walk away before we're in too deep."

"Any deeper and I'll drown." He sucked in a breath like he was preparing for that exact fate, but he didn't budge even an inch.

"Is love supposed to feel like your heart is outside your body?"

A preternatural stillness swept through his limbs, but he was listening.

"That's how I feel when I'm with you, like my heart is standing beside me instead of inside me. Each hit, each cut, each bruise hurts me too, like it happened to me instead of to a wholly separate person. I drive myself crazy thinking in circles about Atlanta, and I must be plucking your last nerve, but part of me died with Maud that night, and the rest of me wasn't sure about how to start living again after Atramentous." I swallowed hard. "I've been on life support since you arrived. Now I've been told it's getting cut, but not when, and I can't help but fixate."

Linus shifted his weight forward, leaning toward me, but he kept his feet planted on the sidewalk.

"I'm so tired of hurting." I studied the position of the moon overhead to give my tears a chance to dry. "I worry sometimes if it slacked off that I wouldn't feel at all, but that's no reason to stay in a relationship that promises pain. I've done that. Loved a man who was bad for me in every single way. Forgave him all the bad times because the good times were so good."

Linus shrank into himself until even the black vanished from his eyes. "I don't want to hurt you."

"I know."

"This is all I am." He spread his arms. "This is all I will ever be."

"I know that too."

Nodding, he lowered his arms. "I can't offer you more."

"You're right." I took the first step. "You can't offer me more."

Lips mashed into a bloodless line, he nodded again.

"You give everything you have to everything you do." I took another step. "That's who you are, Linus."

Neat furrows creased his brow, and the impulse to smooth them away itched in my fingertips.

"I don't understand." He glanced past me, to the van, to the gwyllgi watching the show, waiting to see if I went in or needed a ride home. "I thought..."

"You thought I was here to break up with you."

"Yes," he said, his voice a ragged whisper.

"Then you're out of luck." I spread my hands. "I'm not going anywhere, and neither are you."

"I don't understand."

"You said that already." I took one more step, just close enough I could pat his chest. "Let me break it down for you."

"Please do."

He sounded lost and miserable and...yet. Hope glinted in his eyes, faint but there. I could work with that.

"I'm done with living for the good times when the bad ones stretch for so long I can't see the end if I'm standing in the middle. That doesn't work. It's toxic."

The spark in his eyes guttered, and he dipped his chin, accepting —and misunderstanding—my verdict.

"That's not us." I pressed my palm over his heart. "We're a hundred good times, a thousand perfect moments, a million tiny gestures, before a blip. That doesn't make the bad any easier to stomach, but I like our odds. I want to keep going." I curled my fingers into the fabric of his shirt. "I want to keep you."

Linus gazed down at me, his eyes soft before his resolve hardened. "Come upstairs with me."

"Not the reaction I'd hoped for," I said, releasing him, "but okay."

"I warded the building." He let us in, collected his bag, and led the way up to the bedroom. "We'll be safe here."

Since my last visit, he had set the mattress on its frame and put on sheets. He might not have slept, but he kept up his bedtime ritual. He placed his luggage at the foot of the bed then straightened, his jaw set.

"Sit down." He tacked on, "Please."

"Since you asked so nicely..." Thoroughly confused, I perched on the edge of his bed. "What now?"

Kneeling between my legs, he offered me his modified pen with his left hand while flattening his right on my thigh, palm up. This position put us at eye level, and he had never looked more resigned to his fate.

"There are sigils that force a person to tell the truth," he said. "I would like you to use one of your own design on me."

"No." I shoved him back. "If you can't tell me the truth without being compelled, I don't want it."

"I have told you the truth," he said carefully. "I want you to believe what I said without a doubt."

"I trust you." I searched his face. "I don't need this."

"I do." The pen groaned in his hand, its plastic casing threatening to crack. "Please."

The sigil floated to the forefront of my mind without me calling it, like it had heard his plea and answered all on its own. I drew it on, fingers sure, but my stomach clenched and unclenched at the power he was giving me over him. When I finished, I capped the pen, tempted to break it in half in case he got any more bright ideas.

"Ask me a question you know the answer to, and I'll lie to see how it works."

The sigils from my brain packed a stronger punch than standard ones. I wasn't convinced testing this one on Linus was smart, for myriad reasons, but he would take matters into his own hands if I refused to cooperate. "What is your name?"

"Grier Woolworth."

A red sheen rolled over his eyes, reminding me of the gwyllgi, except this was brighter, unnatural.

"Interesting," he murmured, unable to help himself. "Ask me again."

"What is your name?"

"Linus Lawson."

This time his eyes turned a luminescent green from corner to corner.

Judging by his faraway expression, he could see the colors too, but I wondered, "Does it hurt?"

"No."

Red.

Grin pulling at my lips, I said, "So, it does hurt."

"Yes."

Green.

"Go ahead," he prompted me. "Ask me anything about the night Maud died."

I got the ugliest question out of the way first. "Do you know who killed Maud?"

"No."

Green.

"Other than me, did you see anyone else at the house that night?"

"No."

Green.

"Cletus really is Maud?"

"Yes."

Green.

"Can you separate yourself from her spirit?"

He hesitated. "Yes."

Red.

Annoyed, he sighed. "It would kill me, but it is possible."

"You're bound to...Cletus...until you die?"

"Yes."

Green.

After my chat with his mother, I had some thinking to do, but I still wanted his unbiased opinion while it was there for the asking. "Do you think your mother had anything to do with her sister's death?"

"No."

Green.

"Did you use the sigil Maud taught you to incapacitate Woolly that night?"

"No."

Green.

"That's all I got." I traced his skin around the sigil. "I would have made a list if I had expected this."

"Ask me anything," he invited, the temptation to dig into his past seductive.

"How many lovers have you had?" Horror washed through me in a stinging wave that sizzled in my nape and flushed my cheeks. I slapped both hands over my mouth, but it was too late. "You don't have to answer." Yanking down my hands, I covered his lips instead. "Please, don't answer. I had no right to ask, and I really, really, *really* don't want to—"

"None."

Green.

"—know." I dropped my hand. "None?"

"None."

Green.

Well, minus the red climbing into his face.

"You told me in Atlanta, at the Faraday, that Hubert outing one of your lovers to your mother would be the highlight of his career." I planted my hands on his chest and shoved him away. "And *cupcakes.* When I asked you why women heap on lace and frills like we're cupcakes in need of decorating while men strip down like their perfection can't be improved upon, you explained to me women do it to make their partners feel like their time together is special. *You explained cupcakes.*"

"As far as I was concerned, I was engaged." He landed on his butt and sat there. "I remained faithful."

Green.

"I was in prison for five years."

"I was adapting to this." Black mist whirled between his fingers. "Sex was not a priority at first."

Green.

"And later?"

"My condition, the temperature of my skin, aroused as many women as it repelled. I didn't care. I didn't want them." He made a fist and vanquished the darkness. "All I ever wanted was you."

Green.

In for a penny, in for a pound. I might as well hear the rest of the sordid tale. "But?"

"After a few years, Mother felt I ought to move on. I wasn't ready. She didn't want to hear it. She arranged a date for me. I had my team research the woman's background and discovered her father was in debt up to his neck. He liked to tell people he was a horseman, but the closest he got to the animals was the counter at the track.

"I offered to pay off his debts, all of them, if she would date me for six months. I didn't want sex. I didn't want friendship or companionship. I wanted a warm body I could cart around the city, parade in front of Mother's informants, and then I wanted to go to my loft and be left alone."

Green.

"I spent a great deal of time around women who pretended to be in a relationship with me. A few took me lingerie shopping to keep up appearances." He sighed. "The cost of lace and elastic made me curious enough to ask the purpose of spending so much money on undergarments that wouldn't last the night. That's why I understand *cupcakes.* I experienced the phenomenon myself several times near the end of an affair when a *lover* wanted to extend our arrangement. I always declined. The sex would have felt bought, and the extension only invited hurt feelings."

Green.

"You could have explained all that to me sooner," I said at last.

"Practicing abstinence in your absence, without your knowledge, was one thing." He bent one of his legs then looped an arm around it. "Admitting I have feelings for you after all these years...when you had never seen me in that light..." He sighed. "Pride wouldn't allow it."

Green.

I licked my thumb then smudged the sigil on his hand.

He waited until its power had broken to relax his posture. "What now?"

I pretended to consider him. "Tell me you love me and wait to see if I say it back."

The color washed out of his cheeks. "That hardly seems fair."

"That's how it's done." A shrug rolled through my shoulders. "Boys have to go first."

The ink flaked off his hand, its spell broken. "You're sure you don't want the sigil on for this?"

"You're stalling."

"You're right."

About to show mercy—I had put him on the spot—I stood to exit the bedroom at the exact moment he rocked onto his knees and gathered my hands in his. Heart lodged in my throat, I wished I hadn't dared him to confess his feelings. At least without the sigil, I could tell myself—

"I love you." He stared at my hands like a man attempting X-ray vision. "I suspect I always will."

Amazed to find I could speak, I couldn't help but tease him. "You suspect, huh?"

"I don't want you to burn the marriage contract." He rolled his thumb across my left ring finger. "I want you to honor it." He didn't manage to look higher than my collarbone. "You feel something for me. Over time, you might—"

"You don't listen very well for a professor." I palmed his cool cheek, and only then did he lift his head. "I wasn't posing theoretical questions to you earlier. I meant every word. About *you*."

Neely and Cruz. Lethe and Hood. Those couples had taught me lessons I was only beginning to grasp.

Their love wasn't simple. Practice gave it an effortless appearance, but that was far from the truth. It was a kind word in the morning, a thoughtful meal prepared without request, a kiss before parting ways, a kiss when coming back together. A million tiny kindnesses sprinkled throughout the days, the months, the years.

"You've got baggage. I get that." I sank over him, sat on his lap, and linked my arms behind his neck. "You might be surprised to learn I own a few pieces of luggage myself."

The teeniest, tiniest smile curled his lips, so slight it might have been a shadow indention on his cheek.

"I don't believe you would ever hurt me on purpose." I threaded my fingers through his hair and tugged on his scalp until he tilted back his head, forcing him to look at me. "Every day, for as long as we're together, you'll try to make us work. That's all I can ask."

Hands digging into my hips, he searched my face. "You love me."

"I do." And because he hungered to hear the words, I sighed them against his mouth. "I love you, Linus."

Mist curled off his skin as he met my kiss with teeth, claiming me with sharp nips that gave me shivers.

The taste of my blood ignited a hunger that roared through my gut, and a growl rumbled in my chest.

His guttural chuckle tapered to a husky groan when I raked my teeth over his throat. "Hungry?"

"Starving."

But his blood wasn't the only thing on the menu tonight.

NINE

To ensure Linus got the memo about the change in the main course, I fisted the halves of his shirt and yanked until the buttons pinged off the walls. "Oops."

An arched brow conveyed his doubt. "What do you have against my dress shirts?"

"Nothing." I ruched his undershirt up and over his head too. "I prefer this view."

Just like the first time I touched his abs, tracing the ink there, he sucked in a sharp breath. Chills dappled his skin, the delicate hairs rising as he shivered under my fingertips. I thumbed his navel and raked my nails in a hard line above the button on his slacks. His eyes closed, and his lips parted, and I didn't think he had inhaled since the moment I put my hands on him.

"Breathe," I whispered in his ear. "I don't want you fainting on me."

Air whistled past his lips as he filled his starving lungs with oxygen.

This was honest. This was real. This was...everything.

Before he regained fine motor control, I peeled my tee over my head and tossed it on the floor. Arching my spine, I reached behind me and unhooked my bra. I glided the silky straps down my arms, past my wrists, then flung it away.

I sat before him, halfway to naked, and let him look.

Black swallowed his eyes from edge to edge, and his Adam's apple bobbed twice.

Darkness unspooled around us, inky tendrils spilling into the room, lapping at my thighs. "Um, Linus?"

A tic in his cheek betrayed his annoyance when the black whorls kept spinning off his skin. "I can't seem to control myself."

His frustration was *adorable*, but I wasn't going to tell him that while I was straddling him topless.

Sudden mortification swept through me, and I clamped my hands over my boobs.

"Cletus can't see us, right?" I had always equated his eyes going black with his wraith. "Or hear us?"

As much as I loved Maud, and as fond as I had grown of Cletus, I did *not* want them watching the show.

"I can ward the room to keep him out," Linus offered. "He won't be able to perceive us beyond them."

"That works." Hands on my breasts, I rose. "I'll text Lethe and let her know we'll be spending the day here."

Linus rolled to his feet, collected his pen, and set to work while I got out my phone.

You can head back to Woolly. We're fine here.

>>*You guys are having sex!*

You can't text and have sex at the same time.

>>*Hello? Sexting? It's a thing. Look it up.*

I gotta go.

>>*Gotta go get you some.*

LETHE.

>>*GRIER.*

>>*Remember to use protection.*

>>*Hood keeps condoms in his wallet. I can loan you some if you want.*

Loan implies I would give them back...

>>*Eww. Eww. Eww.*

I'm muting my phone now.

>>*Call me after, and we'll dish.*

Turning off now...

>>*Then Linus must not be doing it right.*

After I muted the phone, I kicked off my shoes, socks, and pants, and set it on top of the pile.

Bent over the threshold, Linus drew on a sigil with painstaking detail that would preserve our privacy while I took the opportunity to apply a contraceptive sigil good for a few hours even if it got smudged.

Then I stood there in my panties, watching him work. I admired the flex of muscle in his back, the utter focus on his task, and my heart swelled until there was no room not filled with him.

He must have sensed me staring. Practically drooling. After finishing the design, he capped his pen and tossed it onto his ruined shirt. He met me in the middle of the room, near the foot of the bed, but he didn't touch me. He just looked and looked and looked until I felt self-conscious.

"I want to paint you like this," he murmured, his hands unable to resist wandering over my hipbones.

"We're beyond pickup lines," I joked, and his cheeks pinkened until I almost regretted the comment.

With his hands on my waist, he guided me to the bed. I sat when the backs of my knees hit the mattress, and he knelt between my legs. With his elegant hands, he traced dueling paths up my sides and over my ribs, his fingertips skimming my breasts. He palmed their slight weight, his calloused thumbs rasping over my nipples until I was panting.

"Beautiful," he breathed and dipped his head, closing his mouth over one aching peak, teasing the hard bud with the edge of his teeth before moving to the other.

He kissed his way down my stomach, south of my navel, and urged me to recline. Hooking his fingers in the sides of my thrift store panties, he eased them down my legs, past my feet, and flung them over his shoulder. He palmed my knees, spreading my thighs the width of his shoulders. Desire flushed his skin, and I fisted the sheets as he sank down and put his mouth on me.

Then it was my turn to forget how to breathe.

He explored me with his tongue until the coil of tension ratcheting tighter in my core sprung loose.

"*Linus.*"

Legs quivering, head too heavy to lift, I stared at the ceiling until I saw him stand out of the corner of my eye. He kicked off his shoes, socks. Unfastened his pants, let them hit the floor.

"I want to look," I said, a quaver in my voice, "but I don't seem to have any bones."

He climbed over me, his skin cool and firm, and kissed the side of my neck. "You liked it?"

"I did." I cupped his face between my palms. "If you tell me you read that in a book..."

His wicked grin was blinding, the widest, most beautiful smile I had ever seen, and it was all for me.

Unable to resist tasting it, I kissed it off his face then ran my finger down his ribs. "More."

Linus slid down my body on the way back to his knees, but I caught him by the shoulders and urged him over me. The restrained hunger in his eyes asked me a question, and I answered, "Yes."

With his feet on the floor and his elbows supporting his weight on the mattress, I had plenty of room to ease my hand between us. Linus's groan turned into a growl when I closed my hand over him. Mist curled off his skin, and he rested his forehead on my shoulder. A shudder climbed his spine when I started exploring his length with my fingertips.

When his breath came in ragged pants and he gritted out my name—a plea, a curse, I wasn't sure—I fisted him, guiding him into me.

Linus wrapped his arms around me, cradling me against his chest, and thrust home in a single stroke.

The pain was sharp but brief, and he murmured soft apologies in my ear as he held me until that bright sting was secondary to the solid feel of him around me, in me. I turned my face toward his, brushed my lips against his, and linked my ankles at his spine. "More."

Pleasure raked across my raw nerve endings each time his hips met mine, and soon I was clawing at his skin, begging for a push to hurl me over the edge, and he used his fingers on my core to send me flying.

His smooth rhythm hitched as I clenched around him, and he groaned my name as he came.

His full weight hit me then, and our hearts raced against one another, sweat sticking us together.

Cinching my noodle legs around him, I begged, "Stay."

"I'm too heavy," he protested, but his knees had stopped working, and he was sliding onto the floor.

Showing mercy, because I was certain I couldn't stand either, I let him go. "Come to bed with me."

I rolled to the far side of the mattress, smiling as I watched him fumble to climb in with me. Linus collapsed with his feet hanging off the end, with his head too far down for more than the ends of his tangled hair to brush his pillow. I scooched lower to make us even, unable to wipe the goofy smile off my face.

"We had sex," I whispered, like it was a secret in danger of being overheard.

"Yes," he whispered back. "We did."

"Do you feel any different?"

Lines wrinkled his forehead as he looked at me. "Yes."

"Me too," I confessed, and his expression smoothed again.

He shifted onto his back, hauling me with him, and I sprawled half on top of him. The weight of his arms made him more real than he had ever been. This was the most physical contact we had ever had, and I didn't mean the sex. I meant him reaching for me, yanking me into his orbit, holding me like I might escape if he loosened his grip. He was initiating for the first time, taking what he needed from me.

And then it hit me. Until this moment, he hadn't believed I was his. He hadn't touched me or kissed me or hinted he might want more. He had followed my lead, given me what I craved, and held his needs in check. He had given me all he could bear, what wouldn't leave too many scars on his heart if I let him go.

Oh, Linus.

"Do you want to shower?" he asked sometime later, his fingers tracing my collarbone.

"No." I yawned, snuggling closer, breathing him in. "I want to stay just like this."

And we did, until the beat of his heart beneath my ear lulled me into a dreamless sleep.

TEN

I woke to a heavy thumping noise that was not the steady thud of Linus's heart beneath my ear, though I heard that too. I waited a full minute in the hopes our visitor would take the hint and leave before I cracked my eyes open.

"Hey," I murmured, vision blurry, "I'm still in bed."

Sheets tangled around my ankles, but there was too much give beneath me for hardwood.

Linus kissed my eyelids, which had slid closed again. "Yes, you are."

"That's...weird." I yawned, forcing my lashes to untangle and stay that way. "Nice, but strange."

"You slept through the day."

"Solving the dream's riddle seems to have worked wonders for me."

"I held you all day," he pointed out. "Don't I get any credit?"

"While your arms are very nice—" I looked at Linus, really looked at him. Combed hair, the ends still wet. Brushed teeth, his breath minty. "You showered."

Mischief twinkled in his eyes. "I held you all day...minus twenty minutes."

"You're also dressed." Sheets whispered beneath my leg when I bent it to test my theory. "I'm not."

Linus traced a chill finger down the length of my spine. "No, you're not."

Smooshing my face against his chest, I groaned. "You stayed awake."

"I did."

"You better not have been mentally painting me again."

He kept his lips zipped while I thunked my forehead against his chest.

"I don't want to come home and find Woolly plastered in nudes."

"You entertain too many guests for that," he said, sounding perfectly reasonable. "However, the basement..."

"You're not transforming the basement into a seedy love den."

"Nudes are art." His fingers tickled over my ribs. "I was thinking more along the lines of a gallery."

"Mmm-hmm."

There was no graceful way to climb off Linus, not when he had draped me over him like a living blanket sometime during the day, but the door kept rattling, and he clearly had no intention of answering it while I was warm and naked on top of him. "Who is that?"

"Whoever it is, they can wait."

Calling out wouldn't do any good. They wouldn't be able to hear us. "You don't sound concerned about our unexpected guest."

"The wards are sound." His eyes twinkled. "I borrowed the design from a brilliant necromancer I know."

"You used Woolly's design here?" Flushed with pleasure at the compliment, I sent my awareness out into the house, but it met no resistance to indicate the dwelling was becoming aware. "Can you tell who or what entered the building?"

"The wards on the bottom floor are light to allow in customers and future staff. The upper floor will be impossible for anyone to attain who has malicious intent." Linus frowned at the door. "I left stewardship of the wards unclaimed, for you. I assumed, if my proposal interested you, that you would want the bond since you would spend the most time here. All I can say for certain is our guest wishes us no harm."

Truthfully, it could only be two or three people. Most likely, it was Lethe or Hood checking in.

"I'll grab a shower." The only thing stopping me from wrapping myself in the wrinkled sheet to make my grand exit was the look in his eyes. "You can deal with whoever is out there."

That was the point when I remembered the bathroom was across the hall here, past our early visitor.

"New plan." I snatched the sheet and made myself a toga. "You distract our guest while I slip past them into the bathroom."

"All right." He straightened his clothes as he stood then followed me to the door. Instead of opening it, he pinned me against it with his hips while he ducked his head to claim my mouth. "I didn't know it was possible to love you more than I already did."

"That's the sex talking." I patted his cheek. "Your hormones will behave after I get on clothes, and you'll return to regular levels of loving me."

Loving me.

Linus Andreas Lawson II loved me.

That, to me, was more of a revelation than the sex. And the sex had been...perfect.

"After last night," he murmured, "that's not possible."

A blush warmed every inch of my exposed skin, and I had plenty. "Are you going to get that?"

Whoever was out there wasn't taking silence for an answer. They wanted in, or for us to come out.

Linus tucked me behind the door, erased the sigil ensuring our privacy, and pulled it open. The light in his eyes extinguished, and the mask of Scion Lawson clicked into place. "Can I help you?"

"Where is she?"

The blood warming my complexion a second ago drained from my face. "Boaz?"

"Step aside, Lawson."

"No," Linus said, his voice gone cold. "I don't think I will."

Before they came to blows, I stuck my head around Linus. "What are you doing here?"

"You didn't come home. Amelie called this morning, frantic. Woolly had been ringing the phone at the carriage house off the hook, but she couldn't go to the main house to see what was wrong, so I went to talk to Woolly." His gaze roved over me, and I saw the moment understanding dawned. "You spent the day here." Boaz gritted his teeth. "With him."

Bumping Linus aside with my hip, I got between them before it got ugly. *Uglier.* "I appreciate you coming to check on me. I feel like a dirt sandwich for not checking in with Woolly, and I'm sorry I worried Amelie, but I'm fine." The fact he was standing on the doorstep of a purchase I had just learned about made me ask, "How did you know to look for us here?"

"I was assigned to you, remember?" Boaz raked his fingers through his hair. "I keep tabs on your movements."

The violation stung anew, and that surprised me even more. I ought to be used to his strings of tiny betrayals. "I need to shower, and we need to get home to reassure Woolly."

The plan was to inch past him and shut the door behind me, putting a slab of wood between them, but I hadn't noticed the sheet was stained crimson on the edge until Boaz fisted the material, staggering like someone had punched him. He dropped the cloth, his eyes glinting with cold fury.

"Did he bother taking off his fancy clothes before he fucked you?" His hands balled at his sides, knuckles popping as he faced Linus. "Did he take your virginity, or did you have to do it yourself? He's fantasized about this for so long, he probably creamed his pants before he touched you."

Using what Midas had drummed into me about being a woman taking on a male opponent, I drew back my arm and launched a right hook that snapped his head to one side. Something cracked. I think it was my hand, but I didn't care. I threw my shoulder into the next punch before he shook off the first hit, and his utter shock was comical.

"Get out." Knuckles throbbing, I massaged my hand. "Now."

"Grier—"

"Do you hear yourself?" I cradled my arm against my chest. "You've lost your ever-lovin' mind, Boaz."

"This is not how it was supposed to happen." He swept out his hand, indicating the sheet. "You let him take it. *Him*. Goddessdamn it." He wiped a hand over his mouth. "Are you getting back at me? Is that it?"

"Linus didn't take anything from me," I said, sad and tired and over this. "And this has nothing to do with you."

Eyes tight, he shook his head. "You don't mean that."

"Lethe." I didn't raise my voice. I didn't have to. "Come here, please."

There was only one reason why Woolly would have fretted enough to reach out to Amelie, and that was if the gwyllgi had stayed to protect me. Hood and Lethe must have slept, among other things, in the van. And they wouldn't have let Boaz or anyone else in without escorting them, whether our guest knew he had been tailed or not.

I spotted her blue hair first and her furious scowl next. "Escort him out of the building."

"Sure thing." She moseyed over to us. "Just one thing I have to do first."

Lethe snapped out a roundhouse kick to his jaw so fast her leg blurred.

Boaz hit the floor on his back with a grunt, and she put her foot on his throat, pressing to make sure she had his attention. And then she smiled, and I almost wet my pants for him.

"You might think you're insulting Linus when you talk smack

about him, but you're really insulting Grier. She wouldn't be with a guy who treats her like dirt. Note how she's not with you anymore?" She applied pressure, and he sucked in air between his teeth. "Even if Linus were literal pond scum, he would still be floating above the waterline. Even if he was a water snail eating pond scum, or water snail poop made of pond scum? Yep. Still better than you. You've sunk low before, but stay down there much longer, and you'll drown."

Hood walked up behind her, and he smiled down at Boaz, all teeth. Lethe ignored him and kept venting.

"Grier loves Linus. That's all you get to know about them. That's all you need to know. She. Loves. Him. And you know the best part? He loves her back. Actually loves her. Puts her needs ahead of his own, that kind of thing. I would go into more detail, really break down how badly you've failed as a man, but it would fly right over your pig head, and I'm too hungry for this BS." She rubbed her belly. "And now I'm thinking about bacon."

"I'll handle this." Hood bent down and fisted the front of Boaz's shirt, using it to yank him to his feet. "You order breakfast."

"I love you," she said, stomach growling.

"You love bacon."

"I have a big heart," she protested. "There's room enough for both of you in it."

After they had gone, Lethe turned back to me. "He's an asshat. Don't let him get under your skin."

"I screwed up," I admitted. "I should have called Woolly or Oscar."

"Grier." She clamped her hands on my shoulders. "You're allowed to make mistakes. You're allowed to live your life. You're allowed to enjoy yourself." She shook me. "So you forgot to check in. It happens. Apologize and move on." She smiled. "I'm proud of you. You put yourself first for like twelve whole hours. That's got to be a record." She shot a look at Linus from under her lashes. "I want all the deets, but let's wait until we get back to Woolly. I'm going to need popcorn for this."

With a wink, she set off down the stairs, leaving Linus and me alone.

His chill fingertips skated across my shoulders before drawing me against him. "Are you all right?"

"This is not how I imagined the morning after, but I'm good." I wrapped my arms around his waist and let the tension drain away. "You okay?"

"We have to do something about Boaz. This type of behavior is inexcusable."

"Request-a-transfer do something, right? Not *off with his head* do something?"

"I'm not going to kill him." His expression shifted into thoughtful lines. "Unless he leaves me no choice."

That sounded like him holding open a door waiting for Boaz to walk through it.

"He needs space to get his head on straight, not have it separated from his neck."

Linus stroked down my spine, a smile playing on his lips.

"That's not a murder smile, is it?" I jabbed him in the chest. "I thought you weren't the possessive type."

"I will never cage you." He took my hand and kissed my fingertips. "Not with love or otherwise."

"Keep sweet-talking me, and I might have to hold on to you."

"I'll bear that in mind." He nudged me across the hall. "I'll bring you a change of clothes."

A bit of last night's glow had returned while I was in his arms, and it carried me through the shower. But, try as I might, I couldn't banish the specter of Boaz. Part of me had always expected to share the morning-after experience with him, but not like this.

Amelie's disinheritance. His engagement. Our estrangement. His mother stepping down as head of the family. Him stepping up.

He had been through a lot, and I sympathized, but I was done being his verbal punching bag.

I had to get him out of my life, and I wasn't above asking the Grande Dame for help evicting him.

AFTER MY SHOWER, Linus brought me one of his button-down shirts and a pair of cotton boxers. I could have worn yesterday's clothes—they weren't that rumpled—but I wasn't going to say no to him fussing over me. Plus, I had that whole shirtdress thing happening after I rolled the long sleeves up to my elbows and belted the fabric at my waist. Those were trendy, right?

At least with his undies on, I wasn't in danger of flashing my butt getting in the van. My poor boobs, however, just had to hang there. Linus didn't seem to mind me going braless. Really, he ought to be used to seeing my boobs jiggle since bras were the first thing I lost in times of crisis.

We met Hood and Lethe downstairs, and we all walked out to the van together.

Boaz was nowhere in sight, but Hood's knuckles were scraped, and Lethe looked far too pleased with her mate.

"I ordered breakfast." She popped me on the rump. "We gotta vamoose, or the food will beat us there."

"Hey," I yelped. "That hurt. This shirt isn't all that thick."

"Oh, that's right." She snickered. "I'm used to you wearing jeans, but you slept here last night, and you didn't pack a change of clothes. You were too busy having *sex*."

I refused to blush.

Fiddlesticks.

Okay, my face was on fire.

"Grier had sex," she sang. "Grier had sex."

"Hood," I pleaded, "a little help here?"

Lethe rested her hand on his thigh, her nails trailing upward, and fluttered her lashes until he caved.

"Linus had sex," he chimed in. "Linus had sex."

"I quit the pack," I grumbled. "I'm going lone wolf."

"You can't quit," Hood said, "and we're only half wolf. You're actually zero wolf. So there's that."

The ride home was more of a ride of shame than anything. Lethe and Hood sang jaunty tunes about how much sex I had last night, and Linus was no help at all. He didn't manifest his scythe or offer to cut off their heads or anything useful. Mostly he just sat there, a tiny smile playing on his lips, and pretended not to hear their caterwauling.

Back home, Woolly barged into my head before Hood threw the van in park. Her panic and relief clashed in a halting melody that made my ears ring. She bulldozed into my memories, discordant noise vibrating in my back teeth, and saw last night through my eyes. The complete quiet on her end startled me into a new blush.

Mortified, I dropped my face into my hands. "This night keeps getting better and better."

"Oh." Lethe plastered her face against the window. "I think that's Joe."

"I can't remember the last time you were this excited to see me," Hood remarked.

"The last time you brought me bacon," she answered before hopping out and sprinting to the curb.

"Lethe and bacon sittin' in a tree," I grumbled as I stepped out into the driveway. "C-R-U-N-C-H-I-N-G."

Chuckling under his breath, Linus emerged behind me and slid his cool fingers in mine. The happiness on his face, there for anyone to see, made my chest ache that he couldn't be *this* Linus in our world. But his status made him a target, and so did mine. People wanting to hurt us would take aim at those we loved.

"I need to go check in with Amelie." I heard the resignation in my voice, but it needed doing. "Why don't you help Lethe bring in her order? I'll be right there."

He squeezed my fingers once then left to help my friend juggle her armload of bags and drink trays.

"How mad are you on a scale of one to ten?"

I whipped my head around at the sound of Amelie's voice. I hadn't realized I had turned to admire the view as Linus walked away until I glanced back at the carriage house to find her standing in the doorway.

"Maybe a three." I shrugged. "You did the right thing."

"I would have called anyone else if I had known anyone else to call."

"I get that." I used my modified pen to write a number on her palm. "However, if I vanish in the future and you can't find the gwyllgi, I want you to call this number. He'll know what to do."

Her lips moved over the number as she committed it to memory. "Who do I ask for?"

"Midas."

Perhaps not the best option considering the fact he struggled with control around Amelie. The darkness in her rankled his animalistic nature, which viewed her as sick prey in need of culling. But she didn't need to know that, and it's not like I had any better options. Hopefully, she would never need to test his restraint.

"He was the blond, right?" Her focus zeroed in on where we used to spar in the garden. "Blue eyes?"

"He would have to drive down from Atlanta, but he's worth the wait."

Chin lowering, she asked, "Boaz stuck his foot in it, didn't he?"

"Your brother is under a lot of stress, and he's making bad decisions. Talk to him. Or Adelaide. I met her at the ball, and she seems to have a good head on her shoulders."

"No one else in your position would have put up with us this long."

"The three of us have a lot of history. Just because I don't think we're good for each other now doesn't mean I don't care. I do. I want you to both be happy."

"You are." She cocked her head. "Happy, I mean."

A dopey grin crept up on me. "I am."

"I'm glad." She smiled, and it was genuine. No shadows. No undercurrents.

"I should go." I hooked a thumb over my shoulder. "Woolly is going to give me an earful—if she lets me back in the house."

"I have a paper due tomorrow." She ducked her head. "I should get back to proofreading it." She snapped her fingers. "Oh. I almost forgot. Check the inside of that shell you showed me. There's an inverted Z. I thought it was scarring from the moon snail, but it's the signature of a local artist. She creates jewelry from what she collects on Tybee. Earrings are her most popular item. She does a good job of making pairs from intact clams so they're a perfect match. Calls them shellmates."

"Nice detective work," I praised her. "I'm not sure what it means, but it must mean something."

Otherwise, Cletus wouldn't keep circling the issue.

"Whatever I can do to help," she said, and I could tell she meant it. Not from boredom, but earnestly.

We parted ways, and it wasn't as awkward as the last time. Maybe next time would be even easier.

I took the stairs onto the back porch, expecting Woolly to lock me out or bean me with the door when I was halfway through it, but I walked right into the kitchen and found her buttering up Linus while he sorted the mail, tossing petitions addressed to me in the trash as per my request. Their bond was fainter than ours, so I'm not sure how they communicated. Images were simplest. That was my bet.

Crinkles gathered at the corners of his eyes when he saw me. "Have you discussed this with Grier?"

Braced for the worst, I rested my hand on the nearest wall. "What are we discussing?"

Woolly projected babies and cribs into my head. Kids running down the halls with his hair and my eyes. I lost count after five, but there were—wait a cotton-pickin' minute—*three* cribs. Triplets? No. *No, no, no.* Hearing the Marchand family was lousy with fraternal twins was terrifying enough, but three infants? At once? Plus the five others she had decided she wanted? I might as well never leave the hospital. I would end up a baby factory operating out of a posh delivery suite.

"Um, Woolly," I began. "It's a bit early in our relationship to think about children."

More images flashed. Changing tables. Bouncing seats. Swings. Highchairs. Strollers.

"Pump the brakes." I snatched my hand back. "I'm not popping out a kid per room. You've got *a dozen*."

Woolly dimmed the lights, her presence storming off across the house in a fit of pique.

"I saw this going differently in my head," I admitted to him. "I figured she would tear me a new one for staying out all hours of the day without calling in. I didn't expect her to pitch a hissy fit because you didn't knock me up on the first try."

Lethe glanced up, a bacon strip hanging out of her mouth that she slurped up like a spaghetti noodle. "There was just the *one* try?" She shoved a box of meat toward Linus. "Eat that. It will help build your stamina."

Linus flushed crimson, and his dark-auburn hair paled in comparison. "I'm not having this conversation."

"It's okay to ask for help." She rubbed her stomach. "Hood didn't get it right out of the gate, either. He's an old pro now, though. I bet if you asked him nicely, he would give you tips. He might even draw you a few pictures. You're an artist, right? He would be speaking your language."

Before she could ask for a pen and paper, he pointed toward the hall. "I'm going upstairs."

He didn't say if it was for a shower, which he had already had, or clean clothes, which he already wore. I don't think he put much thought into the statement beyond blurting what guaranteed to get him out of the kitchen and away from Lethe.

On his way past, he handed off a postcard featuring the picturesque North Shore Mountains. There was no postmark, no note, and no signature, but it was the third blank postcard I had received since Taz went into hiding. I assumed she must be using Elite contacts to pass them to me, but I had yet to catch her coconspirator in the act, though I had a good idea who was responsible.

The picture wasn't much, but it let me know she was okay, and that had to be enough.

The Marchands were out for blood after Taz shot Heloise to save me. She wasn't safe in Savannah, maybe anywhere, until they considered that debt paid.

After tearing the postcard into tiny pieces, I dumped them in the trash, afraid of leaving a paper trail someone might follow back to her. With that done, I stared down Lethe and anchored my hands at my hips. "You ran Linus off so you could hog all the bacon, didn't you?"

"Yep." She opened the box she'd offered him. Only a grease smear remained in the bottom. "He doesn't eat much that I've noticed, but there were no snacks in the van. After noon, it got dire out there." She placed her hand across her heart, staining her shirt. "But I persevered. For you. Because you're my friend."

"There's a convenience store a block down and several restaurants. There were also two bags of takeout containers, candy wrappers, and soda bottles in the back we had to step over to get in the van in the first place."

"What are you saying?"

"That you're a black hole that sucks down anything with caloric value within a fifteen-yard radius."

"I'm pregnant."

"Your baby is so tiny, it could be mistaken for a pinto bean."

"Don't listen to her." She clamped her hands on either side of her stomach. "She's just mad Linus gave out after one round."

"Lethe." I clamped a hand over her mouth. "You can't say that in front of your child."

"Trust me, growing up gwyllgi, it's going to hear worse. He or she might as well get used to it."

A shiver in the wards prickled my nape, and I sought out Woolly to ask what was out there.

Still grumpy, her consciousness flowed toward me like molasses stored in a fridge.

"Lethe."

I cocked my head at the muffled sound of a man's voice.

"Lethe Kinase."

Without waiting for Woolly to interpret the scene, I jerked the door open to find a squat man slabbed with muscle standing in the driveway. That was as close as Woolly let him get, and he had worked up a head of steam over being denied his grand entrance.

"I challenge you," he bellowed. "I challenge you for second in the Atlanta pack."

Hood raced in from the side yard, but he was too late. Magic boiled around Lethe, splashing up her legs.

"No," he breathed. *"No."*

Lethe didn't hesitate. She rocketed toward the property line and tackled the man mid-shift. Foam boiled over her lips as she sank her teeth into his ruff and slung her head until his blood stained her mouth red.

Shrieking like a stuck pig, the challenger dropped to the ground on his side, thrashing in her grip, trying to escape, but I could have told him that wasn't happening unless she let him. Panicked, he twisted onto his back, eager to flash his underbelly and end it.

With a snarl, Lethe released him, allowing him to submit. Already I breathed easier. It was over. *Phew.*

Tail swishing, she glanced back at Hood, huffing at him for doubting her prowess.

With preternatural swiftness, the challenger lunged for her tender belly.

Hood roared, his agonized cry a promise of retribution.

I was too slow to stop the challenger from locking his jaws on her abdomen, but blood ran through my fingers, hot and wet, before I understood I had cut my hand with my knife.

A circle snapped into place around me, and I sketched a sigil on its surface, slamming my hand against it.

Magic shot from my palm, pierced the challenger's chest like an arrow, and he fell dead on the spot.

I didn't need to call on my necromantic powers to tell his heart had stopped beating.

Lethe shifted to human. She collapsed on the ground, cradling her ravaged stomach as blood spilled through her fingers.

Linus ran past me, yanking off his dress shirt, and knelt at her side. Expression tight, he pressed the balled fabric to her wound to staunch the bleeding. The look he offered me was grim, and my knees wobbled.

"I can't fix this," he said, his eyes full black. "The baby..."

On my way to them, I sliced my hand until the blade hit bone. Blood dripped down my wrist, and I didn't waste time with my fingertips. I used my entire hand to draw an enormous healing sigil across her abdomen.

Necromancers weren't healers. We didn't save lives—we offered second chances—but I had to try. I had purged Linus several times. I could do this. I had to do this. For Lethe. For Hood. For their unborn child.

More blood. More pain. More symbols.

Designs flashed, alien in my mind's eye, and I bathed Lethe in my blood without slowing down to figure out what each one meant.

I had to trust my gut, and my gut said I had one shot at getting this right.

About the time my head started swimming from blood loss, a shimmering veil of incandescence settled over her like a shroud. Before my eyes, the ragged edges of the wound knit together, and the blood reabsorbed into her skin. One final pulse lit her from the inside before the glow receded into her pores.

"Get her..." I panted, "...to your..."

Healer.

The world spun around me, dark as the backs of my eyelids.

ELEVEN

"*L**ethe.*" Head swimming, I jerked upright, groaning when the world sloshed. "Where's Lethe?"

"Woolly offered her one of the guestrooms," Linus said. "She's staying down the hall until she recovers."

The gwyllgi wouldn't be happy giving up their den in the woods, but I was glad to have her under Woolly's roof where we could keep tabs on her.

Throat tight, I forced my lips to move. "The baby...?"

"Their daughter is fine." He caught me against him before I slid off the mattress. "You saved her."

"Lethe?"

"She was eating a hamburger the last time I saw her." He laid me back against the nest of soft pillows on what I realized was my bed in my room. "You're the only one in danger at the moment."

"I don't feel so hot," I admitted.

"You need to feed." Linus pierced the tip of his index finger with the knife he bought to replace the one I stole from him and stuck it in my mouth. "You must replenish what you lost. This is the fastest way."

Copper hit my tongue, and I moaned. This wasn't how I'd pictured feeding from Linus, if we ever got that far, but I wasn't complaining. He was *delicious*. Better than a fresh hot chocolate from Mallow delicious.

This much blood straight from the vein was a thrilling rush I hadn't expected, his familiar taste amplified tenfold. Richer, bolder, he intoxicated me, and I got drunk on him.

It didn't take much. As a vampire, a *half* vampire, I was a total lightweight.

"Your color is better," Linus mused. "Do you need more?"

"Can't hold 'nother bite," I slurred. "Bite. *Bite?* I didn't even use my teeth." I meant to poke at my canines, but I shoved my finger up my nose. For a second, I worried it was stuck, and that made me laugh harder. "I don't have fangs. Do you care if I don't have fangs?"

"I love you just as you are," he assured me, removing my finger before I scratched my frontal lobe with all the wiggling I was doing trying to free it on my own.

"You're okay with being finger food?"

"Yes."

"'mkay."

Head thunking back against the pillows, I slept.

"I HAVE A HEADACHE," I groaned, eyes opening on a dark room. "Got any aspirin?"

Two pills dropped on my outstretched palm, and a glass of cold water followed. "You're a cute drunk."

"I've been drinking your blood every day for months—years. Why did it make me loopy this time?"

"You've been drinking two tablespoons of blood diluted in a smoothie." He sat on the edge of the bed next to me. "There's no way to know how Maud was feeding you, or your mother for that matter, but they must have diluted it as well for you not to notice the taste.

You drank the better part of a cup last night, as near as I can tell. That's eight times your usual amount, and it was pure."

Woolly prodded me gently, her concern a pang in my temple, and I pushed reassurance her way.

A commotion drew my attention to the lawn. "What's going on out there?"

"The family of the gwyllgi you killed is howling for blood, literally."

"That dirtbag challenged for second in the pack. What did he think was going to happen?"

"Dominance battles are rarely to the death," Hood said, entering the room. "Most end in submission."

This one should have—it would have if the challenger hadn't cheated *after* tucking his tail.

"He tried to kill Lethe," I protested.

"No." A vicious edge sharpened his tone. "He tried to murder our child, her heir. It was a political move."

"How is that any better?"

"I'm not chastising you, Grier." He bowed his head. "There will be repercussions for what happened last night, but I don't blame you. I thank you. From the bottom of my heart, I thank you for saving our child."

"Ernst Weber attacked after submitting to Lethe," Linus argued. "He acted dishonorably. Lethe won the match. We were all there. We will act as witnesses if required."

Brow furrowed, I glanced between them. "Weber was the challenger?"

"Yes." Hood sighed. "His family has been pack for eleven generations. The alpha won't like this."

"Let me know if I can help." I sat up and swung my legs over the edge of the mattress. "Anything I have, anything you need, it's yours."

"Thanks." Hood crossed to me and gave me a brief hug. "You understand the concept of pack better than he ever did."

"Can I visit Lethe?" I peered through the door into the hall.

"Does she feel like having a visitor?"

"She's sleeping now." Hood softened his expression. "I'll come get you when she wakes."

"We'll be downstairs," Linus told him. "Grier needs to eat, then she and I have to talk."

Hood returned to his mate, and Linus stood to leave so I could shower and dress.

Woolly's presence lingered in the room, so I asked for privacy through our bond.

A vibrant image of kids playing on the lawn flashed in my head, but she vanished after her parting shot.

"You don't have to go." I folded then unfolded a corner of the sheet in my hand. "You could stay."

"All right." He covered my hand with his. "I'll get my grimoire and wait on you out here."

"I don't know if I ought to feel glad you didn't misunderstand the invitation or sad you didn't offer to get slippery with me."

"You're worried about Lethe." His cool touch soothed. "You won't believe she's all right until you set eyes on her." He laced our fingers. "What we had wasn't about sex, and what we have now isn't either."

Mischief prompted me to lean in close. "You do want to have sex again, though, right?"

"Yes," he choked out. "I do." His cheeks turned rosy. "When you're ready."

I rocked forward and planted a smacking kiss on him. "I just had to know."

He touched his lips. "What?"

"You still blush." I slid off the bed and winked at him. "I was going to miss it if you'd stopped."

"I doubt sex has cured me," he said dryly.

"Good." I headed for the bathroom. "I like knowing you're as affected as I am."

Humming under my breath, busy looking as innocent as possible,

I stripped in the doorway.

"How could there ever be any doubt?" he murmured and decided to join me after all.

AFTER A SHOWER that didn't do much to get either of us cleaner, we headed downstairs for breakfast. Linus started blending, and I was about to check in with—brace for it—the Grande Dame to see if the Elite had uncovered any leads in Odette's disappearance, when Cletus swam into being beside me.

He trailed his icy fingers along my cheek in hello, and it stunned me anew that he was Maud, that she was here, and that I had never connected his touches with hers.

For Linus's benefit, I pinned on a bright smile. "What news?"

The wraith leaned forward, infringing on my personal space, but I wasn't alarmed until I heard Linus shout as Cletus enveloped my entire head in his hood.

The world fell away, and a void whirled around my face. Frigid wind slapped my cheeks, and through my watering eyes, I squinted as a scene swam into focus.

"I cannot go back," a soft voice murmured from beyond a gauzy veil I couldn't part. "I will not."

"My love, you must." Shadows twisted before me, twining into the forms of a man and a woman locked in an embrace. "There is no other way."

Straining to hear more, see more, I plunged deeper into the darkness, but the couple swirled away.

The oppressive gloom shifted colors to gray, and Corbin stood before me, looking at Cletus.

"Grier," he said, addressing me directly, "so far I'm being treated like a prince. The clan isn't thrilled with my sudden arrival, but Lacroix is winning them over to my side. He can hold the minds of an entire room of vampires who have sworn blood oaths to him." He darted a quick glance behind him at a door. "The clan masters are resistant to Lacroix's demands, but he always gets his way in the end. Their people..." He shook his head. "They have no clue what's happening around them or to them."

A thud against the door had him turning away from Cletus.

"I don't know what your grandfather's agenda is yet, but he's gathered between nine hundred to a thousand vampires here if my math holds." He looked back at the wraith. "We have to free these vamps. I can't imagine anything good will come of this, and that's not just my prejudice speaking. He's got the numbers and the control to force the Grande Dame to submit to his demands." He shrugged. "Whatever they are."

The transmission swirled away, and sensation returned to me in a rush of tingles.

Fingertips bit into my shoulders, and light stabbed me in the corneas while I thrashed like I was drowning.

"I'm okay," I gasped. "I'm okay." Linus clamped my face between his palms to hold me still. "I'm okay."

"You keep saying that," he said, eyes searching mine, "but it's not convincing me. What did it do?"

For him to relapse into calling Cletus an *it* instead of a *he*, even if *he* was a *she*, meant he had been in serious panic mode.

"He showed me...things." I cut my eyes toward the wraith. "I always assumed there was a skull in there, but there was nothing."

"There is, and there isn't."

Wiping a hand over my face, I rid myself of the darkly creeping sensation. "Did he show you too?"

"No." He indicated the wraith hovering in a corner like a kid in time-out. "He seems to believe he reports to you now."

A wraith fused with his soul who had decided I was his master sounded like a recipe for disaster.

Good thing I didn't plan on breaking up with Linus any time soon.

"He was spying on a couple having an argument. I couldn't see them, and I couldn't hear them well."

"He must have been incorporeal at the time. His level of substance affects the clarity of his visual and audio feedback."

"Why would he show them to me?" I considered the shadow figures intimate conversation. "Do you think he was snooping on Lacroix?"

"It's possible," Linus allowed. "That would explain why Cletus remained hidden."

"After that weird blip, he cut straight to Corbin." The way he addressed me and not Linus made me wonder. "Hmm."

"Dare I ask?"

"Corbin is using Cletus like a video diary, and he's addressing his entries to me. Maybe that's why Cletus brought the message to me instead of you?"

"The fact a wraith can reason out that it should bring a specific message to a specific person is worrying enough without it risking a secondary bond through sharing its power—however briefly—with you."

Forgetting about Corbin for a second, I asked, "A secondary bond?"

"It's rare, but it has happened. Wraiths choose who they bond to, and some bond to multiple people."

"That drags fragments of your soul through other people, though."

"Yes." His lips twitched. "You begin to see why bonding with a wraith is dangerous."

"You're saying Cletus could bond with me too? If he makes that decision, do *I* get a say? Or does he dunk me in his hood one day and bam! We're three-way soul mates."

"A normal wraith wouldn't initiate contact with a necromancer, let alone a bond. It would decide between the practitioners courting its favor. But Cletus is not a normal wraith. His behavior becomes more erratic as time goes on. I can't predict what he might do if he felt your life were in danger."

The wraith cocked his head as he listened to our conversation, and I hoped Linus hadn't just given Cletus any ideas. That he had his own ideas was, apparently, a bad thing.

"Back to Corbin." I would have to digest this latest tidbit later. "He says Lacroix has gathered upwards of a thousand vampires to him. They're sharing a clan home. Corbin says they're under his thrall. That he can control a room full of the blood-sworn vamps. He suspects they might not be there of their own free will or acting under their own power."

"Lacroix is dismantling the Undead Coalition." Linus folded his arms across his chest. "Why?"

"Corbin isn't sure yet." I told him the rest. "He says Lacroix has the numbers to overthrow the Grande Dame."

Black swirled off his skin as Linus went preternaturally still. "Is Mother aware of his location?"

"I meant to fill her in when I visited her at the Lyceum the other night but..." *we ended up talking about you,* "...we discussed Odette's disappearance, that segued into Maud, and then she asked me to leave."

"Maud is a tender subject for her." He drummed his fingers on his elbows. "I need to see her. She must know about this. Any threat against the Society, no matter how vague, must be reported to the Grande Dame."

"I'll grab my kit."

"You're coming?" He dropped his arms to his sides. "To the Lyceum? To see my mother?"

I suppose I deserved that. The Lyceum wasn't my favorite place nor his mother my favorite person.

"I made the call to shelter Corbin. I embedded him in Lacroix's inner circle. She's your mother, but she's also the Grande Dame. She's going to act in the Society's best interests." And in her own. "I'm not letting you face the consequences alone. Besides, the intel he's feeding us ought to get him and me off the hook."

The outline of his tattered wraith's cloak flickered over his shoulders then vanished. "And if it doesn't?"

"Then we hope she feels the same way as Woolly," I said with a wink, "and we offer her our firstborn."

Linus gaped after me as I hit the stairs to collect the backpack of supplies from my room.

I don't think he moved the entire time, including his mouth, which still hung open when I returned.

"Give me some credit." I crossed to him and tapped under his chin until his teeth clacked together. "Do you really think I would hand over our kid?"

Dazed, he stared down at me. "Are we having kids?"

Woolly rustled the curtains in the living room, and the lights dialed up so bright a few bulbs shattered into glitter like she was tossing it at a parade.

"Maybe. One day. I've got my hands full with Oscar for now." I picked at the buttons on his shirt. "Does that work for you?"

No hesitation. "Yes."

Both of us had baggage from our childhoods, and both of us would be gun-shy about strapping it onto the backs of the next generation. We had been raised in different worlds by women with very different standards, skills, and strategies on child-rearing. Not to mention I was goddess-touched. What would that make any child of mine? Mix in Linus's status, and we had to hope the Eidolon condition wasn't hereditary as well.

"You must have had more sex if you're down here planning how many kids you're popping out."

I pivoted toward the stairs and spotted Lethe at the top.

"Lethe." I sprinted up to her for a hug that turned bone-crushing when she reciprocated. "You should be resting. I was coming to visit you. You didn't have to get out of bed."

"Grier." She clamped her hands on my shoulders and held me at arm's length. "You healed me." She ran her fingers through her hair in emphasis. It was longer and showed a good three inches of brown roots. "I am one hundred percent back to normal. Better than normal. Look at my arms." White lines once marred her tan skin, souvenirs from dominance fights over the years, but they had vanished. "I don't have a single scar. I'm as pink and shiny as a new baby." She wiggled in place. "Speaking of Baby, she's been dancing the samba for hours."

"The baby...moved?"

"Yes." She laughed. "Look at this." She peeled up her shirt, a saggy tee borrowed from Hood, to reveal a noticeable bump. "Watch it."

A few seconds later, a flutter twitched above her stretched navel and then another and another.

Head swimming, I sank onto the topmost step. "What did I do?"

"The healer has never seen anything like it. He ultrasounded me while you were sleeping. The baby is six to eight weeks ahead of schedule, judging by her size. And it is a girl. A *girl*. We have a grainy black-and-white printout to prove it. How cool is that?"

"Very." I tried for more enthusiasm. "That's fantastic."

"You saved her." Lethe dropped beside me and slung her arm around my shoulders. "Do you get how amazing that is? You saved her life. We owe you a debt that can never be repaid."

"You don't owe me anything." I leaned against her, glad to have someone to prop me up while this sank in. "I only wish I had been faster." That I had never had cause to test my skills on her. "There are...repercussions...to using my magic in certain instances."

"Linus told us about Amelie. He explained the possible complications."

Bless him for trying to spare me even that small pain.

"I've healed Linus several times without him showing any of the side effects you've mentioned."

"You saved my daughter's life." Lethe stood and helped me to my feet. "I don't care if my bun pops out of the oven tomorrow. She's going to pop. You did that."

"Bun? Oven?" I forced a laugh. "You're hungry again, aren't you?"

"Only always."

"I have to go," I started. "We're off to see—"

"—the Wicked Witch of the Deep South? Yeah. I heard."

"You've got a bad habit of eavesdropping." A habit that carried over from her work at the Faraday, no doubt.

"People who share secrets in public can't complain when they're overheard."

"We're in my living room."

"Technically, we're standing on the staircase. It's a literal gray zone."

"Mmm-hmm." I noticed Hood lurking in the hall. "Return the patient to her suite, please."

"Gladly." He swooped in, scooping her into a bridal carry. "Call if you get into trouble."

"Oh no, you don't." Lethe started kicking and elbowing him. "Either you're going with her or I am."

A low growl rumbled through Hood's chest, but Lethe didn't bat an eyelash.

"I promise not to leave the house." When that didn't work, she sweetened the pot. "Out of respect for you, and my blood pressure, I won't even peek out the curtains into the backyard to count the number of sniveling cowards I'm going to have to eviscerate to reclaim my honor."

"You have a notepad on the nightstand," Hood countered. "You're making a list of names."

Lethe rounded her pretty green eyes. "Those could be baby names for all you know."

"We're not naming our daughter 'Fucking Rat Face Marsha Dover' or 'Flaming Asshat Rhonda Bent.'"

"'Flaming Asshat Rhonda Bent' Kinase." She tried and failed—spectacularly—at looking innocent. "We can call her Hot Buns for short. I can picture it now. Mom, the Alpha of Atlanta, presenting her firstborn grandchild as 'Little Ronny Hot Buns.'"

"You're clearly delusional and require extensive bedrest," I told her. "I'll be forced to order copious amounts of takeout so that you don't have to leave your room until we get back." I checked with Hood. "The healer is still here, right?"

"Woolly offered to let Shane stay the next few days to monitor Lethe."

"Good." That was one less thing. "We'll meet you at the gate."

Hood set out with Lethe while I used an app to order the items she yelled for as Hood carried her away.

Linus greeted me in the foyer, breaking off a conversation with Woolly to smile at me. "Ready?"

"Hood is tucking in Lethe, and we're meeting him at the gate."

Anxious about Lethe, about the baby, about Odette, I forgot the challenger's family had set up camp.

Woolly kept them off the lawn, but they were scattered along the edge of the property. I counted seven men and four women. They spotted me and started calling for Lethe's blood. They dressed well enough, in jeans and tees for the most part, casual, normal, but the flash of their teeth and crimson sheen in their eyes outed them as supernaturals.

"Woolly?" I shut the door behind Linus. "Can you make sure Lethe doesn't have to hear this?"

A few notes of a bolder melody swelled around me as she ramped up the wards to muffle the noise.

"We'll ask Mother to send a contingent of Elite to clear the property. We can't risk the neighbors getting interested in the gathering." Harshness edged his voice. "And, while I respect that physical challenges to dominants are necessary for maintaining a healthy pack, I won't allow you to be caught in the crosshairs of a power bid."

The tattered cloak materialized around his shoulders on a chill breeze that blew hairs into my eyes.

"Where do you think you're going?" I clamped my hand over his wrist before he stepped off the porch. "You're not leaving without your sigil."

The scythe had appeared in his hand by that point, and his deep cowl flickered like a hologram.

Another woman might have felt silly sweeping the hair away from his nape and drawing on a sigil designed to keep him safe, but I didn't have that problem. He led a dangerous life, and I made it even deadlier by association. I would do anything to keep him safe. A few scratches of my pen were nothing.

Amusement glinted in his dark eyes when they met mine, but he let me fuss over him with a tiny smile.

"Now we can go." I capped my pen, took his hand, and we bolted for the gate. "Hood ought to be on his way."

From here, the gwyllgi couldn't get to us, but we had an ideal view of the scope of the problem.

Now I counted a dozen more strangers loitering in the road and along the edge of the woods.

The odds sucked, but hopefully they wouldn't be a factor for Hood. I still had no idea where he parked the van since he didn't use the garage at Woolworth House, but he must have mapped out a back way to reach it since he always beat us to the gate.

"There's Hood." Linus touched my elbow. "We should hurry."

The cloak and scythe earned him nods of respect from the gathering as we passed the stragglers.

A few of them sniffed in my direction, their eyes popping wide in realization I was pack.

The confusing combination of a necromancer packmate and a potentate in hunting mode helped us escape unscathed, but I was grateful they didn't ID our driver. I would have hated to kill another gwyllgi.

One incident might earn me a slap on the wrist, but two? That would draw the pack's—and through them, the alpha's—attention to me. All I needed was for Lethe's mom to rule that being pack meant the other gwyllgi could challenge me to settle their scores too. If that happened, the measures they had taken to protect me just might condemn me in the end.

TWELVE

The Grande Dame met us at the door to her office, all smiles. For Linus. She enveloped him in a hug that ended with a kiss to each of his cheeks, which she patted for good measure. He sighed, resigned to the routine, and I wanted to tell him to treasure these moments while they lasted. One day, all he would have left of her were these memories.

"Grier, dearest." She gave me a light hug that skimmed my shoulders. "I have good news for you."

Sweet relief swirled through me. "You found Odette?"

"In a manner of speaking, yes." She ushered us in, and we took seats across the desk from hers. "It turns out, one of her benefactors owned the bungalow on Tybee Island where she has been residing for some seventy-odd years. The man died, a Rufus Sowell, and his widow decided to liquidate his assets. Since she has no use for Odette's *talents*, she evicted the seer. Her possessions were boxed, the house cleaned, and the property listed by a local realtor."

"I don't understand." I leaned forward. "Where is Odette?"

"We have yet to locate her—she takes her clients' privacy quite seriously—but we have no reason to believe she's been harmed. As a matter of fact, she left a note for the realtors. Something about a leaky faucet." Her pause invited me to admit I was already aware of that fact, but I kept my mouth shut. "I'm not sure why she hasn't been returning her phone calls, or why she hasn't contacted you, but she had a hand in this. I can't imagine her ordering movers about under duress, so we must assume she was a willing participant."

"That makes no sense." I slumped back in my seat. "Why wouldn't she tell me?"

"My understanding is the eviction was sudden." A smile curled her red lips. "While packing away his belongings in his study, the widow found compromising pictures from her husband's youth that featured Odette prominently. Learning he let her live rent free on a property she hadn't realized they owned didn't sit well with Matron Sowell."

"That explains her getting kicked to the curb," I allowed, "but not why she wouldn't tell me. Or why the house was dusted with powdered bronze."

Wherever she had gone, she had come back to oversee packing. The note was proof of that. But she hadn't breathed a word of it to me.

"The indelicate nature of the situation may have embarrassed her," Linus offered, covering my fidgeting hand with his. "She's a private woman. Having intimate secrets from her past broadcast throughout the Society would strike a painful blow to her pride. She might have assumed you wouldn't come looking for her since she called to let you know she would be out of town. Avoiding calls also makes sense if she doesn't want to expend the emotional effort of explaining her new circumstances."

"The bungalow was her home, has been for as long as I can remember."

Resolve hardening to granite, I decided I would buy back the property. Money wasn't the problem. Odette was plenty wealthy. But the scandal would attach a higher price tag for any of her patrons who wanted to help. Our connection was well-known, thanks to her friendship with Maud, so the widow might not sell to me either out of spite.

Not that I could blame her. That kind of betrayal hurt, and scandals like these ruined family names.

"My advice is to wait," the Grande Dame intoned. "If she hasn't made contact in a week, I'll divert more resources to locating her."

"Thank you."

As much as I wanted to believe otherwise, it sounded like Odette had left by her own choice. That didn't explain why she, or anyone else involved in the move, would have dusted the place with bronze powder, but Odette kept various herbs, metals, and minerals for brewing potions. The answer might be as simple as a mover dropping a jar, it shattering, dust coating the floors, and them not cleaning up after themselves.

"You didn't come to talk about Odette," the Grande Dame said, studying us with predatory interest. "What brings you back so soon?"

Linus took a breath to launch into his story, but I squeezed his fingers and cleared my throat.

"Corbin Theroux showed up on my doorstep a few days ago."

The Grande Dame cocked her head at me. "Corbin Theroux showed up on your doorstep."

"Yes."

"The minimum-security facility where he was being held was no Atramentous," she demurred, ignoring my flinch, "but I don't see him escaping without help."

The total absence of shock confirmed my suspicions she was aware of his current fugitive status.

"We had the same thought," Linus said pointedly.

They fell into a staring contest where accusations were hurled and deflected without a word spoken.

"I don't see him here." She flicked a glance at the door. "Did you leave him at Woolworth House?"

Unable to read her, I blundered on. "I no longer have custody of him."

"You understand he's a criminal, correct? I reduced his sentence after his change in circumstances. The research value attached to his condition was worth the trade. Considering he is now one of the very creatures he once hunted, I judged his flight risk to be low. He has no friends, no family, no money, nowhere to hide. Without Society protection, Corbin would be hunted and killed. If not by vampires, then by his own kin."

The continued evenness of her skin tone, the lack of mottling from rage, kept me talking. "I'm aware of his crimes. He confessed them to me."

The Grande Dame arched a perfect eyebrow. "And you, in your infinite wisdom, decided to intercede on his behalf?"

"I did." There was no point in lying. "I'm responsible for his condition, and I feel a certain obligation to him."

"We're not their mothers. We're their creators. They wake fully formed with no need of our protection, ready to go out into the world." She sighed. "All of us feel the bond between ourselves and our progeny, but you must learn to ignore that tug. Otherwise, it will pull you under as your tally of offspring rises."

That was a disconcerting thought. "I found a better situation for him."

"Do tell." She steepled her fingers. "I'm all ears."

"I presented him to Gaspard Lacroix. Grandfather has adopted him into his clan."

Faint wisps of black threaded Linus's fingers, tickling over mine, but he remained otherwise composed.

The Grande Dame didn't sprout fangs or horns. She didn't start screaming or hopping up and down on her desk. Nor did she offer an intern the opportunity to do it for her. She didn't call for the sentinels either, which, honestly, was the more likely scenario.

Her utter lack of reaction convinced me we had been right on the money, about everything, and that she had guided my hand in this.

"You understand you could be imprisoned again for the crime of aiding and abetting a known criminal?"

A punch of cold blasted from Linus, and my fingers grew stiff as a fine layer of ice crusted my knuckles.

Ignoring the numbness spreading up my arm, I lifted my chin and became Dame Woolworth. "I do."

"I would have thought you would do anything to remain on this side of the gates of Atramentous."

A shiver zinged down my spine, and the edges of my vision frayed, the gaping maw of the past eager to swallow me whole, but the fused mass of Linus's and my fingers promised I would never be alone in the dark again.

"I should have contacted you the moment Corbin arrived at my home," I said, failing to mention he only knew where I lived thanks to her dropping breadcrumbs. "I saw an opportunity, and I took it. I apologize for not consulting with you first, but I believe the intel he's gathering will more than compensate for our crimes."

"Our," she echoed. "You want to bargain for yourself *and* him?"

"I do."

"Very well."

She speared Linus with a look devoid of all warmth of maternal pride, warning him not to interfere. This was the Grande Dame issuing an order to the Potentate of Atlanta. The midnight fabric of his wraith's cloak fell from his shoulders, signaling the shift from personal visit to business meeting.

And there I sat between them with only the unfinished mask of Dame Woolworth for protection.

"Corbin estimates that Lacroix has gathered one thousand members to his cause and counting." I struck with the most brutal numbers first. "He witnessed firsthand as the master vampire held the minds of an entire room of his blood-sworn clansmen."

A cold light sparked in her eyes. "What evidence do you offer to support these allegations?"

"We can only guess at Lacroix's numbers, but there must be a list of clans who have defected from the Undead Coalition. You can start by tallying those numbers and adding them to his ledger."

Slender fingers curling, she lowered her arms. "As to your secondary charge?"

"He controlled the entire room, aside from those with natural immunity, at the ball."

"You've been telling secrets," she chided her son. "Did she figure it out on her own, or did you show her the footage?"

Footage.

As the home of the current Grande Dame, the manor would be under heavy surveillance. Add a masked ball into the mix, plus the expectation the master vampire responsible for the Undead Coalition crisis would attend, and the Elite would have kicked security measures up a notch.

Betrayal pricked me, sharp and swift, and my fingers went slack. Linus tightened his grip like he was afraid this might be the last straw, that I might walk out on him for not telling me. His shoulders rounded in anticipation of what I might say or do, and I hated that we still doubted each other.

The first test of my new resolve shouldn't come so soon, but here it was, the decision mine to make.

I chose him.

One of the easiest calls I've ever made.

"Lacroix offered to mitigate the loss of life by holding Balewa's fledglings in his thrall." I tightened my fingers until my nails left crescents in his skin, ensuring he couldn't get away either. "When she sicced her vampires on me, he gave me the means to break free and lure them away from the crowd."

"The magic you performed on my lawn was unlike anything I have ever seen." She sounded almost proud. "Linus has tutored you well."

Ah. That would explain the pride.

"Yes," I agreed, bumping my knee against his. "He has given me quite the education."

Pink tinged his cheeks, so out of character for the austere mask of

Scion Lawson that the Grande Dame scrutinized him until a light sweat beaded on my upper lip.

Maybe pulling the tiger's tail had been a bad idea.

I really did *not* want to admit I was sleeping with her son.

"I was cognizant of lost time," she said, thankfully letting the matter drop, but keeping her keen eyes trained on her son. "I was searching the crowd for Linus when the sensation hit me. I located him, and then he was gone. Vanished. I might have blamed his status for the blip if you hadn't disappeared as well. I checked the footage myself to see if it was an isolated phenomenon and understood Lacroix had enthralled an entire ballroom full of necromancers as well as vampires who weren't blood sworn to him."

Framed that way, I began to understand the convenient timing of Corbin's escape.

She had watched herself ensnared by Lacroix, utterly helpless against him, and she had panicked. And when she got tired of wringing her hands, she did what she did best. She started plotting ways to save her own skin.

"Then you've seen the evidence for yourself." I held her stare. "What more do you need?"

The Grande Dame dithered a moment. "How do you know you can trust him?"

"He was a vampire hunter. He dedicated his life to protecting humans. Lacroix made it plain he takes no issue with vampires killing them. Corbin has no love for our world, but he'll ally with us because it's the right thing to do. He'll stand with us to hold on to a sliver of his humanity."

"I've asked myself a hundred times why you spared him. Why his light called to you in that dark place. A vampire hunter. You couldn't have chosen a worse progeny. That's what I thought when I heard the news. It's one reason why I kept Corbin out of the limelight instead of introducing him at my inauguration, and yet I have developed a theory."

Shock at my change in circumstances, at learning I had progeny, at discovering I was goddess-touched and what that meant, had shrouded that night in a hazy fog of memory, but I had assumed she wanted to keep the Deathless vampire's existence under her hat to preserve my secret. There was no explanation for him that didn't involve me. Odds were good her pride had battled with her common sense, and common sense prevailed.

She had a goddess-touched necromancer and a Deathless vampire, proof of my power, in her pocket. She had all the time in the world to play her hand. There was no reason to call so early into the game.

"I believe in your moral code, Grier," she said, "even if I can't always afford to share your altruistic impulses."

Altruistic impulses. Most of us just called it like it was—basic decency.

"I am convinced you saw something in him worth saving," she continued, "that yours wasn't a random act of kindness, but you correcting what you perceived to be an injustice." She laughed softly. "Perhaps, with your judicious streak, you should have become a potentate."

A faint crease, barely more than a shadow, hardly a smile, bracketed Linus's mouth.

I kicked him where his mother couldn't see for having the audacity to find her amusing. "Perhaps."

Although I had agreed with her, she didn't seem pleased by my response. She must have expected me to recoil from the suggestion, but Atlanta had given me a unique perspective on the duties of a potentate, and the job requirements didn't scare me anymore.

"Do you have any idea what Lacroix plans to do? He's dismantling the current vampire ruling body. That leads me to believe he intends to institute his own. While such coups are frowned upon, they are a legal gray area since no vampire has challenged the government we established for them." Her nose wrinkled at the insult. "Are you aware of a credible threat against the Society that would enable us to move against him?"

As much as I hated admitting it, "Not at this time."

"I'm willing to extend a little faith. You are family, and my son believes you acted in the Society's best interests, or he wouldn't be sitting beside you."

Unsure if I ought to feel comforted or threatened, I kept my mouth shut.

"You have thirty days to produce evidence that Lacroix is a threat to the Society. Beyond that, we will be forced to act in our own interests. We will apprehend Corbin and interrogate him. Your role might come to light, seeing as how you helped him evade authorities, and that would be unfortunate."

"The Elite would launch an investigation into how he managed to escape from prison," Linus intoned, his voice hung with icicles. "Given the person responsible did laudable work to free a notorious inmate from Atramentous, if they were to be found guilty of aiding yet another inmate, one with Corbin's history, with yet another familial connection, the Society might question their ability to uphold the Society's laws without bias. They might even be viewed as a sympathizer."

"Darling," she said, and the temperature in the room dropped ten degrees. "Are you threatening me?"

"Understand me," he said as he stood. "I won't be parted from Grier again."

The Grande Dame's lips thinned when he used our joined hands to help me rise. "I see."

Linus guided me from the room with his palm resting on my spine, and I didn't look back.

Only after we reached the elevator and the doors had closed behind us were my nerves steady enough to ask, "Was that wise?"

"I won't be parted from you again," he repeated, cupping my face, "unless it's by your choosing."

"You're a brave man." I rose onto my tiptoes and pressed my lips against his chilly ones. "Angering your mother, and your boss, might not end well for you."

"I don't care," he said, and I believed him. Caring what happened to him was my job.

The elevator stopped, and we exited into the lobby of city hall. "Where do we go from here?"

"I must speak with Commander Roark." He escorted me to the waiting van. "He's expecting me at the Elite barracks. It's his help we need to roust the gwyllgi."

"I'll go with you." The heated nature of his last encounter with Boaz didn't inspire a lot of confidence that he would escape another meeting unscathed. "I could use a walk to clear my head."

Linus knew me well enough to guess the reason I wanted to go with him, but he seemed more amused than offended. "All right."

After telling Hood where to meet us, we set out for a moonlit stroll to the barracks.

Fresh air and clear sky cleansed me of the fear slicking my skin after the Grande Dame's threats. I might have imagined the night as romantic if the oppressive sensation of watching eyes hadn't drawn my attention toward the darkness gathered under a streetlamp to our left.

"I see it," Linus murmured. "Keep walking."

Within a few minutes, we were level with the disturbance. At first, I thought he meant to walk past, but he snapped his arm out and fisted the clot of night air. He hauled it to him, and I stumbled back in shock. The writhing mass could have been his shadow.

Ambrose.

"What are you doing here?" I searched the night for signs of Amelie. "How did you escape the wards?"

"The wards you set contain the necromancer, but they do not restrain me." A funhouse mirror version of Linus solidified in the smoky whorls. A dybbuk selected its own appearance, but it could only do so once. So long as he was bonded to Amelie, he would be a pale reflection of Linus. "What have you done? Why is this all I am? Why can I not control that fleshy shroud?" Insubstantial fingers raked the air near my head, lost in the churning dark. "I am full of power, brimming with—"

"Enough." Linus took out his pen and drew a sigil on his palm. He held it open beneath the dybbuk, and the creature wailed as it was sucked down into the design where it disappeared like it had never been there at all. "The Elite will have to wait. I can't contain Ambrose within me for more than an hour or two without absorbing him, and Amelie won't survive a separation for long."

Fear pounded in my chest, and I jerked a nod at him while dialing up Hood. He met us at the curb with a frown, and we blazed a path straight for Woolworth House.

THIRTEEN

The population of gwyllgi on my lawn had exploded since we left. There was nothing for it but to shove through them until the wards sealed behind us. Hood had to park the van, and I hated leaving him to find his own way, but Amelie might not survive us waiting to escort him. He had made it out, and I had to hope he could make it back in.

Linus and I sprinted for the carriage house, not bothering to knock on the door. We found Amelie in a limp sprawl on the rug in the living room. Popcorn littered the floor, a bowl overturned at her feet.

"Amelie." I hit my knees beside her and checked her pulse. "She's alive."

Linus joined me, his expression grim. "We have to return Ambrose to her."

"I don't understand." I brushed blonde waves away from her face, and my heart clenched. "It's been months. I thought he would weaken, that we could exorcise him. Instead it looks like he's learned a new trick, that he's just as powerful as ever."

"The tattoo might have complicated things." He lifted the edge of her shirt and started drawing a series of sigils across her abdomen. "There was no other way to save her. She's alive because of you."

"Will she be...?" I hated the dots for connecting in my head. "Have I created another Eidolon?"

"You didn't create me." He glanced at me. "I am what I am by my own choice."

"No, you're not." I trailed the back of my hand against his cheek. "You did this to yourself for me."

Linus closed his eyes, savoring the contact, then resumed his work. He didn't contradict me again. We tried hard not to lie to each other.

"And to answer your question, I'm not sure." Linus pressed his palm against Amelie's abdomen, and magic punched through the contact as he pushed the dybbuk back into his cage. "Ambrose is powerful, but he can't manifest as more than shadow. We need to make sure that's the extent of his capabilities." He watched Amelie a moment then sent another wave of energy through her limbs. "We may have to bind them tighter, shorten his tether, for her to survive him. Otherwise, he might wait her out. The death of her body would sever their connection. He would be free to find another host."

A wraith might wait to be courted, but a dybbuk hunted for its next mark until he secured a willing host.

"You're saying we have to make him a permanent fixture, or he might kill her."

"Yes."

A sharp gasp filled the room as Amelie gulped oxygen. Her hazy eyes focused on me, and she reached out with trembling fingers. "Grier?"

"Hey." I clasped hands with her. "How are you feeling?"

"My head hurts. I must have hit it on the coffee table." She grimaced. "Did I pass out again?"

Linus examined the back of her skull, and he pulled back bloody fingers. "I can heal that if you like."

"I like," she mumbled. "Please."

While he drew a healing sigil on her arm, I watched the cloudy quality leave her gaze. "What do you remember?"

"I was watching *Attack of the Killer Moth from Space and His Five Caterpillar Wives.*" She kept a straight face, like that was a totally normal title for a film. "The last thing I remember is making popcorn during the intermission."

The occasional classic kept a momentary pause in the middle where the theater would have stopped the film while they changed reels or, later, while moviegoers refilled their drinks and purchased fresh popcorn and candy.

"Ambrose paid us a visit." I gave her room to sit upright. "There wasn't much to him, but he manifested in downtown. He was following us." Thinking back to my scare on Abercorn, and the creeping sensation in the woods at Woolworth House, I admitted, "I think he's been following me for a while now. Several days at least."

"But I haven't lost any time until now," she protested. "None of the signs Ambrose was surfacing were there. I would have told you." What little color she had leached from her cheeks. "You don't think I had anything to do with this?"

"You have a stellar alibi," Linus said. "You were unconscious when we arrived, and you would have died within the hour if we hadn't returned him to you. I think it's safe to assume you didn't agree to this power exchange."

"D-d-died?" Her fingers brushed the tattoo on her ankle. "I thought this contained him."

"That was the idea." I touched the design, hissing when it scalded me. "Linus, the sigil is hot again."

Curiosity bright in his eyes, he probed her skin with his fingers. "Interesting."

When he got lost in his thoughts, I poked him in the chest. "Interesting how?"

"I set the wards on the carriage house. They're my design, drawn in Maud's blood. There is no link to you or your magic whatsoever."

He pressed his fingers to the ink until the tips sprouted blisters he examined with utmost care. "This might be our breakthrough."

Meaning he might have figured out how to dissolve the connection between Amelie and me.

The hope was too big. I couldn't swallow past where it lodged in my throat.

"I fainted when the wards at Woolworth House were attacked." Amelie mulled it over with a frown. "What does it mean that this is happening again?"

"I'm not sure," I said, and it was the truth. "Do you want to call Boaz to come sit with you?"

"No." She climbed onto the couch and stretched across the cushions. "I'll be fine."

"Amelie," Linus began. "I regret to inform you there is a hard decision ahead of you."

Bless him for attempting to once again shield me from pain, but I wanted to tell her myself.

"Ambrose may be attempting to kill you." I leaned against Linus, borrowing his strength. "You may have to choose bonding to him—permanently—or taking your chances."

Amelie closed her eyes. "I deserve this."

As much as I wanted to absolve her, I couldn't. She had committed crimes as Ambrose. Horrific ones.

"I ought to be noble and say I'll let him end this, but I don't want to die." She stared at the ceiling. "I can't atone if I choose the coward's way out, and I don't want this stain on my soul when I meet the goddess."

"Amelie..." I started but then stopped, unsure what comfort I could offer her that wouldn't be a lie.

Sensing my dilemma, she put on a brave face. "Will dusk work?"

"Yeah." I smiled, the edges brittle. "That's fine."

"I think I'll call Boaz after all. Just in case." She palmed her phone. "I wish I could see both my brothers again, but my ex-parents would never let Macon visit."

Ex-parents. The reminder of how alone she was made my chest tight. I would have pleaded her case to see her little brother, but the Pritchards hated me too. They would never let him go anywhere with me.

"We'll be in the rest of the evening." Linus took my hand. "Call if you start feeling peculiar."

"I'll do that." She resumed her fascination with the ceiling. "Thanks. For saving me. Again."

"You made bad decisions." I curbed the urge to go to her, hug her, tell her everything would be okay. "That doesn't make you a bad person."

"I don't believe that," she said softly. "I always wanted what I couldn't have. Power. Magic. Reputation. I should have let it go like everyone else does. Instead I paid for it in blood, and blood will always stain my hands." Her lips curved. "I wanted a reputation, and boy did I ever earn one."

Linus curled his fingers around my elbow. "We'll return at dusk if you haven't contacted us by then."

Until he pulled me back, I hadn't realized I had taken a step toward her.

Amelie had been my best friend since I came to Savannah. We might not be friendly anymore, but I still loved the girl I remembered, the friend who never let me down, and it cut deep not to offer her comfort in her time of need. But Linus was saving me from myself, from an addiction I couldn't quite kick, and I was glad he was there to stop me from indulging an old habit.

Woolly opened the door for us on a faintly glowing surprise that rocketed into my gut.

"*Oomph.*" I staggered back with an armful of ghost boy. "Oscar, hey kiddo."

"I took a long nap." He yawned against my neck as I carried him in. "I'm still sleepy."

"You can rest as long as you want." I fretted over his paleness. He wasn't back to full strength. "Woolly and I will be here when you wake up."

"I know." He pressed icy lips to my cheek with a smack. "I just didn't want you to worry."

"Thanks for checking in." I kissed him on the forehead. "Now go back to bed. Don't worry about us."

Fading as he drifted higher, he vanished through the ceiling, and Woolly followed to tuck him in.

"I'm going to check on Lethe." I started for the stairs. "Did you want me to let you in the basement?"

"I might as well be productive," he said, all but rubbing his hands together.

"Don't have too much fun without me," I teased, opening the door for him. "I'll be down soon."

After he stepped into the gloom, I headed up the stairs to Lethe's room.

A teenage boy with blue-black hair that fell past his hips was backing into the hall when I arrived. When he turned to go, he spotted me, and the wire-rimmed glasses he wore slipped down his nose.

"You must be Grier." He stuck out his hand. "I'm Shane Doherty."

"Nice to meet you, Shane." We shook, and his elegant fingers reminded me of a surgeon. "How is she?"

"Right as rain, thanks to you, but out cold." His smile crinkled his eyes until they almost vanished in the folds. "I've never seen the like. Your gift is truly amazing. You're a great healer, Grier." He motioned me across the hall. "I thought we might speak easier in here." He led me into the bedroom Woolly had assigned him. "I appreciate your hospitality, by the way. It's a lovely home you've got. This room is nicer than my own." His nostrils flared as he scented the air. "Would it be rude to inquire if you've had a female guest stay in here recently?"

"A family friend spent the weekend here not too long ago. She burns incense. It helps with clarity in her visions."

Shane canted his head to one side. "She's a seer then?"

"Yes."

"Might she be the famed one from Tybee Island? If you don't mind me asking."

"Odette Lecomte." The rolling cadence of his accent made me smile. "You're not from the Atlanta pack, are you?"

"No." He leaned against the dresser. "I made Savannah my home some years back. Eighty or ninety it's been, I suspect."

"You look sixteen," I protested. "How have you been alive that long?"

"I'm a fair sight older than sixteen, lass." He adjusted his glasses. "Lethe told you about her pack's origins?"

"A gwyllgi mated a warg, and they claimed the offspring belonged here instead of in Faerie."

"Aye, that's about the gist of it." He winked. "Let's just say I'm a distant relative."

A distant relative...? But that meant Shane was a full-blooded gwyllgi. From Faerie. He was *fae.*

A thrill shot through me. "I never thought I would meet someone like you."

"Nor I," he confessed. "Our kind don't much traffic with outsiders, and yet you're pack. I wouldn't be here otherwise. I couldn't risk the exposure."

Not only a fae, but an illegal one. I seemed to be harboring more fugitives by the day.

"All of this—" I gestured around the room and to myself "—is a long story."

"All the best ones are," he said, easing into my personal space. "I would very much like to know more about you. Any necromancer who befriends an alpha's daughter and calls a renowned seer a house-guest must be someone worth knowing better. Are you amenable to that?"

"Friendship works." I took a step back that bumped my hip against the doorknob. "I'm in a relationship."

"More's the pity."

There was something about Shane that made me smile at his flirtatiousness. Probably the accent.

"Maybe one day," I said, aware it was a dangerous offer, "I could pick your brain about being fae, and you could pick mine about—"

"Your long story?"

"Yeah." I laughed under my breath. "That."

"Have Lethe call me when maybe one day comes." His eyes twinkled merrily. "But for now, if you don't mind me saying so, keeping your schedule is draining." He covered a yawn with his hand. "I'm going to turn in early."

"Oh. No. Not at all." Grateful for the excuse, I backed out of the room. "It really was nice meeting you."

"Grier..." He pocketed his glasses and stared at me with eyes so ancient their weight glued my feet to the floorboards and made me wonder if his lenses weren't meant to offset the eerie sensation. "I am an old thing, and a patient one. A woman such as yourself comes along only once or twice in forever. Lethe knows how to get in touch with me should you maybe one day change your mind about other things."

"Ah, thanks."

I shut the door then sagged on my tired bones in the hall.

"Fae must obey the laws of hospitality."

"*Fiddlesticks.*" Clutching my chest, I whirled on Linus. "You almost gave me a heart attack."

"He can't harm you or beguile you while he's your guest without greatly impinging on his honor."

I anchored my hands on my hips. "You were eavesdropping?"

"Yes." He didn't sound embarrassed at getting caught, either.

"Care to tell me why?" I glanced back at the door, remembering those ancient eyes set in a youthful face, and shuddered. "You can't have been worried I would cozy up to him."

"Fae are tricksters, and they can't be trusted."

"How did you know to come up here?" I tapped my foot. "I left you on your way to the basement."

"Hood knocked on the door almost as soon as you closed it behind me. He warned me Shane was a friend of the family. A very *old* friend of the family. Old things tend to get covetous when a new bauble catches their eye. Some have trouble accepting no for an answer."

For Hood to warn Linus, I must have been in greater danger than I imagined. But I hadn't felt threatened. Shane hadn't made me feel like I was seconds away from him spiriting me away to Underhill to play faerie bride for him.

"I'm not a bauble," I grumbled, sadly used to people viewing me as a thing to be owned.

A frown gathered between his eyes. "I know that."

"I know you know." I frowned back at him. "It just bugs me when people treat me like I'm not a person."

The creases on his forehead deepened. "I know that too."

Unable to help myself, I crossed to him and smoothed my thumb across his brow. "You know everything, huh?"

"No." He dropped his gaze to the floor. "I don't."

"I'm teasing." I slid my arms around his waist. "It was a play on words."

"You used to call me a know-it-all."

"I also used to wear diapers and eat boogers. What's your point?"

"I want to make you happy."

"You do make me happy."

"No one has ever..." He closed his mouth, thinned his lips, then tried again. "You do more than listen to me. You hear me. I don't want to drone on until you tune out and I lose that."

"You're a brilliant man, and I love how your mind works. You don't have to hide that from me. This—*us*—is your safe place. *Our* safe place. We can be ourselves when we're together." I pressed a kiss over his heart. "I won't tease you again. Not about that." I grinned up at him. "Everything else is fair game."

The muscles in his jaw relaxed, and he managed a tight smile, but I saw through it.

After being emotionally isolated his entire life, he struggled with intimacy. His touches were still calculated, hesitant, our conversations stilted at times as he sorted through his layers to find the man beneath them all.

It would take time for him to trust he could be himself with me, that him—unmasked—was who I truly wanted. He might never initiate touch as often as I did, but that was okay. He had embraced all the broken parts of me, and I was just as willing to love all his jagged pieces.

"It's getting late." He traced the curve of my smile with a fingertip. "There's something I would like to discuss with you in private before we go to bed."

We.

Go to bed.

Like...together.

Gulp.

With so many extra bodies in the house, I understood his caution. "You want to head downstairs?"

"We could go to your room, or mine."

I wet my lips then made my decision and led him by the hand to mine. "Are you going to set the ward, or do you want me to?"

"Would you mind?" He extended his pen toward me. "I love watching you work."

A pleased flush heated my cheeks. "How can I say no to that?"

I knelt near the threshold and began drawing a series of interlocking sigils I plucked from the depths of my subconsciousness with barely a thought. Magic pulsed in the air, thickening, and then my ears popped.

"Would you like to check my work, Professor Lawson?"

"I felt it seal." He wiggled a finger in his left ear. "Impressive."

"What did you want to discuss?"

"Amelie."

"Ah." I sat on the bed and pulled my legs beneath me. "The impending deadline?"

"No." He perched beside me. "This is about Ambrose."

"That's a fine line, but okay. I'm listening."

"Have you considered why Ambrose might have been following you?"

"Revenge?"

"In a manner of speaking, yes." He rested his hands on his thighs. "I suspect he's been trailing you, testing the length of his tether, waiting to see how far he could go before Amelie died." He rubbed his palms across the fabric. "The thought occurred to me that he might be hoping for a host exchange."

"Wait until Amelie is on the brink of death, then approach me with an offer to let her live if I agree to bond with him?" I tugged down my hair and massaged my scalp. "But he can't just flit from host to host. She would have to die for the connection to break. That, or we would have to exorcise him, which would kill her too."

"Either way, she's dead, and he would have your word that you would host him next."

"That would mean he doesn't know that we know separation would kill her."

"A dybbuk tells their marks whatever they need to hear to believe the lie."

"But he messed up tonight. He got caught before he could put his plan into action." I dropped my head back and sighed at the ceiling. "That ought to make me feel better than it does."

"There's one more thing worth mentioning."

"I'm ready." I braced for impact. "Hit me."

"There's a possibility your design wasn't the cause of Amelie's episodes."

Lightness spread through me, a ray of hope, but I shaded my heart against it. "You think Ambrose was testing his cage even then?"

Reflecting on the first night Amelie collapsed, I had to admit the symptoms fit.

Ambrose would have had to time each of Amelie's original fainting spells to coincide with a strike against Woolly to cast blame away from himself, but he was sly. The attack on her wards offered him camouflage, a way to flex his muscles without alerting us to his strength.

Linus shifted his weight, and the mattress dipped beneath us. "Do you remember what Heinz said when he came to the house to treat Amelie?"

"That her condition reminded him of when new bonds are formed between necromancers and their familiars. Sometimes the animal pulls too much energy from its master, and the drain knocks the kid unconscious." There was no polite way to ask. "The drain Amelie is experiencing, is that how it is for you?"

"I've had several years to chart the edges of my endurance, but yes. I must feed, or I can't function. I learned that the hard way, during the early months when the hunger drove me out of my mind."

I flinched before I could school my features, and he covered my hand with his.

"I didn't understand what had happened to me. I had to research my condition as best I could, and that's how I learned how to survive." He speared his fingers through mine. "Once I understood, I was able to regain control over myself and my impulses. Amelie will be able to build on my experience. The transition to permanent host won't be as traumatic for her as it was for me."

"Are you sure?" Their situations were similar, but they weren't identical.

"Ambrose was feeding on ghosts, vampires, and other paranormal energies. With a host to anchor him, he was self-sustaining. Now he's dependent on her for sustenance unless she lets him hunt, and he's too dangerous to be allowed off leash. Amelie has no experience with this type of hunger, but she can learn to control it—and him —in time."

As selfish as it sounded, I couldn't stop the thought forming. "This means I might be able to practice."

The funny thing was, I wasn't sure I wanted to be a practitioner anymore. There were vampires aplenty in the world, if you asked me. Was there a need for truly immortal ones who could spawn even more vampires? I had no interest in birthing a dynasty of purebloods, creating yet another caste to divide their population. I enjoyed using my magic, learning new skills, but I didn't want the extent of my resume to read *makes Deathless vampires*.

Linus had opened my eyes to a whole new world of possibilities in more ways than one, and I wanted a chance to explore them, to decide what dreams the new Grier would chase.

"We can't be certain without further testing, but this gives me a new avenue to research. It's a promising lead." His grip tightened. "It's more than we had before."

"You'll figure it out." I rested my head on his shoulder. "I'm not in any hurry to procreate."

Linus chuckled at that, no doubt remembering Woolly's mortifying baby fever.

"You should get some rest." He stroked my back. "Tomorrow promises to be a long night."

I curled against his side. "Will you stay with me until I fall asleep?"

"Of course," he said without hesitation. "I'll go change and pick up a few of my books."

"You can use one of those clip-on lights if you want." Most of his research materials were physical books while he did his pleasure reading digitally. "I don't mind."

"I read well enough in the dark."

After he left, erasing the privacy sigil on his way, I dug around in a drawer until I found an old nightlight. I plugged it in on his side then collected a few extra blankets from the hall linen closet. He might not spend the whole night in bed with me, but I wanted him comfortable.

And then I changed into a lacy pink thong and a low-cut blue crop top because there was such a thing as *too* comfortable so early in a relationship.

As much as I want to say he found me in a scandalous pose and fell on me, ravaging me, I was unconscious the second my head hit the pillow.

Guess he wasn't the only one who enjoyed the glow of a night-light and the weight of extra blankets.

FOURTEEN

Wisps of the dream swirled through my head to mingle with the memories Woolly had shared with me. I didn't wake screaming or on the floor. But I did gasp alert to the sensation of cool fabric under my cheek and faint snores rustling my hair.

Barely daring to move, I tilted my head back and peered up at my first glimpse of Linus in a restful, natural sleep. His black-frame glasses had slid down his nose onto his upper lip. A book splayed open beside him, his fingers twitching as if turning pages in his dreams. His hair was pulled back from his face, and I indulged in the opportunity to admire the splash of freckles across his cheeks, the soft curve of his mouth, the hard line of his jaw.

He was beautiful, and he was mine.

The swell of emotion behind my breastbone almost choked me, and I couldn't breathe easy until I buried my face in his shoulder. Allowing my hand to roam across the lean muscle of his chest, I slid my hand under his tee and traced the ridged contours of his abdomen.

Chills dappled his skin, and his chest rose in a great wave. "I fell asleep."

"I noticed." I teased the elastic waistband of his pants with a fingertip. "Have good dreams?"

The air punched from his lungs when I wrapped my hand around his hardening length. "I'm still dreaming."

"Then consider me your wake-up call."

I shimmied down his body, ducking under the covers along the way, and straddled his knees. The dark gave me confidence to tug his pajama bottoms past his hips and explore him as he had me, to learn what touches arched his back, how much pressure made him writhe, and how he tasted. Everywhere.

When he was a boneless puddle beneath me, I climbed up him and flopped on his chest. "Hi."

Wrist pinned over his eyes, he grunted. It was the least eloquent thing he had ever said to me, yet I glowed with his praise.

Five minutes or a hundred later, he grasped my hips, his fingers easing under the scrap of lace. "These distracted me all day."

"Good." I shifted just enough that my slouchy top slid off my shoulder, exposing the top of one breast. "They distracted me too." The lace itched, and it had crawled into places underwear should not visit. "Next time, I'm going to stay awake long enough to seduce you and then change back into granny panties. These are meant to be seen and not slept in."

"Let me help." He hooked the sides of my panties with his thumbs then slid them down my thighs. "Better?"

"Much."

And it got even better after that.

A TEXT MESSAGE burst the bubble Linus and I had existed in since waking. Fresh from the shower, we sat at the bar in the kitchen while I ate, and he read the news on his phone. I set aside the Canadian bacon I didn't have the heart to explain wasn't really bacon long enough to check my cell.

"Amelie is ready." I swiped my thumb over the rest of her message. "Boaz wants to be there. She's asking if that's okay."

Attention on me, Linus set aside his phone. "It's your decision."

"I won't deny her the comfort of her brother unless he forces us to remove him."

"All right."

Fingers hesitating over the screen, I double-checked with him. "You're really okay with this?"

"I stopped caring what Boaz Pritchard thinks or says or does after spending five minutes in his company. I believe I was ten at the time."

"Burn." I chuckled. "I didn't know you had it in you."

"I tolerated him, for you. After his recent behavior, I don't owe him even that much civility."

When he was right, he was right. "I want to check in with Lethe before we head to the carriage house."

"I made her a plate." He collected it from the oven and passed it to me. "Hood bought her a mini fridge earlier. She ought to have milk and orange juice up there." He flicked a glance at the refrigerator in front of us. "We're missing a few cartons, and what's left was strategically placed to conceal their absence."

"That sounds like Lethe, all right." Food must taste better after it's been stolen. "Back in a few."

I hit the stairs and knocked on her door, surprised when she answered it herself.

"I thought you were on bed rest." I picked up a piece of sausage and stuffed it in her mouth before she could growl at me. "I don't have long, but I wanted to see how you're feeling."

"I'm healed," she muttered between vicious chews. "Shane says so."

Telltale prickles burned my nape, but I worked to keep my expression neutral when she mentioned him.

"He hit on you." The wonder in her voice made me cringe. "Shane wants in your pants."

"He was a gentleman about it," I deflected, edging past her to set her plate on the nightstand.

"Don't sweat it." She adopted a bland expression. "If he didn't know there's no room in your pants before, he knows it now."

"*Lethe.*"

"Oh, Linus." She fell back on the bed and writhed, arching her back. "Oh, goddess. Yes. Yes. *Yes!*"

I could have cracked an egg on my face, and it would have sizzled. "I don't sound like that."

"You two got busy a few doors down from gwyllgi. Trust me. We *all* know how you sound."

Thanks to my body's insistence it make up all the sleep I had been doing without the past several months, I had forgotten about warding the room before I put the moves on Linus.

"What the hell is going on in here?" Hood appeared in the doorway, eyes on his wife. "Are you two watching porn?"

"I was just showing Grier how I imagine her O face," Lethe said sweetly. "Based on what I heard, anyway."

Wiping a hand down his face, he looked between us. "What is wrong with you two?"

"The list is long, and my time is short." I patted him on the shoulder on my way out. "Take care of our wife."

"Our—" A snarl rent the air, but it was hard to hear it over Lethe's cackling.

He made a grab for me, and I suspected he would have tickled me to death, but I flew down the stairs like the hounds of hell—or a really pissed-off dog-lizard thing—were on my heels.

The laughter in my throat died when I spotted Linus waiting on me. He carried a bag of supplies slung over his shoulder. It wasn't his usual necromancy gear, but I could see jars of ink bulging in the pockets. This was his tattoo machine and supplies.

The lightness of the evening drained away like I had never teased him under the covers or tormented Hood with my friendship with Lethe.

"We should go," he said when I couldn't find any words to encompass what was about to happen.

"Okay." I pressed my palm against the doorframe on my way out. "Hold down the fort."

Woolly's presence glided through my senses, leaving calm in her wake.

The walk to the carriage house kept my mind looping on the trips I had made through the garden to visit Linus, how each of those interactions had chipped away at my heart until he had carved a niche all his own.

Linus let me take the lead, and that meant I got to experience the joy of Boaz opening the door firsthand.

"Grier," he rumbled. "Come in."

Blinking in surprise at his nearly polite tone, I stood frozen on the threshold.

"I owe you an apology," Boaz said gruffly. "Both of you."

Amelie entered the room, and her amazement mirrored mine.

"There's no excuse for what I said and did." He told this to the trim in the doorway above my head. "Adelaide ripped me a new one after I explained the bruises." His jaw tightened, drawing my eye to the heavy purple and green mottling on his skin. "She deserves better than to hear I got beat up for showing my ass. She deserves better than me, but I'm what she chose." He lowered his gaze a fraction, to the level of the peephole mounted in the door. "I'm going to do better by her, and that means we're getting out of Savannah for a while after the wedding."

"Okay." That checked one item off my to-do list. "Space sounds like a good idea."

"Linus..." He bit the inside of his cheek. "I'm an asshole, I'm always going to be an asshole, but I could be less of an asshole to you going forward."

Linus had the grace not to rub salt in the wound. "I accept your apology."

"Is that what that was?" I wasn't so graceful. "It sounds more like a list of his shortcomings to me."

"I swear to the goddess," a feminine voice muttered from the office. "He's hopeless."

Adelaide stepped out wearing jeans and a pink top with her blonde hair up in a ponytail.

"Hey, Grier." She glared at Boaz. "I threatened to send him out here with notes on index cards, but he convinced me he could handle it."

"I apologized," Boaz gritted out. "He accepted."

The frown lines bracketing her mouth deepened. "What about Grier?"

"I'm not going to ask for her forgiveness." His jaw flexed. "There's no excuse for what I've done."

"Well, you got that much right at least." She shot Linus a tentative smile. "I'm the home-wrecking harlot." She extended her arm. "You can call me Adelaide."

"You're a woman making the best of the hand she's been dealt," he corrected her. "I'm Linus."

Mischief sparkled in her eyes. "You're even prettier up close than you were from across the ballroom."

The look Boaz cut her promised there would be words later. Loud ones. Ugly ones.

He strode out into the garden, and she watched him go, an exhale sending loose hairs skating over her cheek.

"I should go smooth his feathers." She shrugged when I started to warn her off that plan. "I live to ruffle them, so it's the least I can do." On her way past Linus, she said, "You really are pretty, but I'm sorry to have objectified you. I'm teaching Boaz a lesson that ought to enable us to spend the rest of our lives together without one of us ending up in a premature grave. So far, blunt force seems to be the only effective way of getting through to him."

Linus actually smiled after she left. "I like her."

"I do too." As long as she kept her heart out of their bargain, their marriage just might work.

"Me three," Amelie chimed in. "She will be the making of him." She shrugged. "Or the death of him. Definitely one of those things." She clapped her hands together. "Let's do this."

"You're sure?" Linus scanned her face. "You want to bond with Ambrose for the rest of your life?"

A tremor shook her hands, and she squeezed them tighter. "The only other option is death, right?"

"The dybbuk has discovered how to work around the tattoo you already have, and he can slip the wards to leave the house. We could establish stronger wards, if you like, but that's a temporary solution. Your indenture is almost up, and I'm guessing you don't want to be confined a moment longer than necessary. Fixing the wards won't address the issue."

"I'm grateful to Grier for everything she's done for me, but yeah. I'm looking forward to freedom."

"You're sure you want to do this?" I pressed. "I'm not saying death is the better alternative, but I want to make sure you understand your options. We could reinforce the wards to give Linus time to figure out a workaround."

"It's a fitting punishment." Her knuckles turned white. "I wanted him, now I've got him. For life."

A pang rocked me, and I reached for her. "Amelie..."

"I can handle this." She stepped back before I could offer her comfort. "I need the scales to balance before the slate gets wiped clean."

Unsure what to do with my hands, I tucked them into my pants pockets. "What do you need from me?"

Linus understood I was asking him, and he guided me to the office, away from Amelie, to give us privacy.

"I need you to design a new sigil for her." He stroked a finger across the bend of my right arm. "I'll also need some of your blood for the ink. I believe it's the only thing strong enough to contain him permanently."

"If we're wrong about Ambrose being the problem all along, she'll be bound to me."

"If we're wrong about Ambrose, she already is, and we'll have to break the connection before she moves out either way."

Nodding, I sank into the chair behind the desk. Linus offered me a pad and pencil, and I plumbed the depths of that well of knowledge burbling in the back of my mind. A design rose to the surface, and I fished it out, studied it, and then started drawing.

When I finished an hour or so later, Linus stood over me with something like awe softening his features.

"You never cease to amaze me." He traced the pattern with his fingertip. "This is perfect."

"All I did was remember." I shrugged off his praise. "It's no big deal."

"Show me another necromancer who could do the same, and I'll agree with you."

Cheeks heating, I didn't fight the compliment a second time as I extended my arm to fulfill my other obligation. "Do you want to do the honors?"

"I have more practice." Linus trailed his fingertips over the ripe veins. "It's your call."

"I trust you."

After pressing his cool lips in the crease, he sterilized the area then drew the blood he needed.

"Weird," I mused. "I don't get hungry when I smell my own blood, but I salivate over yours."

"You wouldn't get hungry for human flesh if you smelled a steak on the grill."

"Nice try, but no cigar. They aren't comparable." I narrowed my eyes on him. "Just admit it. You're delicious. This is all your fault."

"I'm delicious," he dutifully repeated, "and this is all my fault."

"Am I interrupting?" Amelie stood in the doorway, wavering on the threshold. "I can come back."

"I was just teasing Linus." I smiled with what I hoped passed for reassurance. "You're fine."

"How much longer do you think this will take?" She fidgeted. "I've made up my mind, but I want it over."

"We're done." I stood, offering Linus the drawing. "He'll mix up the ink, and we'll be ready to start."

She chewed on her bottom lip. "Do you think you could wait outside?"

"I..." A pang rocked me. "Sure. Whatever you want."

"I'll take care of her," he promised me. "I'll get you if there are any complications."

"All right." I lingered for a moment, but the look on Amelie's face said she wanted to bolt. Clearly, I was as much of a trigger for her as she was for me. "I'll go keep Boaz company."

Linus stilled, just for a second, half that, but it was enough to betray his hesitation.

"I'll be right outside," I reassured him. "I'll let Lethe take out her pent-up aggression on him if he gives me any lip."

"Call me if you do." An infinitesimal smile made an appearance. "I would like to see that."

Amelie looked like she might want to argue against her brother taking another beating from a pregnant gwyllgi, but she must have decided it was smarter not to antagonize the guy about to ink her.

Outside, I found Adelaide, but not Boaz. "Where did he get off to?"

"He's walking the perimeter. All these gwyllgi have him nervous." She rolled her eyes. "Or so he says. I think we can both tell he's worried about his sister."

She had claimed one of the Adirondack chairs I kept meaning to sand and repaint but somehow never got around to doing either. I plopped down in the one next to her, and it groaned a complaint and leaned to one side.

"I could fix that for you," Adelaide offered. "All I need is some wood glue and a few screws."

"I might have that in the garage." We stood, careful not to collapse our seats, and went to investigate. "We'll be safe that far."

Guiding her to the garage still crammed to the rafters with boxes full of Boaz memorabilia—and his bike—made me feel like I had been caught naked with him on the couch in her living room. She would take one look at my collection, gathered over a lifetime of living next door to him, and see with her own eyes how deep the wound had cut.

Sucking in a breath, I rolled up the garage door and flipped on the lights.

Adelaide was drawn straight to Wilhelmina. "That's his bike, isn't it?"

"Yeah." I flinched away from all the rest. His leather jacket, gloves, helmet. They had been tossed on her seat like he would be back at any moment. "Matron Prichard wasn't hot on him parking a bike in her driveway, so he got in the habit of leaving her here. He's done it for years."

It doesn't mean anything, I almost added, but that would have been a lie.

"This one is yours?" She wandered over to Jolene. "She's beautiful."

There was too much history with that bike between him and me to give her a full answer, so I settled for a simple one. "Yeah. Her name's Jolene."

Smiling, she trailed her fingers over the handlebars. "Like the Dolly Parton song?"

The lyrics rose in my memory, the poignant plea—one woman to another—not to take her man.

The bike's name had never bothered me. Boaz had christened her, after all, but I still got chills.

"Any luck with the tools?" Her gaze panned the space, landing on a high school football jersey here, the lion costume from an elementary school play there, then a plastic crown fit for a prom king. "Do you need any help?"

"They should be right here." Sure enough, I found what she required, including an electric drill with a set of drill bits and an extension cord. "Success."

After I flipped off the lights and rolled the door closed, Adelaide kept staring where Willie sat.

As much as I didn't want to know the answer, I had to ask, "Everything okay?"

"Yeah." She yanked her gaze from the garage and helped me carry the supplies. "I just had no idea what I was up against." She looked back once. "Until now."

FIFTEEN

Adelaide and I repaired both chairs and set them aside for the glue to dry, leaving us nowhere to sit. I could have asked Woolly to give her a temporary pass for the back porch so we could make use of the swing, but the old house had spotted Boaz on the grounds, and she was not happy about it. Introducing Adelaide as his fiancée might get the poor woman banned for life.

"He really does feel like an ass," Adelaide confided while arranging our supplies in a neat pile.

"Good." I cringed to remember the confrontation. "He ought to after the hissy he pitched."

"He's torn between wanting to throttle Linus for getting in your pants, the way an older brother would kill anyone who touched his little sister, and wanting to be the one who—"

"Yeah." I cut her off with a sigh. "I get it."

"Your first time is supposed to be memorable." Her smile tried valiantly to salvage the awkwardness of the situation. "All things considered, I doubt any of us will forget yours."

A groan rattled the back of my throat when I heard it framed that way, as a social event to be discussed.

I would never forget. That much was true. But the memory would forever be divided between the perfect day Linus and I spent tangled up together and the morning after when Boaz shattered the illusion that I could live in those perfect moments.

"You can always come bang on my door the night after I say *I do* and hurl accusations at me if it helps."

I whipped my head toward her. "You're a...?"

"Yep." She angled her chin higher. "There was no time for boys. I was too busy taking care of my sister."

"I don't know what to say."

"You're looking at me like I'm on death row instead of engaged." Her eyes glittered, laughter or tears, I didn't know her well enough to guess. "Boaz has enough experience for both of us. I'm sure it will be fine."

The door to the carriage house opening spared me from wondering if I had worn the same weary resignation on my face when discussing Boaz's past conquests. The light tone, the sad eyes, the tight mouth. Yeah. I liked Adelaide. But I wondered how much of that was because I saw so much of myself in her.

"Amelie is resting," Linus announced. "I used a sigil to help her sleep while her body adjusts."

"Oh good." Adelaide's relief appeared to be genuine. "I'll let Boaz know when he gets back."

"I'll tell him myself." Linus cast me an amused glance when I stiffened. "I need to discuss the gwyllgi issue with him. It would save us a trip to the barracks."

Uncertain how far to trust him, amusement or not, I inched closer. "Do you want me to come with you?"

"I can handle Boaz," he assured me. "I can behave myself."

"Mmm-hmm." Linus was at his most dangerous while cool and collected. "Meet me in the library after?"

Linus couldn't gain access to the basement without me, but I didn't want to pique Adelaide's curiosity.

"We can resume our filing," he said without missing a beat. "I won't be long."

"I'll go in and sit with Amelie." Adelaide shifted her weight toward the carriage house. "We have to stay in this section unless we're with you, correct?"

"Yes." I pointed to the safe areas. "Don't take the security measures personally."

"I hate when Boaz barges into my house like he owns the place, so I understand."

"As easy as he makes it, I can't blame him for this. Not all of it anyway. The added layers of security are more to do with recent threats against me than anything personal."

"Threats against your person sounds personal to me."

"Right?" I laughed. "I better go. I have a lot of work ahead of me."

"It was nice seeing you again." Adelaide waved. "Maybe one of these days we'll bump into each other on purpose."

"Maybe so."

Before I retired for the night, I took a moment to examine the gwyllgi issue. More of them crowded the lawn now than ever. They stood in small clumps, which was odd. Distant relatives lumped into family groups, maybe? Shrugging it off since Linus was on the job, I headed in the house and called out to Oscar. "You up for an adventure?"

"Sure." He drifted through the ceiling until he landed on me and attached himself piggyback style. "Will there be gold doubloons or pieces of eight?"

"Not this time. You'll have to finish your treasure hunt when you're feeling better."

"Can we pretend?"

"Sure thing, kid."

The basement door decided to give me fits and expected me to spill blood to enter. Since it didn't take much, I picked at the pinprick scab left from where Linus had drawn blood and smeared a crimson dot across the lock with a fingertip. It snicked open, and we entered the void.

A swirl of darkness more substantial than the rest swept past me. *Cletus.*

Eager to hear news from Corbin, I jogged down to the library and waited for the wraith to find me.

"Do me a favor," I said to Oscar. "Focus really hard and bring down the scrolls from that pile."

The stack brushed the ceiling, and it was easier sending a ghost boy than pulling out a ladder.

As I turned to address the wraith, he enveloped me in his hood before I could blink.

Ice cold shattered through my veins, and my head swam. The faint scent of rose water coated the back of my throat, a phantom memory, and then Corbin wavered into view.

"Lacroix taught me to feed tonight. He took volunteers. Humans owned by vampires." A vein bulged in his forehead. "*Owned,* Grier." He wiped a hand over his mouth. "I learned to take what I need, and he taught me the cost of mercy. He killed them. Drank them down in front of me when I refused to kill them."

Static fuzzed the picture, making me think time had lapsed between his first memo and his next.

"He spends more and more time in his quarters." Corbin shifted his eyes to the door. "I'm under house arrest after I broke up a blood orgy in the parlor. I'm trying, Grier. God knows I am, but these people—these *things*—they're hedonists. Every night is a spectacle, some new horror Lacroix dreamed up the day before. There's a woman with him now." He wet his lips. "She loves him. Real love. His lure isn't to blame." He gazed into the hood, right at me. "She's not a vampire, definitely not human. Necromancer, maybe? They have history. Decades' worth based on the fights they've been having."

The door burst open behind him, and a vampire rushed in. "Who are you talking to?"

"No one," Corbin said, and the vision ebbed to darkness, but not before the vampire in the doorway locked gazes with Cletus.

Expecting the wraith to cut me loose, I flailed when the void held on.

Muffled voices drifted to me, and the flicker of movement hinted at another vision, but it wasn't Corbin.

"She won't be controlled," a woman protested. "You are a mad thing to believe it possible."

A man countered her, "An impossible thing has merely yet to happen."

"Fool."

"For you, yes." The figures intertwined. "Always."

Lacroix.

Cletus was definitely spying on Lacroix and his mystery woman.

The sound quality was crap, but who else could it be?

I came aware on the floor of the library, staring up at the ceiling and the battle taking place there.

"You killed her," Oscar shrieked at the wraith. "You killed Grier."

Oscar held a scalpel tight in one fist and sliced the air in front of the wraith to keep it away from me.

A low moan was the only defense Cletus could manage, and it's not like getting cut would hurt him.

"I'm..." I swallowed, tasting roses and dust, "...not dead."

"You're not?" The ghost boy froze with his weapon at the ready. "Are you sure?"

"Pretty sure." I rubbed the back of my head. "I don't think it would hurt so much if I hadn't survived."

A blue-tinged missile launched at my chest, and I fell back, grimacing at the pain.

"I was so worried," he cried against my throat, his black tears saturating my collar. "I couldn't get him to stop. He wouldn't listen. He just kept making you look."

"He's learned a new trick." I patted Oscar's back. "He's not hurting me. He's showing me things he's seen that he thinks might help us."

"Oh." He drew back. "I guess that's okay then."

His outline wavered, and he grew lighter than air in my arms.

"Do you need to go rest?" I ruffled his hair. "You fought a hard battle."

"You did promise me adventure."

"I try to deliver."

Yawning, he started drifting higher like he had been pumped full of helium. "See you later."

"I'll be here."

After he left, I hauled myself into a chair I angled toward Cletus, head throbbing with my heartbeat.

"You've got to stop ambushing me. I could have hurt myself if I hit the table on the way down. Let's make a rule that you don't show me Corbin's messages unless Linus is here to play witness, okay?"

The wraith bobbed once in acknowledgment then spread its hands, waiting.

"Corbin," I addressed Cletus the way he always did. "We're coming for you. Just hold on a little longer."

Cletus groaned softly then vanished to relay his message.

Lacroix must not be used to dealing with someone who could form their own opinions and who held their own beliefs. He wasn't winning over Corbin. He was alienating him. While he might be used to whispering conversion in someone's ear, he would have to yell a lot louder before Corbin went deaf to the cries of the humans they toyed with away from the Society's prying eyes.

There was nothing for it. We had to get Corbin out of there before Lacroix provoked him into a fight he couldn't win.

Light taps on the door announced Linus had arrived, and I climbed the stairs to greet him.

"How did it go?" I massaged my scalp. "Will the Elite help with our gwyllgi infestation?"

"Yes." He frowned at me. "There's no pack in Savannah, so they can be rousted for causing a disturbance." He touched my wrist. "Headache?"

"Cletus sucked me into the void. No one was here to catch me this time, so I bumped my head on the floor when I nailed the landing."

Concern caused darkness to pool in his eyes. "Want me to take a look?"

"Let's do this in the kitchen." I entered the hall. "I'm fresh out of focus for tonight."

He cupped my elbow and guided me onto my usual stool. "Are you sure you don't have a concussion?"

"I didn't fall that hard." I patted the spot next to me until he sat. "Did Cletus check in with you this time?"

"No." He twisted until our knees brushed. "You'll have to fill me in on what your wraith reported."

Tempted to laugh at the jab, I posed a theoretical instead. "Do you think Cletus knows?"

"That he's Maud?" Linus scratched his thumbnail along one of the veins in the marble. "He must retain some knowledge of his former life. It's obvious he cares for you, and he has habits that remind me of her. But it's hard to say. Whoever he is now, he's not her anymore. He's someone else. Some*thing* else."

"Oddly enough, that makes me feel better." I covered his hand with mine, smiling to realize there was no difference in temperature between his skin and the stone. "I wouldn't want her trapped in that form, aware of her diminished capacity."

Linus watched me trace the length of his fingers. "What did he show you this time?"

While I filled in Linus, I noticed the volume rising outside and nudged Woolly to muffle the noise before it disturbed Lethe. Assuming she wasn't hanging out the window, yelling obscenities at the gathering. Again. That would explain the increase in volume, actually.

"How about you?" I tapped the knuckle on his pointer finger. "How did it go with Boaz?"

"He left Adelaide to watch over Amelie while he reports in. I doubt he would have gone if the gwyllgi weren't setting up camp so close to the carriage house."

"He's worried they might come for us with torches and pitchforks."

"His sister is confined to the structure. She would be trapped if the pack embraced extreme measures to flush out Lethe."

Dread licked along my insides at the thought. "A fire at the carriage house could spread to Woolly."

Wards or no wards, Woolly would be at risk. We had never tested her against something as mundane as fire.

"It will never come to that," Linus assured me.

"How can you be sure?" I got to my feet and started pacing. "It's been wet lately but—"

A black cloak draped his shoulders, and he gazed at me with eternity in his eyes. "I will slay them all before I let them harm you or Woolly. You've lost enough. You won't lose her too."

Wrapping my arms around myself, I dipped my chin. "I wish the gwyllgi would see reason and leave."

"Their instincts are screaming at them. They won't move except by force or until the imagined debt is paid. The fight disrupted the pack hierarchy. They'll be dangerous—Hood and Lethe too—until a new order is established."

A shiver twitched in my shoulders, and I turned as Cletus swept into the room.

"I thought you had gone back to Corbin." I smiled. "Did you want to see Linus before you left?"

The wraith shot out its arms, clamped onto my shoulders, and dunked me in the pool of shadows beneath its cowl.

Chills raced up my arms and through my body. Teeth chattering, I searched the dark for the message he must be carrying, but there was nothing. And then...there was light.

An empty ballroom. Corpses strewn across the floor. Humans. Dozens of them. Drained to empty shells.

I sucked in a gasp, breathing in more of that faint rosewater scent that screamed *Maud*, then the vision overtook me again.

"You have been reporting my movements to the Grande Dame." Lacroix struck Corbin across the cheek. The resounding *crack* made me wince. Judging by the purpling bruises on his face, it wasn't the first time. "How much of what you have seen have you told her? Confess, and I will show mercy."

"I don't report to the Grande Dame," Corbin spat. "You're paranoid."

"Lies," Lacroix hissed.

"Believe what you want, you will anyway."

"We must strike before the Society moves against us," Lacroix decided, then motioned a slender vampire to join him. "Rally our clansmen." He clasped her on the shoulder. "We move tonight."

"As you wish, Master." She pivoted on her heel, facing Cletus, who must have been hovering in a shadowed doorway, and I swallowed a gasp of recognition. "What are our orders concerning your granddaughter?"

"Bring Grier to me." He pointed a warning finger at her. "Do not harm her."

"What about Scion Lawson?"

"Kill him." He bared his fangs. "His corrupting influence has been the root of all this."

The vampire tasked with rallying the clan passed beneath Cletus, and our gazes almost clashed.

"Set your strongest wards around Woolworth House," she whispered. "The city won't last the night."

The vision swirled away, and I came aware with Linus supporting me.

"Get back to Corbin." I swatted at the wraith. "Don't let him out of your sight."

Linus drew me closer. "Grier?"

Jaw tight, I gazed up at him. "We have to extract Corbin before Lacroix kills him."

Eyebrows climbing his forehead, I recalled for once he was the one waiting for an update.

"They spotted Cletus." I clawed at him to regain my balance. "Lacroix is mobilizing his clan."

Linus swore under his breath. "Do you have any idea where they plan on striking?"

"No." I propped my legs under me. "But I know someone who might." I wobbled to the stool and sat. "I saw Becky. She's posing as a vampire. She infiltrated the clan."

Linus's expression cleared when he understood. "Boaz's partner."

"She faked her way into the manor where I was being held by posing as a newly turned vampire. Her backstory painted her as a doctor in her previous life. She saw me once, to patch me up after I cut my foot on a piece of ceramic. She's the one who kept urging me to take in the fresh air in the gardens out front. My keeper, Lena, grew suspicious of her and asked her to go. I never saw her in that role again." Thinking back on her appearance in the vision, I admitted, "She looked the same. As Dr. Heath, she was already established within the clan. She must not have burned that identity in case she needed it in the future."

"We need to go to the Lyceum." He pulled out his phone. "I'll call Mother. She must rally the council and the remaining masters."

"Gathering all the biggest targets in one confined area is making it easy for Lacroix, don't you think?"

"Not if we use the video conference suite." He spared me half a glance, his lips curving. "The others will remain safe in their homes. We'll be the only ones at risk."

Video conference suite sounded far too modern for the Lyceum. Its addition must be his civilizing influence. Half the dames and matrons probably required tutors to navigate the system. Or hired tech wizards to cheat the learning curve.

"I'll get Hood." I could have called him for a pickup, but I needed to grab my bag. I didn't want to be caught unprepared if the vampires beat us to the Lyceum. "Be right back."

He wasn't listening. His entire attention centered on his phone, on the warning he was conveying to his mother.

Upstairs, I knocked on Lethe's door. "Hood?"

He came to the door barefoot with a book in his hand. "Everything okay?"

"Not exactly." I filled him in on the vampire situation. "We need a ride to the Lyceum."

"I'm going with you." Lethe poked her head around the door. "I'm not letting you face that alone."

Hood ground his teeth so hard I worried they might snap under the pressure. "Give us a minute."

After nudging Lethe back, he shut the door. Their growled conversation grew heated, and I left them to battle it out while I gathered my kit from my room. I hesitated only a moment before reclaiming the goddess-touched artifact I had never returned to the basement and shoving it down the front of my bra. I made a pit stop in Linus's room to pick up his bag, in case he needed it, then headed downstairs.

Linus waited at the front door, phone pressed to his ear, arguing with someone in another language.

I raised my eyebrows, but I don't know why I was surprised to glimpse yet another of his facets.

Loaded for bear, I told Woolly to guard the fort then bounced off the door when she slammed it in my face.

"*Fiddlesticks.*" I checked my nose to see if it was broken. She did have a history of violent assault via wood panel. "That hurt."

The locks snicked into place, and she curtained the windows to darken the room.

"We have to go to the Lyceum." I rested my hand, thankfully not bloodied, on the wall. "People will die if we don't help."

The lights flickered as her resolve faltered, but she refused to bend.

"What's goin' on?" Oscar appeared at my side and rested his head on my shoulder. "Why's she mad?"

"She doesn't want me to leave. She worries I'll get hurt."

"Will you?" The ghost boy turned his bottomless black eyes on me. "Get hurt?"

"I'll do my best not to come home with more holes in me than I've already got."

Linus made a choking sound, but I was sure he would be fine.

That appeased Oscar, who drifted over and laid his hand over mine where I touched the wall. "You gotta let her go, Woolly."

The old house groaned around us, refusing to budge on her stance.

"I would be dead if she hadn't saved me. Really dead. Gone forever." He mashed his cheek against the wall. "You have to let Grier go so she can save other people who need her."

Slowly, the locks turned, and the door swung open.

"Thanks, girl." I patted Oscar on the back and cast him a conspiratorial wink. "Keep an eye on Oscar while we're gone."

On cue, Oscar faded a few shades, and Woolly swaddled him in her consciousness.

"Thanks, kid," I mouthed, and he grinned in response before she whisked him back to his room.

Yep. Definitely a bad influence.

Before Woolly thought better of it, I stepped onto the porch with Linus flanking me. We made our way to the driveway, and my eyes rounded at the number of gwyllgi congregating on the property. The number had swelled even more since yesterday.

We didn't have to wait long for our ride to roll up to the curb, and I counted all three gwyllgi present. Shane passed on the ride, claiming he wanted to scout ahead. I wasn't sure if that was code for get out of Dodge or if he meant the offer, and I didn't press. I did not want land on the bad side of a fae.

Hood glanced back at me. "The Lyceum, you said?"

"Yep," I confirmed. "Drive like there's not a baby on board."

Lethe reached across the console and rested her hand on his thigh. She slid her hand down to his knee, in a slow glide that made me blush. As I was averting my gaze, I saw her slam his foot down on the gas pedal with a maniacal spark in her eyes.

"I was wrong," I cried when the back of my skull bounced off the window. "There's a baby on board. A big one. Maybe more than one."

Lethe just cackled and pressed Hood's leg harder.

SIXTEEN

T he drive to city hall was anticlimactic. Normal amount of traffic. Normal amounts of humans on the streets. Normal amounts of everything. All that changed after Linus and I entered the video conference suite at the Lyceum.

An entire wall was dedicated to what looked like fifty-inch televisions. Each family didn't get its own screen. They shared in groups of six, cutting down on the number of devices required to make it all work and the trauma they experienced when stepping into this century. Bringing humans back to life as vampires? Plausible. Teleconferencing? Clearly witchcraft. That meant a few matriarchs had to travel to whichever neighbor was hosting the video meeting this time, but no more than a few miles. As usual, the dames lorded over the uppermost level while the matrons held court beneath them, and the vampires occupied the lowest tier.

Dames and matrons roared over the din in a feeble attempt to be heard above their neighbors, both in the room with them and in the collective. Underscoring the insanity was the grating sound of vampire incisors scraping. Their agitation gave me chills.

The Grande Dame was the first to mark our arrival, the only

person physically in the room with us, and she swept her gaze over Linus, barely breathing until she assured herself he was whole. I earned a cursory glance, but the stilted show of concern was all the attention she paid me.

Guess she was still miffed about her son siding with another woman over her.

"Linus, darling." Ice crackled in her voice as it filled the room. "I have gathered the council as you requested. Now be a dear and tell us what this is all about."

Clearly, she was annoyed with him too. She knew the reason why we were here. She wouldn't have gathered everyone otherwise. Feigning ignorance gave her leeway to act as shocked and horrified as the rest of the gathering. Or, if the mood soured, just as retaliatory for us having wasted her time.

"We received word tonight that Gaspard Lacroix has mobilized his clan," he said. "He plans to attack the Society."

Gasps poured through the speakers, and a few dames rose from their seats, flapping their arms like chickens with their heads cut off, an illusion aided by their headless figures on the screen, before a glare from the Grande Dame seated them.

"He chafes beneath Society rule," he continued. "He has all but dismantled the Undead Coalition to clear a path for his vision for a new governing body for vampires."

"We must leave," a dame shouted from her spot between two matrons, one of which must have been hosting her. "If what he says is true, we must return to our homes."

"What about our families?" a matron shouted. "We must warn them."

"That is why I requested your presence," he intoned. "It was critical that you all understand the scope of the threat."

"What do you mean?" The Grande Dame played her role to perfection. "What haven't you told us?"

"Lacroix is a powerful Last Seed, an ancient. He will be using compulsion to lead the attack. You won't be able to reason with these vampires. Even if you know them, they are not themselves. They will not listen."

Sharp intakes of breath ricocheted across the screens as true panic set in.

"All of the city's Elite will be on the streets tonight, as well as every available sentinel. I've called in requests for aid from the surrounding cities and put them on alert." He panned his gaze across the various screens. "Go home if you're not already there. Bar your doors. Hide your families. Call the Lyceum if you're attacked, and help will come."

At that point, not even dirty looks from the Grande Dame kept people in their seats. They fled to their own homes and families, leaving us with a view of empty chairs, some toppled over in their haste to exit.

"Might I have a word?" The Grande Dame hadn't budged from her position. "In my chambers?"

"Of course." Linus inclined his head. "We'll be right there."

Until he mentioned it, I hadn't gotten the hint it was a solo invitation. Forcing the issue that he was with me might do more harm than good in the long run, but we had no time for bruised egos.

"You must be certain of this information," she said after the door to her office closed behind us.

"We are," Linus confirmed, ignoring the single chair in front of her desk.

As much as I wanted to believe, especially under these circumstances, she wasn't so petty as to send in an underling to remove one of her chairs prior to my arrival as a direct insult to me, this was the Grande Dame. I hadn't seen her birth certificate or anything, but I wouldn't be surprised to learn Petty was her middle name.

Smirking at the empty chair, she sat. "Do you have anything besides Corbin's warning to support your claims?"

"The wraith showed me a vision of Lacroix giving the order." I stared her down. "He ordered a woman who appeared to be one of his lieutenants to rally their clansmen." I watched her carefully for signs she was in the know. "When she turned, I recognized her. Becky Heath, Boaz Pritchard's partner. She's an Elite and a Low Society necromancer. She must be using the same magical augmentation as before to pass as a vampire. That means the Elite can corroborate our story."

A flash of temper heated her tone. "I am aware the Elite have launched their own investigation."

The truth smacked me upside the head, and I laughed in her face before I could strangle the sound.

"They already had their operative primed." Kudos to her, she made an excellent vampire in my opinion. "Becky has an established identity within Lacroix's organization as Dr. Heath. She infiltrated them once, and she did it again."

Lucky for me, she couldn't shoot lasers from her eyeballs.

"That's why," I continued, "after you viewed the recording from the ball, you sent Corbin to me. You wanted your own mole, and you knew I would take responsibility for him. It was a perfect fit. Lacroix would indulge me, I would protect Corbin, and we would report on Lacroix in exchange for your forgiveness." A cold smile curved my lips. "You're a master at knowing which screws to twist to get what you want, but you know that. You wouldn't be Grande Dame if you weren't manipulative."

"I am not an enemy you want to have, Grier."

"Nor am I," Linus said softly. "You're meant to be the invisible hand moving pieces behind the scenes, but you forgot to wipe off your fingerprints this time."

A cunning light sparked in her eyes, one I might blame on pride under other circumstances. "What is it you want from me?"

"A clean slate." He rested his hand at the small of my back. "You pardon Grier for her part in your scheme and any fallout that results from Corbin Theroux aligning with Lacroix."

"And you pardon Corbin," I chimed in. "This isn't the life he wanted, but he can find new purpose with the right guidance. He's an advocate for human rights, and his voice deserves to be heard. He could be instrumental in restructuring the Undead Coalition with modern ideals after Lacroix has been dealt with."

The Grande Dame didn't look at me or otherwise acknowledge my existence.

"Corbin has put his immortal existence in danger to gather information that might save lives." Linus took up the fight when it became obvious the Grande Dame had no intention of discussing terms with me. "His freedom can be contingent on monitoring for an agreed-upon period of time to ensure he doesn't slide back into old habits, but I believe he's earned a chance to see what he can make of his new life."

"Very well." She drummed her fingernails on her desktop. "I will forgive Grier for her part in Corbin Theroux evading recapture. I will also pardon him, if he consents to one hundred years of service as a sentinel with the option for promotion to Elite." Before I could protest, she continued. "The sentinels will give him a sense of purpose, and they will afford him the camaraderie he lacks without his hunter brethren. He must acclimate to our world and his place in it by living in the barracks for the first twenty-five years in order to foster goodwill among his detractors."

There were no vampire Elite. Even the position of sentinel would ostracize him, like he needed any help standing out.

"We can't accept that deal on his behalf," I protested. "He has a right to—"

. "He is a fugitive and a murderer. He has no rights that I recognize."

Jaw set, I bit my tongue to avoid fanning the flames of an argument that would consume me.

"There's one more condition." The Grande Dame rose. "I want Linus to marry Dame Austen's daughter, Flora. It's a good match. She comes from good stock, and she's witty." She toyed with the pendant hung around her neck. "Linus will also be returning to Atlanta at the end of the month. He has duties to his city and a career he has been neglecting. Flora will meet him there. I'll consent to a fifty-year engagement, a generous offer considering her age, but I expect a marriage and grandchildren at the end of that period."

Austen. Austen. Austen.

Flipping the surname over in my head, I almost laughed when I recalled who she meant. Flora. The older woman. About ten years Linus's senior. She toasted me at the ball when I rescued Linus from his gaggle of eligible bachelorettes.

She might fill a pool with Dom Pérignon for me to swim in after she caught wind of this.

Darkness pooled in the corners of the room, pulsing with Linus's heartbeat. "No."

"Defy me on this," she warned coldly, "and I will strip you of your title and your inheritance."

"I told you once already," he said, "and I won't repeat myself."

I won't be parted from Grier.

That's what he had promised me, and he meant every word.

The Grande Dame's ultimatum transported me back to the ballroom, to our first dance, to what I told him.

It doesn't have to mean forever to still mean something.

Forever was potential without realization—unless you seized the moment and lived your life to the fullest.

For the sake of my pride, I really, *really* hoped Linus was ready to be seized.

I was finished dealing in stolen futures. I wanted to embrace the possibilities. Hands and heart wide open.

"He can't marry Dame Austen's daughter—or anyone else." Scrounging up my courage, I met his eyes while I bumbled through the rest. "He's already engaged." I couldn't tear my gaze from his, too afraid I would miss his true reaction and glimpse only a manufactured one. "To me."

The breath punched from Linus's lungs, his exhale a high-pitched whistle through his nose.

Across from us, the Grande Dame's knees buckled, and she sat down hard.

"You have the marriage contract?" Her jaw hung open. "How?" She looked to Linus. "You've seen it?"

"I have." The edge of his lips twitched. "It's authentic."

Fuming, she snapped her teeth together. "You're—you're—*happy* about this?"

"Grier Woolworth has just claimed me as her fiancé before the Grande Dame of the Society for Post-Life Management. Her declaration is binding and serves as an official announcement of our intentions to be wed." A genuine smile cracked his façade, and the real Linus seeped through. "You ought to be thrilled. This is exactly what you wanted for me, and it's exactly what Maud wanted for Grier."

Nostrils flared, she protested, "That was before."

"Grier and I were different people then." He shook his head. "It wouldn't have worked."

"We had to get broken before we fit together," I added.

Corny, yes. Necessary, also yes. Honeymoon period, remember?

"Go." The Grande Dame swiveled her chair until its back faced us. "*Now.*"

Linus cupped my elbow and led me down the empty hallway to the elevator.

Our footsteps echoed, but I couldn't hear much over the roaring in my ears.

I had claimed Linus. In front of the Grande Dame. In front of his *mother*. And I hadn't asked first.

"Linus..."

Guiding me into the booth and boxing me into a corner, he cupped my face in his hands, his thumbs caressing my cheeks, and stared down at me. "Tell me you meant it."

"I shouldn't have sprung this on you. There's still Atlanta to consider, and your job, and your life, and I didn't even ask first. I just blurted it out, and you can't take back a declaration like that." A bit of the sparkle left his eyes, and I grew desperate to earn it back. "There was no dinner, no candlelight, no roses." I palmed my forehead. "I don't even have a ring for you."

"I don't need those things," he said softly.

"You deserve those things." Sinking onto my knees before him, I gathered his hands in mine. "I botched the first half, but I can do this much right." Sweat turned my palms slippery, and I had trouble holding on thanks to the tremors in my fingers. "Linus Andreas Lawson, will you marry me?"

Black swirls eddied across the surface of his skin. "You only ever had to ask."

"Is that a yes?" I reached in my pocket and came up with a bread tie, a knife, and a gum wrapper. "I need to be certain before I put a not-ring on it."

"Yes."

"Good." Dizziness swept through me, making me lightheaded. "Then hold still so I don't stab you."

After I pulled the bread tie from my pocket, I wrapped it around his finger and twisted the end closed.

"It's not much," I started.

"I'll cherish it always," he said, smiling as he turned over his hand, admiring the twist like I had given him the Hope Diamond.

Coming from the same man who had kept the packet of oatmeal I once tossed him in lieu of an apple, I might have to wait until he fell asleep then slip the ring off him when I was ready to replace it with the real deal.

Metal hit my back, and my breath whooshed over my lips. For a heartbeat, I didn't understand why my knees no longer touched the floor.

Linus had pinned me in the corner, his hands beneath my thighs, his hips wedged between mine.

"I will make you happy," he promised. "You won't regret choosing me."

Not for the first time, my heart cracked in two for this man who had no idea of his worth.

"I'm the lucky one." I linked my arms behind his neck and my ankles at his spine. "You have nothing to prove." I tangled my fingers in his hair and drew his face down to mine. "Not to me."

I tasted my name on his lips and sighed into his mouth. His grip tightened, turning possessive, and I arched my spine, not caring one whit if I was putting on a show for the cameras.

An ear-splitting wolf whistle was my first clue the doors had opened, the digitized click of a camera shutter on a cellphone the second.

"This is going to look amazing on your bridal shower invitations." Lethe kept clicking. "Sure, most of your guests will die of shock over the audacity of two Society titans having the gall to fall in love, but they'll get over it. Or they'll die clutching their pearls. Either way, I'm good."

"We didn't tell you we were engaged," I pointed out as we exited the booth.

"You done in there?" she called to a door labeled *Security* then turned to me. "You'll thank me later."

"Oh goddess." I slumped against Linus. "This won't end well."

Hood emerged with his finger speared through a CD he set spinning with a flick of his wrist.

"Got it." He presented it to me. "Happy engagement."

"Is this...?" I tried to swallow, but my tongue stuck to the roof of my mouth. "My proposal?"

"Yes," Lethe trilled. "I teared up, and it wasn't just the hormones." She walked over and punched my shoulder. "You did great. I had no idea I was practice. I would have made you sweat if I had known you had this planned, or at least asked for more donuts." To Linus, she said, "Welcome to the pack."

"Thank you," he said, drawing me against his chest while I struggled not to die of embarrassment. "Did you make a copy, or is this the original?"

"It's the original," Hood confirmed. "It was broadcast live to the security room, but those personnel have evacuated. No one saw, except us, and that's the only recording."

"Good." Linus took the disc from my hand and snapped it in two, tucking both halves in his back pocket. "I prefer the memory to the recording."

"You're no fun." Lethe huffed at Linus then glared at Hood. "That was really the only copy?"

"Sorry." Hood spread his hands. "Just following orders."

Shane burst into the lobby, his blue-black hair plaited down his back. "We need to move."

Turning from Linus, I faced him. "What now?"

"Vampires," he breathed. "Hundreds of them."

Guess we had been right about where Lacroix would strike first.

Lucky us, we were standing on ground zero.

SEVENTEEN

We fanned out on the sidewalk, watching the slow advance of what could have passed for one heck of a massive ghost tour or other sightseeing group. Except for the fangs. Sharpened incisors were out on display, despite us being in downtown, in full view of any humans who might be out for a late-night stroll through the squares.

"The Grande Dame—" I rocked back toward the lobby, but Linus caught my arm.

"She'll use the tunnel to escape if it looks like the Lyceum will fall." He measured the distance from the oncoming horde and us. "We have to leave before that's no longer an option. We must get behind the wards at Woolworth House until we devise a plan of action."

"We'll be trapped if we do that." I searched his face for indications he planned on duct taping me to a stool in the kitchen until the danger passed, but I found only grim resolve, the certainty he knew better than to ask me to stay behind. "We have to get Amelie, and Adelaide if she's still there, inside Woolworth House. We need to warn the gwyllgi too. After that, you and I are going out there, we're finding Lacroix, and we're putting an end to this."

"Count us in too," Lethe said. "We can't harm him, but the others aren't protected."

"Let's hash this out on the way." Hood reeled open the van door. "Get in."

After he ushered us into our seats, all except for Shane, who promised to meet us back at Woolworth House, Hood mowed a path through any vampires too slow to yield the road.

"The Grande Dame would have been more vulnerable at her home or during transit," I mused. "The updated Lyceum security will be a much harder nut for Lacroix to crack."

"The Lyceum is more than a building," Linus countered, "it's a symbol. The seat of Society power. If it falls, it will strike a blow to the morale of necromancers everywhere."

Hood stomped on the gas, with no help from Lethe this time. "Then shouldn't we stay and fight?"

"There are, at most, a dozen people in the Lyceum. The population of Savannah is around a hundred and fifty thousand." Linus watched as city hall grew smaller behind us. "We were wrong about the scope of Lacroix's coup. He might be marching on the Lyceum, but he's doing it in clear view of humans." His troubled gaze met mine. "The fact the Elite and the sentinels never made it to defend the Lyceum tells me they're fighting elsewhere in the city."

"Lacroix wants Savannah," I realized. "That would explain why he recruited in such numbers, and why he disbanded the Undead Coalition first. The Society is insular. With him controlling the majority of the vampires, he has seized our only allies. We're on our own."

"Not your only allies," Lethe corrected. "You have us, and we can call on the pack."

A tremulous hope welled in me. "Will your mother sacrifice her people to save ours?"

"No," Hood answered ahead of her. "Lethe would have to stage a coup and seize control of the pack or form her own."

"You can't risk that in your condition." I reached into the front passenger seat and jabbed her in the shoulder. "Do you hear me? You're not putting your child at risk for this. It's not your fight."

"You're family." She twisted around until she faced me. "I get that yours has left you hanging in the past, and I hate that. I wish I could undo what was done to you, all of it, but I can't. All I can do is show you what it means to be pack and promise you that you will never be alone as long as Hood or Midas or I are drawing breath. Our teeth and claws are yours, just like you've proven your blood and magic are ours."

Stupid tears overflowed my cheeks. "Thank you."

"Don't thank me yet." She chuckled. "Do you have any idea how much it costs to feed a gwyllgi pack?"

"I'm willing to offset the costs," Linus offered, grinning. "It's the least I can do for my future in-laws."

More tears wet my cheeks at his easy smile, and I unfastened my seat belt so I could plop down on his lap and bury my face in his neck. "I should have proposed on Abercorn."

After he confessed he wanted me to honor the marriage contract, I should have said yes. I should have asked him, so he could say yes. I should have—

"You weren't ready." He stroked his hands up and down my back, soothing me. "You needed more time."

"I used to believe I had all the time in the world, but now I understand that's a youthful illusion." I let my lips trail over his skin as I spoke. "Atramentous aged me. I spent an eternity there. The bright-eyed teen they incarcerated had waited and waited and waited for her life to start." For Boaz to wake up one morning and tell me he loved *me* and not some other girl. "But she died in her cell, alone, without doing much living at all." I darted out my tongue to taste him, and he shivered. "I'm not that Grier. I'm tired of waiting. I'm done sitting on my hands. I'm not wasting a minute of my second chance on second-guesses. I want to live, and I want you to teach me how."

"We can figure it out," he said, a shiver in his limbs. "Together."

The private moment slipped through our fingers when Hood turned down my street.

"We've got movement ahead," Lethe called. "Hard to tell if it's friendly or fangy."

"We're going to put you out at the gate." Hood slowed. "We'll meet you inside."

Linus and I were out before Hood rolled to a complete stop, and he burned rubber to escape unmolested.

Thankfully, the milling crowd was all gwyllgi. No vampires in sight. Not sure I would call them friendly, but they weren't...well... Actually, they were kind of fangy. But they weren't with Lacroix, and that's all that mattered now.

We jogged to the carriage house and banged on the door. Nearly a full minute later, it swung open to reveal Amelie in pajamas with her hair matted from tossing and turning on her pillow.

"Hey." She rubbed her eyes. "Adelaide and Boaz just left if you're looking for them."

"Vampires are attacking Savannah," I blurted, guiding her back into the living room.

"*What?*"

"Boaz didn't call to warn you?"

"He was mother henning me. I muted my phone so I could sleep."

"Linus is going to strip the wards from the carriage house, and we're going to walk you over to Woolworth House. You're going to stay there and help defend her while Linus and I see what we can do to help the city."

The sleep vanished from her eyes between blinks. "Okay."

"Pack a bag, quickly." I shooed her toward her bedroom. "You have until he finishes, and then we have to go."

With renewed purpose, Amelie ran into her room and closed the door behind her. Drawers opened and shut, and a loud zipper rent the air.

"Do you need another set of hands?" I stood over Linus, who crouched in the doorway with a frown.

"No." He wiped a rag wet with horned owl tears over the sigils carved into the wood. "Thank you."

With a clock ticking in the back of my mind, I nodded. "I'll go check on Amelie."

Leaving him with a modified pen in hand, I set off down the hall and almost smacked into her.

"I'm ready." Two bags hung from her shoulders. "I unplugged everything and turned off all the lights but this one."

"Thanks." I hadn't even thought that far ahead. "You beat Linus."

"I've had a lot of time to make a packing list for when I got out of here. All I had to do was check off each item as I tossed it in my bag."

"Smart."

"Bored," she countered.

Back in the living room, Linus was capping his pen and standing. "I'm done."

"Excellent." I exited into the garden and he followed, then we turned to wait on her. "Come on, Ame."

The use of her old nickname jolted her focus away from the wards and onto me.

"Here goes nothing." She jumped across the threshold and landed in the grass. "Well, I didn't explode."

Linus was already moving toward the back porch. "What kind of ward did you think I set?"

"The kind meant to keep a killer away from your girlfriend?"

"Linus doesn't explode people," I reassured her. "He's more likely to cut off your head."

"Yeah." She rubbed a hand across her throat. "I remember."

During her time as Ambrose, she had glimpsed Linus in all his dark glory. The vision haunted Amelie, and she used to have night-mares about him separating her skull from her spine. As usual, I said the exact wrong thing to her. About to apologize, I smacked up against Woolly's wards and bounced off them.

"What is your deal?" I rubbed the bridge of my nose. "Are you hinting I need rhinoplasty?"

The old house rattled her shutters, her lights flashing like a disco.

Linus stood on the porch, safe within the wards, so that was something.

Hood, Lethe, and Shane stepped out of the kitchen to join him, and that puzzled me even more.

"You're going to get your cornices in a bunch now? Really?" I flung out my arm toward Amelie. "She's in danger if she stays in the carriage house, and we can't let her run around unsupervised. The Grande Dame would have a cow and force me to listen to it moo for the rest of her life."

"Maybe if you leave the wards on the carriage house down?" Amelie adjusted her bags. "That way I could escape if they come here."

"Woolly," Linus said, "be reasonable."

A bolt of lightning struck my skull and filled me with images of Amelie, Boaz, and—now that she had a face to go with the name —Adelaide.

Woolly crammed me to overflowing with her perspective on my heartache. Every tear, every sob, every tissue balled up and flung across the room. Every plea to the goddess, every red-rimmed eye, every hoarse voice.

"I get that she hurt me. I get that Boaz hurt me. They hurt *us*, but this is bigger than bruised feelings. She will die if she's left undefended."

The ward's hum turned sharper, a bow sawed across violin strings, her attempt to drown out what she didn't want to hear.

"Lacroix will come here. He's ordered his vampires to take me. He will burn the carriage house to the ground if he thinks torching my friend will draw me out of you." I rested my palm on the barrier. "But I won't be here. I will be with Linus, trying to save as many lives as I can. That means if you turn your back on Amelie now, you're the one who will have to live with the memory of her screams and the guilt of knowing you could have spared her life and chose not to care."

The ward rippled, its song growing fainter, and my hand sliced through the air.

Woolly turned off every light, curtained every window, and her consciousness arrowed toward Oscar's room.

The message was clear. Amelie could stay, but that was the extent of hospitality she could expect.

"It's fine." Amelie hesitated before the lowest step, bit her lip, then let the wood accept her weight. "I'm in." An exhale moved through her shoulders. "I can take it from here. I'll call if we have any trouble."

"Thank you." I walked up the stairs and wrapped my arms around the nearest column. "Your heart is a giant marshmallow, you know that? It's part of why I love you."

The porch light flickered to life, its warm glow a benediction.

Linus trailed his fingers across my shoulders then walked out onto the lawn. Hood and Lethe followed.

"I have to go." I withdrew with a final pat. "I'll text Amelie, so she can give you regular updates. This time, I promise I won't forget."

The front door swung open on a sigh of wind through the eaves, wiggling a bit, inviting Amelie in.

Woolly really was a big softie, even if she nurtured her grudges like Maud's prize-winning roses.

With that done, I joined the others in the grass to face the gwyllgi issue. The Elite had their hands full. No help was coming from that quarter. And we were about to enter the fray, meaning the gwyllgi could track down Lethe and ambush her.

"We need them," she said to no one in particular. "I'm going to challenge their leader."

"Lethe." I grabbed her arm. "Please, don't do this. Not for me."

"Can you imagine the stigma my child would carry if I was in

HOW TO LIVE AN UNDEAD LIE   243

Savannah when it fell, if it comes to that, but did nothing to help? I would be branded a coward, and I would deserve the title. I won't have my daughter's reputation tainted by my actions—or worse—my inactions."

Wrapping my arms around myself, I bit the inside of my cheek until I tasted blood.

"Grier." She enfolded me in a hug, the swell of her stomach pressing against mine. "I can win this. I won't make the same mistake twice. They've proven they fight without honor, and that means I don't have to play by the rules either."

"You got this," I croaked, because it was what she needed to hear.

"Damn skippy." She released me then turned to Linus. "Trap her in a circle if that's what it takes. Don't let her interfere. We need to end this. I need a clean win. As clean as it's going to get with this crowd." Traitor that he was, he agreed. With a nod, she pulled Hood into a kiss that singed my eyelashes from watching them. "Get ready to break out your pom-poms. You guys are my cheering section."

Careful neutrality shrouded Hood's features, transforming him into just another spectator in the crowd.

Thanks to Linus, I understood what that disconnect cost him. He was locking down his emotions, going cold.

"I'll do my best," he said gruffly then knelt and pressed a kiss to her belly button. "Keep your momma on her toes, sprite."

A hush settled across the yard as the three gwyllgi approached the ward holding the pack at bay.

Lethe stepped out in front, the point to their triad. "Who among you is dominant?"

"I am," a thin woman with black hair barked at Lethe. "You killed my brother."

"Your brother fought dishonorably," I yelled, "and he deserved what he got."

"Grier," Linus chastised. "You heard Lethe."

"She told you to stick me in a circle if I tried to interfere. She didn't say squat about smack talking the other team. She told us to break out the pom-poms. Well, this is me cheerleading."

"Stick a muzzle on her," the woman snarled. "She's an outsider. She has no place here."

"You're standing on her lawn," Lethe said dryly. "That means it's literally her place."

Hood chuckled under his breath, and the woman's hackles rose.

"I challenge you," the furious woman shouted. "We fight to the death."

"Dominance fights are until first blood or until one of the challengers submits," Hood said. "There's no need for another packmate to lose their life."

"I'll fight," Lethe allowed. "You win, I die. I win, and you all help protect Savannah from the vampires."

The woman frowned at the part where Lethe glossed over her impending death, not yet understanding that Lethe wanted to spare her. "Agreed."

Magic spouted up Lethe's legs, bathing her in crimson and washing away her human visage. She melted into a muscular beast that was one part Komodo dragon to one part bullmastiff. Dusky scales protected her vulnerable spots, and a reddish-blonde ruff stood on end around her blocky face. Needlelike teeth filled her mouth, and her smile curdled my blood.

Her opponent was slower to shift, and her other form was smaller. That didn't make her any less deadly.

Small fighters learned quickly how to even the playing field or they got dead fast.

The challenger rushed her, a snarl twisting her lips away from her sharp teeth. Righteous fury propelled her at breakneck speed, but it dulled her wits. Lethe stood her ground, legs braced wide, claws sinking in the dirt, ready to end this.

For the baby's sake, I mentally pleaded with her to dodge the strike, but the resounding clash when their bodies hit made me flinch.

A steady growl poured from Hood's throat, and his eyes gleamed a furious red.

"Breathe," Linus whispered in my ear, but it was no use. "Lethe is second in the pack for a reason."

"Rip her throat out, Tess," a man called from the innermost ring of spectators.

The challenger, Tess, took the order to heart and lunged for Lethe's neck. This time, Lethe whirled aside and let Tess collide with the crowd. Some scattered, others flung her back in the ring they formed on the lawn.

"Please be over," I chanted, eyes squeezed shut. "Please be over."

"You're pack now," Hood said, wrapping an arm around my shoulders. "You have to watch."

His grip hurt, and the tips of his fingers had shifted into claws, but I didn't say a word as blood wet the sleeve where his hand rested. This was his mate, who was carrying their daughter, and I could deal with a little pain if it kept him steady.

Linus's frown promised violence when he spotted the spreading crimson stain, but I shook my head.

Nodding once, he took my hand, the metal twist of his engagement ring stabbing me.

If it had been jabbing me this whole time, the way it must have been poking him, I would have yanked it off and chucked it in the weeds by now.

Okay, okay, fine.

I didn't have the heart to toss an engagement token either. I would have tucked it in my pocket, though. Not Linus. He would wear it until I twisted it off myself, and then he would shelve it wherever he kept his treasures. I had to be the lousiest rich girlfriend a guy ever had the misfortune to date.

For Hood's sake, I forced my gaze back to Lethe. Tess was, as predicted, a spry and dirty fighter. Lethe was elegant, vicious, and... she was holding back. "Why hasn't she ended this?"

"She could have killed the girl before Tess finished shifting."

Hood kept his eyes glued to his mate. "But it would shame Weber's family, and that's what started this whole mess. She's letting the girl land her hits, playing to the crowd, allowing them to think she's getting the beating she deserves."

"She's getting hurt," I protested.

"This is our way. Lethe has no choice but to uphold the rules if she wants to be alpha one day."

The clock must have run out on Lethe's patience when Tess started nipping at her sides, perilously close to her vulnerable stomach. When Tess sprinted in to take a larger bite, Lethe whirled, catching the girl's front forepaw in her jaws and crunching down with an audible snap.

Tess shrieked an animalistic cry that tapered into a soft whine as she toppled onto her side.

Lethe circled her, lowered her head, and closed her jaws over the girl's throat in a gentle hold.

The younger gwyllgi urinated on herself, and the pack lost interest in the show.

Lethe had won. Tess had shamed herself and her family. It was over.

Satisfied her point had been made, Lethe released Tess and gave her room to stand.

Lip curling, Tess rose—and lunged for Lethe's throat, bloody teeth bared.

"*Lethe,*" I screamed a warning that came too late. For Tess.

Using her greater reach, Lethe clamped her jaws around Tess's throat and sank her teeth in. She didn't shake her head to shred flesh the way I had seen Hood do, but she didn't let go when the pitiful thing ripped out her own throat trying to escape the reprimand.

Tess's body hit the ground, and the light faded from her eyes.

Lethe shifted forms above her and knelt to check her pulse. "Dead."

A solemn hush fell over the gathering, and a man who looked to be in his thirties stepped forward.

"Grief made Tess act with dishonor," he said. "After Ernst, you must believe it's a family trait."

"The thought had crossed my mind," Lethe replied dryly.

"I have no excuses for them and only an apology for our part in this sham of a challenge. You have served as second to Tisdale for decades, and you have never been unjust in your punishments." He tilted his head to one side, exposing his throat. "Let us prove ourselves." He held the pose. "Lead us. We will follow."

"I regret this was the cost of your revelations, Devlin." Lethe stared at the dead girl. "She was a promising dominant, and she will be mourned." She scanned the gathering with a critical eye. "You heard the terms. Vampires are attacking Savannah. Fight with me, for me, and you will earn back the honor you've lost. Otherwise, I will be forced to give your names to Mom. I think you can all guess how well that will go for you. Whether I'm here or in Atlanta, I am her heir, and you have all challenged my position. Count yourselves lucky I don't require each of you to fight me to retain your own rank."

A whimper worked through the gathering, and a few people hit the ground, belly-up in human form.

A text message chime jerked my attention to my phone and away from the gwyllgi drama.

>>*Is Amelie safe?*

The number was unfamiliar, but it could only be Boaz.

She's staying in Woolworth House for the duration.

>>*Goddess bless and keep you.*

Has Lacroix been spotted yet?

>>*He's walking down Bull Street, headed for the Lyceum.*

Linus and I will be there in ten. We're bringing gwyllgi backup.

>>*I'll let the others know they're friendlies.*

Hood touched my arm and gave me a moment to pull my thoughts from the texted conversation. "Yes?"

"Can you handle the van?" He had trouble pulling his gaze away from Lethe. "I don't want to leave her alone with them. She's acting as alpha, and she needs a second she can trust at her back."

"We can handle it." I gave him an impulsive hug. "You go take care of our girl."

"*My* girl." Hood narrowed his eyes at me. "I saw her first."

As he stalked off to join his mate, I laughed under my breath. Until another ping drew my attention.

>>*You're clear to make your way to the Lyceum. No one will stop you. If they try, give them my name.*

Are Macon and Adelaide safe?

>>*They're in the panic room with the rest of the family.*

>>*Thanks for asking.*

>>*You don't owe us anything.*

I don't hate you.

>>*You should. I would. Adelaide does.*

Hate is a strong word. She wouldn't waste her breath telling you off if she didn't want you guys to work.

>>*You think so?*

Relationship counseling for my ex is outside my comfort zone. Talk to her. You'll figure it out.

Glancing over my shoulder at Linus, I asked, "How much of that did you get?"

"None." He homed in on me. "Your texts with Boaz are private unless you tell me otherwise."

Ah ha. "How did you know it was Boaz if you didn't look?"

"You grumbled *douche canoe* under your breath when you saw the notification, and I made an educated guess." A smile danced in his eyes. "Lethe is having a civilizing effect on you."

I growled low in my throat, but he wasn't intimidated. His eyes darkened, leaving me tingly all over.

There was no time for testing the flavor of my fiancé's smile. I had to keep on task.

Fiancé.

Linus Lawson was my fiancé.

I had asked him to marry me, and he said *yes.*

Maybe in fifty years, maybe in a hundred, but this—us—was forever.

Focus, Grier.

The curve of his lips beckoned, twitching with his amusement.

Focus harder, Grier.

His tongue darted out to wet his lips, and his smile glistened as he taunted me.

"You have a mean streak," I informed him, tucking in my hormones. "I didn't know that about you."

"There's a lot we don't know about each other." He traced the line of my jaw with his fingertip. "And we have lifetimes to learn."

I nipped his finger when it neared my mouth, and his eyes flared with molten heat.

I might not be a vampire, but I don't think either of us would mind if I accidentally on purpose bit him.

Closing his eyes, he gathered his focus. "What did Boaz want?"

"To check on Amelie." I locked down the warmth curling through my stomach to get back to the task at hand. "I told him she was okay and asked if Lacroix has been spotted. He's marching on the Lyceum, safe behind the first wave, so that's where we head if we want to intercept him. The Elite have given us the go-ahead, and they've been made aware the gwyllgi are on our side."

"I'll drive." Linus set out for the gate. "Boaz might have cleared you, but the Elite won't question me."

The bald statement would have sounded like a brag coming from anyone else, but Linus was a power in his own right. Factor in his mother's title, her current location, and yeah. It made more sense to put him behind the wheel. Plus, I had other texts to send. Calls might be better, but it was harder to end those. Ignoring a written response was faster and easier than a verbal one, and both of those things sounded great right about now.

Linus clasped hands with me, and we set off at a sprint down the street. The neighbors on the other side of Woolly were shut-ins, an older couple who hadn't left their home since Maud adopted me.

Tabitha and Ron Meyer. They were High Society, from a dying bloodline. They had no children, and the only guests they entertained hoped to worm into their good graces to avoid the Meyer fortune being left to the Society to disburse as it saw fit.

"What are we doing here?" The Meyers made for such quiet neighbors I often forgot they were there.

"You haven't wondered where Hood parks the van when it's not in use?"

"Yes." But I wasn't about to admit to my Batcave theory. That would mean admitting I sometimes called him Batman or Bruce Wayne in my head. "Did you make an arrangement with the Meyers?"

"The Meyers passed away three months ago, and their property and fortune went into the Society trust. I purchased this property when it came up for auction last week."

"You didn't tell me."

"Since the property abuts yours, and the house is three times the size of Woolworth House, I thought it might be worth holding on to in case the Kinases decide to make Savannah their permanent home."

"You made this gesture for our friends out of the goodness of your heart, right?" I slanted him a look. "Not to add extra layers of security around Woolly and me?"

"Goodness might be a secondary motive in this case."

"Mmm-hmm."

"I kept the purchase quiet to avoid pressuring them into staying. It's a conclusion they ought to arrive to on their own. If they decide to leave, I'll sell the property. To you." He frowned. "I've kept an eye on the Pritchard property as well, but it appears that Boaz's impending marriage to Adelaide has stabilized their situation. They won't be selling any time soon."

The notion of owning so much land, of insulating Woolly, caused my brain to fizzle in wonder.

An inkling of understanding scratched at my brain. "You own a lot of property, don't you?"

"Yes."

"They're investments, right?" I eyed his back as he led me toward the sprawling house. "You're not trying to buy Savannah brick by brick or anything?"

"I was born here. I do have a certain fondness for the town."

"Am I going to find out one day that Cricket is renting her building from you?"

I laughed.

He didn't.

"*Linus.*"

"I'm sentimental."

"How long have you owned it?"

"About five years."

The length of time I spent curled in my own filth in a cell in Atramentous.

"I didn't have much else left of you," he said quietly. "I held on to what mattered most."

To me.

What mattered most *to me.*

He had no affiliation with the Haints otherwise. He bought the building, ensuring Cricket could run the Haints until she retired or sold off the business.

"You have a big heart." I squeezed his fingers. "A good heart."

"No," he said, leading me up the driveway to the garage. "I have an average-size heart with an average amount of goodness in it." We reached the rolling door, and he paused, turning back to me. "But where you're concerned, there are no limits to my capacity for love or goodness. Or, if there are, I've never found them."

"I'm going to make out with you as soon as this is over." I walked my fingers up his chest. "Consider this your early warning. This is *not* a test."

Eyes twinkling, he unlocked the garage and hauled the door up to reveal the van...sitting next to yet another identical van.

Resisting the urge to rub my forehead, I walked into the gloom. "Do luxury vans multiply in the dark?"

"Your pack keeps growing," he said reasonably. "Purchasing a second vehicle is prudent, I think."

Without the gwyllgi hogging the front seats, we claimed them. He slid behind the wheel, and I got in beside him then pulled out my phone. As he rolled down the drive, my thumbs started flying.

I hit Marit up first.

Where are you?

>>You remembered I exist!

Where are you?

>>In the office, where else? What's up?

You need to get somewhere safe. Lock the doors and windows. Don't come out until morning.

>>What's going on? I haven't seen anything weird on the news.

The streets are dangerous tonight. Trust me. Please. I'll explain everything later. I promise.

Depending on how things shook out tonight, all our covers might be blown.

For my human friends, I was willing to risk the fallout with the Grande Dame over edifying them.

Come to my house if you don't have anywhere else to go.

>>I'll take you up on that. Dad's out of town, and you're closer.

>>I'm flattered you chose me for your zombie apocalypse team, btw.

Rolling my eyes, I texted back. *Amelie is there. She'll let you in.*

>>Cool. See you guys soon.

With that handled, I touched base with Neely. I would have hit him up first, but I was pretty sure he was still in Atlanta with Cruz. He might not like it, but I could warn him off coming home until this blew over.

You need to stay out of Savannah.

>>Hello to you too.

I'm serious. It's not safe here.

>>*You couldn't have told me this four hours ago? We just got back. I have a family thing this weekend.*

Come to my house. Bring Cruz and anything you might need to spend a few days.

>>*You're scaring me. What's up?*

You remember the wreck in Savannah? It's like that. But worse. The whole city will be on lockdown soon.

>>*Promise me answers when I get there?*

Since I wouldn't be here, the promise was easy to give. *Sure.*

The only human left to warn was Cricket, and I waffled over getting her involved. We hadn't spoken since I resigned as a River Haint, and I hadn't bumped into Detective Russo in weeks. The break from the latter had been nice. Granted, it was harder for Russo to stalk me now that I didn't have a set routine. Still, I couldn't let it go. I had to warn Cricket and hope she had enough faith in her least trustworthy former employee to listen without demanding all the nitty-gritty details.

Bring the guides in. End the tours early.

>>*Refunds costs me money and earn me bad reviews. Give me a damn good reason first.*

The streets aren't safe tonight. Not for them, or you, or anyone.

>>*That's not an answer.*

You love your Haints. I know you do. Do this for them. Keep them safe.

>>*You owe me answers in the morning.*

I was running up quite the tally. All I could do was hope I could afford to pay the bill when it came due.

Thumb smoothing over the screen, I considered dialing Russo. She had the resources to issue a blanket statement to the city that could save lives. Except I couldn't tell her the truth, and nothing but the truth would convince her to put her neck on the line for me with the department.

Humans would die if Lacroix was targeting Savannah versus the Society, there was no way around it, and they wouldn't be the only casualties. An emergency bulletin or evacuation order would incite panic. Innocents would flee into the night to escape a fictional fate only to experience a very real one.

The best thing for the humans would be keeping them in the dark and hoping they were safer there.

Basically, business as usual.

"We're here." Linus broke into my thoughts. "They ought to be, but Bull Street is clear."

There had been no Elite checkpoints, either. Meaning Boaz had overestimated their ability to contain the situation.

"What is his endgame?" I wondered. "Lacroix can't mean to out vampires to humans."

Vampires, for all their inhuman strength and longevity, could die.

"He's made it clear he has no love for humanity," Linus said, parking in front of city hall. "However, he ought to appreciate the danger humans pose to us all."

"Unlike us, they're vulnerable in daylight." They might terrorize the city tonight, but tomorrow the residents of Savannah, paranormal or otherwise, would be free to retaliate. "Whatever statement he's trying to make, he only has until dawn to do it."

"Lacroix only needs to take the Lyceum." Linus got out and waited on me to join him. "His people could retreat belowground during daylight hours, and the recent security upgrades would protect them from retaliation while they slept. At dusk, they would be free to roam the city and wreak havoc on the supernatural—and mundane—population."

"Goddess, my family is one rung short of a ladder on both sides."

"We don't get to choose our families." He examined the exterior of the building. "What they do, how they act, is not a reflection on us."

Having just witnessed the gwyllgi pack, one family within its ranks at least, commit the same mistake twice, I wasn't so sure. I would be judging the rest of them by their traitorous tendencies until they proved themselves trustworthy. Better to be careful than dead.

"I'm going to text Boaz, let him know we're here."

"All right." Linus drifted toward the back of the van. "I'll gather our supplies."

We're at the Lyceum. Standing on the front steps. Where are the vamps?

>>E. President Street. They changed direction about three blocks ago.

"What's on E. President Street?" I called to Linus. "Boaz said—"

"The tunnel mouth exits at Liberty Terminals. Mother keeps watercraft docked nearby in the event of an emergency." Linus slammed the doors shut, locked the van, and slung my bag across my shoulders before doing the same with his on himself. "We have to go. The rear access is the weakest entry point."

We set out at a run, and I had never been more grateful for all the practice I had gotten lately.

"What about your mother?" He hadn't mentioned her once.

"A Grande Dame can't allow the Lyceum to fall on her watch." He stared straight ahead. "She'll be deposed if she runs, and she knows it. She'll stand and fight."

"The title isn't worth losing her life," I protested. "Surely she can see that."

"All she sees is a threat to her power."

There was no easy answer for that, and it had to hurt him to know she was choosing to go down with the ship rather than join her son in a life raft.

The recent insult to her pride didn't help matters, but she had another think coming if she planned on going out in a blaze of glory for the sole purpose of burdening him with the knowledge that if he hadn't hurt her feelings, she might have listened to reason and gone to her own safe room at their family home rather than sit at her desk and wait for the vampires to descend on her.

All right, all right. Even she wasn't that much of a drama queen, and I doubted she would sacrifice herself so early in her career— before distinguishing herself as a rival to Maud—over a tiff with him.

Her ego was too inflated to believe she would actually lose her son to me. She might think it was an infatuation he would get over now that he was living with the real deal and not the *unobtainable ideal*. But she didn't understand that memory only took you so far.

Perfect example: Boaz and me. My silly childhood fantasies and teenage dreams about him had crashed and burned around me. I got my shot with him, and it started out with a bang, but we still went up in smoke.

Linus might have held a vision of me in his mind while we were apart, but the first time I woke him screaming in the night from across the lawn, she swirled out of his grasp. The Grier he loved as a boy hadn't made it out of Atramentous. Not all of her anyway. But, as he got to know the new me, and I got to know him, I wondered how I hadn't seen him for what he was back then. I had been so blind. But I saw him now, and I would never look away from him again.

We skidded to a halt where General McIntosh Boulevard curves into E. President Street, and my stomach dropped into my feet.

There must have been five hundred vampires, enough to fill every seat in the Lyceum, tromping their way toward the not-so-secret tunnel entrance. Out of the vampires Lacroix had taken, more than a few would have been escorted through the Grande Dame's private entrance during their long lives. And it would have cost him nothing to coerce the location from them while they were under the spell of his lure.

"What do we do?" The Elite were nowhere in sight. I spotted the bodies of a few sentinels, slumped in the road, their weapons trampled under the vampires' feet. "We can't take on so many alone."

"Lacroix must have ordered the power to the Lyceum shut off," he murmured. "Otherwise, they would have left guards at city hall in case anyone used the elevator to escape out the front. They're placing all their eggs in one basket."

"The lights were on out front," I reminded him.

"The Lyceum is on a separate circuit, so we don't have to explain to the city why their power bill runs so high."

Huh. I always assumed the Society had placed someone on the board who kept two accounting ledgers. One for the city and one for the Society. His way was simpler.

"Wait—what?" If the power was out, the elevator was out, meaning there was no way out. Period.

Linus wove black mist through his fingers. "Anyone still down there is penned on both sides."

Ice spread through my veins when I fully grasped the implications. His mother, the Grande Dame, was entombed in the bowels of the Lyceum. Without power, we couldn't bring her up through the front elevator. Without manpower, we couldn't carve a path through the vampires to bring her out the rear.

"Tell me what to do." I flattened my hand between his rigid shoulder blades. "How can I help?"

"We need to pinpoint Lacroix's whereabouts. Once Lethe and Hood arrive with the other gwyllgi, they can distract the horde while we attempt reasoning with their master."

"And if we can't?"

Midnight fluttered on the air around him, cloaking him in a gauzy shroud. "We kill him."

EIGHTEEN

Nestled between buildings and hidden behind a dumpster to help mask our scent, Linus and I watched. Lacroix was easy to spot. We didn't see him, exactly, but the knot of vampires frothing at the mouth in the center of the mass gave us a pretty good idea of where to find him. He wouldn't be out there walking alone where the Elite could pick him off. He would be hiding among his followers, using them as a living—or undead—shield.

"Now that we've found him," I asked Linus, "how do we get to him?"

"No word from Lethe?"

I checked my phone again. "No."

Just to spite me, it pinged once I stuck it back in my pocket.

>>*All hell is breaking loose. Get ready.*

What's happening?

>>*The pack is tearing its way through the rear guard.*

Thanks for the heads-up. We're moving on Lacroix.

There were other, less pressing, notifications. Marit, Cruz, and Neely had reached Woolworth House. They were safe within her wards. Cricket had pulled the Haints in and sent them home early. They wanted answers and updates, but all I could do was mute those conversations and hope I could get back to them later.

"That was Boaz." Nerves tingled in my fingertips. "The pack has already made their move."

Linus kept sweeping over the vampires with his gaze. "Then we wait for our opening."

"Let me refresh your sigil." I unbuttoned his dress shirt a few inches then tugged on the neck of his undershirt until I could draw on bare skin. I stuck to the impervious sigil and prayed it held fast against Lacroix and his vampires. "I brought the artifact. Goddess-touched necromancers are half-Last Seed and half-necromancer, so it makes sense it would work against them too."

"Good thinking." He arched an eyebrow when I removed it from my bra. "I had no idea you hid such fascinating things in there."

"You can strip-search me later." I winked at him. "For now, let's go knock some vampire heads together."

A heavy dose of bravado never hurt anyone, right? Between Linus and the pack, I would just be the mouthpiece for our operation, and that suited me fine.

Cool fingers closed over my upper arm. "Your sigil."

"Already done." I showed him my arm. "I got bored around the time that one guy walked past holding his cellphone over his head in one hand while blasting 'The Electric Slide' from the Bluetooth speaker in his other."

His wannabe boombox was giving away his age. He was too young by vampire standards to be a threat, except to our eardrums.

Over the din of their incisors scraping in a rhythmic, nails-on-chalkboard screech that made my ears ache, a chorus of throaty howls raised the hairs down my arms.

The cavalry had arrived.

Within minutes, Lethe found us. Crimson drool strung from her jaw, but her tail wagged. Hood was right on her heels, ears perked, a growl rumbling through his thick chest.

"We think Lacroix is there." I pointed to the tightest clot of vampires. "We need to reach him, see if I can talk sense into him. His people are supposed to capture me, not kill me. Worst-case scenario, they march me right to him."

"Worst-case scenario, he cages you." As the crisp words left his mouth, the night unspooled around Linus. "We'll have to fight our way out past every vampire in the streets if he catches a whiff of you."

A ball of dread formed in my gut, worry he might leave me behind. "What are you saying?"

"That I want you to be careful." He palmed my cheek. "That I want you to take every precaution."

Confirmation he saw me as a partner and not a damsel sent relief swirling through me.

"Stick close." He brushed a lingering kiss over my lips that curled my toes. "You never know when I might need saving."

Lethe made wet gagging noises and staggered closer. I plastered myself against Linus to escape, and for other reasons, but she kept coming. Trust me when I say Lethe's morning sickness was worthy of *The Exorcist*. Two legs or four, it didn't matter. Regan MacNeil only wished she had Lethe's range. Projectile vomiting was truly an artform, one I didn't appreciate. At all. Even a little.

Hood's chuffed laughter as he nipped her on the ear clued me in to the joke. Namely, me.

Without a backward glance, Lethe bolted for the chaos, barking orders as she ran.

Hood pinched the back of my shirt between his teeth and jerked his head over his shoulder.

"You want me to climb on your back?" I squinted at his withers. "You're not that big."

"You don't weigh much." Linus flexed his hand, and his moonlit scythe materialized in his palm. "Trust Hood to know his limitations."

Easy for him to say, he was walking. "Do you remember how much I hated horseback riding lessons?"

"What I remember is you getting caught skinny-dipping with Boaz in the pond behind the barn."

A flush crept up my neck. "I'll just get on Hood then..."

Linus gave me a boost, and I straddled the gwyllgi, fisting my hands in his ruddy fur.

Nerves jangling, I sought out Linus. "Be—"

Hood lurched forward, and my teeth clacked together at the roughness of his gait.

To keep my feet from dragging, I had to hang on to his neck and plaster myself down his back. I drew my legs up behind me, hooking my ankles on his spine, and held on for dear life.

Ahead, Lethe carved a path through the vampires that Hood took with lengthening strides. Based on the screams behind us, Linus was carving a more literal path with his scythe.

Blood spattered my cheeks until I had to press my face against Hood's neck to shield myself from the gore.

A sharp yelp snapped my head up in time to see how stupid I had been.

More than a dozen slavering vampires had converged on Lethe, and she was surrounded.

Lacroix wasn't using his people as his vanguard. The coward wasn't here. The knot of vampires hadn't been concealing him. They had been corralling several dozen fledglings with bloodlust brightening their eyes.

We had fallen for their ruse, and with us in the middle of their circle, the vampire guards closed ranks behind us, trapping us among their ravenous charges.

"Protect Lethe," I shouted to Hood over their snarls. "I'll stick with Linus."

I leapt from his back before he could protest, tucked into a ball, and rolled to a stop at the base of an icy cloak spun from starless skies and nightmares.

"He's not here," I stated the obvious. "What do we do now?"

"We try not to die," Linus said as black swallowed his eyes from corner to corner, "and we take as many of them out as we can."

"Good plan."

Fighting back to back with him, romantic as it sounded, was impossible unless I wanted to risk accidental decapitation. The scythe required a range of motion my presence behind him would impede. Close-quarters brawling would have to be good enough.

A vampire stalked me as I moved away from Linus, charging the second I was outside the scythe's lethal reach. All I had to do was hold the stake. He impaled himself on it, gaping in shock as blood flowed over my hand. I yanked my arm back at the same time I kicked him in the gut. His corpse slid off the tapered end with a sucking noise, and I grimaced. How did Corbin stand it? Murder was so...*messy*.

"New plan," I called to Linus. "I'm going to set a circle, and we're going to see how many vampires I can take out at once."

The small knife in my pocket wasn't much of a weapon, but I kept it razor sharp. It parted the skin covering my palm, and blood flowed. I made a fist and squeezed, drawing a tight circle in crimson.

"Lethe. Hood. Get in here."

The second their paws crossed the barrier, I grasped the back of Linus's cloak and hauled him in. The magic sprang closed around us, and the horde bounced off the impenetrable barrier.

With blood still dripping down my hand, I cupped my palm and dipped my fingers, writing sigils on the ward as fast as my mind conjured them. When I had five lined up, I smacked my palm against each one.

Blasts of energy as bright as daylight swept out into the crowd, incinerating them where they stood.

"Goddess," I breathed. "It's never done that before."

The pulse usually shoved vampires off their feet. A solid hit knocked them unconscious. It had never killed anyone. This time, it vaporized them. And from the ashes of their destruction strode Lacroix, without a scratch on him. We had been right about his hiding spot, we just hadn't been able to single him out from among the rabid fledglings.

"A goddess-touched necromancer is at her fiercest when protecting those she loves," Lacroix intoned. "I had wondered if you had it in you." He examined the remains of three dozen charred husks, all that remained of his fledglings. "I see now it was foolish of me to question if my son had bred true."

"Savannah is my city, not yours." I drew several more sigils. "Leave now, or I will burn you to ash."

"You can't harm me, that ought to be evident." He chuckled, indulgent, but his eyes gleamed with malice. "I have lived a long time, Grier. Long enough to know how to protect myself against goddess-touched necromancers. I would never have engaged with you otherwise. As you might suspect, I enjoy being alive, and I've got lifetimes of experience in staying that way."

He reached into the opened neck of his button-down shirt and produced a quarter-sized medallion stamped with intricate sigils. The design scratched the back of my brain where my genetic memory resided until I understood its purpose was similar to the sigil I drew on Linus, with one important caveat. Lacroix's protection extended as far as my blood and my magic, and the blood and magic of others like me.

Lacroix was that cocky, that bold. He had only warded himself against circumstances beyond his control.

"The stake is an heirloom, I presume?" Lacroix eyed it covetously. "Perhaps we can arrange a trade."

Asking would have given him the upper hand, so I waited for him to spell out his demands.

"Come with me of your own volition," he said, extending his hand, "and I won't kill your betrothed."

Shaking my head, I walked up to the edge of the circle. "You already gave the order."

"I did." He let his arm drop to his side. "I can take it back."

"No deal." I eased between him and Linus. "You'll kill him as soon as you secure me."

"Ma coccinelle."

Fear ignited in my chest, roaring through my limbs, as the crowd parted behind Lacroix. "Odette?"

Vampires escorted Odette, her frail arms trapped in their immovable grips.

Messy white braids slid across her face, and blood speckled her dress. She was missing a shoe and her glasses too. The vampires might not have been restraining her so much as preventing her from face-planting. She was almost blind without them.

"We discovered this treasure on the edge of the city." Lacroix grinned, his fangs lengthening. "If memory serves, she was one of your mother's dearest friends. Your adoptive mother favored her too, yes?"

"Let her go," I rasped. "Please."

Odette was family. I couldn't lose her too.

"Ah." He clucked his tongue. "I see you have recalled your manners."

"Whatever he wants," Odette cried, thrashing in their hold, "do not give it to him."

"I'll trade myself for Odette." I heard myself as if the words echoed back to me from across a long distance. "Just don't hurt her."

Behind me, Lethe and Hood had gone eerily silent. But it wasn't Lacroix they were staring down with murder in their eyes—it was Odette.

"Don't blame her," I told them quietly. "This is my choice."

Linus rested his hand on my shoulder. "No."

That was the entirety of his argument.

No.

I wasn't certain that had been all he meant to say, or if that was all that came out. He wasn't a man who relished repeating himself.

I won't be parted from you again, his bottomless eyes reminded me.

The breadth of his devotion left me with an impossible choice. Either I condemned Odette...or him.

Cool fingers speared through mine as Linus entwined our fates. "Lower the wards."

The gwyllgi pair whined behind me, their crimson eyes focused on Odette like she was the biggest threat on the street.

"This isn't her fault." I scratched them both behind their ears. "Don't hurt her."

Lethe lunged at me, closing her mouth around my hand but not biting down hard enough to hurt.

"I have to do this." I wiggled free. "Odette is family."

The hairs stood upright down the length of Hood's spine, and he snarled at Odette with pure loathing.

All I could do was hope they would obey my wishes. I was out of time to reassure them. Lacroix wouldn't wait for my answer forever.

"Give me your word you won't hurt the gwyllgi," I grated from between clenched teeth. "Linus and I are more than a fair trade for their lives. Let them go. They won't give you any more trouble." I cut them a sharp look. "They'll go back to Atlanta, where they belong."

"You must believe the two of you stand better odds of escape together." He rolled a shoulder. "The boy is leverage. You will not be kept together, but perhaps you will be rewarded with supervised visits if you do as you're told."

Heart a panicked bird in my chest, I held on tight to Linus and used my toe to break the line.

The ward fell, and Lacroix's grin widened until it stretched from ear to ear.

Movement in the crowd drew my eye past my grandfather to a blood-drenched gwyllgi barreling down on us with murder in his eyes.

"Stop," I yelled. "*No.*"

His enormous paws struck Odette in the chest, and she fell back, thumping her head on the asphalt.

"Get away from her." I rushed over, yanking his fur, pulling him back. "She's with us."

Red magic splashed over my hands, up my arms, sucking me down into the beast's transformation.

Strong arms cinched around my waist and ripped me back as power consumed the creature, and a man's form emerged with a booted foot pressed against Odette's throat.

Shane.

"For the longest time, I thought you were dead, witch." His outline rippled, the beast eager to tear from his skin again. "You'll wish you were, when I'm done with you."

"Shane, no." I struggled to get free, but it was a very human Lethe —not Linus—holding me back. "Don't hurt her."

"I'm not going to hurt her." He applied more pressure, and she gurgled. "I'm going to kill her."

"Lethe, let me go. *Please.*"

Lethe didn't say a word, but her whole body trembled against me as she fought the compulsion.

A compulsion that shouldn't have extended to protecting Odette. *No, no, no.*

There had to be an explanation. Lethe might not be able to tell me, but Odette could explain.

"Please," I begged, glancing back at Lethe. "Don't make me hurt you."

Blood dribbled from the corner of her mouth, dripping onto her shirt. Her labored breaths stirred the hair at the base of my neck, a rasping wheeze of sound. Panicked she might kill herself to save me, I searched out Linus for help. But he was staring at Odette with a peculiar expression drawing his forehead into tidy rows.

Hood retained his gwyllgi form, and blood *drip, drip, dripped* from his eyes as he took laborious steps closer to his mate...and Odette.

Torn between loyalties, I went limp in Lethe's arms to give her some relief then sought out Shane. "What's happening to them?"

"The NDAs the pack use are fae made. They're nasty pieces of work," he said. "The magic woven into them will kill anyone who breaches their terms. Lethe is fighting it for you, and Hood is fighting it for her." He slanted me a look. "Whatever they know about this woman, they're bound from speaking ill of her. They have no way to warn you, but I can, and I will."

Tears sprang into Lethe's eyes, and she rested her forehead against my shoulder as sobs overtook her.

"I don't understand." I stroked her hair until Hood shifted and gathered her in his arms. "Odette was one of my mother's best friends. She was one of Maud's confidants. She's like an aunt to me."

"She's Lacroix's lover." Pity shone in his eyes, but he shook his head. "She—"

Horror pitched me forward, but there was nothing I could do, nothing I could have done.

Lacroix was an ancient, and he was fast, and he was ruthless. Even more so than the fae.

Between one blink and the next, Shane's body hit the pavement.

Lacroix dangled the severed head from a silky rope of blue-black hair.

Odette closed her eyes, her limbs trembling, and sobbed when his blood spattered her.

"He talked too much." Lacroix tossed the head away and cleaned his hands with a handkerchief one of his followers offered him. "Now that we can hear ourselves think, I await your answer."

Shock made it difficult to turn my head away from Shane's corpse. The brutal attack had come so swiftly...

Swallowing the metallic taste in my mouth, I wet my lips. "No."

Hidden behind the mask of Scion Lawson, Linus gave no indication if he agreed or disagreed with my change of heart, but the comforting weight of his arm draped across my shoulders.

"You would let her die?" Lacroix knelt beside Odette and toyed with one of her white braids, now stained crimson. "She means so little to you?"

A sour taste coated the back of my throat, and I picked at the scab on my palm, taking comfort in the warmth of the blood slicking my fingers. Magic in my hand, eager to come when I called on its power.

Odette might have been the one who bumped her head, but the impact had shaken me too.

"You cut your house-sitting duties short," I said quietly to her. "You saw a vision of me in a car accident in Atlanta. You saw I got banged up, but you didn't stick around Woolly to welcome me home or meet the gwyllgi." I thought back on what Amelie told me at the time. "You blamed an allergy to dogs, but you've played with strays on the beach. You even took one in for a while. You never sneezed, not once."

Slowly, Odette opened her milky eyes, and her brow furrowed. "I did see, but you were fine. I—"

"You made excuses for not visiting me after the Kinases settled in, but you've never liked to travel often or far. When I asked you to visit Amelie, and you checked if the gwyllgi were still here first, I should have suspected you had history with them. Why else would their presence have mattered to you?"

Thanks to the NDA, it's not like they could have outed her, but their behavior would have tipped me off that something was wrong.

Lacroix watched me now, listening as I worked it all out, balling the handkerchief in his fist tighter.

"I should have been suspicious when you used your vacation as cover for moving out of your bungalow, but you're family. Why would I think twice about anything you'd told me?" The more I rambled, the more I made sense, and I hated that I couldn't stop. I wanted to bury my head in the sands outside her candy-colored home and pretend the ground wasn't crumbling beneath me. "Your bungalow was dusted with powdered bronze." I curled my fingernails into my palms. "Why would you do that? Why would anyone do that? Unless they knew I would go looking for you. Unless they knew I used gwyllgi for security. Unless...they had something to hide."

"I visited a client, as I told you," she croaked, tears spilling over her weathered cheeks. "I was notified that the bungalow's owner intended to sell while I was away. I paid a company to move my things. I have only just come back."

Vision wobbly, I let fresh blood fall to the pavement, sealing the ward I had smudged earlier.

"You left a note for the realtor about the toilet in the master bathroom." I raised the circle around us, protecting us, and only then did I let my own tears fall. "You're lying, Odette."

"*Bébé*, no."

"The Elite had the handwriting analyzed. The results came back positive. It was yours."

Eyeing Lacroix, she arranged herself in a seated position. "Those tests mean nothing."

"This doesn't mean anything either." I reached into my pocket and retrieved the ark shell Cletus had given me the day I went searching for Odette on Tybee. "A million of these must wash up on beaches all over the world. But this one—it's identical to a shell I found pressed into the concrete patio at the estate where I was held captive, right down to this."

I held it up for her to see, my thoughts racing over what it meant if I was right. Unless she convinced me otherwise, she had been there when the patio was poured to leave her mark on...her home. The estate where I had been kept, not only as a prisoner, but as a baby. The estate my mother had escaped from.

The implications spun out in widening circles that made me dizzy with understanding of what debt Hood and the Kinases felt they owed me.

Her scent reminds me of a young woman to whom I owe a blood debt.

That's what Hood had told me.

I couldn't save her, but perhaps this might help me balance the scales.

The young woman I reminded him of, the one he couldn't save, was...Mom.

And that meant Odette knew everything, and she had never told me. Any of this.

"The hole was so small on the original, I didn't notice it at first. Granted, I was also drugged at the time. But I saw it again the other day, when I met with Lacroix. I even took a picture since I didn't understand the connection." I turned it this way and that. "The holes are in the exact same spot. Moon snail predation might explain one hole in a matched shell, but two? The reason for that, and their identical size and shape, is they were earrings once upon a time."

Odette raised a shaky hand to her throat, her milky eyes glassy with unshed tears.

"The whorls on the inside I thought were scarring is an artist's signature. She makes jewelry from what washes up on Tybee." I tossed the token to her. "At first, I thought Cletus brought me a shell from the beach. I couldn't figure out why he fixated on it, but now I think he must have found the orphaned half in your house during our second trip."

The bungalow might have been stripped down to the magnets, but a shell? Found in a beach house? That wouldn't draw a second look from most people. Lucky for us, Cletus wasn't technically a person.

"No," she cried. "Grier, *no*."

"The wraith monitoring Corbin Theroux is mine." I doubted Linus would mind if I laid partial claim to Cletus. "Think very hard about what I might have seen and heard before lying to me again."

The couple Cletus had shown me in flashes between Corbin's reports—it had been Odette and Lacroix.

"Visions from a wraith are distorted," she protested. "You can't trust everything you hear or see."

"A wraith's entire vision might not translate, but it knows what it saw."

"Wraiths are not sentient," she argued. "They only know what they are told."

"What about Shane?" I jerked my chin toward the body cooling beside her. "What did he know that was worth his life?"

The cozy invitation into his bedroom hadn't been seduction, it had been subterfuge. He scented Odette in the room he had been given, and he wondered at our connection. The fact he had been aware of her location but hadn't acted until now made me wonder if this wasn't her first time using bronze powder to deter nosy gwyllgi.

"I did not kill him," she protested. "You saw—"

Automatic weapons fire peppered the night, the sharp pops scattering my focus.

The Elite had arrived.

Finally.

"This is your last chance," Lacroix warned. "Come with me, and I will let your friends live. Deny me, and I will ensure you watch the light fade from their eyes as I drain them."

"As much fun as that sounds," Boaz drawled, swaggering toward me. "I'm gonna have to pass."

Boaz kept his weapon trained on Lacroix, and when Lacroix lunged for him, he filled him with a clip.

It didn't matter. It didn't stop Lacroix. It didn't even slow him down.

Crimson sprayed the invisible barrier as Lacroix's wicked fangs severed Boaz's carotid with a shake of his head.

Momentary paralysis overtook me, my heart a drumbeat in my ears. *"Boaz."*

His name became my battle cry as I smashed through the barrier and landed on Lacroix's back.

The ancient's primal roar caused my hindbrain to twitch with the urge to flee—fast and far—but I held on and clenched my fingers around the stake. With every ounce of my strength, I plunged the sharpened end into his flesh. Thanks to him bucking like a bronco desperate to unseat his rider, my aim sucked, and I pegged him between his shoulder blades instead of in his heart.

Lacroix might have protection against a goddess-touched necromancer and her artifacts, but the reality of a stake plunged beside his spine until the tip protruded from his chest was hard to ignore.

Hands slick with gore, he groped at the point, trying to yank it out so he could heal.

One look at Boaz had me sliding off Lacroix and sinking to my knees. That happens when they buckle. Your weight carries you down, and your kneecaps crack against the pavement.

Lethe and Hood might be out of commission unless Lacroix moved against me, but Linus was in my corner. Always. I trusted him to watch my back while I did what I could for Boaz.

"You idiot," I growled, tempted to slap him. "What did you think you were doing?"

With my trusty pocket knife, I sliced open my palm and gritted my teeth as the blade parted tender skin.

"Saving...you..." he wheezed. "Love...you."

Eyes prickling with unshed tears, I tuned him out to focus on the vault of knowledge locked away in my head. A standard healing sigil wasn't going to cut it. I needed more, stronger, but panic was paralyzing me. I took the best fit, honed the design to fit the application, and covered Boaz in looping swirls from head to toe.

Light erupted from his pores, blinding me. I raised my arm to shield my eyes from the brightness, but it was too late. The after-image of his outline was seared into my retinas.

If anyone figured out I was incapacitated, they might as well slather on the butter. I was toast. But just because I couldn't see didn't mean I could afford to sit on my hands. I tested Boaz's throat, and his pulse thumped under my fingertips. I ran my palms over his neck, past the damage from Lacroix's fangs, over his chest and down his sides.

Blood turned my palms sticky, but he was mending, the skin knitting back together. The fluids he'd lost couldn't be replaced, but this would keep him alive long enough for us to get him away from the carnage.

"Stupid girl." A haughty sigh warned me I had company before her grapefruit scent cut through the stink of viscera. "I thought you had moved past this infatuation."

Jaw dropping, I rubbed my eyes. *"Clarice?"*

"Tilt your head back." The Grande Dame pinched my chin between her fingers, and the tickle of a brush caressed each of my cheeks. Magic whispered over my skin, and my sight returned in a swirl of sharp colors that cut my eyes in time to see her staring down her nose at me. "You'll do."

"I was a sitting duck until you came along."

The implication, that I was shocked she didn't let the battle handle the problem of her future daughter-in-law, was plain.

"I love my son." Her red lips thinned, a trait she had passed on to Linus. "And he loves you. It's an affliction he's suffered for a number of years. You loving him back?" Her gaze clashed with mine. "That...I did not expect. I always wanted better for you than Boaz Pritchard, but Maud wanted the best for you."

It went without saying *the best* was her son. I wasn't about to argue when I agreed with her.

"When you were...sent away...I thought the separation might free him from his fascination, but I see now I was mistaken. Whatever hold you have over him is irrevocable. For him to remain in my life, I must accept my grandchildren will come from you."

Grandchildren.

Between her wish list and the one Woolly slapped me with earlier, I would be birthing litters of tiny, redheaded Woolworths.

"Now." She capped her ink jar and tucked away her brush. "Explain yourself."

"Lacroix attacked Boaz. I attacked Lacroix." Squinting against the vibrancy, I searched for my grandfather. "Where is Odette?"

"Odette was here? I didn't see her." She frowned down at me. "Lacroix was gone when I arrived."

Sick to my core, I had to warn her. "I have reason to believe she may be working with Lacroix."

A flicker of true fear darkened her features, and then she spoke the words that turned my heart to stone. "Where is my son?"

NINETEEN

Another time, I might have relished shoving the Grande Dame away from me so hard she fell to the pavement on her butt with an undignified grunt. I might have even rewound the moment, savoring it, replaying it until it burned in my memory, never to be forgotten. But the raw panic fluttering behind my breastbone left me too lightheaded to care.

"Grier," Boaz whispered as his eyes started tracking. "What...?"

"Stay put and don't die." I whirled toward the Grande Dame. "Keep him safe."

"Me?" Flicking the grit from her palms, she examined her scrapes. "Do it yourself."

"I can't," I shouted, leaping to my feet. "I'm going after Linus."

Incredulousness painted her features sharp enough to cut. "He can take care of himself."

"We'll have to agree to disagree. I'm not hanging back and hoping for the best." I summoned the wraith, hoping I wasn't sacrificing Corbin in the bargain, and watched with a heavy heart as he cocked his head at the Grande Dame as if recognizing her. "Stay with them."

Cletus billowed, his cloak spreading in an inky spill through the air.

"I'll take the gwyllgi with me," I promised him. "Protect them. Please."

Before the Grande Dame could argue, I sprinted away. Lethe shifted and fell in beside me, Hood flanking her on four legs.

Fighting was tapering off around the edges as the vampires retreated toward the tunnel mouth, making our job simpler. Pack members herded the cowards attempting to escape the slaughter back toward the waiting Elite, who staked them without mercy.

Putting their distraction to good use, we fled the chaos.

About to paint on a tracking sigil, I glanced over at Lethe. "Can you find Linus?"

A short bark confirmed it, and the gwyllgi pair slowed then dipped their noses toward the pavement.

Seconds later, Lethe threw back her head and bayed at the moon before breaking into a sprint.

I ran as fast as I could, counting on Hood to help me plow through the remaining vampires. Sweat poured into my eyes, and my hair stuck to my face. Lungs blazing, I gulped air and pushed my legs until the burn migrated from my calves, up my thighs, and into my side.

Lethe kept howling, her cry raising the hairs down my arms.

Hood caught the scent a moment later, and he joined in the hunting song.

An alley loomed ahead, and they shot through it like bullets fired at a target.

Darkness swirled around two figures clashing at the dead end, and blood soured the air. Linus's familiar scent hit the back of my throat, hunger and fear churning in my gut. A darker smell clogged my nose, Lacroix's blood, thick and metallic.

Heedless of the danger, I rushed into the miasma armed with only the blood in my veins and the sigils in my head.

Linus had gone full dark. He was all tattered fabric and moonlit blade, soul and bone, a wraith come to life. He flowed with his scythe, each arc a vicious slice that rent the air. He moved like a dancer familiar with the steps, able to follow their patterns without thought.

But if Linus had gone dark, Lacroix had gone feral. The stake protruded from his chest, and his blood drenched his clothes. He bared fangs thicker than my pinky finger that dripped with viscous saliva. Slices marred his face and throat, the wounds healing slower thanks to massive blood loss.

Eager to assure myself Linus was all right, I scanned what I could see of him. Once I confirmed he appeared unharmed, I could breathe easier. The sigil was holding strong, keeping him safe. Now I just had to take out Lacroix before that changed.

Powerful the sigil might be, but his sweat could dissolve it. A lucky scratch from Lacroix could void it too. I couldn't risk either of those happening. I had to take Lacroix out before he gained the upper hand.

Without my life endangered, Lethe and Hood were no good except for moral support. I had to factor them out. This was between Lacroix, Linus, and me.

Searching the alley, I prayed to the goddess for a weapon to materialize. When I spotted a stack of rotted pallets, I ran for them. Bracing my foot on a cracked slat, I eased my fingers under the plank and yanked up. It snapped off in my hand. The width made it unwieldy, but its sharp end was what mattered. I broke off a second one then advanced on Lacroix.

Linus locked gazes with me, and I shivered beneath the alien coldness in his expression. There was no hint of my Linus in his gaze. This was the Potentate of Atlanta, the Eidolon, and the cruel edge to his features made my breath catch. Proving he read me, no matter what mask he wore, he made an elegant turn that shifted Lacroix's back fully to me, a perfect opening.

Clutching a stake in each hand, I lunged for my grandfather. This time I didn't miss, and I drove the wooden shards through his heart.

The fight drained out of him, and he sank to his knees, his eyes wild and inhuman. The look he turned on me promised vengeance, and I took a healthy step back.

"For your crimes against the city of Savannah, the Lyceum, and the Grande Dame, I hereby sentence you to death." The wicked blade gleamed when Linus raised it over his head, and I shut my eyes so I didn't have to watch my grandfather, monster he might be, die. "Justice is served. May the goddess grant you peace."

A whistling noise telegraphed the scythe's deadly arc to my ears, but there was no resulting thwack as blade met bone. No indrawn breath. No thump as Lacroix's head rolled across the pavement.

Daring to crack open my eyes, I sucked in a ragged gasp at the wicked athame slicing into Linus's throat.

"Release him," I snapped, shifting to one side to see who had ambushed him and then wished I hadn't.

"I offer a trade, your Linus for my Gaspard."

As much as I wanted to blink away the sight of Odette holding Linus at knifepoint, I had to accept this was the real her, that the woman I had known and loved since coming to Savannah was a figment of my imagination.

That didn't make losing who I thought she was hurt any less.

"All right." I lifted my hands to show her they were empty. "Let him go, and I'll allow you both to leave the city."

"That is fair," she conceded. "I accept."

"Was any of it real?" I hadn't meant to ask, not while Linus's life hung in the balance, but it came out all the same. "Did you love Mom or Maud or me at all?"

"I loved Maud," she said quietly, "but she adored Evie, and when there was no Evie, there was still you."

I didn't need her to spell it out. I could read between the lines just fine. That was a big, fat *no*.

She hadn't loved Mom, she hadn't loved me. Her tolerance must have been an act for Maud's benefit.

Doing what I do best, I shoved all that hurt, all that pain, all that misery, into a mental box and twisted the key, locking it away where it couldn't distract me.

"Lower the knife." I pulled on my Dame Woolworth mask, its austere indifference the best defense I had against letting Odette know how much she had hurt me. Though she had known me long enough to see through the cracks, I still held on to the edges for all I was worth. "Step away from Linus. Once you've released him, I'll back away from Lacroix."

"Gaspard is wounded. Moving him will prove difficult. Forgive me, *bebe*, but I must even the odds." Without flinching, she drew the blade across Linus's throat. It shouldn't have given him a paper cut, not with that sigil on his body, but Odette had come prepared, it seemed, with a goddess-touched artifact. A crimson line carved his throat, and blood gushed down his chest. "He won't die if you treat him quickly."

Horror wobbled through my knees, but I kept them from buckling as I rushed to catch him as he fell.

"I've got you." I wrapped my hand around the front of his throat. "I've got you. I've got you."

I eased him down onto the pavement, his gaze locked with mine, unflinching, like he wanted to make sure my face was the last thing he saw.

"Sorry in advance," I teased in a broken voice, unable to break his stare. "Promise I'll buy you a new one."

After ripping open his buttoned shirt, I hacked away his undershirt and used it to staunch the bleeding. He held the fabric in place while I sawed the pocketknife across my palm. Spots danced in my vision, and I slipped to one side, dizzy. Biting into my bottom lip until my eyes watered, I regained my focus.

Using his chest and abdomen as my canvas, I smeared jagged sigils that curled like thorns over his sides.

The most ridiculous thought crossed my mind, that the sharp edges had pierced his soul to cage it in his body, but it flittered away on a breeze smelling of garbage and pennies.

More blood. More pain. More sigils. More magic.

I gave it my all.

It wasn't enough.

The vicious slash wasn't healing. It wasn't *healing*.

The goddess-touched artifact used to inflict the wound must have made him resistant to my magic.

"Odette," I begged, desperate. "You have to help me."

Lethe butted me in the shoulder with her blocky head, and Hood padded closer too.

I didn't have to look back to see Lacroix was gone, and Odette with him.

I made a fist, squeezing out every drop, and delved into the farthest recesses of my genetic memory. I scooped a sigil from the bottomless pool of ancient knowledge and applied it in concentric circles.

Magic shimmered over Linus's skin, coating him from head to foot, but there was no blast of energy this time. No light. No miracles.

For a moment, a vision from the nightmare superimposed itself over us.

For a moment, he was Maud, lying in a pool of blood, already dead.

For a moment, I was that younger Grier, hunched over my adoptive mother's body, her blood on my hands.

But she had been gone when I found her, her blood ice on my fingers. Linus was still here.

He was still here.

Cut deeper. Cut harder. Cut faster.

More blood. More pain. More. More. *More.*

Slowly, so slowly, his eyelids slid closed, and his lips parted on a soft exhale.

"You're not leaving me too," I screamed at him. "Linus. *Linus.*"

"Grier," Lethe said gently. "Let him go."

"No." I shrugged her off me. "I can—"

Hood cut in, his voice barely a whisper. "Do to him what you did to Maud?"

The verbal slap cleared my head and shocked me out of my panic spiral.

Up the well-worn stairs to my mind, I ran, as fast as my feet would carry me.

Mom. Maud. Amelie. Boaz. Odette. Linus.

I couldn't keep going like this, not when I lost everyone I loved, not when I was alone.

Again.

Always.

Slamming the mental door behind me, I curled in a tight ball, in my safe place, and shut my eyes.

TWENTY

"**G**rier."
　　"*Grier.*"
　　"*Grier.*"

The name echoed through the vastness of my mental hidey-hole, soft and inviting.

"*Come back to me.*"
"*Come back to me.*"
"*Come back to me.*"

The voice warmed me, and I uncurled from the fetal position to peek at the door leading down, down, down, back to that other place, the hard place, the ugly place.

I didn't want to go back. I didn't want to remember. I wanted to stay here, with nothing.

Having nothing meant having nothing to lose.

"*I love you.*"
"*I love you.*"
"*I love you.*"

Wary of who had the power to rouse me, even in my safe place, I padded over to the door and turned the knob. The comforting scent of cold tingled in my nose. Crushed herbs and dirt. Familiar things. Wonderful things. But I couldn't remember why those things mattered so much.

Nudging the crack wider, I eased through and took the stairs back down into my body.

"You can't leave," a coarse voice rasped. "I won't let you go."

The first name to pop into my head was Midas. The beautiful, ruined voice. The gentleness of it.

But hearing his voice had never made me weep, and I couldn't stop the great heaving sobs that wracked my chest.

"Open your eyes," he said, a sandpaper whisper. "Look at me."

"No." I bawled until I hiccupped and choked on my denials. "You might not be real."

"Shhh." Blessedly cool fingers lifted my hand to an equally cool throat. "I'm real."

Daring my lashes to rise, I studied the pressed shirt in front of me. The fabric looked expensive, that was promising. The buttons gleamed, a match for all the ones I had sent pinging across the floor in recent months. Heart pounding, I kept traveling higher, checking off all the similarities that gave me sickening hope I wasn't hallucinating.

The skin of his throat, once smooth and unblemished, had a fresh scar that I doubted any amount of necromantic magic could erase. And I didn't care. Not one whit.

Courage mounting, I examined his chin, noting the auburn stubble. Higher still, I found his poor nose, flawless even after Woolly had broken it. Pale lashes and then...navy-blue eyes.

"Linus."

"I'm here." He trailed his fingers across my cheeks, and tears glistened on their tips. "So are you."

"How?" I clutched his wrists. "Oh goddess, I didn't—?"

Understanding my fear, he shook his head. "You healed me."

"I thought I'd lost you." I stared at my hands. "I couldn't counteract the blade's magic."

"You saved me." He rubbed his throat. "I wouldn't have survived until the healer arrived otherwise."

I almost asked if Shane had treated him, but no. Shane was gone. Lacroix had killed him.

An immortal being snuffed out of existence as if he had never been. Such a waste.

"Heinz." Linus answered the question I hadn't asked. "Boaz dispatched him to our location."

The savage attack on Boaz felt as distant as a nightmare. "He's okay?"

He hesitated. "Yes."

My pulse kicked up a notch. "What aren't you telling me?"

"You healed him. Completely."

The awe in his expression made me nervous. "What do you mean —*completely*?"

"He has no wounds or signs of ever having been injured. In his entire life. He's a blank canvas. Even his scars have been erased." He traced my fingers, marveling at the power in them. "He also has a new leg."

"A leg?" I yelped, jerking upright. "A whole new leg?"

"Not an entire leg, no." Amusement curved his lips. "Just from the knee down."

"I didn't mean to do that." I wouldn't even know where to start. "I didn't know I *could* do that."

Maybe Lacroix was right, and love for Linus and my friends was the key to unlocking my full potential. I had witnessed shades of this phenomenon in Lethe's healing, in her child's growth spurt, but this was next-level bizarre for a necromancer. We weren't healers, but maybe...I was?

"He hasn't complained, if you're concerned he might want his prosthetic back."

"Do you think that's why I couldn't heal you?" I wiped my damp palms on my thighs. "I ran out of juice?"

"I believe Lacroix was right, that goddess-touched artifacts counteract goddess-touched magic."

"The weapons we forge can be used against us as well as by us."

"We have yet to discover the limits to your power. This lends weight to the argument the Marchands, and others with regular contact with goddess-touched necromancers, would require a means of controlling them."

Nullify our magic, and we were left defenseless against the power of fellow necromancers and the raw strength of vampires. While I understood the Marchands' healthy fear of what they created, I wasn't thrilled to have experienced their precautionary measures firsthand.

"Any word on Corbin?" I didn't sense Cletus. I hoped that meant the wraith was with him.

"Lacroix has him confined to a cell. He's safe, for now. The clan home has been warded against wraiths, but Cletus is keeping an eye on the property. We'll know if Lacroix attempts to have him moved." Linus cupped my cheek in one hand. "We'll get him back."

Corbin gambled his fate on my ability to protect him, and he lost. I owed him. More than I could pay.

We had to get him back. He had more than earned his second chance, the opportunity to shape his own future, and I intended to give it to him. But that wasn't the reason why my throat was closing in a fist.

Shaking my head, I had to admit to the utter selfishness twisting my gut into knots.

"Odette almost killed you." I rubbed the heel of my palm over my chest, but my heart still ached. "You almost died."

"But she didn't, and I didn't, thanks to you."

"That's not good enough." I drew my legs under me. "I have to learn more about my condition, and fast. I need to understand the limits of what I can do, of what those artifacts can do." I raked my fingers through my knotted hair. "I have to learn how to make my own, how to arm us against Lacroix."

"There's only one place you're guaranteed to find those answers," Linus said, and his mouth crimped into an unhappy line. "The Marchands must have archives on your condition since they breed for goddess-touched necromancers. They have artifacts, that much we know for certain. It stands to reason, given the fact Marchands forged the weapon Heloise used against you, they have the knowledge you seek."

The Marchands, who had written Mom off, written me off, who blamed me for the death of one of their own. I doubted they would welcome me back into the fold at this point, but that didn't mean they wouldn't have a use for me. That was a happy thought. Still, the trade would be worthwhile if it meant we could save Savannah, and ourselves, from Lacroix.

Happy to take a break from my family, I shone the spotlight on his.

"You haven't mentioned how the Grande Dame fared," I said carefully. "How is the city?"

"Mother evacuated the Lyceum after we left, herself included, and joined the Elite in their barracks." He sounded surprised, and proud, and surprised to be proud. "She led the others through the tunnel to safety. They escaped before Lacroix arrived and sealed the entrance behind them."

"Does that mean the Lyceum is secure?"

"Yes and no."

"That doesn't sound good."

"The protections Mother put in place before she left kept the vampires out of the Lyceum itself, but they've taken city hall." He kept his expression carefully neutral. "Odette is holed up there. Lacroix too. He was too weak to evacuate before dawn. Savannah's Elite have the building and the tunnel mouth surrounded. Reinforcements arrived from our neighbors, and they're sweeping the town for Lacroix's people."

"What do the humans think is happening?"

"A cat five hurricane." He massaged his temples. "The solution isn't perfect. Hurricanes aren't like tornadoes. They don't just pop into and out of existence. They're tracked for days or weeks in advance, and a tropical depression just passed over us."

Unable to resist, I tucked a lock of hair behind his ear. "Tell me they're calling it Hurricane Clarice."

Naming the storm after her was the least the meteorologists she had in her pocket could do to honor the woman paying them to fabricate a catastrophic event.

"A mandatory evacuation order has been issued for the city, and there's a curfew in effect we hope will reduce the victim pool for night feedings for those who can't or won't leave. That's all we can do. Try to minimize the casualties."

"How are Lethe and Hood?"

"Mourning Shane." He took my hand. "And regretting their parts in what happened, their inability to warn you, to share what they know."

"I will admit, I was struggling." Sometimes you had to weigh the value of keeping a secret against the good revealing it might do, consequences be damned. "Now I understand the contracts they sign are nooses they can't slip without hanging themselves. They couldn't have warned us, no matter how much they wanted to, without dire consequences like the ones we saw when Lethe tested her bonds."

A knock on the door had me peering around his shoulder. "Oh. Hi."

Amelie stood in the doorway, her fingers twisted into knots. "I just wanted to see if you needed anything."

"I'm good." I adjusted the cover over my legs. "Thanks."

"Thank you," she croaked and dove for me. "Thank you for saving him."

With her in my arms, I closed my eyes and let the tears come. "Your brother is an asshat, but I couldn't let him die."

"He really is," she sob-laughed against my neck. "Thank you, Grier. I mean it. *Thank you.*"

"It's okay." I stroked her hair while she cried in my arms. "He's fine. You're fine. I'm fine. We're all fine."

As far as lies go, it wasn't a bad one.

Over her shoulder, Linus pointed toward the door then slid out of the room, leaving the way open.

"Hey," Neely called, "no one told me there was a party going on in here."

Cruz scowled at us from the hall. "Are all-girl parties usually so...damp?"

"They're called tears." Marit hip-checked Cruz out of her way. "Yanno, the salty liquid that pours down your man's face when he watches *Titanic* or *The Notebook*?" She flopped down on the bed next to me and took a deep breath. "Are you going to tell us what's really going on here? Or do I have to tickle it out of you?"

Amelie shook her head after I cast her a questioning look. "I haven't told them anything."

"That needs to change, starting now." Cruz seized the reins of the conversation with practiced ease. "You invited us over before this superstorm hit the news. How did you know it was coming when no one else did? Why didn't you evacuate if you had advance warning? Better yet, why didn't you tell us to get out instead of holing up in its path?"

"Throw on the brakes." Neely touched his husband's shoulder. "Give the girl a moment to process."

"I need answers too," Marit said. "I have to think of my dad, our family, and our employees."

"Get Linus." I patted Amelie's hand. "I want him here for this."

"Are you sure?" She shifted forward into a protective stance. "After this, there's no going back."

"They deserve to know." I drew myself up taller. "I trust them with the truth."

"You better," she groused. "Your neck is on the line here."

A thoughtful expression crossed Cruz's face. "Amelie knows," he surmised. "She's always known."

"Yeah," she admitted. "This is my secret too."

Neely dipped his chin, his face crumpling at the exclusion, and Cruz kissed his temple.

Amelie went to fetch Linus, and she returned with him and Lethe in moments.

Marit stood and joined the Torreses, a united human front, and it was surreal seeing them all together.

I swung my legs over the edge of the bed, and Linus sat on one side of me while Amelie took the other.

He took my hand in silent confirmation he supported my decision, and I held on until my bones creaked.

Lethe posted herself against the wall, her eyes narrowed on the three humans in our midst while Hood remained in the hall at their backs.

The unsettling realization settled around me that the gwyllgi had penned them in to see how they reacted to the news humans ranked lower on the food chain than they had always been taught.

"We aren't human," I told them. "We're necromancers."

A hush spread through the room.

"You...raise the dead?" Neely's hand lifted to his throat, and he paled. "As in *zombies?*"

"As in vampires," Amelie corrected.

"Vampires," Cruz echoed.

"That is..." Marit speared her fingers through her hair. *"Freaking awesome."*

Neely examined Linus and then Lethe for signs of rot or dripping eyeballs. "Are you necromancers too?"

"Yes," Linus said.

Lethe didn't answer, and neither did Hood.

"Danill Volkov," Cruz said, eyes narrowing on me. "He's one of you?"

Leave it to Cruz to see the big picture before the others finished studying their individual puzzle pieces.

"A vampire, yes."

He kept plowing onward, a hard glint in his eye. "And the woman who rammed Neely in Atlanta?"

"She was a vampire," I admitted. "You were right when you said the accident was my fault. Vampires had targeted me, and Neely paid the price."

Usually, Cruz ran hot. This was Cruz downright glacial. I wasn't sure which was worse. "We're leaving."

"No," Neely said, sounding tired. "We're not." He dragged his gaze to me. "Make it good. This is your only shot at convincing him you mean us no harm."

Thankful he had given me that much leeway, even if he did make me sound like an extraterrestrial, I launched into the big sell.

"The same vampires who attacked us in Atlanta have seized control of Savannah. They're holed up in city hall until dark, so there's a chance you can strike out in the morning if you want to evacuate. We'll have to secure a route and an escort, but we can make that happen if it's what you decide is best for you." I included Marit. "Any of you."

"We can wait until morning to leave," Cruz started, "but beyond that—"

"Good grief," Lethe huffed. "Stand back and try not to wet your pants."

Red magic splashed up her legs, sloshing onto her shoulders, and it drained to leave her gwyllgi form.

Too late to stop her, I dropped my face into my hands.

A thud had me searching out the source.

"Cruz."

The ballsy lawyer sat where his knees had buckled and gawked at Lethe. "What the hell is that?"

"Lethe is a shifter," Hood said from behind them. "So am I."

The boom of his voice reminded them he was there, and they scattered from the doorway.

"Who's a pretty girl? You! You are! Come here, puppy," Marit cooed. "Can I pet her?"

"Uh, no." I fisted Lethe's ruff to hold her steady. "She eats people who annoy her."

Neely knelt beside Cruz, draped an arm around his shoulders, and stroked his back.

"You're handling this better than I expected," I admitted to Neely.

"How long have I worked for a ghost tour company?" He scoffed. "You think I haven't seen things I can't explain? Do you know how many of our guests come back with photos or video of orbs and apparitions? They're all over the website." He screwed up his face. "Come to think of it, a lot of those tours have you credited as the guide."

"Ghosts are attracted to necromancers," I admitted. "I did use that to my advantage."

"I'm not judging you." He ran his fingers through his perfect hair. "We all use the gifts God gave us to our best advantage."

Mentioning we worshipped a goddess was oversharing, so I just nodded, grateful for his cool head.

"This explains a lot," he mused. "Your disappearances."

"Yeah." Fingers clenching on Linus's, I wet my lips to explain, but nothing came out when I tried.

"Enough." Linus put an end to that avenue of questioning. "That's enough for now."

Grateful for the reprieve, I let his ruling stand. Even so, it took a full minute for my heart to slow.

"The world is bigger and more dangerous for you all than it was yesterday," I said, "and I'm sorry for my part in that, but I'm trusting you each with the truth. I care about you, and I want you to be safe. I don't think that's possible anymore, not without you understanding the scope of your involvement in our world."

Cruz had recovered somewhat, enough to articulate a question for Linus. "Who are you?"

"Linus Lawson," he said levelly. "I'm Grier's fiancé."

"Fiancé," Neely gasped. "Forget this other-world nonsense. When did this happen? Where's the ring?"

Linus held up his hand, showing off his twisted band with a proud smile.

"I don't understand." Neely looked to me, expectant. "You don't have a ring, and he's got...a bread tie?"

"Our society is matriarchal." I chuckled at his horror. "I proposed to him. He'll be taking my last name."

"You bent a knee for him, and that's the best you could do? Money is tight, I get that, but come on. You could have saved up and bought him a gold band at least." His indignation on Linus's behalf earned him a smile from my amused fiancé. "You can always buy him something nicer later." He held up his own left hand to showcase a platinum band inset with diamonds. "This is my upgrade."

Linus made a fist, protecting his ring like he expected Neely to pry it off his finger. "I like this one."

"Lawson," Cruz repeated. "You're Clarice Lawson's son."

"Yes," he confirmed. "I am."

"You're telling me I've been working for a vampire the past four years?"

"We're necromancers," Linus said with infinite patience, "but yes. Mother required a human agent to manage—" he stopped short of dragging the Society into this "—her interests."

"She chose you," I told him, "because you're a brilliant attorney but..."

"Nothing Mother does is without a reason," Linus agreed. "Your connection to Grier is no doubt what brought you to her attention, but given Grier's circumstances at the time, there's no reason to believe she recruited you with ulterior motives."

"I'm going to resign," Cruz announced. "I want no part of this."

"Resign from a sweet gig," Marit chimed in, "and she's going to wonder what soured you on the deal."

"You don't understand," he snapped. "These people, their world, nearly cost my husband his life."

"Babe," Neely began.

"You could have been killed, and I never would have known the truth." His scowl cut deeper. "Not that I'm convinced I believe their version of events as it is."

Lethe growled to remind him she was still in the room, but she had made a tactical error. She let him adjust to her presence then allowed the topic of his husband's wellbeing to heat his blood. Cruz might have been ready to faint when the paranormal steamrolled his practical side, but he would dig in his heels and stand firm for Neely.

"How can I protect him from this?" His gaze shot to me. "What do I do to keep him safe?"

"The less people who know you're aware of our world," Linus advised, "the better."

Cruz snarled up his lip at me. "I will never forgive you for this."

All I had to offer him were two words barely worth exhaling. "I'm sorry."

"You're sorry?" Cruz chuckled, bitter and hard. "You should have let him go. If you loved him, if you cared about him at all, you would have cut ties after Atlanta." He spread his hands. "But here we are, in your home, in your world, and he's in more danger than ever. That's not love, Grier. That's not friendship, either. It's selfishness, pure and simple."

"That's enough." Neely stroked a hand down Cruz's spine. "Grier is my friend. I might not have known what I was signing up for at the time, but I don't regret having her in my life."

Leaning into Neely's touch, Cruz popped his mouth open on a blistering retort his husband cut short.

"I love you, but you don't get to make this call for me." Neely gazed down at him. "I hate that we're in this situation, that I led them to you through my friendship with Grier, but we're in this up to our necks. Our best chance at survival, at maintaining a normal life, might be embracing the *paranormal*."

This was my opening, and I didn't just walk through—I sprinted.

"You can walk away now, and I won't reach out again." Coward that I was, I addressed the offer to Cruz to avoid the moment when Neely chose his husband, his safety, over the dangerous friendship I offered. "Or you can all take positions within my household, so I can protect you."

"You have that power?" Cruz sounded doubtful. "You can do that?"

"I do, and I can."

"How?"

"Clarice Lawson is our elected leader," I confessed after Linus gave an infinitesimal nod. "Her maiden name was Woolworth. She was my guardian's younger sister. Our families are the most powerful within our society."

Neely rolled in his lips before popping them out again. "But all the ramen—"

"I got cut off from my inheritance for a while, and things were tough." The hows and whys of my sudden poverty got glossed over so as not to terrify them right out of the gate. "I had to earn my own way, and I ate more peanut butter and jelly than I want to admit." Ending my highly edited backstory on a high note, I tried for a convincing, pro-Society smile. "My title has since been reinstated, and my inheritance returned to me."

During my spiel, Cruz had shifted his focus onto Linus. "Grier's fortune is on par with your mother's?"

A smile played on his mouth. "Grier is the wealthiest woman I know."

Neely gawked at that, but Cruz just nodded. "Can I have a moment to discuss this with my husband?"

"Of course." I cut Hood a warning look, and he let them pass. "Marit?"

"I'm good." She rolled a negligent shoulder. "This is the coolest thing. Ever. I want to pick your brain, but that can wait." A laugh escaped her. "Except I have to know." She drew in a sharp breath before exhaling her question in one go. "The ghost on the Cora Ann... Did you have anything to do with that?"

"The ghost was a boy. He was murdered on the boat back in the twenties, and his remains were walled up in the engine room. He was haunting the steamboat." Again, I tiptoed around the absolute truth. "He was already showing violent tendencies. I can't say for sure my presence helped, but I don't think it hurt."

Amelie and Ambrose had each played a part in how those events unfolded, and so did the Elite, but I had to ease the humans into this world if I wanted them to keep their heads above water.

"You saved my life." Marit offered another shrug, this one less fluid. "That makes us even in my book."

"I'm glad to hear it." And I was. I wanted us to be okay. I wanted us to remain friends. I might have given up playing human, but I didn't want to cut them out of my life. "Are you okay to stay here for a bit, or do you want to leave?"

"Are you kidding me?" She threw back her head and laughed. "I'm not missing a minute of this."

Glad someone was having a good time, I lapsed into silence while Amelie and Marit chatted softly.

The kiss Linus pressed against my temple helped settle the jitters from waiting on the Torreses' verdict.

An hour and change later, Cruz escorted Neely into the room, a grim line tipping his mouth into a frown.

"I remember the night Amelie dragged you into Cricket's office to beg a job for her bestie," Neely began. "I knew you and I would be friends after you watched me apply makeup with your jaw hanging open like I was the one working magic." Neely steeled himself, and Cruz took his hand to offer support. "But the truth is...I don't know who you are, really."

The bottom dropped out of my stomach, and I nodded miserably, bracing for the letdown.

At least he hadn't called me a *what* and not a *who*. He was letting me down gentler than I deserved.

"What I do know is you're a kind, thoughtful, generous, and funny woman. You're loyal, strong, caring, and have excellent taste in friends." He shared one final glance with Cruz before telling me, "You're worth the risk, Grier."

"Thank you." I shot to my feet and hugged him until he grunted. "I won't let you down."

"Talk to me about joining your household," Cruz said after a period of time he tapped out with his foot.

"I can poach you from the Grande Dame." Given I had just stolen her son, she was not going to be thrilled with me, but she admired ruthlessness. With the right spin, she might come to view my personnel growth as personal growth, evidence I was adapting to my new station as Dame Woolworth. "I don't have a legal team. You would be it, unless you hired on more staff. I would match your salary and benefits."

He inclined his head, considering the angles. Money never hurt, but the ability to build his own team, to run his own show, would appeal to a man like him.

Amused at Cruz's distraction, Neely asked, "Does that mean I get to be your official bean counter?"

"Sure." I grinned, an idea forming. "You might be able to fit in accounting as a part-time gig."

"Oh?" His eyes glittered with interest. "What did you have in mind?"

"Linus owns a building on Abercorn he's generously offered to lease me so that I can open my own ghost tour company. I'm going to need help deciding on a theme and designing a look to go with it." I smiled at the possibilities sparking behind his eyes. "I suck at branding."

The pity laugh he uttered confirmed he was raised too polite to point out the obvious.

"On the topic of branding, I need a consultant who can help me perfect my style. Now that I'm an heiress again, I have to look the part."

"Oh, fun." Neely clapped his hands. "I'm on extended leave from

Haint Misbehavin' during my convalescence. I can use the last two weeks as my notice to Cricket."

"Cricket will hate to lose you." Just thinking about the size of the hole his absence would punch in that company sparked fresh guilt.

"Cricket will manage. She always does." He dusted imaginary lint off his shirt. "Besides, I set her up with my protégé. My second youngest sister is filling in for me. Erin doesn't have my experience yet, but she's a natural. Cricket will be trading in a Torres for a Sanderson, but it would still keep the job in the family."

"I don't have their credentials," Marit said, glancing between the Torreses, "but I grew up helping Papa run River Street Steam. I can help in the office with scheduling and payroll." She winked at me. "I run a tight ship."

"I would like that." Tears brimmed in my eyes. "Very much."

"I'll contact Mr. Hacohen," Linus offered. "He can start drawing up the paperwork."

The trio exchanged a nervous glance, but excitement thrummed in the air around them.

"Employment with me doesn't mean severing ties with the human world." On the contrary, our survival was dependent upon the mortal hunger for immortality. "Keep your friends, stay in touch with your family. All I ask is that you don't share our secrets. Our existence depends on hiding ourselves from humans."

"Humans," Cruz echoed, eyes sliding toward Lethe.

"I'll prep the NDAs," Hood said, folding his arms over his chest.

A flash of blood leaking from the corner of Lethe's mouth filled my head, and my gut roiled with guilt.

"I can't do that to them." I pushed the hair from my eyes. "I wish I hadn't done it to you."

Lethe bumped her head against the back of my hand, and I scratched behind her ears.

"Have it your way," he told me before pegging the humans with his best feral glare. "Endanger my mate, or Grier, and I will let Lethe tear out your throats."

Cruz tucked Neely behind him. "Don't threaten my husband."

"Where's a fainting couch when you need one?" Neely leaned around his husband, defusing the tension in the room with a wave of his hand as he fanned his face. "All this testosterone is giving me the vapors."

"Let's pick this up at dusk," Amelie offered. "You guys have all been through a lot tonight. Go rest, talk it over amongst yourselves. We're all happy to answer any questions." Slipping on her tour guide persona, she ushered them into the hall. Tone bright, she chattered all the way downstairs. "Who's hungry? I make a mean cup of hot chocolate. It's not Mallow, but..."

Her voice trailed to an indistinguishable murmur, the promise of a snack enough to tempt even Lethe.

After the hall emptied and the staircase cleared, I shut the door on the world.

We had a meeting with the Marchands to arrange, a trip to Raleigh to plan, a house full of humans to protect, a lawn full of gwyllgi to feed, a city to reclaim, and the Lyceum to defend, but I wanted to pretend, just for a little while, none of it existed.

Linus perched on my bed, his pressed slacks and neat shirt contrasting the crumpled sheets.

He caught me admiring him and smiled in a self-conscious way that told me he still had no clue what put the sparkle in my eyes when I looked at him, but he was a mirror, reflecting my own wonder back at me.

Reaching behind me, I twisted the lock with a satisfying *click*.

Strolling over to Linus, I planted both palms on his chest and shoved him on the bed.

Cheeks flush, he found my hips with his hands as I straddled him. "What are you doing?"

"I'm forgetting." Leaning forward, I planted my palms to either side of his head then ducked until my warm exhale skated over the chilly skin of his throat. "How's your memory, Professor Lawson?"

His fingers dug into my flesh. "Who?"

Laughing, delighted he was playing with me, I peeled my shirt over my head. "I like you."

"You love me," he said, and I heard him marvel at it.

"I do." I unhooked my bra and tossed it on the floor. "What are you going to do about it?"

Eyes gone dark and hot, he flipped us, pinning me beneath him. "I'm going to love you back."

And he did.

Over and over.

Until his sweat coated my skin, until my hair knotted around his fingers, until the jut of his engagement ring drew blood I licked off his fingers.

Until the world shrank to just the two of us.

ABOUT THE AUTHOR

USA Today best-selling author Hailey Edwards writes about questionable applications of otherwise perfectly good magic, the transformative power of love, the family you choose for yourself, and blowing stuff up. Not necessarily all at once. That could get messy.

www.HaileyEdwards.net

ALSO BY HAILEY EDWARDS

Gemini Series

Dead in the Water #1

Head Above Water #2

Hell or High Water #3

Gemini Series Novellas

Fish Out of Water

Lorimar Pack Series

Promise the Moon #1

Wolf at the Door #2

Over the Moon #3

Araneae Nation

A Heart of Ice #.5

A Hint of Frost #1

A Feast of Souls #2

A Cast of Shadows #2.5

A Time of Dying #3

A Kiss of Venom #3.5

A Breath of Winter #4

A Veil of Secrets #5

Daughters of Askara

Everlong #1

Made in the USA
Middletown, DE
26 January 2019